A Cycle of the Moon

a novel

UMA PARAMESWARAN

We acknowledge the support of the Canada Council for the Arts for our publishing program. We also acknowledge support from the Government of Ontario through the Ontario Arts Council.

Front Cover: Kirtana Venkateswar Iwamoto
Back Cover Photo: Christine Vogt-William
Design: Peggy Stockdale

Parts of "Chander" appeared in an earlier work titled, "The Door I Shut Behind Me." Excerpt of poem on page 83 from "Yussouf" by James Russell Lowell (1819-1891).

Library and Archives Canada Cataloguing in Publication

Parameswaran, Uma

    A cycle of the moon : a novel / Uma Parameswaran.

ISBN 978-1-894770-62-0

    I. Title.

PS8581.A688C92 2010   C813'.54   C2010-904790-7

Printed in Canada by Coach House Printing

TSAR Publications
P. O. Box 6996, Station A
Toronto, Ontario M5W 1X7
Canada

www.tsarbooks.com

Contents

Family Tree

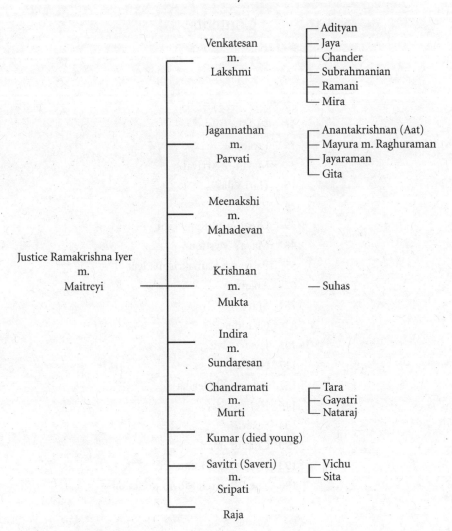

Justice Ramakrishna Iyer
m.
Maitreyi

Venkatesan
m.
Lakshmi
— Adityan
— Jaya
— Chander
— Subrahmanian
— Ramani
— Mira

Jagannathan
m.
Parvati
— Anantakrishnan (Aat)
— Mayura m. Raghuraman
— Jayaraman
— Gita

Meenakshi
m.
Mahadevan

Krishnan
m.
Mukta
— Suhas

Indira
m.
Sundaresan

Chandramati
m.
Murti
— Tara
— Gayatri
— Nataraj

Kumar (died young)

Savitri (Saveri)
m.
Sripati
— Vichu
— Sita

Raja

Other characters:
Vasudevan: Ramakrishna Iyer's younger brother
Kamakshi: Ramakrishna Iyer's widowed sister
Radha: Vasudevan's daughter
Maru: Ramakrishna Iyer's sister's grand-daughter
Krishnaswamis: parents of Neela, who is engaged to Anant
Maya: Chandramati's friend and house-guest
Devika: Suhas's cousin on her mother's side
Vijay: son of Ramakrishna Iyer's youngest brother, Balaraman; engaged to Devika

Prologue

It was a tense autumn the year Mayura came away from her husband saying she was never ever returning to that uncouth, lustful monster. Everyone in the family was affected by her presence to a greater extent than they had thought likely. A sense of collective guilt emasculated the men even while they lectured her on the moral duty of returning to her wedded husband. A sense of outrage mingled inexplicably with secret sorrow alienated women from themselves and from each other. No one knew what to make of her or of themselves. Partly to give Mayura a lesson in life, partly to unburden themselves of the weight of memory, relatives and friends found themselves impelled to tell her, or think about, their life-story.

And meanwhile, she moved among them as though nothing, nobody, could touch her. And those who thought they had, retreated, scorched.

Mayura's Arrival

THE NEWS SPREAD QUICKLY, as such news will, that Mayura had come to her parents' house and was very adamantly refusing to return to her husband. Why should a young woman, wagging tongues asked, who was married hardly three months, return to her parents? Deepavali was two months away. That was when a bride's first homecoming should be, with her husband leading her into the house after her mother, with song and prayer and kumkum-turmeric-arati welcoming them at the threshold.

It could be that she was already pregnant; women of Judge Ramakrishna Iyer's family conceive quickly we know, but even so, where was the hurry? That should be the bride's second visit when, escorted back by her father in the seventh month, the golden hue of pregnancy on her filled-out skin, she enters her mother's home at an auspicious time of an auspicious day. It could be that she was just visiting; we know these modern girls observe no traditions and consult no almanac before undertaking a journey, pay no heed to ancient wisdom that forbade travel southwards on Thursdays, east on Mondays and Saturdays, west on Fridays and Sundays, and north on Tuesdays and Wednesdays. But wherefore this rumour that she was not ever going back to her husband? It could not be that her husband had packed her off for the standard reason—to extort more dowry from his father-in-law by dredging up one of the many trivial complaints such as that the bride's aunt's sister had insulted the groom's niece once removed at the wedding, or that the diamonds in the groom's ring were not as big as had been stipulated, or some such blown-up grievance. No, it could not be that because even had this been fastidious 1945 instead of 1965, the bridegroom's party could not have complained on any score, so lavish and perfect had been the celebration.

It was surely Justice Ramakrishna Iyer's best celebration to date. Having married off four daughters, and several nieces, the old man was an undisputed authority in conducting weddings, as he was in everything he undertook. The entire function followed a pattern that had been perfected through the years. The family astrologer was the first to be closeted with the judge. Once the date was fixed, and the muhurtham, the hour when the tirumangalyam should be tied round the bride's neck, others were called in—the family purohit, the jewellers, tailors, caterers, nadaswaram musicians, builders. The judge gave the orders, the parties concerned worked out the details.

So had it been with Mayura's wedding. A week before the wedding date, the builder brought his workmen and started constructing the pandal. The judge supervised in person while the men dug the holes for implanting the stout wooden posts necessary to support the thatched roof. One could never be too careful with these sluggards, he felt. To spare themselves an extra hour's work they would not dig deep enough, and the next thing one knew would be the whole pandal coming down on the guests. With each wedding the canopied hall had been made larger because the list of invitees had grown longer as the family expanded and became more renowned. Mayura's mother, Parvati, vociferated loudly against the structure but, of course, out of the judge's hearing, and Jagannathan did not dare pursue the matter with his father after his first suggestion had been firmly rejected by the indomitable patriarch. It was Parvati's vain ambition to have the wedding at Abbotsbury, the place favoured by anybody who was anybody in society with a capital S. But the judge summarily dismissed the suggestion that his grand-daughter be married at "one of these mushroom show centres that are sprouting all over Madras." A girl must be married at home, the judge had blasted anyone (and at every wedding there had been at least one) who suggested that they rent one of the fashionable halls that were so exceedingly convenient and comparatively inexpensive. A girl should be married at home, not at an exhibition hall.

Head cook, jeweller, flower vendor, milkman, chauffeurs, all of them stopped by the judge's veranda and made their obeisance before going on to Jagannathan's house that stood farther behind the main house. And every evening, Jagannathan reported to his father on the work done and the work yet to be done. Like a feudal lord, the retired judge had presided over the preparations, and like fief-holders the pundit, the head cook, the hired hands (all of whom had worked at many such occasions and knew the judge's meticulousness and eccentricities) carried out his injunctions.

The wedding ceremony lasted all morning. The judge did not approve of modern ceremonies where the pundit abridged the Sanskrit verses, passed over some of the rites, and compressed the entire ceremony so that guests could attend the morning muhurtham, have the wedding lunch, and still reach their offices in good time. He insisted that the pundit enunciate the verses clearly. "Don't murder Sanskrit," he had shouted at this eldest daughter's wedding much to the dismay of the pundit who shut his ears at the use of so inauspicious a word as murder. The judge also insisted that the pundit explain in detail the meaning of the different steps and vows that the young persons were taking. Whether bride and groom heard it or not, the judge, seated in his cane-woven chair, leaning forward on his silver-headed walking stick, heard every word, and nodded his head in approval.

As always, Mayura's wedding too had been witnessed and blessed by the judge's friends—old men and women who were part of the intellectual aristocracy that had been at its peak in the twenties and thirties. The men wore a gold-bordered cotton turban, off-white jubba, silk-bordered dhoti, and an angavastram with a red and gold trim. The women wore nine-yard saris that seemed to have more gold than silk, and their two-carat diamond earrings flashed red and blue on their ear lobes as they shook their heads in conversation. With each wedding in the community, this group was getting visibly smaller, and they sat longer after lunch reminiscing about those who had passed on since the last social occasion. Members of the younger generation were more active and numerous and yet it seemed that they formed only the periphery of the morning function, overshadowed by the august presence of aging aristocrats.

The judge washed his hands of the festivities once the wedding lunch was served in traditional style—the only detail that had changed was that the guests sat on chairs and tables instead of on silk mats on the floor. He refused to have anything to do with the anglicized reception held in the evening. With habitual forthrightness he had said, "That farce has nothing to do with the wedding. It is just a public paying back of social debts by my son. From a hundred feet away you can make out the three categories of invitees; if Jagannathan rushes out in welcome you'll know it is a fellow higher up in the government or political hierarchy, if the invitee shakes hands with Jagannathan you'll know it is a colleague, and if a fellow comes with joined palms and ingratiating smile you'll know it is a subordinate. Mind you, even if you miss the greeting protocol, you can't go wrong once you see the wives . . ."

Despite the old man's views, a reception had been held at every wedding the family had celebrated during the last twenty years. As always, the bridal couple sat through the evening on a velvet-upholstered chesterfield, alone in spite of streams of guests and their mumbled congratulations, uncomfortable in their new, expensively heavy dress and tinsel-woven rose garlands that scratched their necks which sweated profusely despite the standing electric fan positioned especially for them. A well-known musician whose fees were known to be high gave a full two-hour concert from a specially constructed dais while unhearing guests moved along tables that were continually replenished with vadais and bondas, almond-flavoured milk, laddus, sandwiches, coffee, ice-cream and cake, an assorted variety of Indian and westernised delicacies.

At Mayura's wedding, the dowry was displayed in one of the rooms of Jagannathan's house, and select guests were given a conducted tour while others who chose to walk in were politely greeted by a distant relative, positioned there for just that purpose, and diverted back to the pandal. Mayura's mother got the idea that this would be a safe and innovative fashion to start in order to show off the trousseau in a less cumbersome way to more people than the old custom of taking close friends to the "safe room," as the little room tucked between the dining hall and master bedroom was called. The jewellery was on the centre table in a glass display case borrowed from the jeweller's showroom (execrable exhibitionism, but that's none of my business, the judge had said) and in another showcase were selected saris from the trousseau, neatly folded, a corner of each turned up to reveal a triangular piece of the pallav: colourful Conjeevarams, shimmering Banarsis, soft silks from Kashmir, georgettes from Mysore, mirror work and batik, embroidered cottons, all in the colours and designs in vogue, all with matching cholis and slippers. Though they were nowhere visible, every woman who entered the room left knowing that there were two dozen sets of lingerie and other items, including Bridalform bras smuggled in from the United States at fifty rupees apiece. Dinnerware and kitchenware filled several tables. True, there weren't too many silver plates and bell-metal tumblers and brass kudams but those were things of an age long past. This was the age of stainless steel and electrical gadgets. There were enough pots and pans of steel to blind one as they caught the sunshine through the glass windows and reflected dancing beams onto the ceiling. Jagannathan had modernised his house, replacing the old-fashioned windows with their wooden shutters and iron bars with large glass windows in slim, rectangular frames. To satisfy the curiosity of guests who might want to know just how heavy the pots and pans were, there were two large pans on the table. There was nothing discreet about the armed guard in uniform who stood ostensibly at the gate, but clearly with his attention on the guests who entered Jagannathan's house. Nowadays an armed sentry was a common sight at Nalli's and Radha Silks and all the high fashion sari and jewellery emporia, and considered quite inoffensive, and so why not at a wedding? Guests had their own opinions about this new fashion of glass display cases, but it might become the vogue for all one knew. Parvati had the reputation of being a very innovative woman who gave lavish parties both at Gymkhana Club and at home.

Yes, it had been a capital S Society wedding all right, complete with journalists and photographers. And the guests had been pleased with the extravagance (in addition to the usual blouse-piece, the women had got a silver kum kum box in a brocade gift bag), and had gone away acclaiming that the day had been celebrated with the eclat and publicity befitting the social status held by Jagannathan and the judge.

But now when news got around, as such news will, that Mayura had returned, people reviewed the wedding day and inscribed it with a new palimpsest. The groom had a dull expression, did you notice? Such a contrast to the glow of intelligence that runs in Ramakrishna Iyer's family ... The young man, Raghuraman's his name isn't it, has a good teak and mahogany furniture business in Bombay, we were told, and plenty of wealth made by his grandfather in Burma, but no culture. What can you expect in the son of a Brahmin-turned-merchant who had lived in Burma long after the war, no less? It was one thing to have lived there when it was part of the Raj, at a time when civil servants were posted in Rangoon as a matter of course, but who would want to have lived there so long after the two countries had gone their different ways? So huge and hairy he hardly looked a Brahmin . . . Did you notice the smallness of the groom's party? It is never a good sign when relatives don't turn up, a quarrelsome family do you think?

Our Jagannathan is a shrewd fellow. He'll manage to patch it up . . . Mayura is a stubborn girl. Her grandfather's pride and arrogance shows all over her . . . I've always held that girls should be married young, else they become shrews. Mayura is twenty-two if a day . . . And I still say Parvati doesn't know how to bring up children. If I were her I'd send Mayura back to Bombay by the next flight.

Very few had anything nice to say about Mayura, for she had an air about her that made others feel inferior. Her personality was not like others' in the family; there was an alabaster regality about her. With her slim figure made fairer and slimmer by her magyar-sleeved blouses of the softest material and colour, georgette saris that clung to her body, and her gliding gait, she looked like a mermaid princess. Even tradition-bent women had to grant that costume jewellery and sequin-sewn saris that would look cheap and out of place on others looked perfect on her. Anyone else with her straight, thin hair would despair of rigging up any coiffure that was passably neat, but she innovated the most elegant hair-styles with little twists of her fingers that not only stayed secure but seemed expressly designed to blend with the time of day and the very mood that she wished to portray.

The girl refuses to talk, Lakshmi says, it is so odd. Could it be that he is not quite . . .

That had been Parvati's first suspicion. That Friday afternoon, when Mayura got off the taxi, burst into tears and rushed into the house saying, "I hate that man, if man he is. I am never going back, never," Parvati embraced her in anguish, already assuming the worst. And when her daughter did not reply to her "What's it? Isn't he all right . . . ?" her fears were confirmed. She groaned, "O what have I done to my darling? How were we to know? In those days our barber would have attended on him and told us if . . . oh it is too terrible, oh my poor child . . ."

"Don't be silly, mother," Mayura said, suddenly cold and dry-eyed. "You women can think of only one thing, pah, you are no better than him." Parvati's relief found vent in anger. "Why have you come back, you shameless creature, why have you come to disgrace the family?"

Having seen Mayura alighting from the taxi, Lakshmi, wife of Jagannathan's elder brother Venkatesan, came in. As on every Friday, she had washed her hair and was drying it over a wicker basket through which the fragrant herbal powder sprinkled on live coals wafted the Friday morning smell all the way to the judge's veranda, where he sat in his mahogany easy-chair. After forty years of following ordained customs, Lakshmi's first instinct at seeing Mayura was to tell her to stop at the threshold while she prepared an arati plate of turmeric, water and kumkum to welcome her, but volcanoes had started erupting even before she could tie her hair into a knot. She now tried to pacify Parvati who was ranting. "At least go upstairs out of hearing of servants," she urged them.

"I don't care who knows," Mayura shouted defiantly. "I am not a hypocrite whatever else I might be." Mayura had never liked her uncle's soft-voiced wife who had won the reputation of being an ideal daughter-in-law. Mayura believed it was by sanctimonious docility that Lakshmi had managed to have Ramakrishna Iyer eating off her hand.

The taxi driver had, meanwhile, placed Mayura's suitcase on the veranda and from his pocket had taken out change due from the currency notes Mayura had handed him before getting out of the cab. He stood uncertainly for a few seconds and then pocketed the bills and change that no one seemed to want. With a wink at the maid, he went to his cab and drove away. The maid placed a bucket of wet clothes under the clothes line and took her position undisguisedly behind the door. But Mayura soon went upstairs to her old room and shut the door. Parvati started crying in little sobs. Lakshmi consolingly put her arm around the weeping woman and led her upstairs. The cook, noting that the scene of action had been taken beyond their earshot, joined the maid who went back to the clothes line. They were joined by the driver of a navy blue Chevrolet, who had come from the Krishnaswamis with a note for Parvati. The maid was only too eager to tell him the news. Figuring he would not be welcomed at this juncture, he gave the note to the maid and stood at the well a little longer, flirting with her as she filled him in on other details about Mayura.

Half an hour after Mayura's arrival, Parvati telephoned her husband at his office. He was talking to representatives from an Employees' Union when her call came through. Her shrill voice vibrated over the wire like a taut steel string of a violin. "Mayura is here. She has left her husband without even telling him." He drew in his breath. Mayura here? What was the hysterical woman saying? And so loudly too. He hissed back, "I'll call you later," and hung up. He turned with a smile to the Union spokesman. It would be disastrous if they'd heard. The Union had resorted to mudslinging, and Jagannathan, always jealous of his reputation, trembled to think of what they might do. If at this crucial juncture when a settlement was about to be reached, they came to know of any scandal connected with the government arbitrator, they would exploit it whether it was relevant or no, and muckraking journalists would take it up.

Jagannathan turned to his visitors with a smile, "Pardon the interruption, you were saying . . . ?" After they left, he ordered his peon not to admit anyone. He then phoned his wife and got the details. Accustomed to his wife's breathless narration, he picked out the important facts and erased minor details so as not to clutter up his concentration. Mayura had not discussed anything or even hinted at the possibility of her departure. She had just left a note and walked out of the house half an hour after Raghu left for his office early that morning.

Jagannathan called for a telegraph form. There wasn't one in his office. The clerk called the peon who hurriedly adjusted his cummerbund and turban and ran in. The clerk told him to get telegraph forms but Jagannathan interrupted the clerk and handed a sheet to the peon. The peon smirked at the clerk and turned to go. Jagannathan called him back, checked that he had his son-in-law's business address correct and ran his eyes over the message: Mayura just arrived stop Greetings to you stop Jagannathan. It sounded okay. He despatched the peon. "Bring extra forms," the clerk called out, reestablishing his authority. The peon pretended not to have heard. His smirk lingered in the air, guaranteeing that the clerk would soon get back at him.

Jagannathan dismissed the clerk from his room and took out his personal stationery. The letter took him longer than he anticipated. He knew what he wanted to write but it did not read well. He had grown so accustomed to dictating authoritative letters that anything he wrote had a touch of arrogance. And one could not afford to be arrogant towards a son-in-law at any time, least of all when he had been deserted by one's daughter. At last the letter was written. Mayura had always been greatly attached to her family and to Madras. What she had done she had done in a bout of homesickness. He apologized most sincerely for her impetuosity. Would Raghu kindly excuse the hasty action of a wilful child and wait a few patient days while she overcame her nostalgia? He addressed the envelope to the home address and sent off the clerk to mail it with express delivery stamps.

A few minutes later he felt the letter would reach very late and that the telegram had been too bald. He wrote out another message. Excuse Mayura's burst of homesickness. Stop. She has never been out of Madras before. Stop. Shall personally escort her back next week. He reread the message. It would reach only at night, perhaps only tomorrow morning. He could phone his son-in-law but not now, not with the kind of bellowing one had to do calling long-distance; in the evening perhaps, but what if Raghu didn't return home from the club till midnight? Best send an express telegram and follow it up with a phone call, if possible. He stretched his hand to ring the bell but then decided this was too personal a message to be entrusted to anyone. Jagannathan walked downstairs to the telegraph office in the next block.

That Friday afternoon, Ramakrishna Iyer stretched himself in his reclining chair on the veranda outside his study as was his habit after lunch. And, as was his habit, he took off his spectacles and closed his eyes after he had read all he wanted to read in *The Hindu*. He looked old and serene with his eyes closed, very different from the alert dynamism of his usual self. Now one noticed his long wiry frame, his thin sharp nose that burgeoned out fleshily at the end, his white crown of hair above a high forehead, the asymmetry of his face accentuated by the uneven thickness of his lower lip. When he was awake, his eyes dominated his personality and one was conscious of little else. They were small and scintillating, luminous like the eyes of an animal caught by the beams of a car's headlights on a dark night. They moved swiftly as though sweeping the entire scene into themselves with a single glance. If one saw them at close range, one would perceive the white edges of his aging iris and the excess fluid in which his pupils darted, but it was not often that anyone dared to look straight into his eyes. Now, as he lay with uncreased forehead, his penetrating eyes closed, he looked like a sage of old, emanating yogic serenity. Only the skin hanging loosely in criss-cross webs on his neck showed his seventy-six years.

He could hear Parvati's voice carried across the shimmering stillness of the midday heat. He knew Mayura had returned. He concluded that since Jagannathan had rather spoilt the child, she had taken the first plane to Madras on feeling the first pangs of homesickness. He noted that her return was causing a lot of excitement. There was far too much running to and fro between the different houses. Women were like that, weepy and excited at the sight of a bride. A bride on her first visit to her parents' house evoked in all who saw her some vicarious pleasure and pain. Women re-lived their virginity and deflowering through her. Also there was the pain of realization that she who for years had been part of the family was now a visitor. She belonged to another family now, she belonged to a man, a stranger, and that hurt.

Ramakrishna Iyer had gifted away not just one daughter but five including his niece; gifted, yes, that was the word, kanyadaan, the Sanskrit sacraments were cruel there; they brought out all too unequivocally the irrevocability of the gift to which men and gods were witness. Celestial beings had been called upon by name—the Eternals of the uppermost heaven, the immortal denizens of the sky, the presiding deities of the eight directions, the gods of the elements, the sages and enlightened ones, invited individually and collectively to bear witness that he, Ramakrishna Iyer, was gifting away a maiden.

"Vayu, god of wind, come with all thy retinue and bear witness that I, Ramakrishna Sarma, son of Venkatesa Sarma, grandson of Venkatarama Sarma, great-grandson of Ramachandra Sarma, descendant of sage Bharadwaja, do now in the presence of Agni give away this maiden decked with ornaments of gold and silver and that gem that surpasseth worldly treasures, virginity . . . Varuna, come with all thy retinue from thy ocean realms and bear witness that I . . . do give away this kanya decked with ornaments of gold and silver and that gem that surpasseth worldly treasures, virginity . . ." He had called on deities and mortals to bear witness to his disclaiming of all rights over the maiden. Kanya! what wealth there was in that single word when used for the last time! For, immediately after the father ceased, the man standing before him by the sacred fire continued, "Woman, step down and join me . . . This yoke I place upon your shoulder and call you to walk by my side in fruitful harmony even as a pair of bullocks walk in step . . . come woman, and join me."

As he now went over the Sanskrit mantras, the old man remembered Indira's wedding. Twenty-three years ago, already that long? they had sat on this same veranda, he and Maitreyi, alone with their aching hearts.

The workmen were dismantling the pandal, stacking coconut-frond panels one on top of the other, and rolling the strips of coloured cloth that had canopied the hall. A servant woman who had been with them since Indira's birth was weeping loudly, tears coursing down her cheeks from collyrium-stained eyes. Lucky, they could cry uninhibitedly at weddings and funerals, whereas Brahmins, indoctrinated through generations to stoic impassivity could not slacken the rein on their emotions. Maitreyi sat silent, occasionally wiping her eyes with the edge of her sari.

Here was the silver plate of turmeric-coloured rice-grains with which the assembled witnesses had blessed the bridal couple, and here the green lumps of henna that had reddened the edges of her feet and fingers, there in the corner were piled what remained of the coconuts and betel leaves given in gladness to the guests, and at the middle of one end of the pandal was the sand heap from which emanated the burnt smell of ghee that had fed the sacred fire around which the young man had led her seven times and made her his.

The two of them were alone, their loved daughter gone away from them, and all the others gone to see her off. Now they would be at the railway station, loading her rich dowry into the baggage car of the Calcutta Mail. Yes, his sons would do everything with all due care and efficiency just as his elder daughter and other women in the family had smoothly carried off the festivities.

He looked at his wife. Poor woman, it had been a great strain, this parting. He would never forget the poignancy of her last embrace as the bride touched her feet with a broken "Ma." The house would be desolate now without their lovely cheerful daughter—ah poor child, how she had cried all day long, poor girl, to leave her home for a stranger's . . . and yet her life was before her, theirs was behind. Was it for this that he had lived and begotten children—to give them away in marriage and be left only with memories? Harder was their lot than hers for she had her life before her, yes, that was the irony of it all—that she would forget all this pain of parting and parents and the past in her first kiss.

He said it aloud, "Yes, that is the irony of it all—she will forget all this pain of parting and her parents and the past in her first kiss."

Maitreyi wiped her once-bright eyes. "As I did in mine," she said.

Indira was now living down the street, and yet Ramakrishna Iyer felt the pain of that parting as keenly now as he had then. Reliving that moment, he could not remember if Maitreyi had said it as a statement or as an inflected question. Maitreyi had a way, a wonderful way of opening his eyes to little things and big. He sighed. The wick and the oil, one needs must go before the other, as the adage said, but the flame goes out with the first, why hadn't anyone put that truth in any adage or proverb?

He heaved a deep sigh and composed himself for his siesta.

Hari Vilas

JUSTICE RAMAKRISHNA IYER WAS a barrister of an earlier age. His life had the chiselled clarity of the master sculptors of old. In the spring of 1904, at the age of fifteen, he left his ancestral village on the banks of the Kaveri and came to Madras. He graduated with distinction from Presidency College and then went to England to study for the Bar. He was admitted to the Bar, and returned to the law courts of Madras just as the war clouds over the Balkans started spreading all over Europe. He went on to become a legend for his oratory and stinging wit.

His older brother died while he was in England. Five months after his return, his father died suddenly, as though satisfied that he had fully carried out his worldly responsibilities, having just got his youngest daughter married off to a rich landowner. At the age of twenty-four, Ramakrishnan was head of a family of three younger sisters and two very young brothers, his mother, his wife, and his brother's widow and daughter. He insisted that his sister-in-law and niece would be better off in the city than in her parents' village. As indeed they were. His was the parental house to which all three sisters came for the birth of their children. He took guardianship of his brothers, Vasudevan and Balaraman, and paid for their education.

On his return from England, his marriage which had taken place when he was fourteen and his bride six, was consummated, and in the next fourteen years he begot seven children. Like his peers, he built himself a large house in Mylapore on a two acre plot of land studded with coconut palms. He named his estate Hari Vilas, and his house Maitreyi Nivas, after his grandmother, so he claimed to others, but it was named for his wife, whom he loved with a passion that only the two of them knew about.

They explored each other's body and mind in all kinds of ways that was assumed to happen only in poetry and at a purely figurative level. Only his younger daughters, with their childish intuition, knew about it, and had seen how his eyes twinkled and the corner of his lips smiled when he was with her.

He had his eldest daughter, Meenakshi, educated at home along with his niece, and had them take music lessons with a master who came to the house three times a week. His niece wished to have a career, and he encouraged her, but also supported her when she decided to revert to the traditional role of getting married and raising a family. When Meena was fourteen he got her married to a promising college student of eighteen, the only son of a poor widow. The boy did well and entered the Financial Service.

Ramakrishna Iyer had his sons educated in the sciences. When Venkatesan graduated from Presidency College, he sent him to Cambridge even though Venkatesan would rather have stayed home with his pregnant wife. It was soon after Venkatesan's departure that fate made its first gash on Ramakrishna Iyer's blueprint, the outline of which he had drafted early in life. His youngest son, Kumar, who was showing every sign of being a mathematical prodigy, died of typhoid just before his tenth birthday. The barrister handed over the pending cases to his juniors and shut himself in his private library.

The library was a long, narrow, high-ceilinged hall. It projected out like a chapel, and the huge, magnificent circular stained glass window on the narrow wall completed the effect. Its tall, narrow, arch-shaped glass windows and its sloping pantiled roof of twice-baked tiles that shone clear brick-red through the years gave it an air of seclusion and sanctity even now when it was surrounded by other houses. For years it had stood like a monastery in its own coconut grove, connected to the house by an umbilical cord.

Here the barrister spent eleven months, completely eschewing the law books that lined the shelves which acted as dividers between his study and the rest of the library. He spent the first four months reading and re-reading English translations of European classical literature and philosophy; then he moved to the Sanskrit texts. Whenever he was not in the library, he was at Higginbothams, placing orders for books. From time to time, he received a long envelope from an agent in London, and cartons of German commentaries on Sanskrit classics. A shrewd bookseller in Allahabad sent unsolicited parcels of Sanskrit texts and translations and commentaries along with an itemized bill that ran to hundreds of rupees. The bookseller knew the amount was never questioned and always promptly paid.

Two weeks before Kumar's first death anniversary, Ramakrishna Iyer came out of his library into the house. He told his wife, "I am back. My money-making tongue is itching to work." After his first day back in the courts, he said, "I feel ten years younger," and his wife placidly commented, "Which means you are out to work yourself and those around you to death." "You don't look as though you've ever felt the taskmaster's whip," he said, looking fondly at her. "I have had a whole year to recoup," she answered.

They looked at each other in a way that made Indira and Chandramati blush to the pores of their teenage pimples.

The barrister started accepting cases again but a judgeship was his goal. His tongue continued to bring him more wealth and prestige. Though he used it less and less outside the courts, when he did, his words had the same knife edge that characterized his legal arguments.

He took up his blueprint once more. He built a house by the side of his own but farther back from the gate, for Venkatesan who, on his return from Cambridge, was to take up a teaching position at a local college. He extended his house at the back, adding rooms and a second staircase and independent entrance so that Jagannathan could settle down at his legal practice on his return from London. He had long ago mapped out a career for each of his sons: teaching, law, medicine, engineering in that order. He had also decided that all of them would settle down in Madras, in these houses he had built for them.

Soon, Maitreyi gave birth to a daughter whom they named Savitri because Yama, who came for her mother with his noose of puerperal fever saw the child and desisted from tightening the noose. Eighteen months later, Raja was born, and he brought a flood of fortune to his father, so people said.

Like a careful architect, Ramakrishna Iyer had drawn a blueprint for his life. When he was made a judge, the final detail fell into place. The eddying circles of rejoicings at Maitreyi Nivas reached collection boxes of temples and charities.

That year Venkatesan returned from Cambridge with academic laurels. Indira was married into a very rich, very well-known family.

Six months later, Jagannathan cut short his stay in London without completing his studies for the Bar because the climate threatened to puncture his lungs, so he said; the truth was that he missed the easy life he had led at home, and having had a taste of the marriage bed with Parvati before he left, he missed it more than he would own and did not have the strength to contain himself or the temerity to grasp whatever was accessible as so many of his fellow-sojourners in the Empire's capital did. He tried to bury himself in his studies but he was not built for concentration; he attended several meetings of the nationalist group working underground in London for India's independence but flinched from the risks involved. Also, war was looming. Whereas his brother had left because his work was done, Jagannathan panicked at the prospect of being in the midst of a war that might cut him off from home. The only gamble he indulged in was one in which he would lose nothing or gain a princedom; he wrote the Indian Civil Service examination. A month after that he wrote to his father about how the English climate threatened his lungs. He knew what the response would be; and so he packed his bags and waited. Within a week of receiving the expected cable, he left London for Madras and Paru's arms. In due time news came that he had passed the ICS examination and he was called to join the envied hierarchy.

But Fate made its second gash soon after that. Maitreyi, who had never wholly recovered after Savitri's birth and had hidden it effectively from her husband and even from her doctor, died after a short illness. Ramakrishna did not break down this time. Nor did he retire to the library. He impatiently shrugged off condolences, and those who came to sympathize went away condemning him for callousness.

O that a judgeship should turn one's head so! Later, when they saw his new asceticism and liberal donations to philanthropic organizations, they adulated him and hailed him as one of the patriarchs of the intellectual aristocracy. He ignored that also. And so, later still, people called him arrogant and tyrannical. But they respected him just the same.

After Maitreyi's death, his younger sister, Kamakshi, took over the care of the younger children. Kamakshi had been widowed at the age of twenty-two, and had returned to Hari Vilas with her infant son, Shanker. Always deeply attached to Ramakrishna and Maitreyi, she now devoted herself to nurturing their youngest children, Savitri and Raja. Savitri came to be called Saveri; no one knew whether it was Kamakshi's choice, since Yama had taken Maitreyi after all, or Raja's lisping that had changed "Savitri" to "Saveri," but it was to be Saveri then on for all except her father.

As years went by, Ramakrishna's sons and sons-in-law left Madras to follow different careers. Venkatesan alone never left Madras, or even the college he had joined on his return from Cambridge. The only move he made was from the new house back to Maitreyi Nivas, and he made it because Jagannathan wanted the new house.

Jagannathan's work transferred him from one city to another for the first few years. When he was posted to Madras, six years after his return from London, he had several reasons for not wanting to live in the main house. He had many visitors; he had to give parties that lasted half the night; he had to go on tours leaving Parvati to manage the big house on her own; and there were other reasons that were nearer the core of his dissatisfaction and could not be put even into discreet admissions—their father was getting more testy about his diet than Paru cared to cater to, and even more important, the judge made no bones about telling his son's visitors what he thought of their under-the-counter dealings; at a time when Jagannathan was eager to be in the good books of both Imperial and the imminent Independent governments, his father's lambasting of the growing corruption within government was an embarrassment that Jagannathan wanted to avoid. In short, Jagannathan wanted the new house and he took it after a spate of one-sided talking.

He need not have given any reasons, for Venkatesan, mild man that he was, asked for none. But the younger brother, habituated to long, specious arguments and negotiations, gave a string of smooth-tongued points—his numerous visitors disturbed Father's routine, the older house was bigger and therefore more suited to Venkatesan's growing family, Lakshmi was such an excellent housewife compared to untrained Paru (who, having rich parents had never entered a kitchen until she got married, but that could not be mentioned since Lakshmi's father was not well off, and so it would appear snobbish) and Father liked Lakshmi, and so on. Jagannathan moved to the new house and Venkatesan moved nearer his father.

The year he turned sixty, the judge moved to the next phase of his life-plan. He cleared parts of the coconut grove and built more houses, one for each of his other sons and an extra one—the Fifth House as it was called—to house his daughters and families when they visited. He did not consult any of them. Never at any time would it have struck him that he should; he did, however, make some allowance for their personal preference by making both floors of each house have just two mega-sized rooms within which they could build walls as suited them. The ground floor also had a kitchen at the side and two bathrooms for the family. Krishnan and Jagannathan extended their houses to their needs. The Fifth house stood as it was, and served as a dormitory for guests, as study space for college-going children, nap-space corners where the servants had their naps or stored their extra clothes, for they had their baths at the well; and storage areas where everyone stacked up cartons of stuff that were meant to be dealt with later but never were.

His special obsession lay in the area of bathrooms and toilets for servants. He insisted that all servants take a bath before they entered the house in the morning, and he ensured that they and any children they brought to work would use the row of three toilets built along the back wall, instead of using the coconut grove as servants usually did. He personally inspected the toilets from time to time; and yelled the roof down if the tiles on the floor and walls were not sparkling white. Years later, when indoor plumbing became the rule rather than the exception in city houses, he put in toilet bowls and insisted that they too be kept sparkling white. This resulted in a great deal of argument among the servants, who thought it was the sweeper's job and not theirs to clean toilets. Of all the family stories that his children and grandchildren would tell their children, the story of him haranguing someone he had caught using the bushes or grove was surely the most hilarious one.

Once all the houses were ready, he legally gifted away to his sons the houses he had built for them, so that "nobody need wait for me to die." Maitreyi Nivas alone was his, and that would go to Venkatesan after him. Twice he had taken the steps towards formally changing the ownership papers but both times he had stopped his lawyer from going ahead. He could not bring himself to signing away his Maitreyi Nivas.

He was the only one who loved the old house. Its front was indeed imposing but in the modern context it looked grotesque as did the rest of the house. A tall, wide grilled gate resembling the entrances to old English manors opened into a neatly gravelled driveway that forked around a velvet lawn and merged at the porch. At the centre of the lawn was a lily pond and around the edge were flower beds with a profusion of seasonal flowers. At the far end was a little pond, an area on which the gardener did not spend much time.

The house seemed to be sitting at an awkward angle to the gate. An aerial view of Maitreyi Nivas gave the impression of a paper kite with an oversized face, the narrow library wing being the tail. The large veranda that ran along the side and where the judge spent a lot of time nowadays, gave him a view of the other houses so that any grandchild who wanted to escape his vigilant eyes pretty well had to take the back door of the compound wall, which he personally locked at eight o'clock every evening and opened at six o'clock every morning. As the grandsons grew older and came home later, they learnt to climb over the back wall, even if it meant having to tresspass on properties that had been built upon more recently.

Maitreyi Nivas bore the impress of several schools of architecture, not all of which were necessarily in harmony with the rest. Ionic pillars in pairs ran along the front veranda. The walls of the main hall had arabesques carved at a height of six feet. Each room had several niches for oil lamps in case electricity was temporarily cut off during rains. The master bedroom upstairs had a mansard roof while the rest of the house had a flat terrace. Gargoyles gaped their ugly mouths from terrace walls. When Sheila, daughter of the judge's brother, Balaraman, visited the house one summer, she wrote a creative description where she called it "a grotesque structure facing the wrong way, side toward the road, with a row of twin pillars that support nothing and serve only to entrap the chubby legs of Hari Vilasians; huge windows each with four doors painted a ghastly green, numberless rooms big and small but all square and bare ..." Ramakrishna Iyer had called her to his study and kept her there an hour and a half explaining to her the whys and wherefores of the design—the twin pillars gave an architectural balance; the house was at just the right angle to receive the sea breeze; green is a soothing colour; the less furniture there was the less surfaces to harbour dust, and moreover, sitting cross-legged on the floor kept the body supple. Furniture should be functional, and beautiful only if their beauty was not a hindrance, how often we see fragile figurines on teapoys no less fragile which discomfited both host and visitor, who could not sit comfortably for fear something would be knocked down.

The same hotch-potch mixture of styles characterized interior design and decor. Framed pictures lined the walls, many wedding photographs and family and college groups, but still more reproductions of famous paintings. In heavy rosewood almirahs with glass fronts there were exquisite figurines of china and glass. Delicately chiselled marble busts stood on crudely heavy tables. On either side of a painting of Aurora, cymbals in hand walking out to wake the world, was a Ravi Varma reprint of a scriptural tableau. Each piece of art was well-chosen but their settings and background were often jarringly incongruous. Radha, another of the judge's nieces, was aesthetically upset by this on her first day in the house. She told her father, "Unless one has the single-minded concentration of Arjun, who on being told to shoot a bird saw nothing but the pupil of the bird's eye, I don't see how anyone can appreciate the beauty of a bronze Nataraja when it is flanked by two crude clay potteries shaped by an unknown armless beggar."

Her father, Vasudevan, had replied, "Or unless one sees a cosmic harmony."

When the men came home that Friday evening, the youngsters greeted them with news of Mayura's arrival. Well that is a pleasant surprise, they said; but when each saw his wife's expression he knew that the surprise was not a pleasant one at all. In low tones, in the privacy of the bedroom, each woman told her husband all she knew while he changed into his evening clothes. Raghu was a boor and a sensualist; he gambled, he drank, he possibly had had several serious affairs besides any number of minor flirtations; his friends were as dissipated and the twelve weeks had been one long orgy of cocktail parties and dinners; his sexual appetite was insatiable; he was crude; he talked about their nights to his friends, not under intoxication for he was never drunk but with brutish frankness, making a big joke of the whole process.

Later in the evening, the men gravitated towards each other with a sense of shared guilt, and they spoke with more than usual fervour of Pakistani infiltration and the possibility of the Chinese striking before winter set in.

Radha

THE FIRST VISITORS WERE the Krishnaswamis. How they came to know the
news within hours of Mayura's return was a mystery, their driver's note
having been ignored by Parvati since all it asked for was for her to phone
back with the address of a common friend. The women in Hari Vilas had
decided this was a purely adult affair about which the children need not
be told any details. After the first storm, they had moved back to their
routines so that even the youngsters had not sensed anything out of the
ordinary on their return from school or college. Tomorrow would be
different. That evening in the cheri the servants would spread the news
spiced with genuine and imagined eavesdroppings. Then, the initial sense
of shame and pain overcome, the women themselves would want to share
their sorrow with friends.

But that the Krishnaswamis should so soon know of her stormy
return was mysterious. News travels fast, as such news will, but so fast?
Parvati was disagreeably jolted when she saw the navy blue chauffeur-
driven Chevrolet purring through their gate on the driveway just as
daylight was changing to twilight. One look at Mrs Krishnaswami's face
was enough to figure out that she came in search of confirmation of
some scandalous rumour. Parvati was jolted. But only for a moment.
She was as much a connoisseur of dissimulation as any at the Club. She
went out to greet her visitor effusively as becomes dear friends who are
to be shortly related. Less than twenty days ago, Krishnaswami and
Jagannathan had exchanged coconuts and fruits and, over a short religious
ceremony, betrothed Krishnaswami's daughter Neela to Jagannathan's
eldest son, Anantakrishnan. An engagement party—just for the family

and close friends they kept assuring but everyone knew it would be a gala affair at the Gymkhana Club with at least six hundred invited guests— was scheduled for Sunday, the fifth of September.

Mr A Krishnaswami was a short thickset man who looked shorter and more thickset in his official outfit. He had a satisfied look of achievement on his fleshy face. Once, his face had been lean and his expression angry and intense, and it was to that steely young student that Jagannathan had given his affection in London thirty years ago; to that half-contemptuous, half-sympathetic friend that he had confided his lack of courage to join the underground freedom workers of whom Krishnaswami was one. Krishnaswami had played his cards even more carefully than Jagannathan, had worded his newspaper tracts with diplomatic tour-de-forces that impressed the nationalists without offending the rulers, had judiciously courted imprisonment late in 1946, and won a secure and powerful though unspectacular position in the Congress government.

He always wore khadi, a khadi suit with Nehru collar, and when in Delhi he wore his white cap at the same angle as the Defence Minister did. He studiously picked up a working knowledge of Hindi. Recently he had been making his speeches in Tamil because he was astute enough to see into the future; he could not see too far but far enough to be secure at his post. Even after years of kowtowing to politicians, he felt extremely uncomfortable doing all this, and was more at home in English clothes and language and atmosphere. Which is why he opted to be a member of the English-oriented Lake Club even after it became known as the strong-hold of British Raj conservatives, and why he liked Jagannathan with whom he still played tennis as he had in their London days. Between these two men there was a bond of affection as genuine as lay within their capacity. It was a deep bond, but through the years, associations and circumstances had shaped their interaction. "We were together in London in the late thirties," each had told third parties scores of times since the thirties. The tone had undergone some change since the days when Jagannathan was a Collector in the British Raj and Krishnaswami a nationalist Congress worker. Today Krishnaswami was a deputy minister in the Congress government and sometimes when he introduced Jagannathan to a newcomer with the familiar words, Jagannathan heard a nuance that reminded him he had once sobbed out his fears for his

personal safety and had begged this man to release him from his obliga-
tions to the Cause.

Mrs Krishnaswami, as always, was a step of ahead of her husband as
they walked up the driveway. They just dropped in, she said, on the way
to the Club. On the spur of the moment she had asked the driver to turn
right on Lloyd's Road instead of left. Else they'd have phoned ahead they
were coming. "You know how it is, I do things just like that," she clicked
her fingers, "and how is everybody?"

While they ran through the required social jargon, her eyes roved
round for Mayura, of whose arrival she had got news from the driver.
The driveway was long; probably they had hustled the girl out of sight
and would not even talk of her. Jagannathan's hearty words came as a
disappointment. "We have a pleasant surprise," he said, "Mayura is
here. Raghu is on a business trip to Delhi, and so she came down here,
and of course we are not going to let her go till after the engagement
party."

"Isn't that wonderful!" Mrs Krishnaswami exclaimed with appropriate
gestures.

"And Anant will be here Friday next. He is planning to drive down with
a couple of friends instead of taking the day train."

"Oh! that will be so fatiguing, the dear boy. And where is the sweet
child?" Mrs Krishnaswami had a habit of emphasizing certain words
rather exaggeratedly for effect. Mayura, overhearing the conversation
from the adjoining room, gritted her teeth. She wanted to walk into their
midst and say, "Yes, what you heard is quite right. I have come away
from my husband without even telling him." She heard her mother's
safe reply, "She went out to visit some friends," safe in that if Mayura
did enter at some point, she could feign surprise about seeing her back
so soon.

"Yes, of course, the dear girl must be dying to meet old friends. We
never know how much we miss them till we go away, isn't that right? That
is why we do hope Ananta will settle down in Madras. Neela loves Madras
so much. He could open a clinic in Adyar."

Where the rich old hags are, Mayura thought, whose boots the
Krishnaswamis lick, nouveau riche storekeepers with huge gauche houses,
whose bribes work back and forth between business and politics. I don't

know how Father could arrange such a match. I wonder how much dowry they plan to give, it must be either a fortune or nothing depending on which way the pendulum is swinging at this particular time. But that is none of my business, any more than it is hers to come prying around with her scandal-scenting nose.

Mayura started out for her room. The staircase was in the hallway alongside the living room. Parvati, sharing a sofa with Mrs Krishnaswami, heard the swish of silk in the hallway and caught her breath. She tried to look casual as she glanced past her guest's shoulder. She saw the pallav of a sari moving up the banister and Mayura's hand sliding under it. It was quite likely that her visitor would have seen more of the girl who was going upstairs. But the farce had to go on. "Maybe that's Radha returning from her day with the student team from abroad," she said enthusiastically.

"There was something about them in *The Hindu* this morning," Mr Krishnaswami said.

"Oh, there's been news about them even in *Ananda Vikatan*, and Radha's name was mentioned too; what an honour for the dear child," his wife added.

And the talk turned to the students, to Mrs K's disappointment.

Coffee was offered and refused, offered again and accepted; imported Brittanica crackers and home-made sweets were served, superficial conversation continued for another twenty minutes and then the visitors left, to Parvati's relief.

That Friday afternoon Radha was at a window seat in the bus. It had been a tiring week for the members of the International Youth team and their local hosts. But their visit to the Theosophical Society Gardens with its famous banyan tree had refreshed the foreigners from the fatigue of giving speeches at various colleges and visiting an endless string of factories and projects. The representatives of the local colleges were feeling the relief that comes to amateurs who have successfully completed a professional undertaking; for, though groups came every year and went through near-identical itineraries, the local committees were different and to the student-members in charge of the organization, the conducted tours organized for the visiting students was a mammoth project. The visiting team would soon be leaving and everything had gone off perfectly.

Radha alone did not share the feeling of relief. She was in the throes of pain at the imminent parting. The team was leaving at two o'clock and it was now noon. She looked unseeingly at the young man in front of her. His blond hair was straight and long and his face peculiarly hairless because the hairs on his intentionally unshaved face merged invisibly into the skin. His profile was sharp and melancholic. One could well have expected him to say what he did on being asked what gift he'd give India. Instead of talking about economic aid or cultural exchange, he had said, "The beauty of our midnight sun." Radha did not need to look at Nikolaus Maris who sat next to her to know his features. He too was typical of the image that people had of his country. He was Hermes come alive from the colonnades of Greece. Bold brown eyes, a head of sleek black hair, olive-skinned, broad-shouldered, he spoke with a charmingly faulty accent and the overdone enthusiasm of those on goodwill tours.

Radha had monopolised him on the various bus-trips, and they had not talked of statistics and agricultural and political conditions as the others so painstakingly did. They spoke of Greece, the land of her birth, the only land she had known till four years ago, and the only land she wanted to know at the moment. She thought nostalgically of their house, albeit small and precariously standing on the slopes near Acropolis along with a hundred other cluttered houses, where she had lived for sixteen years before coming to Madras and Hari Vilas.

Her father, Vasudevan, had been chased out of the country in 1930 by the British government for his nationalistic activities. He wandered through Europe, and when he drifted into Athens he saw the Aegean and the Acropolis, he saw the people, the poverty, the beauty all so akin to his own land, and he remained there. There he married and there his children were born, and there his sons remained, Greek in name and nationality, but his youngest child and only daughter he named Radha and her he brought back with him when he returned to his native land after an exile of thirty-one years.

Vasudevan was the only parent Radha had known, her mother having died when she was eleven months old. They had lived on the second floor of her grandmother's house at the foot of Acropolis and they continued to live there. Her father, old at forty-one, spent his free time near the Parthenon, sketching the sculptures around him and those in his mind, often with Radha playing nearby. He sketched with black pencils and crayon on large sheets of paper, and when a curious tourist happened to stop by he would hold him with theories he had formulated on Indo-Hellenic culture, and he would show him his sketches where he had superimposed broad-hipped Uma on Venus, and Hercules on Bhima the better to show the similarities and differences of sculptural traditions. The bewildered tourist would then escape and from a distance click his camera to take a picture which he could project later at home gatherings and Church socials with a commentary of his meeting with the loony Yogi on the Acropolis. Radha grew up by his side, listening to his stories of the Hindu epics and Greek myths, his exposition of the fundamentals of Indian and Greek sculptures and his theories on why the caryatids in Greek temples were flat-chested and in flowing robes whereas the friezes on the pillars of Hindu temples were full-bosomed and nude . . . Sometimes he spoke of the national struggle, as though it belonged to a time as ancient as the temples he described. For him it was. For years he had greeted sunrise on the Parthenon and sat dreaming of the day the sun would rise on an India independent of British shackles. The sun did rise one morning on an India which was free at last of the flag that he had burnt at public meetings, but Vasudevan did not return to see the tricolour for which he had been exiled. Months passed into years and he still spent his mornings on the Parthenon and his evenings in the garden at the foot of the hill.

Living worshipfully in the shadow of his memories, Radha grew to cherish her other heritage and yearn for the inheritance that waited for them beyond the seas. But as she grew up, she found she could not live any more in two worlds at the same time. In the one she had no companion except her father. And her father was old, and the world around her was young, and so when she entered middle school she turned away from her father and the world that was his. She longed for a common Greek name, she did what others did with greater zeal so that she could merge herself the more indistinguishably with the world around her.

Soon after her fifteenth birthday her father received the letter. It was from the Government of the Republic of India, and it invited Vasudevan, Indian national and distinguished citizen, to return to his homeland which remembered with gratitude and appreciation his dedicated service and sacrifice in the cause of freedom.

Why such a letter was written and at whose recommendation, why his country should have remembered him only thirteen years after independence, Vasudevan did not know. He did not care very much at first, for he had long stopped reading the news from his motherland which depressed him greatly whenever he came across it perforce. A man enslaved by a stranger could appeal to his brother, but to whom can a man enslaved by his brother appeal?

For six months Vasudevan read and reread the letter embossed with the seal of the Republic of India and wondered why it had come to torment him into hope and longing. Then he decided to return.

Radha turned to him once more. She was more excited than he was; here was proof at last that his sacrifice had not been in vain, that his patriotism was recognized by a grateful country. Her father was a hero.

Eleven months after the letter reached him Vasudevan sailed from Athens accompanied by Radha. As the ship neared Bombay he spoke less and stood alone, an old man alone with his fears. Radha could not share them for she could not comprehend what there was to fear and brood over. As they sailed into the harbour she thrilled with nervousness and gratitude. This is my father's land and mine.

The welcome they received far exceeded anything she had expected. They stayed in Bombay four days and then left for Madras. More civic receptions, newspaper interviews and adulatory meetings awaited them. People poured into Maitreyi Nivas all through the day. Her uncle, Ramakrishna Iyer, behaved with extraordinary rudeness. On the fourth day he opened the front gate that had stayed closed for years and put up a placard on the side gate, "Visitors! Use the other gate." He partitioned off the house from the two rooms at the front that he had prepared for them, and hung placards everywhere else, "Visitors, keep away from here." On the fifth day the Governor visited them and amiably making conversation with the judge asked, "Does your brother find it tiring to receive so many visitors?" The judge promptly replied, "I don't know about him but I know that I am sick and tired of so much lip-service and hypocrisy." On the ninth day the judge had them removed to Jagannathan's. "You, no doubt, will welcome all these blabber-mouthed white caps. I have no use for them," he told his son.

For two months the Government made no offer of a job. Then Vasudevan got a letter inviting him to work at the Government Archives in Delhi on a consolidated salary of three hundred and ten rupees per month, and there was a rented flat that came with the job. "If you think you can get two square meals a day on that pittance you are a cruddy fool, Vasu," the judge said, and tore up the letter. Radha remonstrated with her father that night about his brother's inordinate arrogance but her father only said, "He is a good man, though his tongue is a whiplash."

The next day Ramakrishna Iyer came into their room and said, "Enough of this bootlicking to the Congress blackguards. You stay right here and start your work. Visit Madurai, Bangalore, Halebeid, Kashmir, if you will, but don't talk any more of selling yourself for a miserable sinecure."

Forty years ago Ramakrishna had owned a Victoria and a Model T Ford, both of which were kept side by side in a massive garage of stone along the back wall of Hari Vilas. This structure he now built upon and soon Vasudevan and Radha moved into their own house.

They settled down in Madras. People forgot the hero. A dream faded and the sky showed deep crimson gashes. Life entered a commonplace rut. Radha passed her matriculation and then joined Queen Mary's College. It had the reputation of being one of the best in the city but to Radha it was a cage. She was disgusted with the students around her. They moved in small spheres; those who did not herd into class and engage themselves parrotwise in memorizing Boyle's Law and Avogadro's Hypothesis spent their time talking of fashion, movies and boys. Somewhere, no doubt, there were intelligent young men and women but she never seemed to come across them once she stepped outside Hari Vilas. For long hours she stood on the topmost terrace of the college staring out at the ever-roaring sea, pining for the land of her birth as her father staring at the Aegean had pined for his.

Now, with Nikolaus beside her, she felt an intense nostalgia; speaking her language with someone other than her father had borne her on the crest of a wave for a week and now she was being hurtled down.

The bus moved slowly along the beach road, and someone was singing something that everyone was supposed to hear and to join in the chorus.

In the lull she thought, He'll be going away soon. Back home, back to life, back to her country. Her country, yes, this was her father's land but not hers. This land had given them nothing for his patriotism. It was terrible to be poor. When they had arrived the whole country acclaimed him but had done nothing for him. And now even his homecoming was stale.

They should not be poor by rights. It was all lies that young Srikant had told her father once, "We want to give you comfort. We would like to give you all the best. But how? We who wish to give have nothing, nothing to give. Nothing at all except our own dreams and disappointments. You were exiled working for a subject nation. And now you have to work as hard for the same people, free only in name." These and other things they had said, Srikant and his friends who visited her father regularly even now. And she had been satisfied that her father got the admiration due to him even if he did not get material comforts.

But now she felt that it was all lies, all lies. If they wished, they could make him rich and renowned—others who had sacrificed less had received much more, a few days in jail had given men ministerships—but they did not wish. That was the stark truth. They had cast him off like a rotting fish. These people had no appreciation for nobler values. Oh, how she hated India. How she wished she could return home!

"Have a cigarette, come on, you've been refusing too often," Nikolaus said. "No, no thank you," she said, once again offended at being offered a cigarette.

A few minutes more and he will be gone, the only person who had attracted her in these last two years. A few minutes more. He said as much. "Time has passed all too quickly, sweet one." He reached for her hand but she pulled it out of his reach and pretended her hair needed patting down.

"This reminds me of the road to Cape Sounion, the sea following, ever following, but that is more beautiful, is it not?" he said.

Radha wanted to give him her hand then, and her aching heart. She remembered only too well the winding road along the blue Aegean, blue, sparkling blue such as found nowhere else, all the way to Aegeus' rock where the old man had stood watching for the white sail as she so often stood on the veranda of the college, looking out at the sea with an empty heart sapped even of longing.

And yet when he stretched his hand again, again she withdrew.

Now they were at the University hostel where the foreign students were staying. They got off the bus and Nikolaus kept patting her shoulder and telling people how much he enjoyed her company. And vaguely she resented this familiarity.

As she turned away she knew that another dream had ended and as sharply. There was no going back for her. These three days had shown her that. She had already become part of Hari Vilas, of Madras, of India, infected with inhibition about holding hands, about physical familiarity even as normal as a hand over her shoulder . . . At one point she had told herself, I mustn't feel upset over little things. It is just their way, different from ours, no doubt . . . Yes, she had said it—different from ours, no doubt. Hari Vilas, Madras, India had absorbed her into a rut of conventions. She could not go back now or ever.

She wanted to walk to the sea and stand in the spray of the breakers till death like sleep might steal on me and I might feel in the warm air my cheek grow cold and hear the sea breathe o'er my dying brain its last monotony. Mayura had taught her those lines, and talked about the poets and poetry in her textbooks. How consoling it would be if Mayura were here. But Mayura was far away in her new blisses. Radha realized that she was physically tired. To sleep, sleep away the last four years and wake up on Acropolis!

Radha wandered back to her college, and into the girls' hostel, looking for distraction. Rekha's room was open but Rekha was not there. The bed was not made, Rekha was like that, her room was always open, always untidy. I must go home, Radha thought, and lay down. The pillow had a lingering fragrance of perfumed hibiscus hair oil. She flung it away to her side and pressed her bended knee on it. Just a short rest, she said to herself.

Her sleep was troubled. Deep, yet not totally unconscious. Voices drifted past the room. Rekha came in, "Having a snooze eh?" she asked. Radha woke up then. There was no Rekha. With her toes she kicked away the counterpane and several books fell to the ground. I should be going, she said, unable to open her eyes. She fell asleep. Raghu and she were at the beach. His eyes were dark brown, with pupils that seemed to leave no place for the iris. The setting sun shone on his face, and his pupils were purple and glowing. She dropped her eyes and took a handful of sand. Raghu put his hand under hers and tilted it empty. He lifted it and pressed the nails of her first three fingers to his lips. "Dearest! we are going to be very happy," he said. Radha swam up to sub-consciousness. It was Mayura on the beach, not she. Mayura had told her about it, that he slid his fingers under her buried hand and had drawn it up, that she had withdrawn it quickly, that one of the two loafers near them had laughed and passed a comment that was obviously filthy though it was inaudible.

Mayura hasn't written to me even once, Radha thought sadly. But, after all, she had written only a single letter even to her parents, a brief four lines about their journey being comfortable, the flat being big, the cook having had everything ready for them that evening. She is busy, too happy to remember others, who wouldn't be with Raghu?

Radha dreamed again. There were voices, male voices, the postman's familiar "Post", no it was someone else coming in. How did they get into a women's hostel? What did they want? She should scream. But no scream came to her aid. I am dreaming, she told herself, but I can't wake myself. I am in Rekha's bed, resting after the drive from Tiruvanmayur beach and final farewell to the visitors, I ought to get up and go home. Radha knew she was dreaming but she could not wake herself. Nor could she release herself from the grip of the daydreams and nightmares she had one after another. People came in, prowled around. One bent down to smell her. He had the face of a dog. A while later the men went away. One of them was Nikolaus.

Radha and Raghu were in her house. He was talking to her father. But when she went up to him and laid her cheek against his arm, her father was not there and she was alone with him. "I love you so much," she said, "so much, I wish we could live together forever." "But of course, I am going to be around for a good while yet, you'll have me right by your side till you scream from boredom." The voice was Mayura's, not Raghu's.

Fifteen months ago, when the question of Mayura's marriage was first taken up, Radha had been miserable at the thought of separation from her dearest friend. Often that winter, as they played Mayura's favourite game, Carrom, sitting on the smooth, black-stone floor of Mayura's room, she wanted to fling herself into Mayura's lap and say, Don't get married, not yet, and she wanted to hold on to the long slim legs and never let go, but she knew how much Mayura loathed demonstrative behaviour, and so she refrained. One day, that was the day the father of a young executive had written that the horoscopes were very favourable, Radha had impulsively said, "I'll miss you Mayu, if you get married and go away—" and Mayura had replied, "But of course, I am going to be around for a good while yet, you'll have me right here till you scream of boredom." And that had not been a dream. Nor had it been a dream when Raghu had sat in the rocking chair in their small drawing room, talking to them about Greek and Indian sculptures.

"I would go a step further," he said, after listening to her father's thesis, "I would say that there was a far greater civilization in the past than we have cared to grant. My theory is that the Ramayana and Mahabharata are poems written in a minor civilization that succeeded a far superior one, a civilization which was technically as advanced as the one we live in today." He smiled, his sensuous soft lips pressed together, forcing the laughter to a dimpled scar on his cheek. Radha could not decide whether he was being serious, or having a joke at her father's eccentricity.

He continued, "Just consider this. Suppose a primitive Aztec tribe that had seen the Spaniards, their ships and guns and what-have-yous, and then retreated so far into isolation that they are still living somewhere unknown to us. The first generation or two would have talked of the thunder of cannons and the magnificence of the ships. These stories would have become legends and with generations would have altered. Suppose then that today a poet, a very imaginative poet of this isolated tribe that has not seen a white man since then, was to rewrite the story. He'd exaggerate all he could and talk of a magnificent island that floated to the shore of their land once upon a time, and the tall white gods who wielded thunder, and so on. Do you see what I am trying to say? That the most fantastic descriptions he writes will still fall far short of reality because a poet can only build upon objects and elements he is familiar with. In other words the poets who sang the epics were retelling stories of a supersonic civilization, of guided missiles and television, and possibly even interplanetary travel, but they had to work with comparisons drawn from their own life and exaggerate upon those elements; and so we have Rama shooting an arrow that could pursue its prey to death, Sanjaya giving a first person commentary of what was happening on Kurukshetra several miles away, and Rama being carried in a celestial chariot across from Lanka into Ayodhya ..."

Raghu had continued his fantastic speculation till Mayura, dressed and ready for a walk to the beach, had appeared among them. Raghu had bounded up eagerly and left with a hasty Bye-bye. They were married three days later.

Radha sighed. Mayura was too busy, too happy with new emotions to remember her. With Raghu who wouldn't be?

Radha slept again.

She woke to Rekha's loud laugh. Rekha banged the door once more to make sure Radha would wake.

"Come ye, come ye, and see the resurrection!" Rekha shouted as Radha stretched herself. "I thought you had slept yourself into suspended animation. Would you like to stay and join us at our nosebags?"

"No, thanks. I should be going home."

Radha combed her hair and braided it afresh while Rekha carried on a monologue of how Radha would faint from hunger unless she had a bite of the leather that passed for roti in their dining hall, and of how her crumpled sari was a disgrace that would tarnish the fair name of QMC if Radha walked back on the road in it . . . Radha powdered her face. "I can't get the sleep off my face," she said, ruefully rubbing the deep lines made on her cheek by the rumpled bedsheet.

"You look a perfect terror. Just take care you don't frighten any kids into Buckingham Canal," Rekha said cheerfully, "and don't be so uppity-up," she took out an ironed silk sari from her chest of drawers. Radha looked at her handloom cotton sari that had been crisply starched and ironed in the morning but was now a shoddy heap of wrinkles. She decided to obey Rekha's order and draped the silk sari around herself.

Radha walked out by the front gate and turned her steps toward the bus stop. The sea reminded her of Nikolaus and Greece and pain. She thought about her grandmother, with whom she corresponded regularly but from whom she felt cut off. She did not look to her left but she could not shut out the sound of breakers lashing on the shore. In another half hour the sun will set, the same sun will sink into the Aegean a few hours from now, she thought, her heart heavy with emptiness.

It was another five minutes before she realized that she was standing at the wrong bus stop. Then she decided to walk instead. After all, it was only a mile. It was getting dark. And as she walked back she reassessed what had happened to her. True she could not return to Greece, true the iron rut of Madras life wedged her, but was there not something mystical in this change of the very instincts? Wasn't she exaggerating the stupidity of people around her and their own poverty?

Her father was happy. He had his work and for the last two years the museum had been paying him an honorarium to carry on his research. He looked younger than Radha had ever known him, and he was beyond doubt satisfied with life. Like his brother he had started on a mammoth book project, and he immensely enjoyed his trips to Madurai and Tiruchi and other places. She had to admit she enjoyed them too, for as they walked about the temples she recaptured some of her past worshipful love for her father, and at several temples she could not but be moved by the atmosphere which projected Eternity because, added to the sublimity of the Parthenon was the intensity of life and faith, as living devotees lit real lamps and offered prayers to gods who still dwelt and moved between the sculptured pillars. If her father did not feel himself cheated of renown, why should she? Why did she bear a grudge against people whose homage was, anyway, insubstantial and worthless? Blackguards, as her uncle had said. She appreciated him now, generous, noble man . . . Yes, life had treated them well, and she was particularly proud to belong to Hari Vilas.

Radha sighed, thinking of Mayura miles away. How much she missed her friend only her father knew, and he had been expressing tenderness in the only way he knew, by taking her on his tours and asking her to help him in his work. But even he could not wholly understand because he did not love Mayura. "What do you find in the caryatid?" he asked, "her eyes remind me of the Statue of Liberty's—cold disdain and sullenness looking down from Olympian heights." More than once he had said, "If she, by chance, were to be petrified in one of our temples, straight-lipped, slim-hipped, small-breasted, why, my whole lifework would become untenable and meaningless!"

Her father was at his writing table when she reached home. "I've had a long day," Radha said cheerfully, entering the room. Already Nikolaus and nostalgia belonged to the pain-pleasure of the past.

"Did you come by Jagannathan's?"

"I didn't go in. Do you want something from there?"

"I just wondered if you'd met Mayura."

"Mayura here?"

"Er . . . well, yes."

"What is the matter?"

"She has come away from her husband, leaving just a note behind. It is her idea of drama, I guess."

Radha looked at him, eyes dilated with fear and disbelief. "Come away?"

"Forever and forever, so she says," he said with a dry chuckle.

"But she's married to him. To Raghu!" Radha cried in a high treble.

"Oh well, she has her reasons, one needs must suppose."

"She can't do that, she can't." Blood seemed about to spurt out of her eyes because another dream had ended and the sky bled crimson gashes.

Great-Aunt Kamakshi

"I THINK YOU SHOULD go back, Mayura."

Mayura looked disdainfully at her great aunt, Kamakshi. Drily she replied, "You are not the first to tell me that."

"Nor the last, of course. But such pat retorts are not going to help you any."

"You are not the first to accuse me of impertinence, nor the last, of course. I have heard nothing else these five days."

"I pity you."

"I've had plenty of that too, Athai," Mayura cried impatiently. "I came here to be alone. I didn't think anyone, least of all you, would climb two steep flights of stairs to come to the afternoon heat of the open terrace."

Kamakshi looked at the peepul leaves above them. The breeze rustled through the tree like gold-leaf temple bells tinkling in the wind. "Beautiful place."

Mayura impatiently ripped along the rib of a palm leaf by her side and threw it away. Kamakshi picked up the torn leaf and started plaiting it.

Kamakshi was more of Hari Vilas than anyone except Ramakrishnan. Widowed within six years of marriage, she had lived here all these years except for a few years with her son after he had taken up his first job, in Trivandrum. The wrinkles on her face showed clearer and deeper because she was fair. The black of her eyes were whitish grey but still lustrous. Her hair was more grey than black. Her forehead was narrow, but because it was unadorned with kumkum and because her hair was combed severely back, it seemed wide, like her brother's.

Mayura ignored her presence for the next few minutes, leaning against the parapet wall, with closed eyes. The old woman was undeterred. She too sat on, silent, plaiting the green frond after carefully slitting it into thin strips, still held together at the top. Suddenly she recited, "She shall lie with earth above, and he beside another love." The young woman opened her eyes. There was something ludicrous in an old woman intoning in English.

"I didn't know you picked up even Housman along the way," she said sarcastically.

"Ramakrishna has been kind."

"He has a mania for teaching English. I didn't know he had instituted an essay prize in so many high schools until a friend of mine got it."

"He is the kindest man I've ever come across."

Mayura looked curiously at her great-aunt. At sixty-eight, she was still sturdy enough to climb to the terrace without wheezing. Her skin and eyes were old, but she did not have any of the physical weaknesses of age. People had often told Mayura that she resembled Kamakshi not only in her features but in her flailing sarcasm. In an old woman it was okay, they said, but in a young woman it was not okay, no way.

"It is a long time since I read anything except the newspaper in English, or had the desire to, but some lines remain imprinted forever in one's mind."

"Well, I should think there are better quotations to remember. Anyway, he may lie beside a new love each night even while I am alive for all I care. And for that matter," she laughed, "do you remember the other lines in the poem, something along the lines of, he shall lie with clover clad and she beside another lad?"

"Would you? Now, when he is alive?"

Mayura dropped her eyes, unable to meet the other's. If the old woman's voice or eyes had been in the least shocked, Mayura would surely have said, Of course, yes. But the eagerness, almost the plea, in the question startled her. Composing herself, she scornfully said, "Anyway, it is immaterial. Sex is not essential to living. You should know that better than anyone here."

"So you can't, isn't that the answer?" Mayura was again startled, now by the hissing triumph in the words. After a pause, Kamakshi said with a groan of despair, "We are too tied down to our inherited values of one-man-for-life, unconsciously and inextricably trapped by Brahminical ideals to be . . ."

"Promiscuous?"

"Some of us will drive ourselves to that, but we won't take the obvious path of remarriage."

"Come, Athai, many do it now. Things have changed since your days. Widow remarriage is accepted nowadays, you know."

"Would you take another man?"

Mayura was thrown out of her usual composure, and found relief in anger. "I don't know. I . . . I haven't thought about it. I am sure I'd remarry if I were widowed. I . . ."

"But you won't be widowed. Put yourself in the proper perspective. The pressure, and I don't mean social, external ones, I am talking of our inner thinking feeling self, is as weighty in you as they were in me. Remarriage— we in our day were thrown off by the idea of widow-remarriage as you are by remarriage after a divorce. Where does that leave you? You are not going to be a widow, but a divorcee. And you will never know a man's embrace."

Mayura had not thought that far yet. Between "separation" and "divorce" there was an ethical chasm, and she had not come to all that yet. But her aunt's blunt words had stirred her lips into quivering, and she struck out. "I can do without sex, I tell you. Haven't you? And haven't you done more with your life than others do with a husband and children?"

On her second return to Hari Vilas, Kamakshi had plunged into work, and there was no field of social service in Madras and environs that had not felt her influence and benefited by it. Orphaned high school students still lined up at the fee-cashier's desk with cheques written out by her. Destitute women still came to see her though she had retired several years ago. Mayura would not admit so to anyone, but she had admired Aunt Kamakshi, and had vague aspirations to follow in her footsteps. The other woman she admired was almost the opposite of Kamakshi; Maya was Aunt Chandra's friend, an artiste who seemed to live totally for herself. To work, to create, to transform. She would do it, now that she was on her own. In marriage, one could never be on one's own, she had very quickly realized, not if one is bound to a boor, a lascivious drinker who wanted to fawn and fumble every minute he was home. If he had been otherwise, a studious academic with a sensitive mind engrossed in philosophy or physics . . . what use dreaming? It was too late, too late. But she could work.

She could see an exciting active life ahead of her. Soon, as soon as nagging aunts and solicitous uncles stopped counselling. When and if they stopped counselling.

"Work is no substitute for, for sex as you so bluntly put it."

"Oh!" Mayura looked at her aunt with new recognition. "Was it that important for you?"

"It is not the body I am talking about, though that itself is reason enough why you should go back. Yes, sex, home, children, these mean a lot. You turn your back now on married life. You might plunge, if you are ambitious, into work. But then, you'll see your ambitions to change the world are only pipedreams. A time will come when you realize how futile your life has been. It will be too late then; you can't get back your husband, you can't have children . . ."

"Husband, children, as though these are the only things in life."

Kamakshi shook her head. "I didn't mean to say all that. You have something in you that upsets, distracts, diverts people into irrelevancies. That is not at all what I was thinking about." She wiped her face, as though to erase the past few minutes. Then in an intense tone she said, "We are inveterate romantics, Mayura, idealism is a plague in the family. But your idealism is perverted."

"My ideals are different, that is all."

"Ideals! All ideals should be thrown away. And your ideals. Bah, distorted perversion. You are crying for the moon when you have the power of the dawning sun in your hand."

"Scorching lust."

"What does it matter? Lust, all right, lust. But the lust is real. Your ideals are farfetched, bodiless, inaccessible."

"Why don't you try to find out what they are before you condemn them?"

"You yourself don't know what they are."

Mayura had no answer to that.

Kamakshi continued, "All ideals are insubstantial. We, I mean, average thinking people like me, not pseudo-idealists fattening on their own immaturity, we romanticize ugliness into beauty, pain into pleasure, even failure into martyrdom. We are usually lucky enough to remain entranced. But sometimes we come to a point when we cannot conjure up an illusions, and then we realize the utter meaninglessness of what we've held as sacrifices."

There was a long silence.

Kamakshi threw aside the palm leaf she had plaited and replaited, and stretched her legs in front of her. The story-telling pose, children called it, legs stretched in front, one hand massaging her knee where arthritis had set in, with an even, rhythmical motion. Now her eyes were closed. A patch of sunlight fell on her white hair and darted back.

She started speaking without opening her eyes. Her voice was preternaturally soft, and the words rippled out like the music of a dream, sad, slow, obliviating all else.

"Those were long evenings as we sat in the lonely empty room with dreary rain outside, rain that pours down from the sky unclearing for days the black clouds growing blacker or grayer but always there brooding sprinkling drizzle on the overburdened earth but not quenching the funeral pyre that smouldered now sparking now scorching always smouldering in our barren bodies aching for her. Silence, no words no tears no sad songs in which to pour out, but who can pour out what from emptiness to emptiness? Each thought of what might have been if fate, that moron who snips and slices unfeeling unknowing our hopes and dreams, had not intervened and blighted irrevocably blighted the legacy that was ours paid in full with my naked forehead and my warm blood through years of patience and resignation, the price high price of motherhood in widowhood in this our life our home. He said nothing because he was a man and I because my words deepfelt throbbing with blighted hope and loneliness might yet mock his greater grief. And so we sat in the lonely empty room and thought of her who was with us two springs, happy years so happy one feels it is forever and one forgets the years of subconscious waiting and hoping and praying, of unsatiated longing and unexpressed loneliness. And then came that snip-snippeting moron and left us more alone than ever we had been.

"And I watched my son losing his youth before he was twenty-six, watched him entering our gate creaking gate that closed shut but never quite, with lowered head and slow steps not wishing to enter where she had lived and where nothing was now except emptiness. Shabby clothes, unwashed body, his odour filling clothes chair room that once breathed her jasmine flowers. Silence. Evenings of empty silence with opened books unread, unlaced shoes sweating unwashed socks into the room that once breathed her jasmine flowers. And sometimes I wished Shankar would fling his indoctrinations and let himself go as others fortunate others unbound with racial inherited enslaving principles did, at races, bars, gaming houses, than have this stifling sorrow seeping enervating into his heart his loins.

"One day in the low toneless voice that had possessed him he said I wish I could cry I try to I whip myself into a frenzy of longing that I might cry for very despair. But no tears come because tears are not for men we've been told. Why are we taught it is a shameful act to cry? Something would flow away with tears. Is that why we hoard it in? he said.

"Because of those evenings, dreary rain outside and emptiness within, I was purified of something I had nursed for twenty and more years, a grudge I had whitewashed subconsciously and therefore doubly tenaciously into an idealized state of existence.

"Twenty-two, I was twenty-two when Ramakrishna brought me back here, back home, my home but never my son's. He resented Ramakrishna as only an orphan who knows he is an orphan—everyone tries to make up for his orphaned state with subtle secret sympathy—can resent a guardian. And I, selfish as I was, allowed him to hate because that made him love me more, and I needed his love I told myself, all his love, I selfish possessive deprived hungering unsatiated me took and hoarded in my heart.

"Ramakrishna brought me home, awakened my mind, injected his ambitions into me and goaded and pricked me nagged me threatened me into schooling myself. My mind widened with years and experience but my body remained twenty-two because he was twenty-five forever and I could not dissever—would not dissever because of my preconceived ideals of womanhood, of Sita and Shakuntala and Arundhati who were begotten of man and built up by man to be worshipped by him because he needed to worship and had the power the imagination to mould what he willed—myself from him, it was always twenty-two. And also because it was its own. It never wanted to be its own but had to be because the mind, that invisible tyrant itself enslaved by centuries of dos and don'ts oughts and oughtnots glorifies itself and deludes itself and prides itself in its enslavement, and tyrannizes the body into not wanting, and the body not wanting, the tyrant instead of being triumphant sinks into regret and nurses a grudge a deep grudge that a woman's life should close at twenty-two because of a man.

"And now, though it wrenched me to see my son those long desperate evenings of dreary rain outside and emptiness within, I was purified. At last I did not have to be subconsciously wary as one is wary towards the end of summer of dipping one's bucket too deep into the drying well for fearing of drawing up the sludge that one knows all along is there, and now I could dredge the very bottom and bring out the gob of mire and say, Yes, I resented having to close my life at twenty-two, but no more. There is not and will not be any resentment in me. This I said because I saw my son in the very image of his father and I saw how wretched he would have been had it been I and not he who had been taken away by Them who had written this marriage should end. He would have been as my son was now, his evenings long with dreary rain outside and emptiness within, he who was born to live and love and enjoy life to the fullest, full blooded, active . . . reduced to such wretchedness and stifling sorrow. And I was glad that he whom I had loved so warmly so passionately yearningly had been spared this pain this emptiness. Grateful I was that it had been I and not he that had been bereaved. And I willingly closed my life at twenty-two because it had satisfied that snip-snippeting moron bent on breaking a marriage and yet had enabled him to leave with youth and manhood unsapped by sorrow.

"Another spring came by. I saw that my son had his life to live. That he should not waste it so. And I urged him to start again. And I selected a girl sweet and loving and lovable, and blessed them with grateful heart. The wedding was a quiet ceremony on the summit of the Sacred Hills. And there I remained two weeks while they went to the house that I had prepared for them. And I prayed with peace and gratitude.

"They came to take me home. I watched them coming up the slope, and thanked the gods to see him happy once again. And they came nearer, waving their hands, and I was filled with gladness to see him young and joyful. And they came nearer—my twenty-seven year old son and his bride. And I realized suddenly and hopelessly that my sacrifice had been meaningless, for had it been I and not he, he would have been as my son was now."

*

Mayura turned away from the closed eyes and aging face. She wished the voice that rippled in eddying circles around her like music in a dream after one has descended to consciousness would stop swirling around her.

She dissolved it the only way she knew. She clapped with infuriating slowness. "Athai, if you climbed up all the way to the terrace to tell me the story of your life for my edification, I regret to say you have shot wide of the mark."

Kamakshi clenched her fists. "I didn't mean to talk about myself. But you made me. Your presence among us is a rake that makes us muck into our past. I see it now. Here again we romanticize your plight and feel sympathy and pain where none is needed. But you," she added drily, "you very quickly bring us back to sanity."

Continuing her patronizing, Mayura said, "However, you have taught me something. You are the only one who hasn't talked of duty and all that, but seen marriage as sex. But don't you see? You make too much of the body because you were deprived of it. You owed a grudge to life because your youth was wasted. And half your life was wasted because until youth was gone you could not work, being unreconciled to your body being wasted. But I know and see the whole picture of my life and what it can be if one just turns one's back on sex and gets on with life."

"I thought I was beyond losing my temper, but you, you, oh you uncomprehending fool," Kamakshi thumped the air with her fist as she would a table, "you make me as uncontrollably furious as those passive, perennially pregnant women who could not would not understand that marriage is not mere . . ."

"It is, it is. There again is another of your many and inconsistent romanticisings. Those women know it for what it is—an endless night of intercourse and child-bearing."

"If you knew that, why did you marry?"

"Because I hoped . . ."

"That you'd be one of the fortunate exceptions? And what made you think you were one of the blessed? Your horoscope perhaps?"

"No need to be sarcastic. The point is, I know now."

"The revelation came suddenly? A flash of lightning?"

"Go away."

"Raghu should be flattered, that he was the Bodhi tree under which you got your enlightenment, that told you to foul up a poor man's life. You are no better than men who ruin a woman's life by marrying for a dowry or to get a housekeeper or someone they can beat up."

"Stop it," Mayura said, "oh stop it." And suddenly, without knowing why, she broke into tears.

I didn't want to be sarcastic, Kamakshi thought, but it has been my refuge, my only self-defense all these years. I wish I could cry, Shankar, I wish I could cry.

Maya's Mystique

"AND, MR PROSPECTIVE BUYER, the house comes with a magnificently furnished guest room complete with a live and permanent guest." Hari Vilas youngsters had this and similar jokes about Chandramati's house-guest, Maya. Maya usually lived in Bombay, like the rest of the show-biz crowd, but she made frequent trips to Madras. Sometimes she stayed in a hotel. Most times, she stayed at Chandramati's. When Chandramati's husband, Murti, had set up business in Madras, they had rented the house built for her brother Krishnan since he was in the Railways and came to Madras only on vacations. The duration of Maya's visits was unpredictable. Sometimes she stayed only half a day, and at other times she stayed for months at a stretch. If one met her, by chance, at a party, one would not guess that her mother had died a prostitute, or that she belonged to the film world. Her make-up was so slight, her skin so translucent, her expression so refined, her movements so graceful, and her speech so genteel that one would naturally assume she belonged to a royalty high in the list of princes pensioned off by the government.

Just what she was in the film world few at Hari Vilas knew. The faint air of mystery added to the awe and admiration that the youngsters had for her. She did not act or dance or sing in films. Her name did not appear in film magazines, or in the main credit lines of any film, popular or avant-garde, and yet she was in the social circle of directors and actors. She was an art consultant, Chandramati said with a vagueness characteristic of her, and if one could read the fast moving credits on the screen at the end of films on the Hindi and Tamil screens, one might have often seen her name in the late 1950s.

She stayed at Chandramati's as a friend, and as such she was accepted. At first wagging tongues had wondered why Judge Ramakrishna Iyer's daughter should allow such a person into the house. But with passing years, her visits excited no comment. Her stays were getting much longer. The guest suite in Chandra's house was furnished for and by her. The drapes, the bed, chairs and carpets were all her selections. She transformed the room once in a while with new furnishings that came in large cardboard cartons from Bombay or Delhi, which cartons the younger children gleefully turned into tunnels and caves for their games.

Maya was a quiet guest. No one visited her at Chandra's, and if she kept odd hours, often coming back only in the morning, it disturbed nobody. Even her car was soundless, even though it was one of the hump-backed monsters of an earlier age. It was a dark green Dodge, with chrome trim and a gold-dipped flying horse on the hood. There was a liveried chauffeur on duty. Whenever Maya was home, it stood under the mango tree between Chandra's house and Jagannathan's. Everyone knew it was one of the fleet of cars owned by the Muthu Chetty family who were wholesale grain dealers and operated the largest agency for imported agricultural machines. Some said one of the old man's many nephews was her lover. Be as it may, the car was always at Maya's service when she was at Chandra's.

What most surprised even those at Hari Vilas was that Maya was Chandra's friend. It would have been easy to understand Mukta having such a woman as her best friend. Mukta was a society woman, outgoing, convivial, one who loved parties and the social whirl, who went out of her way to meet exotic people and experiences. But Chandra was a quiet woman, the only docile person of Ramakrishna Iyer's blood. There was no hardness or pride anywhere in her; she had large, gentle eyes; her matronly figure and perennial good humour gave her a bovine look of contentment. She seemed perfectly satisfied with housewifery and sought no social pleasures. Her husband, Murti, was a partner in a well-established firm of chartered accountants and seldom came home before seven. They had once been avid Club-goers, but now were not part of any group. The youngest of their three children was already twelve, and there was no reason at all why Chandra should glue herself to the house. She did not even join one of the women's clubs that met in the afternoons. She observed all the festivals and holy days but without much zeal or enthusiasm, unlike Lakshmi who celebrated them with energetic faith and joy. That such a convention-loving matron should have Maya as her best friend was a source of mystery even for those around her. But there it was.

Mayura was in the deck chair on the front veranda of her father's house. There was silence all around, the silence of siesta hour. But Mayura knew Maya did not have the siesta habit. Everyone at Hari Vilas knew what Maya did or said at Chandra's house because she was one of those persons who interest other people. Mayura held her as a hero, a model of what she might want to be. Now, Mayura was intrigued by Maya's silence. She was the only person, other than her grandfather and Radha, who had nothing to say about her return. Maya had not avoided her the way Radha had, but neither had she spoken anything except of general interest.

Mayura went toward Chandra's house after checking that the Dodge was under the mango tree. Maya was outside, sitting on a cane chair, one of those comfortable chairs, painted light yellow and with glossy green arms and a green diamond that characterised chairs made by Jayabharatam Company. Maya's legs were stretched out, her heels resting on a cane ottoman. The lower edge of her expensive Banarsi silk sari trailed in the grass that was wet and muddy with the morning's downpour. Mayura went to her hesitantly and asked, "I wonder if you have a few minutes to spare."

Maya looked at her without answering, a long, lazy look from beneath her faintly mascara'd eyelashes. She appeared amused. She took her feet off the ottoman and pushed it toward the girl, saying, "Here, or you can pull up a chair from the veranda." Mayura sat down, and immediately felt at a disadvantage, for the ottoman had shrunk her to her ten-year-old self that had held in awe this glamorous friend of Chandra Athai. She said as she had planned, "You are the only one who hasn't said anything about my misdeed," but the words did not sound as light as she had wanted them to be.

"It is not exactly any of my business, is it?"

Ignoring the mockery, Mayura continued, "I come for advice."

The mockery was more unmistakable now, "I thought that was something you had altogether dispensed with."

Mayura bit her lip. "The value of advice depends on who gives it."

"And you think that I, having deserted my husband, am the only person whose advice can have the stamp of validity."

Mayura flushed deeper. "You know why I left."

"There's no one who doesn't, is there? His bed-conduct was not satisfactory. And by what criterion does one who has never known any man judge a man to be lecherous? By those Arthurian tales of Galahad, by Petrarchan sonnets and Urdu ghazals of undying love?"

The younger woman felt humiliated.

Maya's voice was low and uninsulting but gathered impatience as she spoke on. "You are not a child upon whom the mysteries of sex came unannounced. You were not brought up in such seclusion that books were out of your reach, and your reading has not been confined to Victorian novels where 'breast' is never used in the plural. You have lived in a family where marriages and births have been taking place with clockwork regularity. I don't see how you can cling to any romanticized ideas."

Mayura muttered, "You sound just like Aunt Kamakshi."

"A remarkable woman. If she has spoken to you already there isn't anything I need say."

"Not all men are like him."

"Probably not. Most would be worse." Again there was keen derision in her tone.

Mayura sat sullenly silent, unwilling to admit humiliation by leaving. But when she looked up, her face was pathetic, and Maya's became suffused with sympathy. A torrent of impetuous confession spurted out of the girl. "He is vile ... their jokes are so vulgar, so personal, always about sex and nudity and such. For instance, oh, there are so many instances, for instance, the second Saturday I was there, some friends dropped in and we had high tea. It was at the table, and so I couldn't even leave the room. He said, 'Mayura wouldn't be much of a swinger in a nudist colony, but she is a treat, guys, you can take it from me that it is hogwash to say lean gals don't have juice.' I was so embarrassed, I've never been in such company. I thought of pretending I hadn't heard, I thought of walking out, thought of flying into a fury—the words were ready on my lips, after all it wasn't the first time he had said things like that, it started on the very first day, but I was paralyzed, I couldn't move or speak, and I smiled, god knows why I smiled, but I smiled, and one of them said, 'Congrats, Raghu, you've picked a real sport. If I'd said anything like that in my lady's presence, she'd have screamed the roof down here and now,' and another said, 'Mine wouldn't have said a word, just frozen my balls with a look, and walked out of the room and my bed for a week, and you must admit that's hell for a recently reformed guy like me.' And Raghu said, 'I know what you mean about your lady-love. I've intercepted her dagger looks. She reminds me of old man Prasad, a Cerberus of a schoolmaster, I tell you, the muscles of my backside used to harden even when he gave me a casual look in passing, woof.' Then one of them chipped in, 'They harden like hell even in happier circs you know,' while Raghu continued about how he used to be caned on his bare bottom, 'I bet I still have those ferrule marks,' and of course another had to say, 'Does he Mayura?' O heck, they are so crude. And then all those brothel jokes . . ."

Maya shrugged, amusedly contemptuous. "Sexually immature. You can be sure that those who talk like that never actually do anything away from the straight and narrow. All that bragging is a way of sublimating juvenile fantasies. I have often wondered why some men never grow up; I am pretty sure it has something to do with pseudo-masculine boys-only public schools. But they do grow up at some point."

Mayura continued as though she could not stop now. "And not just in talk. He insists on lights and slow striptease while he walks around nude and aroused, oh god, revolting." She put her hand to her face in an agony of remembrance.

Gently Maya said, "Mayura, the point is, do you want marriage or don't you? If you want the state of marriage, you have to accept men's sexuality, and Raghu seemed as good a man as they come."

"But what if I don't want marriage?"

"What then?"

"I can do something with my life as you have with yours. Create beauty, rich experiences . . ."

"You can try, but you won't make it."

Mayura reddened.

"It will be much harder for you than it has been for me, who had some advantages, shall I say." Mayura rose, insulted to tears. Maya motioned her back to her seat. "O, I don't mean you have no looks or talent. It is just that there is no comparison between us. To be born in a family like yours, to be educated in the manner you have been, yes, dance and music thrown in for good measure of course, these are disqualifications for a career like mine. It is easier for the poor to become rich because they have nothing to lose and so can take risks.

"I was born in the gutters. I don't even have the satisfaction, as some of my peers do, of having a devadasi for mother and an accomplished and rich man for father. I was born very legitimately in holy wedlock to a lowly shopkeeper's assistant and a servant woman. My mother took to prostitution only when I was two. So she had nothing to pass on to me, though I used to imagine she was a temple devadasi with art in her veins, and that my father was the film director who was one of her lovers when I was seven. He was a wonderful man, the only father I knew; he got me admitted to a good school and even though he did not stay long with my mother, he paid my tuition all the way through school and college. I used to study like crazy so I could impress him, but he never came back, not even once, though he continued to pay my fees for years, and gave me an education. You Brahmins born to education just don't know what it means—to be able to go to school. My mother knew its worth, knew that was the only other way to get out of the gutters. But it was too late for her. She rose to the top of her new profession," Maya's tone was sad, "because she learnt how to twist her body and for whom to open out her thighs. A night with a waiter in a hotel meant good food for a day, a weekend with a zamindar meant new clothes for both of us, a great asset to start with. Once you dress well, you can climb out of the gutter, the red light ghetto. She did that, and I was her beneficiary. I did not have to go through all that, but I too prostituted myself. At a time when I was sure I wanted to be part of that tinsel world of silver screens, I flirted with those who could benefit me, hirelings, underlings, all the long aisle to the director's office and bed, not one of whom I'd care to talk to now. But I did then. I was an opportunist. I still am, I suppose. But you, you cannot stand naked-ness in a healthy young man, how would you like a flabby belly on yours, and stale breath?"

"There are other ways," Mayura said, stubbornly refusing to give way to the panic that rose within her. "There are . . ."

"It is too late for you to start on a career of genuine art. I mean no offence, Mayura, but you are not and never can be an artist. Now,

Chandra, if I could have met Chandra when she was your age, I would have nagged her night and day, oh how I would have nagged her . . ."

Mayura felt more jealous of Chandra than ever before. But Maya was continuing, "There are too many in the field of pseudo-art for you to get anywhere on your own. And you, priggish nun, will not allow your chaste body . . ."

"Maybe I will, for a price, I will. To reach the peak."

"My peaks are not for you Mayura. You're not a sensualist, though I have a feeling that maybe Raghu is. You are an intellectual snob who won't allow any but another intellectual snob to touch you . . ."

"You, you . . ."

"I know what you want to say. That I can't understand intellectual aspirations. So let's leave that. The present point is that you have too much to lose. See what happened to me. Came a time when I could choose those who gave me pleasure even if they did not materially benefit me, and contrariwise I snubbed those who could help me in my career. Soon no assignment or man satisfied me, and my career came to a standstill. I lost my dare. I think twice now before undertaking anything because I have a lot to lose. And I have become a faithful one-man woman, to my own dismay. If it has been so with me, what can you expect, you people who start at the top of the social ladder, you just can't be good gamblers; and the stake, you must remember it could well be an illusion, an illusory wealth of experience that might turn out to be mere ditchwater."

"Your experiences have not been illusory."

"Not mine, thank god. But I have a body and a spirit. I don't know if you have anything other than mental processes, and that too comes from some hereditary source and not from any defined ability for individual achievement. You're a blind fool who thinks she has high ideals and is wallowing in self-pity that she has been cheated by someone that I thought was rather charming and intelligent."

Mayura did not raise her eyes. In a small voice, she said, "Is that what you think of me?"

"Does it matter what I think of you?" Maya rose and left, lazily trailing her dirtied sari-pallav, with a smile half-amused, half-contemptuous.

Mayura whispered after her, "It matters a great deal. I wish it didn't."

Patriarch Ramakrishna Iyer

RAMAKRISHNA IYER DEEPLY INHALED the fragrance of dawn. It was going to be a beautiful sunrise on the beach. He could see that from the way the clouds conglomerated in the eastern horizon, leaving the rest of the sky deep and clear. Soon the clouds would turn red and orange and yellow, the colours rioting and slashing each other for a brief half hour before withdrawing into grey brooding. Years ago Maitreyi Nivas had shared sunrise with the beach. Later, the vast field to the east of Maitreyi Nivas had been built upon, and a garish colony of houses cluttered the space beyond his compound wall. He did not care to have within his view those little painted cardboard houses built without a frontage and without any sense of beauty or comfort. He made his compound wall higher and stuck fragments of glass bottles at the top while the concrete was still wet. The wall cut off more of the eastern sky but he did not mind. He could visualize sunrise on the beach—streaks of magenta and yellow racing through grey clouds giving way to fiery red where the sea mated with the sky, the sudden brightening of the earth, the sun riding out of the clouds into clear azure.

He walked to his coconut grove. A huge broken frond was hanging dangerously over the path. He made a mental note that rascal Munisami had to be reprimanded. Since Munisami had ignored a drooping frond right on the path, it was quite likely that his negligence had extended to leaving overripe coconuts on the trees. What if a ripe coconut were to fall on some servant child? Good for nothing Munisami. He looked up. The yield seemed to be below average this year; the scoundrel had probably forgotten to salt the base.

He stopped of a sudden and took a deep breath. The parijata tree was in full bloom! Delightedly he walked to the tree at the end of the grove and took in deep draughts of the delicious air. He picked up a handful of flowers. Snow white with orange stalks, they died even as they bloomed, turning brown in the hand within moments of being picked off the ground. Gently letting go of the flowers, he walked up and down the path through the grove. His long-sleeved white shirt was a size too big, the shoulder seams drooping over the arm, but he preferred to wear oversize shirts. Fools strangled themselves in tight collars, not realizing that clothes were made for man's comfort. His collar was buttoned, and he wore cotton socks and slip-on shoes. When the dew is on the grass, one ought not expose oneself to the dampness in the air. His dhoti was tied unevenly around his waist, the front lower than the back, where the lower edge hardly covered his shins. His gait was curiously simian—long arms hanging straight down, palms facing back, shoulders hunched, neck and jaw out-thrust. From time to time he pushed dried burrs on dried twigs out of the path with his silver-headed walking stick.

He noticed that Lakshmi was at the front of her part of Maitreyi Nivas, sprinkling diluted cowdung water on the large square of ground that had been made hard with it over the years. She then brought out an earthen bowl of rice flour and started drawing an elaborate geometric design. She worked deftly, pinching flour between thumb and forefinger, and drawing lines and curves with the expertness of experience. May you always have the rice flour design of well-being in front of your home, he blessed her silently. He watched her from the edge of the grove with affection. A daughter-in-law after Maitreyi's heart, he thought, a good mother, thrifty housewife, devoted wife, indefatigable in her services. Nowadays she tired easily in body, though not in spirit. Had Adityan, her first born, been alive today, she would have a daughter-in-law to whom she would have turned over her responsibilities as Maitreyi had turned over hers. Soon may Chander or Subrahmanian bring home a good bride, he blessed her.

He turned to the path that ran around Maitreyi Nivas. He leaned on his cane and looked at the black letters on the marble—Maitreyi Nivas. Soon he must finalize the papers and hand over the house to Venkatesan. It was hard to bring himself to sign it away, but it had to be done. No one should wait for his death. He walked around the house. He stopped under the nellikkai tree. It had been there when he bought the land. The architect had wanted it cut down, but Maitreyi had begged that it remain. Under it she had built a tulasi matam for a tulasi plant. She prayed daily to the aromatic sacred plant, and once a year celebrated, as is decreed, the wedding of the tulasi to the gooseberry (nellikkai) tree. As the tulasi stood in the shade of the fruitful tree, so would its devotee stand all her life in the protective shadow of her husband.

When I die, he thought, my ashes shall be buried here. Maitreyi will not like it, a tree is to live under, she'd say, not to die under; one's ashes should be immersed in holy Ganga or Kaveri, not buried under a tree, she'd say if she were here. But he would have convinced her, as he had convinced her about so many other matters. Or maybe not. She was a stubborn one, my Maitreyi. He sighed. Yes, he would have his ashes buried here.

And years hence, maybe some day when Subrahmanian's daughter-in-law comes home, and comes to offer her daily prayer to the tulasi, he would address her mind and say:

I heard your husband tell you the day you entered this house that under this ancient tree is buried the ashes of his great-grandfather, founder of this house; this family line. Because they know so little about me, and because my ashes in this earthen jar moved when you crossed my threshold, because I have often heard you wondering about me as you pass and repass this spot while plucking jasmine and roses for your hair, I shall tell you my story, the story of the lineage you have made your own.

> Twelve decades ago I, a boy in years but a man withal,
> left my village home, not in hate, for I loved them all,
> loved my gentle parents,
> loved my sisters cousins widowed aunts,
> Yes, loved even my despot uncle who'd whip me
> if I dodged the morning prayers,
> And loved too the girl born for me,
> my mother's brother's child, just a child
> with all the skinny rawness of a child
> plain and unformed to all eyes save mine,
> Which saw more because she was born for me,
> and I a man within though a boy in years.
> Her too I left that Magha morn and walked eastward.

I was young and the world for me was young
And folks were kind and they could be so
For the harvest had just come in,
Had I not myself been on the fields
While the paddy was being flailed
And measured in its plenty?

Ramakrishna Iyer paused. The opening lines of an autobiography. An autobiography was the last failing of a successful man, an irresistible temptation. A temptation and therefore to be resisted, fought, overcome. And yet a well-written autobiography . . . an irresistible temptation and therefore to be resisted.

Ramakrishna Iyer went in. He glanced at the headlines of the newspaper before taking off his footwear. He washed his feet and hands. He slipped into his slippers and entered his suite. He placed his walking stick in its place on the hat-stand and sat down to work. He stared a while at the wall opposite his table, and Kumar's fever-bright eyes smiled at him from the mahogany frame. Twelve decades ago I, a boy in years but a man withal . . . The phrase lilted in his mind. He took out a clean sheet of paper and wrote, Why do I dread senility when it is but the sweet forgetting of the unrealized aspirations of youth and the incurable decrepitudes of age?

Munisami, the judge's man-of-all-work, reverently picked up the morning's Hindu and placed it on the teapoy next to the judge's armchair. When the master came in from his morning walk, he read the headlines on the first page before going in. Then it was Munisami's duty to pick it up and place it where the master would read it at leisure. Munisami dusted the chair and placed the footstool in position. That phase of his morning work concluded, he moved to the front veranda, sat on the floor and leaned against one of the series of twin pillars.

Munisami was a relic of his kind under the British Raj, abjectly servile, utterly obedient, impenetrably dull-headed. His master commanded, he obeyed. Given a new job, he forgot everything about it once it was completed. However, in his daily chores, his machine-like efficiency was proverbial in Hari Vilas. There was never a speck of dust on the furniture;

never a cobweb even in the most isolated corner of the library; never a patch that did not shine by eight o'clock in the morning in the white tiled bathroom or the black-floored rooms; never a scrap of paper anywhere but under the ivory inlaid rosewood paperweights on the lower right quarter of the table surface in the judge's study. He took several breaks during the day, but could generally be found at Maitreyi Nivas between sunrise and four o'clock in the evening. His day's work done, he joined other men in the cheri behind Hari Vilas, a silent auditor chewing a pleasantly aphrodisiac wad of tobacco that his master forbade on the Hari Vilas premises during the day.

Munisami had walked through life garbed in waterproof ignorance while floods of national awakening and showers of intellectual profundities had drenched the world outside and within Hari Vilas. There were vague landmarks in his life that had grown more vague because of their inconsequentiality. He remembered the Mahatma's visit. Though he had not been privileged to see the great one's physical body, he was carried away by the jubilance of the crowd which welcomed the precursor of the second Ram Rajya, and he had no doubt at all that the Prince of Ayodhya would once again walk through the streets of Madras just as he had eons ago on his triumphant return from Lanka. He remembered the evacuation of 1942 when fire dropped from the sky and the city was denuded of all save himself and his master. For fifteen years he had faithfully placed an X against the sign of the yoked bullocks because though raised in the slums around Buckingham Canal, he was of peasant stock and his blood unquestioningly answered to the call of the yoked bullocks and racial memories of green fields and harvest songs.

But those things were not relevant to the daily routine, and therefore they were inconsequential. The most relevant thing in life was the clock that ruled his master and therefore himself. It was one of his colossal achievements that he could read the time. Only on the face of one clock, it was true, but what did clocks matter once he was outside Hari Vilas? He could read the time on the huge faced Seikosa in the hallway that swung its shiny brass pendulum as it ticked its way to four o'clock.

The Seikosa and Saraswati ruled the master's half of Maitreyi Nivas. This he knew, and this he accepted with humble reverence. He never passed the framed picture of the white-attired peacock-throned goddess

without joining his palms in worship. Paper and the written word were
her domain. He never touched a book directly, but held it with his white
shoulder cloth. And even for the newspaper, he wiped his hands on the
duster before touching it. Not a scrap of paper was to be destroyed except
what was in the cane-woven baskets in each room. That was one of the
master's decrees. The master commanded, he obeyed.

Ramakrishna Iyer wrote voluminously. He jotted down his thoughts,
weighty and casual, on half-sheets of paper tagged in a sheaf and tied to
legs of tables or to nails on the wall all over his six-room suite. It was
Munisami's duty to collect all loose slips of paper from all of the six rooms
and place them under the ivory-inlaid paperweights on the master's
study table. From time to time the master made him burn a heap of
paper. Years ago, when told to do this, Munisami had flinched from the
task. Paper could be sold to shopkeepers who used them for wrapping
their customers' grocery; this burning seemed to be wasteful destruction
indeed. But once the master had caught him sneaking off with part of the
heap, and had given him a long discourse on why such paper ought not
to be sold for crass monetary gain. Munisami did not understand the
lecture but thenceforward he lit the bonfires with ritualistic fervour,
knowing that Goddess Saraswati was somehow involved.

"You lazy good-for-nothing, where are you?"

Munisami leaped to his feet and ran in, duster in hand. The master had
come into the house from the rear and had caught him unawares. The
master continued writing. Munisami took his position near the door,
ready to bow his head over joined palms the moment the master chose to
acknowledge his presence.

Ramakrishna Iyer ran his pen across the page he had written. Why do
I dread senility when it is but the sweet forgetting of the unrealized aspirations of youth and the incurable decrepitudes of age? He rearranged the
words. Why do I dread senility when it is but the sweet forgetting of
youth's unrealized aspirations and age's incurable decrepitudes?

He crossed that out. Too many prepositions in one, the possessives an
aural dissonance in the other. He looked up, and gave Munisami a lecture
on the proper care of coconut palms.

After dismissing Munisami, the judge reread what he had written. He
stopped himself from crumpling the sheets in his hand. The idea was

there, the words would come later. He opened the bottom drawer of his table and dropped the sheets into it.

A boy in years but a man withal, the refrain lured him into contemplating an autobiography. But no. Well, the words were mellifluous, worth writing down. He wrote out the lines he had composed, and dropped the sheet into the bottom drawer.

He sat back in his heavy revolving chair.

After several minutes, he rose and opened one of the Godrej almirahs that divided his study from the rest of the library. On the third shelf there was a stack of school notebooks, all of one kind, with a green cover, sixty-four lined pages, unused. He drew one out, shut the almirah door and went back to his table. As was his system, between the crested name of the brand at the top and the rectangular slot for inserting the name and other details of the student and school subject, he scrawled the title of his new subject—MAYURA. He opened the book and wrote the date on the top left corner—2 IX 65. Under it he wrote: It is almost a week since Mayura's dramatic arrival. Her case has already been considerably wrecked. Everyone knows she should go back. Unfortunately everyone has said as much. It pays in a court of law to say what you have to say in forthright and forceful terms. But not in human crises. The truth couched in words becomes meaningless. Hence the "Ineffable Name," "Yahveh," "Om."

Ramakrisha Iyer closed the notebook and dropped it into the topmost drawer.

Ananta

ANANT WAS EXPECTED ON Friday afternoon. He was driving down with three friends. He had said they would leave at night and drive straight through. Till six o'clock no one was worried and therefore kept speculating aloud what could have gone wrong. Maybe they had run out of petrol. Maybe they had run over some domestic animal and were held up by consequent wrangling. Villagers along the national highway had figured out that those who ran into their goats and chickens would rather pay them some cash and get away than be delayed, and so it had become a game of one-upmanship as to just how much they could haggle before they conceded the game. Because fact was, that the people in the car could simply drive away, unless the villages had some thugs who were ready to manhandle the motorists. The boys imagined aloud some more gruesome mishaps— maybe the petrol tank had burst into flames, maybe they'd bumped off the road in the ghat section and been tossed down a hillside and were being hauled off by dacoits . . .

By dinner time these vocal speculations stopped because most of them were Aat's arrival, but then started eating, sure he would come before they finished. Brothers and cousins converged to Jagannathans' and sat talking of the news from the battlefront, which was sensational enough to drive other thoughts from the boys' minds. Through the day the radio had been on full blast, and the news bulletins had been listened to with rapt attention followed by whoops of excitement. The bulletins did not add much as the day went on, but the repetitions were manna to the boys. A great day, they asserted, a day that would be remembered a long time by every true-blooded Indian. Squadron Leader Trevor Keelor had downed a Pakistani Sabre jet with his Gnat fighter.

In the morning battle, the enemy had lost two F-86 Sabre jets and one thousand two hundred and forty-four men. Onward Jawans, onward to Lahore and victory. Trevor Keelor, hero of the hour, hero unto eternity. Who knows, one of these days we'll see our Vij hitting the headlines. Lucky blighter to be where the action was. Jayaraman resorted to Henry V and orated "He that sheds his blood with me today shall be my brother, be he ne'er so vile this shall gentle his condition . . . and gentlemen now abed in England shall hold themselves accursed when this day is named and any speak who fought on Crispin's day . . ."

They animatedly spoke on. But almost everyone at some or another point irrelevantly interjected a speculation about Aat's non-arrival. Maybe he and his friends had decided to be prudent after all and take the train instead of driving their jalopy. Maybe they had decided to stop overnight at Humpi instead of driving in the dark. At eleven o'clock, everyone dispersed with several repetitions of the tiresome statement, Boys will be boys.

The telephone rang at half past eleven. Mayura flew downstairs and was at the phone before her mother got there from her room a few feet away from the living room where the phone was. "Yes, we will, good night." Mayura banged the receiver back on its cradle.

"Who was that?"

"Who else? The deputy minister's wife asking if our dear Ananta has arrived." She mimicked, "We are so anxious, please phone us the minute you get any news, regardless of what the time."

"You shouldn't be so rude."

"Heck, it is the nth time she's phoned in the last few hours."

"After all, they have as much cause to be anxious."

"Sure, sure, they'll thank god it was before and not after the engagement if Aat is lying dead in a ditch right now."

Parvati knocked her knuckles on the side of her head to express her lamentation. "How can you say such inauspicious things? You have a black tongue. How can you even think of such awful calamities? My darling Ananta."

Aat arrived after midnight. There was commotion as lights were switched on and excited voices relayed the news through Hari Vilas. Several people congregated on Jagannathan's veranda.

Nothing had happened. Nothing at all, just a run of bad luck, a flat tire, some gasket trouble, engine getting too hot, had to be cooled off, oil kept leaking, but everyone was fine. The others had dropped him at the gate and gone their way. All fine. (Parvati immediately promised their household deity a hundred-and-eight coconuts.) The jalopy had just about croaked on them, and they almost thought they'd have to abandon it and take a train after all.

"Silence there! Caterwauling like fishwomen! No sense of time, no regard for others! Waking up all of Mylapore at two in the morning! Is someone dying there? If not, everybody get back to bed." Ramakrishna Iyer boomed from his veranda.

"Ananta has arrived."

"Oh, the bridegroom! Go strew flowers for the bridegroom, strike up the clarinet and drum, for the bridegroom cometh! Irresponsible scamp. Go back to bed, everyone. At once."

Silence descended upon them like a photographer's mantle. The assembly vapoured away. Jagannathan's family continued to talk a while inside the house. The Krishnaswamis were duly phoned. Then Jayaraman and Gita went to their rooms upstairs. Mayura followed a few minutes later. As she climbed up the stairs, Aat addressed her softly, "Sis, what is it?" Parvati clapped her knuckle to her forehead. "Ask, by all means ask, but you won't get to know anything from the dumb pillar. You already know as much as anyone else here. O, how greatly I must have sinned in my previous birth to bear such a daughter!" She went to her room. Jagannathan, with an apologetic grunt on behalf of his wife and daughter, followed her.

Aat had bridged the brief silence that accompanied Mayura's appearance with a casual Hi Mayu! Now, from the foot of the stairs, he greeted his younger sister a second time. They looked at each other for a breathless moment. Then Mayura ran down and pressed his hand on the banister with her own. "Aat, what is it?" she repeated his question back to him with tenderness. Aat leaned his forehead against her hand.

"Are you hurt?"

He shook his head, No, and looked up at her.

"You too?" she asked gently.

He did not reply. Their gaze intertwined.

"Aat!" her whisper encircled him, crushing them in an orgasm of pain.

"Here's an extra pillow, my Kanna Ananta," Parvati's voice preceded her figure. Mayura withdrew her hand and eyes.

"Thanks, Amma."

"Go to sleep, my dear boy, you are looking very tired."

"Yes, Amma," and almost inaudibly he added, "tired to the very marrow of my being."

"Sleep well, darling son."

"Yes, Amma, I think I'll sleep in all morning."

"Come dawn, you'll be rushing off to see we know who," Parvati fondly joked.

Mayura went upstairs. Parvati watched her going up and once again gestured with her knuckles on the sides of her forehead her misfortune at having borne such a daughter.

Ananta did not sleep late. The Krishnaswamis descended on Hari Vilas at half past seven and whisked him away for breakfast. They kept him on for lunch. He returned at one o'clock and joined his family for a second lunch. In high spirits he joined the others in quipping at his own expense. All that afternoon jokes and congratulations were passed and rebounded with enthusiasm. Mayura watched him in silence. So Neela is all right, she thought, whatever it was that had made his eyes large watery bogs of helplessness will vanish soon.

"The Krishnaswamis have certainly put a spell on our boy. Goes for breakfast and stays on for lunch," someone said.

"Krishnaswami not Krishnaswamis. Singular, feminine, single," someone else corrected.

Aat said, "I am trapped. Say, fellows, do you think I could possibly get out of this?"

Jayaraman said, "You can, but Dad will get shunted off to Timbuctoo." Aat joined in the general laughter, but his eyes winced. Mayura noticed that.

"Well, now that you see Neela with new eyes, how does she seem?"

"As Durga to the sacrificial goat."

Jokes, repartees.

*

Mayura sat on the stone wall of the pond at the far end of the lawn. Afternoon shadows from the mango tree fell aslant on the water, and little patches of shimmering white rose against the weedy green of the surface. Mayura pulled a vine that stood stuck to the glutinous inner wall of the pond. The leaves were bright green; water trickled off their waxy surface as she pulled. It was a long weed, a strong weed. It uncoiled itself from the entangled mesh of weeds and lotus roots at the bottom of the pond. The stalk was green and firm in her hand, and as she neared the root it became soft and slimy. The soil on the stone bottom being thin, the root suddenly came away easily in her hand, a little edge of brown gnarled tentacles at the end of a green sodden stalk. Mayura threw it out and pulled at another vine. A single lotus was striving to rise out of the suffocating weeds and its own smothering leaves. It was white, with a yellow tinge at the base of each petal; it had a yellow halo at the centre where a little cluster of stamens rose erect.

Aat came out of the house. He looked like a robust teenager in his corduroy stove-pipe trousers and striped Madras. A triangle of fair skin showed at the open neck of his shirt. He had his thumbs inside the patch pockets on each side of the front, and he thrummed his fingers on his flat abdomen as he walked along. He was looking for his sister. She ought not to have come back. If a deal had been made, good or bad, one had to carry through with it. This he knew, this she must be made to realize. He did not know how effective he would be in his big-brother stance. It had always been she who had led, he who had followed, even though he was fifteen months older. As a child he had been puny and frail, buffeted by constant colds and fevers; she had been rosy and strong; in their early teens she had become thin and stayed slim while he grew into virile manhood.

Not finding her in the mango clump, he turned towards the jackfruit tree, another of their childhood haunts. The swing was empty. But he could almost see their child forms on it, she sitting on the plank, he standing behind her, rhythmically bending his knee to give the necessary push to the swing. Downward, upward, backward, higher and higher till they rocked the world around themselves, king and queen of the seven castles. Aat found himself whistling a nursery song. It was not a well-known rhyme; none of the Mother Goose books had it. They had taken it from a nameless book they called Fun Book. Fun Book had thick pages and a mouldy smell they loved. There were tricks and conundrums, and songs with notations, little wiggly worms that were drawn between four lines.

Aat pushed the empty plank with his foot and turned away. He had to talk to Mayura about herself. A desolate sense of waste overwhelmed him. She had to go back. That too was only another face of waste since this bloke, Raghu, had turned out to be such an uncouth fellow. But once a deal was made, it was binding. That's all there is to it. One had to stick it out. One could hope, of course, that once one started sticking it out, it would somehow become tolerable.

He felt the sun piercing a red spot through his shirt. The sun was blistering hot for a September afternoon. Or was it the change from Secunderabad that made it seem hotter. No clouds anywhere either. Aat looked up for clouds, looked at the sun, and as he turned away his blinded eyes, he saw Mayura at the pond and started walking towards her. The neatly mown grass shimmered into a million zillion ripples, dark and deep, and he felt himself groping for a foothold in the dark. And far away, on the other side of the black ocean was his sister. He felt himself running on water, falling, sinking, bobbing up, running, and she was still far away, inaccessible. He ran, throat parched with his efforts to shout, the voice not emerging from the throttling constriction in his throat, he ran over the water shimmering in a million zillion ripples. And the darkness lifted and the black waves vanished and flower-pots of rose buds came into view and he was standing near Mayura.

He flung himself on the grass and took a deep breath. It was a beautiful afternoon; the sun shone brightly; butterflies flitted over roses and shrubs: big black ones with long wings and a mottled egg-like protuberance at the base of each wing; smaller princess butterflies that had streaks of black and orange on pale yellow wings; the palace menials with their plain yellow uniforms; it was a beautiful day. He looked around for the long grass that was delicious to chew. There were many behind him. Each blade rose out of the ground thick and strong, and then a slender stalk emerged from beneath the sheath, and at the top branched off into long thin blades, each with a white green vein running along its length. Aat pulled out the upper stalk from its sheath and put the lower end of the tender streak of juice into his mouth, holding the blade between his lips. Its soft touch on his tongue soothed his parched throat not by itself but by recalling those long-past afternoons under the jack-fruit tree.

Mayura continued to pull weeds out of the pond. Aat raised himself on both elbows and rested his chin in his cupped hands.

"We seem to have made a sad mess of our lives, sis." He looked at her apologetically. The sentence was a prepared preamble to what he wanted to say about her future. Mayura looked at him. Rebuke rose slowly out of the depths of her eyes like the dot-sized figures in film-trailers, and like them it grew to gigantic proportion, and felled him as it struck his face.

"Aat!" her eyes called to his. He looked at her. "Sis, oh Sis." He clenched his fists on the ground and let his head sink them.

"What is it? Aat, I thought it was over, that you had come through. Aat!" Her voice caressed him, drawing him up into the protection of her womb. Slowly his racking body was stilled.

Without looking at her, he drew a slip of paper from his hip pocket and handed it to her. She unfolded it. It was a restaurant cash memo for four cups of coffee and three plates of rasagolla. She turned it over. "I know I cannot live without you. I will come." Mayura looked sadly at the girlish scrawl.

"It was under my door." Aat's voice was strained but there was no more anguish. His next words came more easily, "Tough luck, isn't it?"

He silently chewed on another blade of grass for a while. "Odd the way things start and end. The first six months were great. You know how pals rally round when they know a guy is interested in someone, bring her into the gang, boost him up when he is low, play him up when she is around, kind of reconnoitre, clear coasts, nose around to find out where she does what. Things were swell for us while we both dallied. But comes a day when a guy sees only her face wherever he turns, in books, on blackboards, on cinema screens, dreams, when he sees her in himself, thinks he is she. Comes a day when they cannot stay away and dare not stay together.

"This was when Father sent this photograph of Neela. I suppose you've seen it, a full length studio portrait, beautiful hair-do, mermaid look sari and all. Beautiful. You have to grant her that. Father sent that photograph carefully packed with cardboard on either side, a letter listing everything about her and all that jazz. I could not stand that picture. I flung it away.

The world had only one face for me and that sweet face obliterated everything else. I wrote a very well-worded masterpiece of a letter to Father,
very polite, very respectful. I said I must complete my studies and establish
a practice before thinking of marriage. True our family had enough wealth
to support seven generations of idlers but a guy must earn a handful on
his own before starting a family and all that, and so would he please shelve
all ideas of alliances for another two years . . . Back came his reply asking
me not to hurry with any decision . . . And all this writing to and fro
made me think. And I decided I wanted Chitra so badly that I'd kick
the world out of my way. I knew Mother would weep the roof down and
Father would shrink himself trying to hide from his circle of friends,
Chitra being of the non-Elect, plain D S P Reddy's daughter. But I was
sure she'd win them all, just like that," he snapped his fingers, "hands
down."

"Then started the long-drawn marathon. I found myself in a rather
ironic fix I'll probably joke about in after years. I found that her old
man, her uncle actually since her father died a few years ago, is more
orthodox than Manu himself. He was ready to whip anyone who wasn't
an Andhra-born Reddy. There's one for our Brahmin ego! I did not give
up, of course. I prepared for a long siege. I almost won. I persuaded her
into agreeing, but then she could never forget that her mother was
obligated to her uncle, who'd rather kill himself than marry his niece out
of caste. So stupid, so humiliating to have to admit that this age-old
bugaboo caste-system has added another two sundered hearts to hang
on its trophy. But there it is. Yes, she loved me, but she did not dare. So
we stopped seeing each other. But that seemed to make us frantic and
more crazily in love. And so we started seeing each other again. We kept
swinging like a goddam pendulum till the main spring broke. She said No
and stuck to her No for a whole month. And that was when Father's letter
came—what conclusion was he to draw from the fact that I had kept
the photograph so long? What did I think of her, a girl beautiful, rich,
educated, daughter of an old friend now high up in the ministry. So high
he could shunt me to Timbuctoo, I could read between the lines what
everyone here seems to know.

"I wrote a reply, short and obedient. A dutiful son even if not a happy
one. I posted that letter and went to the hospital for my four-day rotation.

Pals came and reported she was looking for me; I didn't believe it, you know how pals like to tease a guy. When I returned to my room I found this under my door."

Mayura said, "You could have called the whole thing off. There was a lot of time."

"Father jumped that ceremony on me so fast, I wonder if he'd have done it anyway."

"There was so much time. First off, you could have told Chitra about your letter and spared her humiliation if not the heartbreak. Or, you could have told Father you were retracting."

Aat shook his head. "Forget it, sis, the deal was made. It was too late."

Mayura said with studied pauses, "Not really, tenth of August, this cash memo says. Probably they went to this Park Restaurant just before coming to your room. After looking for you for two or three days. And to think she'd have come to your hostel room with her girl friends, pals who rally around but also broadcast . . ."

Aat hammered his fists on the grass, his body convulsing torturedly. "Stop it, Mayu, don't make me go through that torment again. I had days and nights of it. Stop it. Take your strangling hands off me."

"Yes Aat," Mayura, who had not touched him, threw away an uprooted weed and started pulling at another. Aat sat up and regained his breath.

"You wanted to hurt me," he said.

"Yes Aat."

He rose on his knees and flayed his arms as he cried out, "You've done this through the years, hypnotizing me, controlling my emotions, my very thoughts, right from the time I was a weakling boy. Made me climb trees that I dreaded. That jamun tree, you willed me into climbing to the top just to shake you a few ripe jamuns. And I clung on that green branch, my shirt pocket dripping purple jamun juice, immobilized till you chose to say, Come down, Aat, let us eat them now. Made me race till my legs were ready to drop under me and when I won, I always won because you made me win, you held my sweating face between your hands and smiled at me. Made up stories of Pathans, all the villains in your stories were Pathans, who kidnapped children and hid them in the baggy balloon trousers tight at the ankle and when I hid my face in my hands you drew me into your lap and stroked me into the seven

castles where we were king and queen supreme. Always your rubber boy
to be twisted."

"Aat, Aat, have I ever hurt you before? Think back Aat, have I ever hurt
you?" Mayura pleaded, "I am so unhappy that I couldn't help myself right
now. Think back, Aat."

Aat lowered his arms, sat down on his knees. "No," he said slowly.
"Never. When I am so low I can't sink any further into depression, I call
you and you come, wherever I am you come into my dream and take
my head between your hands and draw me into your lap. It seems so
real that I can't believe it when I am awake but I feel so rested, so swell
when I wake up. Strange, others see you hard as uncut diamond, solid as
sculptured marble, and yet when it is you and me, perhaps you and some
others too . . ."

"No Aat, just you and me."

"What is it, Mayu?"

"You are afraid, Aat."

"Yes, dammit, I am afraid. There is something weird, something scary
about where we are. Don't look at me with your witch-eyes."

"What ugly words you use!" She was deeply pained.

"I use ugly words and you caress me with your eyes. Your husband,
poor bloke, gets only your disgust."

"If I were wedded to him twenty-plus years as I have been to you and
Hari Vilas, yes, I would not turn away in disgust."

"Stick it out twenty years, then. Easy." He spat out the words.

"One needs a base, Aat. One needs to start right, and if the disgust
comes later, it will just be a mood, a passing setback. You and I started
from scratch, with love, affection, mutual protectiveness all the way until
we separated."

"Separated?" Aat's voice was highpitched, lost.

"Yes, Aat, you and I have gone our separate ways. A whole black ocean
between us."

"But I crossed it, right now, just now." He pointed to the other side of
the lawn, a little lost boy uncertain of himself.

"Aat, oh Aat."

His voice was more confident now. "And I'll stay right here, sis, this side
of the million zillion waves. Come."

Spontaneously Mayura stretched her hand towards his. Then she dropped it. "You have your life to live, Aat, go rest awhile before it comes to claim you back. I will see you before Neela comes to take you out."

Aat rose and obeyed her, as he always had. Seeing which, Mayura almost called him back. If she told him to call this whole thing off and stand by Chitra, maybe he would do that too. But either way, he had invaded, perhaps irrevocably, a woman's life. Yes, he might do whatever she told him to. But where would that lead? Who knows where any path leads? Who knew six months ago that she would ever agree to any of the young men her parents had talked about? Who knew three months ago that the prince was only a frog? Who knows now what she would do, could do, should do.

Mayura watched his back all the way till he entered the house. And then she let her heart break all over again. Aat, so close to her all these years, was now on the other side of a black ocean. How could it have happened? And yet the moment he told her what he had done, something had snapped. Like the snapping of her Achilles tendon on the tennis court two years ago. She had heard it snap, the way knuckles crack but much louder, except that it was an internal sound that no one else heard. She had fallen to the ground. There was no pain at all, so clean was the break.

A doctor who was on the next court had come to her right away, and he had said it was the Achilles tendon. You can get it surgically sewn back, he said, if it is done within twenty-four hours; or you can get your leg into a plaster and let it heal by itself. It was like a rubber band, he said. The two parts could be pulled together and sewn, or Nature would take care of it over the next three to six months. Take your pick, he said. She had taken Nature's way.

The rock that had dropped to the bottom of her heart when Aat said what had happened, now started pounding from within. And the pain started. The rough-hewn boulder gnawed off pieces of the walls around her heart as it pounded against them, and then itself started breaking down into stones. The switch on the concrete mixer had been turned on, turning the stones into smaller stones the size of sand so that they snicked off little slivers of the wall of her heart as they spun around. She could feel the walls of her heart thinning out, while the sludge prepared to settle.

Men, what had happened to men nowadays? Or had they always been like that, all those men she had thought of as strong souls in strong bodies, those heroes of the epics and classics she had wallowed in the air-conditioned comfort of summer holidays? Was it just a front? Had it always been just a front these zillion years of civilization?

All the men in the family, so lovable but so stupid, god so stupid, how can anyone be so stupid? Venkatesh Periyappa, wasting his brains and London degree in a small college that did not even have real research students, Father bowing down to corrupt politicians, Uncle Murti crunching numbers for corporate businessmen—but at least they were okay where the family was concerned, loyal to wife and children, but Aat . . . how could he be so so, she could not even think of the right word, so weak, god, why were men so weak; gentle but spineless jellyfish or self-confident, brutish animals. Stupid jellyfish who couldn't stand up for themselves. Aat, that Aat should be one of those contemptible men, who couldn't stand by the woman he loved. How could he do it, how could he put this girl Chitra through all this. God, god, is that what all men are? Mere jellyfish or sexual animals? Princes who turn into frogs, frogs who can never turn to princes?

If I could only cry, something would flow away; no, if I could only howl and scream and howl until I am emptied out of all the sludge and sand of life.

～

4 IX. Each man for himself must decide.

By coercion and anger, persuasion and tears, we only distort our vision: A sensible person, endowed with reason, brought up with a good sense of values, will see the right path for himself.

Interference only brings out the mule in man.

In my generation women earned their freedom. Today's woman demands it. Which is as it should be.

5 IX. Collective guilt is far worse than individual guilt for moral human beings. One can speak about the latter; one can get counsel and consolation; it lightens when shared; it purifies; at worst it wrecks one's life. But collective guilt emasculates the community, members move furtively, seeking to avoid each other, for meeting another is like looking into the mirror when your face is filled with pus-filled boils.

6 IX 65. She is like a beggar at the door who does not beg, who does not speak, but will not go away. He does not even look at you but the guilty ever feel his eyes and the world's on them.

What master mind-readers beggars are! They sit outside the temples, begging bowls in front of them. One who goes to thank god throws them a coin in the gratitude of his heart; one who goes to ask throws them two because himself being a suppliant he needs must be assured of the words, Ask and it shall be given.

Beggars exploit not our sense of compassion but our sense of guilt. And if we pass them by without giving, the more wretched we.

Maru

MAYURA AWOKE TO THE SOUND of nadaswaram music. Ranjani was getting married that day.

Ranjani's house was on the other side of the back wall of Hari Vilas, and for three days the sound of preparations could be heard as workers put up the shamiana and the head cook with his assistants brought in huge utensils and provisions. The previous day, her mother had broached the topic with much hesitation. She had suggested that Mayura join her in the morning for the muhurtham, even if she did not want to stay on for lunch. From the way she spoke, it was ambiguous as to whether she really wanted Mayura to agree. Parvati was indeed ambivalent on that point. She could not decide which would be the lesser evil—for Mayura to attend the celebration so everyone could see that she was all right with whatever was happening to her life, or whether Mayura's absence was safer than her presence which might provoke others to probe and worse still provoke Mayura to say or do something unseemly.

On one hand, Mayura was after all her own daughter and knew how to keep up appearances in public. Her tantrums, her flare-ups, her hurting words, her brooding were reserved for the family. While she preferred to avoid visitors, if she found herself among acquaintances, she behaved with restraint, indeed with seeming pleasure, when speaking to them. She talked about Bombay, the shopping experiences, parties and new friends with such ease that those who heard her wondered if the rumours were false after all. She seemed like any other new bride on a short visit to her parents. At Anant's engagement party, some assumed she had come for the occasion and Mayura's parents had gone along with that perception, saying how glad they were that Mayura was with them at the celebration. But there were others who still had a look on their faces when they met either of them, a look of curiosity and askance that was easy enough to decipher. But without more fuel, rumours could not spread.

On the other hand, Mayura's brooding spells were now longer; and she picked up quarrels easily.

"You don't really want me to come, do you?" she had said aggressively. Parvati ignored the edge in her daughter's voice and said, "Ranjani and you started school the same day, and at one time you were inseparable. She was the one who made us cut a door through the back wall so the two of you could run between the houses. And she was so helpful at your wedding; she was the one who suggested who should do your hair and make-up, remember?"

Mayura remembered it well enough. She and Ranjani had gone their separate ways once they were at different colleges, but Ranjani had renewed their friendship in the days before Mayura's wedding. Ranjani was excited. Since getting married was her one great goal, she had already scouted all the jewellery stores and found out the latest vogue in sari colours and depth of choli necks; she knew which flower vendor provided the freshest flowers, and which hors d'oeuvres she wanted for her own wedding. And now she was getting married. The details had no doubt been picked and pruned by her, and there was bound to be something new and different at the reception. Mayura decided she would attend the reception, and not the wedding ceremony which was way too early in the morning. Her mother had been more than satisfied by Mayura's decision. Receptions were easier to handle; there always seemed to be more young people at the reception than at the muhurtham. Also, people made brief conversations, spoke superficially and moved on whereas the long religious ceremony gave ample time for guests to corner anyone whom they wanted to grill.

Mayura listened to the crescendo of drumbeats. The bridegroom would have just this minute tied the tali around Ranjani's neck. She could not remember that point in her own wedding. All she could remember was that the heavy rose garland was biting her neck at the back, and the deodorant was not working because she could see a patch of sweat in the underarm of her blouse, for her muhurtham had been closer to noon. Perhaps she should have gone to the ceremony after all. Ranjani and she had been inseparable once.

Mayura hoped Ranjani would be happy. No, Mayura was sure Ranjani would be happy. Ranjani had a gift for finding pleasure in everything she did. Whether it was painting her nails without a single smudge or writing pages and pages in her careful script where every letter of the alphabet was slanted just so on every single page, she always showed off her work with genuine pleasure. Mayura could see Ranjani with a big proud smile on her face, waving her stubby pre-teen fingers to let the breeze dry the nail polish that she had stolen from her older sister's paraphernalia of cosmetics. Her handwriting had been her pride and everyone else's grief right through middle school. Every teacher would comment on how that was the way handwriting should be. The neatness of it drove Mayura mad, every "t" crossed just so, every "i" with a dot on it that was a teeniest little circle rather than a dot. In high school, it was Ranjani who talked her into taking the oddest classes during the weekends—macrame, flower-arrangement, a cosmeticians' course. The last had met with severe disapproval by elders in both families, as though they thought a course in how to clean nails and put on make-up meant the girls would end up doing those awful things as a career. But now, as she lazily filed her nails, Mayura thought, why not? There were cosmeticians' salons springing up all over Bombay, and Ranjani could well be running one of these fashionable places where lowly workers did the scrubbing of soles and the owner gave demonstrations on delighted clients who would walk out with a lovely new face and hairstyling. She briefly imagined herself as the owner of a boutique, but no, that required one to speak sweetly to the clients and firmly to the employees, skills she held in disdain.

Ranjani was good at these picky little details. More than that, she derived so much pleasure in them, Mayura had always felt a little jealous. She herself was never satisfied with anything she did, feeling it could have been done a little better. But whether Ranjani's work was good or not, Ranjani herself exuded such a sense of pleasure at its completion that others could see only perfection. As she thought back, Mayura was dissatisfied with herself. Why was she always running down people? Why was she always aiming at some acme of perfection when it was so clear that human beings couldn't ever attain it?

Perhaps she could dress up even now and catch the final moments of the ceremony, the saptapadi that would go on for another half hour. The wedding shamiana was right there, on the other side of the wall with the door through which they had run in and out as children. She could have attended the whole ceremony, awake as she had been since five in the morning. Oh well, she thought, could have, should have, too late.

When she came down an hour later, dressed in a rich Conjeevaram silk sari, there was much activity in Lakshmi Athai's house. Several people had dropped by from the wedding house to Hari Vilas, friends of Suhas and Devaki, who had no doubt invited them over so they could wait here and go back for lunch after the office crowd had finished theirs. She could hear her cousin Maru's unmistakable laugh as she entered her aunt's house. There were almost a dozen young women in the "oonjal room"—as they called the large dining room because of the swing that hung at one end of it. Five young women sat on the swing and Suhas and Maru were setting up some plates on the dining table. All seemed to be speaking at the same time, and everyone was laughing. As Mayura went in, she greeted them cheerfully. "Where were you?" one of them asked her, and she answered she had got up a bit late.

Mayura was testing the waters with her ambiguous answer, to see if anyone believed she had really been there. They seemed to think she had been, for one of them said, "Of course, of course, a new bride gets into that sleeping-in habit very quickly."

"Especially in a new place where no one ever comes visiting," Mayura said without any hesitation. "It is quite a bore, really, husband goes off to work, nothing to be done till he returns."

"After which all the real work starts, hnh?" Again everyone laughed.

"I wanted him to come for this wedding, but not him. He claims there is too much work, not that he has ever missed a single day going to the Club," Mayura said.

"Bombay is so far away, can't he just get a job here?"

Another said, "Wow, I'd be glad to move to a real city. But just my luck, every one Dad has considered lives in Trivandrum or Calicut or some such dump."

Maru said, "Okay folks, here are the snacks on the table, but don't dig in if you want to keep your appetite for the wedding lunch. I would love to stay on in the best city in the world but I am going away a long ways away, A-mer-i-ca!"

"Really? Who is he? Why didn't you tell us all morning while we were just twiddling our thumbs watching Ranju getting dolled up?"

"Didn't want to upstage Ranju, but now I can tell you all about it," Maru said with a flourish. "He has the cutest Adam's apple."

"Oh no!"

"Apples are the ultimate temptation and all that, but an Adam's apple?"

"What does he do?"

"Where is he?"

Maru said, "He is doing research somewhere out in America, Connecticut or Colorado or some place."

"You don't know?"

"Or it could be Arizona or Arkansas."

"Maru, don't be such a space cadet. These are very different places, geographically, Arizona is a desert, why would anyone opt for a place that is hotter than Madras ever can be? Connecticut is okay."

"Nearer New York, is that why?"

"Yeah, the east coast is civilized but the rest of the country, yuk."

"California would be good."

Maru laughed her usual peal, and said, "Kansas, Arkansas, California, Connecticut, who cares? It is difficult to remember who is from where when you are out shopping in a busy market, you know. But I am sure he is the man for me."

"Because of his Adam's apple? Is there anything else special about him?"

"What's his name?"

Maru said, "Sivaraman, now isn't that just so right a name? Maru Sivaraman."

"Siva Sivaa," said one, knocking her fist on the sides of her forehead.

"Rama Ramaa," said another, raising her right hand to her forehead in the usual sign of exasperation.

Everyone laughed.

"I think he's quite tall," Maru said.

"You think, don't you know?"

"Or maybe he looks tall because his face is so long and thin," Maru said.

"Oh goodness, the long and short of it," one laughed.

"Hey, I am not short. Five-foot-one isn't all that short."

"How do you know he is the one?" one said sarcastically.

Another said, "Really, I would like to know what you are looking for. This whole process is so dicey. Tell me, Maru, did it really feel just right? Or is it that you are tired of shopping?"

Maru said, quite seriously now, "I really think he is the man, absolutely he is. He has such beautiful fingers, a pianist's fingers."

"I read somewhere that pianists actually have stubby finger ends."

"So, when did you see his fingers? Did you go to the beach together?"

Maru said, "Oh no, we met in Bangalore as a matter of fact. At Chittammai's house. Amma dragged me off to Bangalore for a wedding, so she said, but then she had me meet three young men, not one or two but three, and all from A-mer-i-ca! August is America season, you know, like December is the Music Season. They come in swarms before 'school starts' as the phrase goes, they call University 'school.' August is their summer break."

"What were the others like? I guess they'd be taken by now," one sighed.

Maru replied, "There was one really handsome chap, like Dev Anand you know, but he seemed too aware of that, I think. I didn't like him. He probably didn't like me either, the way he behaved, but maybe he was okay."

"So, is this guy of yours still hanging around? If so, take care, he probably doesn't have a job."

Maru said, "None of them ever do, you know, these guys who are from out there—all students mostly, 'grads' as they call themselves, which means, as Chittammai so aptly put it, slaves to some professor who has the money to make them do his work. Chittammai liked him. She found out soon enough from his mother that all she wants is to send him back with a young woman who can cook and clean and keep house for him so he doesn't starve himself to death. His mother kept saying how thin he had grown since he left two years ago, absolving herself of the fault for his scarecrow looks I guess."

"Maru, you are crazy, an Adam's appled scarecrow? And you don't even know whether he lives in Tulsa or Timbuctoo!"

"Oh well, my mother knows every detail one needs to know. Give me the list of questions and I will find out from her."

"Did your mother tell his mother you don't know how to cook and clean, or did she praise you sky high for your culinary expertise?"

"Of course she did, praise me I mean, that is what mothers do, what mothers are for."

"So tell us about what he said, he must have said something to make you fall for him."

"The parents did all the talking, as usual, but he did insist on meeting me again on his own, I mean as much on his own as anyone can wangle in these cases. He came with a friend, someone he had gone to school with and who already has a couple of children, can you imagine?"

"Did he come with the kids?"

"Oh no no, but we talked more with him than with each other, you know how things are with such visits."

"Maru, don't be so clued out. So what did he say, like, is he good at cricket? Does he listen to music?"

"I don't know, I'll find all that out once I go there, I guess."

"So all you know is he has an Adam's apple and long fingers and a super-worried, probably super-possessive mother who is going to be on your tail."

"He said the system there is excitingly different from here and one could do whatever one wants, take any courses at the university one feels like, take forever to finish a degree. That is good, isn't it?"

"So why has he lost weight?" asked one, going back to basics. "Maybe he is tubercular."

"Fancy being a scarecrow in the land of milk and honey."

Maru said, "I dunno. I guess food would be easy enough for anyone who can tear into hunks of meat, but for vegetarians it is rabbit food, he said."

"Still a vegetarian, wow, didn't he go to IIT? I thought that is the first habit they get into."

"What is rabbit food?"

Maru said, "Some leafy vegetable, I guess. He said it is eaten with something called a dressing and he didn't know for the first few months that dressings didn't have meat and so he ate the leaves with lemon and salt."

So you talked food all the time?"

"Did you check if he is the kind who would shut you in at home?"

Maru said, "Hey, do I look like I'd let anyone do that to me? One just has to grab life with open hands and run with it. Anyone who comes in my way, beware."

"Easy enough to say that now. It isn't as though you can run back home from that far away if you were getting sick of anything." She looked at Mayura discreetly.

Mayura did not bat an eye. "Yes, that is a good point. One gets very lonesome in a strange place. With no one whom you know, while the guy has swarms of people around him whom he's known forever."

That answered a great many questions to most of the girls in the room. Suhas did not say anything. Nor did Maru, though she had heard all that had gone on in the house from Suhas and Devika. Mayura was grateful that her cousin Maru's presence was taking the heat off her.

"So Maru, is this really pukka? Or is it only that Barkis is willin' as far as you are concerned?"

Suhas said, "Did you know that all that Barkis wanted was someone who cooked well?"

Maru said, "Don't be so bookish, we all know that Barkis is willin' just means one is all set to tie the knot. Now if someone throws a wrench I will be totally and absolutely, irremediably and incurably devastated, heart-broken. I don't know where I can find another Adam's apple as cute as his." Maru said this with due theatricality.

"I wish we all had mothers as capable as yours, Maru, to line up so many boys who live in A-mer-i-ca!"

And all of them sang, "A-mer-i-ca, A-mer-i-ca!"

Chander

A stranger came one night to Yussouf's tent
Saying, Behold one outcast and in dread
Against whose life the bow of power is bent,
Who flies, and hath not where to lay his head.

CHANDER STOOD AT MAYURA'S door and declaimed with all the gestures and modulations he had used as a third-form kid during recitation period. Mayura looked up from the carrom board and burst out laughing. Natarajan, Chandramati's youngest son, said with military crispness, "Permission granted. You may enter Yusuf's tent," and added, as he missed an easy shot, "Permission cancelled. Go away, you bring me bad luck. This is a crucial board and I've got to win it."

"What's the stake?"

"Public announcement of defeat, at the dinner table, by the loser who has to wear a dunce cap."

"Pooh, is that all?"

"You know Mayura'd rather die than accept defeat. Boy, it's going to be fun watching her eat humble pie."

Chander stretched himself on the divan and threw his right foot on his left knee. Chander, like Venkatesan his father, was an academic but he looked more an athlete, one of those who appear on the cover of sports magazines, breathing brawn and vitality. His square face was as smooth-shaven as a baby's bottom he claimed, thanks to Ronson, taking a television commercial pose; his smooth face enhanced the teenage mould of his figure, thin-hipped and long-legged. Today he wore light blue denims with red seams, a broad leather belt, striped shirt with button-down collar and sleeves so short his biceps rippled visibly every time he flexed his arms. He sported a flat-top haircut. It was only in the red capillaries within his eyes and the almost invisible fleshiness under them that Apollo gave place to Bacchus. Chander was home on a six-week vacation from his research associateship at a Canadian university.

He addressed Nataraj. "And what are you doing at home, kid, on a weekday afternoon?"

Nataraj replied, "Thumped into the new cook this morning, can you believe it, the guy has my name, how do you think we are to handle that? and I went into one of my suspended animation acts." Nataraj had a respiratory problem, an occasional muscular spasm in the chest that choked him into breathlessness. The attack lasted only several seconds and occurred only once or twice a year but frightened his mother into a bundle of nerves for days after each attack. She mollycoddled him and he played it up for all he could.

"Can't you see the poor boy is suffering mortal pain? He'll need an excuse for losing as you'll see soon." Mayura was in a cheerful mood now. She had stayed in her room all morning, going down briefly to fill her lunch plate. "So, our dear phoren-returned cousin, methinks you are fleeing someone or something."

"I come to thy impregnable fortress, O Queen, which no pursuer dare enter unbidden and where therefore I am safe safe safe."

Two days ago, soon after Ananta had left, Mayura had locked herself in and refused to come out saying if anyone entered her room without her permission, she would go on a hunger strike. That had given rise to a string of jokes among her younger cousins. No one dared to force their way into her room, knowing she would carry out her threat and starve herself rather than come out on any terms except her own.

Mayura had brooded over the mess her brother had made of a poor girl's life. His eyes had sought hers again and again right through the rituals of prayer and partying that had gone on all of Sunday, but she had looked above him and away. Spineless creature. What right did he have to be happy? Even the morning he left, she had delayed coming down until the sounds of voices told her there would be no opportunity for her brother to talk to her alone. Vulgar brutes or spineless jellyfish, all the men in her life.

But now, since she was in a good mood, Mayura chose to ignore Chander's teasing. She merely laughed and said, "You evade my question, slave, out with it."

"From whom else would I be fleeing, lady, but from those who want to hitch me hiking the one-way trail of matrimony?"

Mayura's finger was poised behind the striker but she paused and looked at him to see if there was a second meaning to his words that involved her. He went on, "The campaign is gathering momentum with deadly rapidity. A carload of women bounced in a few minutes ago. I know a hunter when I see one. And poor Amma just gets swept off her feet even if she doesn't like some of these visitors. She gives them the run of the house; and sure enough they make a beeline for me pushing Amma from room to room till they find me; caught me in my underwear as I was coming out of the bathroom. And they weren't the least embarrassed or apologetic. No sir. I know a potential mother-of-a-bride-in-waiting when I see one. They come with glinting eyes and grim determination, like they had butcher knives tucked in the pleats of their saris, and me a little chicken running every which way. They'd rather leave me dead than unwed. And the worst is that I can't trust Amma any more because I got proof positive she is part of the conspiracy. Yesterday she dragged me off to visit old friends, she said, and I thought all she wanted was a chauffeur, but they turned out to be hunters, no two ways about that."

"Lucky bounder," Nataraj said, "you can get to eat sojji-bajji morning and evening every day."

"Sure, along with the snacks comes so-called music, sheer cacophony trilled out by . . ."

"Tremulous maidens who hope to win the most eligible bachelor of the year," Mayura said. "I can't believe anyone would still go along with the singing thing in this day and age. You asked for it, Chander, word has spread that you will consider only girls who can sing and so you are getting an earful of music at every turn."

Chander made an elaborate gesture of terror. "I am counting the days. If I can withstand them another week I think I'll be home free. Mother will start concentrating on how much she's going to miss me soon and so she will accept my state of single blessedness."

"We'll fight to the bitter end," Mayura said, "we'll pursue you with pundit and tirumangalyam to the very door of your plane."

They laughed.

"Poor Lakshmi Periamma has been torturing herself all the time you've been away that you'll return with a white wife."

· "Me? Fall for a paleface? Ridiculous."

"We'll see."

"Go in for one of those hipless, breastless females? Give me a break."

Nataraj whistled. He pulled an American magazine from the pile under Mayura's bed and flipped through the ads until he came to one he thought adequate, which he passed on to Chander.

Chander dismissed it. "You don't know, kid, all that is like their ice-cream, just fluff and foam."

"Boy, you are a bounder all right."

"My meaning, Nattu, but infinitely better expressed." Mayura said, trying to laugh but feeling very annoyed.

"Seriously man," Nataraj continued, "you might be better off with one of them, you know. I hear they do everything, wash the car, mop floors, do the shopping, and still manage to look like this! I wouldn't think twice about going for one of them."

Chander grunted. "Sure, kid, if you're moronic enough to want your wife to wear the pants in your house."

"Come on, all the men out there couldn't be morons."

Mayura felt a new appreciation for the boy but that did not stop her from pocketing the last black and saying, "Three plus twelve, makes it fifteen to your nineteen. My opening strike."

Chander whistled. "Okay, kid, you are in trouble; you need to concentrate, and so I'd better not talk." He went to the window. Nataraj looked at him with admiration. "Boy, that outfit sure looks zingy."

Chander turned and struck a model's pose.

"You look ridiculously juvenile," Mayura said.

"Sure looks zingy."

"I'd give them to you, kid, if you weren't such a pigmy."

"Just wait, buddy, I'll be shooting up soon."

"I'll mail you some beans, Jack, when I get back." Chander turned back to the window. He let out a wolf-whistle. "Whoa, I am in the wrong place. Looks like Radha had her whole class down for lunch and they are leaving now, whoa, look at them, that one with a pony tail, long earrings down to the shoulder, six inches of midriff and a deep deep V-neck, whoa!"

Natarajan joined him in a trice. "I prefer that one," he said, jerking his thumb toward the magazine.

Chander playfully boxed his ears. "You talk helluva lot too much, kid."

"That's because you talk his juvenile language. You used to be such a sober, sensitive chap, look at you now."

Chander pretended not to have heard her. He pushed Nattu back to the carrom board and sat on the third side.

"You have come home to find a wife, haven't you?" Mayura asked.

"Frankly, yes. It is time to move on. But to find the right girl, aye, there's the rub."

"Shouldn't be difficult, as you have already seen. Give your specifications, boss, age, colour, height . . ." Nataraj said.

"Immaterial and irrelevant. Tolerably good-looking, slim and shapely, of course."

"And?"

"A good cook who won't ever give me sandwiches, I've had enough of those for breakfast, lunch and dinner these two years. Someone who sings classical songs, or plays the veena maybe, I can imagine her on a Kashmir rug in my apartment, playing on the veena, soft-voiced." Chander stopped himself from seriousness with a resounding clap on his thigh. "Say, that's an idea. A sitar, I'll take a sitar back with me. What an idea!" He rose to his feet and walked about, rubbing his hands gleefully.

"It is a lot of fun bantering back and forth, Chander, but I wish you'd act at least as mature as when you left. You've got to be serious . . ." Mayura said.

"Et tu Brute? That's what Dad's been saying. Then fall, Caesar." He dramatically threw himself on the bed.

He had miscalculated the length of the bed and hit his head against the headboard. He eased himself on to the pillow, a hundred thousand nails drilling themselves through a dime-sized bump.

Natarajan laughed at hearing the thud. "Careful, buddy," he said, "don't knock out the little brains you have."

"You've got to shut doors behind you and open new ones," Chander heard Mayura saying from some deep well.

"Someone said that to me centuries ago," Chander said vaguely. The electric drill bored down into his heart with an unrelenting whirr.

The light behind the "No Smoking—Fasten Seat Belts" sign faded. The trans-Atlantic jetliner tore through dense white clouds into the serene blue of the upper sky. Far below, the clouds thinned out into wisps of cotton candy, and the azure of the sky touched the deeper blue of the ocean on which occasional black specks trailed streaks of white. Then there were no more clouds, no more darting streaks, only an unfathomable blue below, above, around.

Chander blinked the glare away and focused his eyes on the book in his hand. The black of the title and the motley orange-yellow-green of the jacket resolved from their hazy halations into a clear spectrum of colours and forms—*The Mahabharata* translated into English by Kamala Subramaniam. His mother had given it to him at the airport half-apologetically, half-beseechingly, at the last minute so that he would not have the heart to refuse. "Keep it on your table," she had whispered, hastily stepping back lest her heartache spurt out of her eyes. She was an undemonstrative, non-interfering mother, and this was the nearest she had ever come to imposing anything on him. She left it to that single moment and gesture to tell him of her prayers for his safety and her hope that he would turn, occasionally at least, to the wisdom and solace contained in the book. Looking at the volume, Chander smiled at the incongruity of her choice—this was the epic that had dissension and deceit everywhere. His smile turned into sad retrospection because he knew his mother very well. She would have preferred a copy of the *Ramayana* or the *Gita* but this was the only English book that the corner shop had on its shelves and she had neither the self-confidence nor the time to get away to a bigger bookstore, with all the activity that had been going on since he got his visa. She was so energetic and in control of her surroundings at home, but once she stepped outside Hari Vilas, she was a nervous and diffident fish out of water.

Chander had made an equally idealistic gesture to himself. On the way to the airport he had stopped the car at Higginbothams on Mount Road to get "some reading matter for the journey" as he sheepishly told his parents; what he had bought was a copy of the new edition of Chandrasekhar's *Radiative Transfer*. It was not his field of study, nor was it one that would or could be read during a journey. Yet, as the car sped him through his last miles on Indian soil, he had an urge to hold that book. To see it was to think of its Indian-born author, and to think of him was to open a world of ambition and inspiration.

"Hello! I am Mr Satish Mundhra."

Chander looked up at the unctuous-faced young man who exuded friendliness and perfumed hair-oil, and who had obviously come from some row behind him. The plane was half empty, it being the last week of September. Chander half-rose from his seat and took the proffered hand. M V Chander," he said in a low voice as though to compensate for the other's crude loudness.

Mundhra sat next to him and started talking about himself. By the oddest of coincidences, he was on his way to the same university as Chander. He also had the same connecting flight from Montreal. When Chander did not offer corresponding personal details, Mundhra set himself the task of drawing out the information. Chander was annoyed. He disliked the custom of exchanging life stories on sight. However, he was as unaccustomed to evading straight questions as he was to asking them. Reluctantly he submitted to the cross-examination. He was twenty-four-years old, had a doctorate from Madras University, was unmarried, had two brothers and two sisters. He had a two-year contract with the University of M at an annual salary of seven thousand dollars.

Mundhra whistled at hearing the salary figure. "Wonderful yaar, you will stay on, of course?"

"Can't say."

"You do have an immigrant visa, I suppose. Canadian Immigration gives it to most fellows who come on a salaried job. Unfortunately, being a student, I don't have that passport to lifelong luxury. Have you calculated how much one can save in two years?" He added up various expenses—for food, lodging, income tax, insurance, car, entertainment—and the total savings came to a six-digit figure in Indian currency.

As the questions and counselling went on, Chander was aware of a growing resentment. He also felt acutely self-conscious each time a flight attendant or passenger walked by. Mundhra, insensitive to his own loudness and Chander's discomfort, waxed more friendly and voluble. He spoke mostly of his own achievements but he interspersed his autobiography with adverse comments on western culture. As the air-hostess leaned across to pull out Chander's lunch table, Mundhra said in Hindi, "Do you see how she sways and leans over? Seductresses all," and he lewdly smacked his lips.

An appetizing aroma of coffee and not-so-appetizing smell of food filled the plane as lunch trays were carried up the aisle. Suddenly Mundhra fell silent, and fidgeted. Chander wondered if he was, perhaps, diffident about the correct use of tableware. Mundhra leaned towards him and whispered, "How does the damn flush work?" He jerked his thumb towards the washrooms. Chander wanted to say, Sure, I knew all along that you had firsthand knowledge of the western way of life. But he softened his sarcasm by saying, "Same as in other planes."

"On the Bombay-London flight I tried all those knobs and taps but nothing happened. The handle isn't in its usual place. I am a man of regular habits," he went on piteously, "my whole day is upset if I don't start it right. I am feeling ill already." His face was a study in misery. Feeling mean for having teased him, Chander told him where to look for the pedal. But his sympathy was all too short-lived. When Mundhra returned to his seat it was with the words, "Our toilet habits are much cleaner. These westerners . . ."

Mundhra carried on in the same trend through the meal; the westerners were far behind in their culinary arts, they had no taste buds, no appreciation for the finer shades of flavour . . . Everything about his neighbour revulsed Chander—his shiny rayon suit, his ornate watchstrap, his plastered hair, his heavy accent, his loud voice, his egoism, his shallow generalizations. As Mundhra droned on, Chander had a sense of being trapped, a premonition that it was going to be difficult to shake him off.

The premonition proved correct. When they landed in Winnipeg, Mundhra took the lead, rather efficiently too. They checked in at a hotel downtown. When Chander came out after a shower he found Mundhra on one of the two beds, busily circling ads concerning inexpensive boarding houses. He had bought both the local newspapers, got a map of the city, information about buses to the university, and already gone through a weekly guide to the city's nightlife that was on the hotel table along with the telephone directory.

"How about going to one of these joints after dinner?" he asked, pointing to an advertisement that promised pleasures. Chander replied that he was not interested. That set Mundhra off again. It was hardly six o'clock. Why go to bed so early? And alone too! (delighted with his joke he repeated it several times.) Surely Chander did not intend to be an ascetic. Didn't he want to celebrate his arrival? Come on, an immigrant visa too! Better start living it up. Do in Rome as the Romans do. (Again, he was tickled by his own wit.) "Boy, I wish I had your visa. Are you lucky or what? Let me see your magic wand." He riffled through the contents of Chander's briefcase without so much as a "May I" and extracted the landing card from the passport. He held it as one would a jewel, and theatrically declaimed, ". . . evidence that the rightful holder is a landed immigrant . . . The magic carpet to health, wealth and happiness—The GREEN CARD!"

Chander drily said, "It isn't green, it isn't a card, and this isn't the United States."

Mundhra ignored him. ". . . a treasure to be guarded forever and aye. Keep it in your wallet." He picked up Chander's wallet and put it in.

Chander stared at the other's thin line of moustache with distaste. Why had he allowed this leech to close in on him? Why had he not parried his questions? walked off to another seat? told him to shut his goddam mouth and go to hell? Was it patience that made him listen to the boor? Was it tolerance that kept him from rebuking? Or was it weakness? Tolerance and weakness, one considered a virtue, the other a vice, but were they after all different words for the same quality? Was it tolerance that had allowed India to suffer wave after wave of cultural and political invasions? Tolerance that prompted Hinduism to be so submissive while missionaries and rulers had drawn away its people and its wealth? Or was it weakness? Nonviolence or cowardice? two names for the same quality, and that quality a national trait for a people who flaunted it by using the more flattering name . . . a nation made of spineless thinkers and unthinking egotists, and Mundhras always led Chanders by the nose . . . because Chanders permitted them to.

Mundhra was saying, "You ask it, we have it. That is the way the wind blows here. And the mangoes you can't get for money you can get with sweet words as you will see on campus."

Chander stood over the other man's bed. Words stormed their way out, virulent, devastating words. Mundhra was a bundle of preconceptions and prejudices, a shallow, selfish, callow brute, pampered by his illiterate community which adulated university graduates as gods on earth. What a community! Gossipy women who at thirty were already elephantine, debauched men idling their afternoons away lolling against dirty bolsters in their fly-infested shops, chewing betel leaves and spitting tobacco juice on the pavements below their shops, selling adulterated sweetmeats and shortweight groceries to poor customers whom they further exploited with usurious loans . . . He stopped, shocked, when Mundhra burst into sobs, "I am a shopkeeper's son. My mother is a gossip, and my wife is fat. My children do play on the street with snotty noses. But I love them. I want them. I would rather have them around me and me on my rope-strung cot in my dung-polished courtyard than this . . . here . . ." He flailed his hands helplessly against the newspaper sheets that rustled and crumpled under him.

Chander's shocked distaste changed to fascination as he watched the prone figure on the bed crying unashamedly. It dawned on him that he envied this man. He envied him for this experience, this feeling of utter lostness in new surroundings, this surging, tempestuous, irrational onslaught of nostalgia for persons and a place. This man could live a life of discovery because he could be moved to tears by longings. In Chander there was no yearning, there was no wonder at the sight and feel of a civilization so different from his own. At that moment Chander forgave Mundhra for everything. He realized that some subconscious feeling of lostness had moved Mundhra into attaching himself to a fellow countryman.

"I'd give anything, anything in the world to see one of my own people, to hear my own language," Mundhra was saying. With a shock of short-circuited sympathy, Chander realized that Mundhra was not talking of his family but of his linguistic community. Here they were, two men from the same country, who saluted the same flag, worshipped the same gods, yet so alien to each other! "My own people, my own language . . ." Could they never be one people unless they had the same language? Was it after all only a language that could hold a nation together in peacetime?

Be that as it may, this man needed to see his own people, and to speak his own language. An idea struck him. He reached out for the telephone directory. "Maybe we could run through a list of names common to your part of the country," he said.

Mundhra jumped up. "Great idea! Let's do that." He unceremoniously grabbed the directory and flipped through the pages, spelling out the names aloud, "No, no Mundhra, no Agrawal, Aggarwal or Agarwal, yes there's one! Manohar K. Sunset 2-6309, what does that mean, Sunset?"

Chander explained, and Mundhra went to the phone. The ensuing conversation was loud and cheerful at both ends of the line. Agarwal was just starting out for the Kohlis' home; they had an after-dinner get-together of Indians on the fourth Saturday of every month; Mundhra and his friend were most welcome; he would come by in ten minutes and pick them up; hadn't they dined yet? no matter, Mrs Kohli would surely have something.

Mundhra was excited. He plastered down his hair and re-knotted his tie. He scooped out his clothes from his suitcase and pulled out a stack of record albums from the bottom. He pulled out packets of paan-beedas from a brown paper bag. "I must take these. Betel leaves dehydrated and powdered, I didn't even know they existed till I was packing up. I bet they'll love it."

Chander felt a twinge of guilt. He too had brought a pound of spiced and scented betel nuts, Madras style, but he was in no hurry to share it with anyone. Spontaneity. That was it, that was what he envied in Mundhra. Spontaneous nostalgia, fellow-feeling, generosity.

At the Kohlis, Mundhra greeted everyone with warm enthusiasm. Chander could not. As always, he shrank into himself when in company. He had always attributed the withdrawal to sensitivity, but now in his mood of reassessing values, he accused himself of innate snobbishness. I am the insensitive one, he reflected, a clod that cannot respond or be touched by any strong emotion.

Mrs Kohli, a smiling, sweetfaced woman with several rungs of fat showing at the waist, insisted on serving them a meal of sorts, promising they would have a lot more of snacks soon. Then they joined the thirty-odd persons in the large living room. Chander, somewhat thawed out of his aloofness, was handed over from person to person, all of whom had the same questions about his work and gave the same assurances on the friendliness of the people and related the same jokes about the winter ahead.

Within minutes Mundhra had become part of the company. Chander noted that he did not use his native Hindi very long. There were people from different parts of India, and everyone spoke English, garnished with occasional Hindi phrases. The children, who came in from the basement from time to time, spoke only English. In India, Indians built walls of "My people, my language," between themselves. Here apparently they couldn't care less whether their children had any knowledge or feeling about their country, religion or language.

At first Chander instinctively shied away from the twang in the children's speech; Mundhra made no secret of his astonishment at their accent, for he had to ask them to repeat everything twice before he could follow what they meant. One of the ladies said how her baby's first words were in their native Telugu but once she started taking him to the park, he started calling her Mommy, and now he couldn't even understand Telugu, leave alone speak it. A man next to her said, "Just you wait a few years and he'll be correcting your English. My daughter is on tenterhooks whenever her friends drop in; she is afraid we'll say or do something wrong."

They spoke with complacent pride. Suddenly the implication of their immigrant status dawned on Chander. Till now he had thought of his landing card only as a needless and tedious formality, a wasteful trip to Delhi for a personal interview at the High Commission that had lasted less than twenty minutes, and had consisted solely of questions that he had already answered on the printed forms. Now, he gathered from others' experiences that it was indeed a precious document, as Mundhra had said, which many of their friends had not succeeded in getting. They narrated the stories with the smugness of people who had "arrived" talking sympathetically of those who had not made it. Chander could not place why he was feeling so isolated and hurt.

Someone asked him if conditions in India were really as bad as the newspapers led them to believe. Conversation stopped and everyone waited for his reply. Just as he started telling them about the drought, one of the women chipped in to tell him in detail about the thousand dollars they had collected, for the soldiers, last year. She spoke in a gushy manner about "the girls who worked so hard" and of the dinner and the folkdances they had arranged. Chander was annoyed that the India-China conflict should have been no more than an occasion for a social bash. But the others seemed to enjoy her loquaciousness. Chander then spoke of the long queues everywhere, for grain, for fuel, milk, medicine . . . They listened with polite sympathy, as though he was sharing some personal grief which was outside their orbit. Roused to anger by their indifference, Chander continued in a higher key of emotion. He spoke of the black-marketeering, the rampant corruption, bribery, inefficiency . . . He was conscious that he was magnifying their indifference and exaggerating his descriptions, but he felt impelled to provoke them into active sympathy and identification. They were not provoked. They politely changed the topic; once again smaller conversation groups were formed, and Chander found himself in a group that was sorting out Mundhra's record albums.

"Do you have any Pankaj Mullick records?" someone asked. Mundhra did not. Another asked for classical recordings. Mundhra drew a blank there too. He had all the latest film hits but no one seemed interested.

"Ah, here is a Saigal," a young man enthusiastically brandished a record. Several others responded, and in silence everyone listened to the first song. Then they spoke of old films, while Saigal sang on in the background. There was deep nostalgia in the air.

What astounded Chander was that they spoke of a distant past. The first among them to leave India had left it less than ten years ago and yet the India they had in mind was not the India they had left but the India of their boyhood, and often enough an even earlier one. The young man who was jubilant at finding the Saigal album could not have heard or seen Saigal who was of the 1940s; so that what he recalled was not even his actual boyhood but dreams of a hearsay boyhood. To some of them trams still trundled by on Madras streets, anti-British slogans and processions still rang through the country, and Lala Amarnath's double century against Don Bradman's eleven was still the greatest event in cricket history.

It was not callous indifference that prompted them to be blind and deaf; it was some nostalgic idealism, or was it escapism? They seemed to have an image in mind, a golden age of romanticized memories. They did not even want to experience those pleasures again as was evident when Mundhra passed a plate of his betelroll packets. They reminisced about the betel-areca shops at the street corners, the vendor dipping into a dozen different tins of spices and liquids to prepare the roll of betel leaf that melted in one's mouth; they talked about the time when they were roadside Romeos clustered around such shops, eyeing college girls as they strolled by in groups, but only a few took Mundhra's packets.

Chander mulled over his own feelings of aversion and fear. What were they? Not Indians any more, nor were they Canadians. Clearly they were a close-knit group; they seemed to have kept their own identity and did not seem to have any affinities with the people or place around them. The women had not changed their costume and none had changed their food habits if one were to judge by the food on the table. But they shied away from all talk of return. They hoped to go back, they said, but Chander felt that their hope was for a time as far into the abstract future as their memory was for an abstract past.

Like the mythological king, Trishanku, they stood suspended between two worlds, unable to enter either, and making a heaven of their own.

Chander moved away to a bridge table in the corner and picked up a deck of cards. His head felt heavy in the smoke- and music-filled air. Mechanically he started a game of solitaire. But the weight was not in his head. It was in his chest, a thudding, throbbing weight. As he flipped the cards in threes and continued with his game, the throbbing stopped but the weight remained, and also an inexplicable sense of loss, anger, contempt.

Chander pulled out his wallet and looked at the light blue piece of paper on the top of which a crown floated above a shield held by a lion and a unicorn. "This card is required for customs clearance and when making application for citizenship. It will also prove useful for many other purposes." He looked at the words as though they held a threat. The passport to lifelong luxury . . . the devil's bait to lifelong exile . . .

He sat very still, staring at the words. He felt a great surge inside him, a swirling, forceful torrent sweeping onwards and dashing furiously against the sluice gates of self-control. For a moment he indulged in the thought of what a relief it would be to let himself be carried away in that current. But years of emotional restraint held their own. He was distorting things—people and values—out of all proportion; being irrational, childish, making an emotional furor over a harmless piece of document two inches by eight that held no more compulsion or threat than his driver's license portended death in a highway accident. Even so, he could not bring himself to replace the paper in his wallet. Someone was approaching his table. Quickly he continued his game of solitaire. A pale short man in his thirties pulled a chair to his right and joined him.

"Enthralling music," he said, "the album must have got into Mr Mundhra's collection by mistake, one would think." His voice was surprisingly rich for his frame, and his fingers surprisingly long and slender. Chander watched him beat his fingers on the table to the rhythm of the music.

"You read characters fast," Chander said.

"He wears his on his sleeve. A bit of a bore but good-hearted. This seems to be a recent release. I thought I had all of Ravi Shanker's recordings."

"Came out a few months ago."

"Beautiful. And rather different from his usual style. The sitar is a sad-sounding instrument and Ravi Shanker . . . just listen to what the maestro does with it. You can almost hear the anklet bells of dancing women. So different from his usual pathos." The music built up towards a crescendo of joy. He continued to soliloquize, "We are a happy people, an innocent people. Our devotional songs are love songs because God is our lover, not our judge. We dance our way into God's arms, not crawl on our knees to his throne. We were not meant to suffer and starve. Nor to exploit and deprave each other."

Chander felt a happy kinship with this man. He extended his hand and said, "I don't think I know your name. Mine is Chander."

"I am Hari Cariappa."

"Delighted to meet you. Your name was mentioned earlier, I forget in what connection."

"As one who's been here longer than most others? Last year's best scientific paper award? Married to a Canadian?" at which Chander's grip loosened and the other's likewise on getting the cue, which withdrawal came through to Chander but it was already too late.

*

Chander was acutely conscious of the weight again. It was there, inert, crushing.

Once: Chander was fourteen. It was his first season in an adult cricket team. His brother Aditya was the captain. It was the final day in the final match of the tournament. Chander was bowled out after forty minutes of steady batting; though he had got only twenty-two runs, he had helped his brother, who was a hitter, to pile up boundaries while he held steady, unlike those before him who had fallen every ten minutes. At three o'clock he had to go home for an hour because he had told his mother he would buy some grocery she urgently needed before dinner. When he left the grounds, they needed twenty-five runs to win the match and the trophy. Twenty-five runs to make in ninety minutes with four wickets in hand. It was easy as eating jam.

But when Chander returned to the cricket field at ten past four, it was empty except for half a dozen urchins playing gilli-danda. He rushed towards home. The boy next door hollered out to him that they had lost, "thanks to the skipper scooping a ball right into the bowler's hands" five minutes after Chander had left. The other wickets had fallen like ninepins of course.

Chander ran into the house and into his brother's room. In blind anger and disappointment he rushed at his brother, intending to hit him with all his might. But the closed fists did not smite. They fell limply on the other's chest and Chander burst into tears. He buried his face against his brother's shirt where the sweat had made a yellow half moon under the armpit, and he sobbed.

That was the last time Chander had cried actual tears. He felt those tears rising now, tears from the depths of some divine despair that had been building up all evening. But he was not fourteen now, and Cariappa was not his brother. Yet, for a moment hearing that rich voice he had thought, seeing those ascetic eyes he had hoped, holding that firm clasp he had felt . . . Chander sat very still and stared at the half-finished game of solitaire, holding three cards in his right hand.

Cariappa picked up Chander's landing certificate and turned it over thoughtfully. Then he pushed it towards Chander's hand and pressed his palm on the back of the cards and the fingers that held them. In a soft voice he said, "Brain drain, heritage drain, how many was India destined to give away? No, that was not relevant. Individualism. I alone am important, not abstract ideologies of patriotism and nation-building, go piss them away down the rivulets cascading through the Nilgiris where the eucalyptus leaves crackling underfoot spark boyish fancies that flame like the sun's glorious spurt of blood before it sinks behind the blue hills where wafts the smell of coffee shrubs between which slither silent cobras that raise their hood to the piper's tune as he puffs his cheeks and contorts his wiry frame at Sulluru station to entertain into coin-throwing the Grand Trunk passengers going north through tiger-dacoit jungles and the plain to where the Ganga flows from the mountains where Himavan rules and Siva dances on snowbound Kailas the dance of joy from which alone doth spring love, laughter, every worthwhile thing . . . and I metapmorphosed into a hybrid way of life ostrich-wise ignore the bonds that break one by one, and grow gray with renown and riches, and children who will never know their lost patrimony, or knowing hold it in contempt."

Cariappa withdrew his hand and Chander suddenly wondered if the words he'd heard had actually been spoken or just communicated with the press of a hand. Cariappa said, "When we leave our country we shut many doors behind ourselves though we are not aware of it at the time."

Carefully steadying his hand, Chander turned the three cards in his hand face up on the table. He picked up the queen of hearts from the open pile and placed it below the king of spades in the second column. "There are many doors ahead of us," he said.

"Chander! are you okay?"

He dazedly opened his eyes, which closed shut reflexively. He felt Mayura's hand on his forehead.

"Did you shut the door, Mayura?"

"Door, what door?" Nattu asked.

"Did you?" Chander's hand gripped her arm.

"Yes," she said, inaudibly.

"But one always wants to leave the door ajar a wee bit," Chander mumbled.

The boy was wholly insensitive to the tenseness in the air but his words were unintentionally relevant, "Can't cut it both ways, not if you want an air conditioned room. Open door, enter door, shut door. No chinks. That's the rule."

"There are other doors ahead of us."

"You are the only one to say so, Chander."

In place of Mayura's face, he saw the inscrutable gesture and godlike look that Hari Cariappa had bent upon him two years ago. So much had happened since that day. Was it that moment that had driven him to the feckless recklessness of wining and dining and womanizing that Mayura had recognized so easily. Yes, he had been sober and sensitive once, long ago, those days in some distant past when he had looked up at the terrace next door and watched Usha drying her hair in the morning sun.

No one had mentioned Usha to him since his return, as though she had never existed. That single line in his mother's first letter, "I am glad to tell you next-door Usha's marriage is on the sixteenth, by grace of God." Had no one guessed? or was it that everyone had and so had said nothing.

"That glassy look in your eyes had me worried for a sec," Nattu was saying, "thought you'd really lost your marbles."

"Make yourself scarce, kid, go back to your carrom, if you dare."

The boy guffawed. "Know what the score is? I am twenty-two and she is twenty-six; and I've pocketed the queen."

They returned to the game. The sound of carrom men and striker hitting and rebounding against the board infuriated Chander. He wanted his mind to feel the solace of utter blankness. How simple it would be if Joan were accessible now. One forgot one had a mind when one was with that entrancing bundle of sheer sensation. Or even Leslie despite her angular limbs because she knew how to move. Mayura too had angular arms, but what was her body like? As a child, he had sat in his underwear with his cousins in the garden tank, squirting water on them. Strange. Here they were, sisters and cousins, all around him, and he hardly knew what they were like inside their yards and yards of swathed silk. Mayura probably had an alabaster body moulded out of whipped butter. Or was it just foam?

Suddenly and irrelevantly his thoughts flashed back to his first long-distance drive in Canada, soon after his arrival. He was with Ken and Jean Townsend, a happy-go-lucky couple who had befriended him on his arrival at the university. While Ken maintained a steady seventy-mile speed towards the fall colours of Kenora, Jean maintained a steady stream of anecdotes from the rear. She had insisted he take the seat in front so he could get a better view.

"Watch out, dear," she interrupted herself.

"What?"

"Didn't you see?"

"See what?"

"That rather biggish animal squashed on the right lane."

"Yeah, so what about it?" Ken shrugged.

Chander looked back. "I don't see anything."

Jean laughed. "We are already half a mile away from it."

Chander laughed, but now his eyes were on the road. Soon he saw the sandy tail of a squirrel. And several miles later a bird in a scraggy red circle. He felt guilt swelling into nausea. "So much blood," he said aloud despite himself.

"I saw a Red Cross slogan the other day that was rather neat," Jean said, "Give your blood to the Red Cross, not to the highways." This time Chander could not muster up even a polite chuckle.

That was two years ago. Two months ago, Susan by his side, he was driving his Volkswagen at a slow twenty miles an hour when he saw a squirrel ahead. Probably the red Mustang that passed him a minute earlier had run over it. The squirrel squirmed, or did it? He slowed down, and he steered deliberately, or did he? and felt a soft bump, or did he?

Perhaps this was the real he, stripped of the protective mail armour of home life. Water finds its own level. But that it should be so low ...

"Damn, double damn," Nattu clouted himself.

"Better luck next time. That makes me Unbeaten Champ." Mayura crowed triumphantly.

The boy was a bad loser. "C'mon, let's have a return game."

Mayura was a taunting winner. "Sorry, time for my beauty siesta."

"Blue funk, that's what you are."
"Don't forget you have to wear a dunce cap."
The boy stomped out of the room.

"Come, Sleeping Beauty, for your siesta," Chander held out his arms. The laugh that should have been the normal answer froze in her throat. She was afraid that he meant what he said. And reflexively her eyes wandered to the tight little bulge under his coarse denim. Ashamed and guilty, she quickly stared elsewhere. One evening, Raghu and she, along with his inescapable gang, were at Juhu beach, and the gang took to girl-watching. Aside, Mayura said to her husband, "Oh stop looking at girls." "J J J for jealousy," one of his friends teased her. Another said, "Know what I think? Your dear wife may not mind infidelity so much as she objects to lack of good taste." Raghu joined in, "And good taste is not admitting aloud that it is a natural instinct in women to ogle as far below the navel as it is for men to look above. Right?"

Mayura looked away but Chander had probably known what she was looking away from. Or perhaps not. He said, "Know what I think? I bet you are fun to sleep with. Lucky Raghu." Again she was shocked and scared at the ambiguity contained in the words. Was he leading up to a talk about Raghu, like everyone else, or was he being more immediately personal?

With an attempt at flippancy, she said, "Probably not. I am too much like the females you described, hipless and . . ."—she couldn't bring herself to say it.

The young man on the bed filled her with strange emotions. He was not the affectionate cousin she had known all her life. Or was she imagining him different? Fascinated and repelled by his likeness to Raghu, was she reading unwarranted meanings in his words and actions? Her muscles were taut with guilt, an emotion entirely alien to her experience with her brothers and cousins.

Then she looked at her cousin full in the face. Coldly she eyed the flesh under his eyes, thickened lips made blacker by constant smoking, red capillaries in his eyes . . . and even as she looked there was a change in him, a vulnerability, or was it in her? and she knew that he had put on a mask of a "bounder all right," that the sorrowful "Did you shut the door?" and the wistful imagining of a south Indian girl on a Kashmiri rug playing veena was the real Chander. Or was it? If it was not, why did she hear Aat in his voice? And if it was Raghu she saw in him, why did her nether lip tremble? If he rose and put his arms around her, what should she do?

He got up.

The hand that lay lightly on her shoulder, was it purely friendly, fraternal?

He patted her on the shoulder. "Time I took off," he said, "and thanks for the asylum. And if you ever want an asylum from anyone here or elsewhere, I want you to know my door at the far north cold and free is always open. Come for a short visit, or if you must for a very long one. I mean it, I can get you admission into some university or the other. It really is a land of opportunity and all that. You can count on me for support, financial for sure, and as much of emotional as I can give, messed up as I am."

He had at last managed to say what he had come to say, not very clearly or effectively perhaps, but he had said it. He would help her get away, if that is what she wanted. Even a short time away might help her figure out what she wanted to do with herself. He wished he could spell it out—the need to place a distance between herself and Hari Vilas, a retreat where she could be alone. Maybe he should write it down, the possibilities she could explore. In a letter one could say exactly what one wants to, without getting emotions all mixed up like a bloody bum. Even if her husband was only half as bloody bummish as himself he wouldn't blame her for coming away.

Mayura continued to feel the light touch on her shoulder long after he had left. Perhaps once Raghu too had been like the Chander of old, her affectionate cousin, romantic and idealistic. Perhaps Chander hadn't changed, merely put on a mask. Everyone puts on masks, everyone had to. And surely Chander has. A man couldn't be one kind of person for twenty-four years and then within two years become something else. And yet Chander had. And if that was so, what about Raghu? Had he once been like Chander of old? Was he still so, under that mask that all of us have to wear? . . . a face to meet the faces that we meet. Or is it that he will one day be what Chander had been? Just as Chander himself might one day return to what he had been—generous, helpful, always alert to others' needs.

*

"I use ugly words and you caress me with your eyes. Your husband, poor bloke, gets only your disgust."

⌒

Justice Ramakrishna Iyer took out the notebook, read over what he had written and added an entry.

7 IX. Am I evading my responsibility? Non-interference, faith in individual maturity, silent disapproval . . . are these only excuses to justify my inaction?
  Inarticulateness is the plague that prostrates the middle class.
  I inarticulate? Words I have always had at my command. What then restrains me? What restrains everyone here? Why don't people talk of pertinent matters instead of delivering mandates from the podium?

He read over what he had written. Inarticulation instead of inarticulateness?

Jaya

MAYURA STOOD AT THE tank near the veranda of Uncle Venkatesh's part of Maitreyi Nivas, talking to her cousin, Mira. She noticed that the tap was leaking and shut it tight. Water collected from the taps served by the City Corporation and used for washing clothes and utensils was precious. Lakshmi came out, shopping bag in hand, giving instructions to her daughter about what she had to tell the cook. As she left, Mira took up the conversation again.

"You talk as though it is an unforgivable sin or a crime or something to be plain looking."

"It is."

"But beauty isn't something one can draw out of a hat."

"Who's talking of beauty?"

"Aren't you?"

"Of course not. You and I are not beautiful . . ."

"But we are young. Jaya is older, she lives in a small town. She has children . . ."

"Heck, so is Sumitra older, and Aunt Chandra, why, your mother looks youthful and pleasant at fifty! And all of them have children and a house to look after and a husband. The difference is in the attitude and cultivation and keeping of good taste . . . smart clothes, personal care . . ."

"Her clothes are clean, homewashed, it is just that they aren't ironed . . ."

"But what atrocious taste! and just look at her children! Unkempt, snotty nosed, who'd believe they are from Hari Vilas?"

"Stop it, stop it."

"Such a sloppy, slovenly woman, I can hardly stand her presence."

"You are talking of my sister." Mira got the words out with great difficulty, her lips drawn tight in shame and pain.

"Too bad you can't be objective. Mind you, affection for siblings exists as a matter of course, but you, I thought, could be objective since the gap in age between you is so much and since you've never really lived with her. You were just a child when she got married and moved away."

"She is my sister."

"And my cousin, my father's brother's daughter, born in Hari Vilas, and therefore part of me."

"That's what rankles you. If she was an outsider, you'd be more charitable."

"Why, yes, Mira, you are very intelligent!"

"Stop being patronizing."

"You understand, and you feel the same way I do I am sure, but on principle you defend her because she is your sister, no matter how clumsy and crude she is."

"Stop it." Mira's unformed mouth was as indecisive as the line of water pashing against the measuring pole.

"It isn't so much what she says as how, so loudvoiced and uncouth . . ."

"At least she doesn't make acrimonious personal remarks."

Mayura shrugged off the comment. She sat down comfortably on the wall of the tank. She said, "Who'd believe she was once spontaneous and enthusiastic? Brimming with vivaciousness and vitality . . . look at her now . . . perhaps it is being married to a small town tobacco-chewing boor that has made her so unbearably crude. Look at the way she walks! As though she has heat rashes on the inside of her thighs."

Jaya who had stopped to talk to Chandra who was on her way out, was now waddling up the driveway with wide strides, swinging her arms in a semicircular motion. She wore a blue cotton sari that stood out in odd places because it was starched but not ironed. And she wore a bright green blouse. Her hair was greasy, her face was mottled and thick-skinned around her mouth and chin. Bitterness had placed a myopic frown between her brows. She had come to Madras to be with the family during Chander's visit.

Mira wished she would go past them silently. She felt intensely ashamed of her sister. And because she knew she ought not, she forced herself to call out, "Did you get an appointment?"

"Not for today. Dr Mani goes into the Operation Theatre after lunch-time. But he was kind enough to squeeze a place for me tomorrow morning. I'll be so relieved after he examines my boy, even if he says an operation is necessary I'd be happy so long as it is Dr Mani who says it. My poor boy has been suffering so much from this earache." She spoke on loudly, and Mira wished she'd clear her throat so the jarring split in her voice would clear.

Suddenly, Jaya turned to Mayura and said, "So, what have you decided?"

Very coldly Mayura replied, "I wasn't aware I had to make any earth shattering decision."

"You know what I mean. I think you should return to your hubby right away."

"How very kind of you to counsel me!"

"Never leave a hubby by himself more than a week. Once they get lonesome you never know to whom they'll go."

"What wifely trust!"

"And more than that, he'll suspect you've been up to something here. Unfair of him of course but men are like that."

"What mutual confidence!"

"Be sarcastic all you want. But I warn you. It happened to me. He'll charge you with infidelity, of carrying on clandestine affairs . . ."

"How flattering for you!"

". . . plaguing me with insults and obscene accusations . . ."

Mayura clicked her tongue in mock solicitude.

". . . the same may happen to you."

"Except that there is a teeny weeny difference, namely, your husband had a concrete basis to rile about."

Mira looked up, scared.

Jaya flushed. "How dare you . . . you know the truth."

"Everyone did at the time, unfortunately."

"What was it?" Mira whispered, half afraid, half curious.

Jaya did not answer.

Mayura shrugged. "Nothing. Just acting Florence Nightingale. Too bad the patient was almost in the altogether."

Stop it. Mira was ashen pale.

"Eleven years ago," Jaya said softly, as though to herself.

"A star cricketer, she once took me to see his batting. A lanky pitch black man, all knobbly bones and joints."

"And still it chases me"

"Spilling gobs of sweat as he returned victorious to the pavilion."

"Just three hours to soothe a dying man."

"If you say so, of course, just three hours."

Stop it. Stop it.

". . . and he the only person who could tell the truth to the unbelieving world, dead, nobody caring, I heard someone say at the condolence meeting at the Union Hall, Too bad we've lost our chance at the trophy, they wept for the loss of a trophy, not for a youth dying. Nobody cared." Jaya continued speaking to herself. She cleared her throat and blew her nose into the pallav of her sari. "Nobody cared."

Mira's face was contorted with fear. No. No.

". . . hustled into marriage . . ."

"Whatever it was, stop it," Mira whispered, about to run.

Jaya caught her arm and pulled her back to her seat on the tank wall and sat down beside her. "You don't know? Little sister, you haven't heard?"

"I don't want to. Let me go."

Jaya spoke in a low voice, with an urgency. "But you must know, little sister. It may be that when you join College you walk up the stairs, your hand on the left banister because girls walk single file along the left while the boys surge up in fours, you are walking up and you hear Skipper tell his friend, Mohan is our only hope next Sunday for I think Govind won't make it to the field by then, and his friend asks, Why where is Govind? And the skipper says, Malaria since last Sunday, a hundred and four degrees plummeting down to ninety-seven, and the other asks, Doctor? And Skipper says, Oh yes, of course, I got the hostel Doc to go with me, and he fears it might be pneumonia plus, tough on Govind, and the other says, Anyone to take care of him? and Skipper says, Sent for his brother who's up in Raipur, but I guess it is okay, just routine medicines and all that stuff, I've been dropping in every day and will go today after the meeting, and the other says, What meeting, and Skipper says it is about the Chepauk pitch that is in real bad shape, and they talk on and you are swept with the crowd and pushed into your Chemistry classroom."

Hands wet and limp.
    Govind is ill.
    The lecturer as usual has come before the bell and filled the blackboard with equations and reactions and you copy down the hieroglyphics on a new page.
    Nobody with him.
    Don't be silly, pals spend half the night talking about cricket in his room.
    The property of mercury as we have seen
    Nobody cares and he is alone
    Silly silly don't be silly
    I should be there nursing him
    Silly silly
    There's no one to take care
    He doesn't even know you
    To go over the physical properties again
    He doesn't but I must go
    You are not even a name to him. Just one of the forty-eight girls in the first year, one of three hundred and ninety-two girls in National College, and he in the fourth year, star batsman, only player to have piled up a century in every match this season.

To repeat, the chemical properties of mercury
    Silly silly
    And it shows 105 degrees
    Silly silly
    "I adored him from the day I saw him. Just chance that I dropped by Aunt Alamu that Sunday morning in September, just chance that my College was playing Medical that day, just chance that Aunt Alamu's house faced the playground, just chance that those two cousins were cheering Medical for all they were worth. But what followed was not chance. I took up for my College not because I knew cricket or cared for National but

just to annoy the boys. I didn't even know what the score was but I bet them a rupee National would win. I didn't know that we had been skittled out for 84 the previous day and had been given an ignominious follow-on because Medical had cashed in a neat 260 for 9 and we were back on the pitch already two wickets down and it was only eleven o'clock. And even as I slapped hands on the bet, the third wicket fell. The boys were jubilant. Govind was next joined by Narasimhan, who was a hitter. It was known that once he got used to the pitch, it was hard to dislodge him and so the boys prayed and cursed that he be bowled out within the first few overs. But that didn't happen. Then both batsmen started hitting out—National's invincible partnership at its best. Boundary followed boundary, the scorekeeper had a hard time keeping up. Lunch break saw the partnership standing at 102 runs, with Govind's at 58 and Narasimhan's at 44. But the boys were still in high spirits. They speculated that once the partnership was broken, the wickets would go down like ninepins. At a generous estimate National would be dismissed before tea with another hundred runs, and of course Medical would easily score the forty or fifty runs in the hour and quarter between tea and close of play. And this was allowing National a lot of room, they said. More likely the National innings would close even before they equalled Medical's score. That would leave them enough time, they said, to pick up the rupees from me and reach Sun Theatre in time for the Tarzan movie. Now that they had predicted the day's play to their satisfaction, they spent lunch hour talking about the players. Govind was the best, and no doubt about that, they said, admiring his strokes, poise, text-book stance right foot forward for the masterly snick, perfect coordination of footwork to limb movement . . . a great bat, a batsman's batsman ˙. . . we must try that favourite boundary stroke of his with that full arm swing, wasn't he taking a risk though stepping halfway down the pitch to take thosetreacherously slow balls full volley? They went on and on about Govind. He was a perfect sport. Remember how he brought that Muslim kid what's his name out into fame the other day by making him face Phadnis all the time instead of that typhoon terror Ahmed. Always took a double run and a single at the last ball so he would be the one facing the terror Ahmed. Helped the kid hit up a decent 21 runs and that's enough for a kid's first match in A team you know.

"Inevitable that I should fall in love with him that lunch hour that September afternoon eleven years ago."

Mayura, without meaning to sound eager, eagerly asked, "Did you win?"

Jaya let go Mira's arm. Her eyes sparkled with elation and her voice was young and vibrant. There was no mistaking the raising of brows and the slight catches of breath that characterised many Hari Vilasians. "After lunch, just as the boys had talked about Narasimhan's tendency to over-eat, he ran too slowly and was stumped out. The fifth wicket fell just as we equalled Medical's score. Govind got his century. He was impregnable, his bat is twice as broad as the wicket, dammit, the boys kept groaning.

"Bowled, bowled, *bowled*, they shouted with each ball. Buck up Buck Up I outshouted them. Out Govind out, they yelled. Go Govind go, I screamed. Each ball became an agony for me, a hope for them. Half an hour before tea Govind was bowled out. He got a standing ovation from the crowd."

Jaya paused and then continued, "As a matter of fact, we lost the match. The Medicos lashed out in a do or die effort, lost eight wickets in half an hour, but they hit the needed runs and won twenty minutes before draw of stumps for the day.

"After that I went to all the National matches. I joined the crowd of girls for whom it was a fad to watch cricket and cheer their team, and so I was one of the in-crowd.

"Do you know what agony one goes through when one's favourite is batting? Especially when one doesn't know much about the game, unlike radio commentators who can see all kinds of details. Every ball is a monster, a fiend, and I cowered at every single ball. Every ball could be one's last. It is not so bad if the guy you are interested in is a bowler because fate doesn't hang in the balance but when it is a batsman who has your heart, every ball is third-degree torture, you are stretched on the rack from the moment the bowler starts his long leisurely run that becomes faster and faster, the bolts tighten when he flings the ball, and you are paralyzed until the moment you see the ball careening away safely somewhere far beyond the wicket. Sometimes, when it is a slow bowler, the ball comes slow and high, and is hit hard and high, and you sit in suspense watching its curve, its direction, the position of the fielders, their distance from the likely destination, you watch it all in one throbbing moment, and you sink back exhausted when at last the ball touches the ground.

"The torture isn't half as intense if you know anything about the game because then you can know the moment the ball is delivered whether it is headed for the stumps or not, you can make out an off break from a leg break from a spin from a noball and you can sit on judgement of the play instead of being victim of its suspense."

There was a long pause. Jaya's voice, that had risen with the excitement of the game, reverted to its low softness. Her eyes lost the fire that had animated them but her mouth still transformed her face to what it had been. Like Mira's, her lips were tremulous, pink, defenseless.

"And now fever is raging. 104 degrees plummeting to 97. And no one with him. I almost sob over the chemistry hieroglyphics. Room 17 Sri Murugan Lodge Keechri Lane, I write on the page. I wake up, startled at the smudge that was slowly spreading on the page. I wipe my eyes furtively. Again I write Room 17 Sri Murugan Lodge Keechri Lane. I knew he lived there. I do not know when I knew that but I know now, and that is all that matters.

"I must have run all the way for it is only 11:35 when I stand outside the Lodge. It is on a lane off the main road. It is a shabby rooming house with men in torn clothes smoking beedies. I stand pertified, but men start staring at me, one passes by me a second time. I collect my breath and courage and rush up the staircase that is between two small stores. The rooms are on the second and third storeys, I know that is how it is with these rooming houses that sit on top of a row of shops. A veranda runs in front of a line of rooms to my left and to my right. The first room on the left is numbered 14. I pause. I tremble. What if there are friends around him? Then I could go away assured there was someone to help him. How am I to know? I turn left and walk beyond Room 14. I go past Room 17. I look through the open door and the open window. There is nobody in. I am relieved and ashamed. He is not even in his room, so well he has gone out. I am relieved and glad. Then I am afraid. What if I am seen here by someone who knows me. In a College like mine, a great many boys know all the girls by face because that is their passtime—to watch us, dangling their legs from the ledge of the veranda walls. My name will be rolled in mud and trampled upon. I envied the Muslim girls who chose to wear a burqa to college. I turn back and walk toward the staircase again. As I pass his room, I peep in and I see him on the cot under the window. He is under the bedcover, so flat and still that I had missed him at first. 'Govind.'

"He does not answer. It may not even be him. I should not enter, but I do. What if it is someone else? There are bottles of medicine on the table. It has to be him. But the world is full of ill people. What if it isn't Govind? But I must know for sure. I go in. It is Govind. I don't know how I know but I know. He is huddled under a yellow counterpane that is wrapped around his waist like an Egyptian shroud. He must have turned and twisted and turned. I shut the door and run to him. His teeth are chattering. I stand by his side and stare at the back of his head, at the straight black hair uncombed and dry. I bend down and pick up the blanket from the floor. It smells of fever and sweat. The bed-sheet, not wide enough to be tucked under the mattress, has crumpled into a straight cord in the centre of the bed. He lies huddled on the other side. His back is wet. His shirt clings to him. I suppose the fever had come down in the morning and was rising again. I cover him with the blanket. I bend down and stroke his hair away from his forehead, and wipe it with the edge of the counterpane. Between the black of his hair and the black of his face is a dark brown strip where the cricket cap had kept out the sun. I stand and stare. And still he shivers. The room is bare: the cot, a table, two chairs, a stool. Two dirty shirts hang on the nail back of the door, a steel trunk is under the bed, one or two pairs of white cricket trousers and some underwear are bundled in a corner, books on the table, socks back of the chair, shoes, cricket shoes, cobweb and dust. I kneel down and stroke his forehead, broad, hot. I have not touched a man's face ever, except for Dad's and that only till I was ten. How shining and wet his three-four-day beard is, and prickly. I cry. How long I do not know but I stop when he moans. He is delirious. Ma Amma, he says. And hot, scalding hot. But his shirt is wet. I smooth out the bed-sheet. I look around for a towel, and not seeing one, I take a shirt from the nail back of the door and wipe his back. Then I see a towel under the pile of underwear and trousers. And he raves. Asks for his mother. Govind, Govind, I whisper. Not knowing how one removes a man's shirt,

I lift it and wipe his back with the other shirt. He tosses about, throws
off the blanket. He pulls at the yellow coverlet shrouding his body and
then gives up and lies still. Ma, Amma. I soothe him give him water from
a flask. There is only half a cup of lukewarm water. I pour it into the cap
of the flask, and hold it to his mouth. Drops drip off his mouth into his
beard. Govind, Govind. I put my arm under his head and try to raise him
so he can drink. He drinks. Still delirious. I am scared. I soothe him, sit
on the bed, and draw his head to my breast and soothe him. I am not
afraid any more. I can sit here forever and forever, his scraggy scalding
head against me. He sleeps. I kiss his face. His salt sweat is on my lips. I
run my lips over his forehead. I could lick away his fever. But I a woman.
I lay his head back and rise. I sit at the foot of the bed and press his
feet that burn my hand through the thin coverlet. The door opens. A
travel-stained man comes in with a shoulder bag. He sees me and draws
back. Then he looks at the number on the door. Govind? I nod Yes. He
comes in.

"'How is he?'

"'I don't know,' I say.

"'I am his brother,' he says. And who are you, his eyes ask. Govind
groans. The man goes to him, draws a chair and sits by the bed. He talks
to Govind. He got the telegram Monday but nobody had any money, it
being the end of the month. However, he came as soon as could borrow
the amount.

"Govind seems half conscious. The man speaks on. Everyone was well
at home. Maybe Govind would be better off at home. They could leave
tomorrow. Malaria was always like that, enervating, and there was nothing
anyone could do about it except sweat it out.

"I don't know why you had to send for me, he mumbles, malaria is only
malaria, but telegrams are always scaring and mother had insisted he come
down.

"The man continues to talk.

"'Ma, Amma.'

"'Govind, I am here, Babu.'

"'Ma, where is Ma?' I put my hand on his. He smiles and goes back to
sleep or unconsciousness. The man goes to the water pitcher and drinks
a tumbler of water. I pour some water into an empty saucepan that's

covered by a notebook, I place it on the electric hot plate on the table and put on the switch.

"'It is good of you to be here,' the man says.

"I continue stacking the books to make more room for the bottles of medicine and for the stove. I almost cut my hand against a blade. I pick it up and also the razor that is among the books, and place both on the windowsill.

"'Has he no roommate, friends?'

"'I don't know.'

"Who are you? his eyes ask. 'Thank you for your help Miss . . .' he waits for me to tell him my name.

"'Even he doesn't know my name,' I say, 'I am not even a face to him.'

"His eyes express his disbelief.

"Govind raises himself on his elbow. 'I thought Amma was here,' he says. We both go to him. He falls back. He looks at me. 'Who are you?' he asks.

"'He is delirious,' the man says. 'Govind, I am here, Babu.'

"'Babu, where is Amma? Call her back.'

"The man does not say anything. Govind closes his eyes. We sit on, the man on the chair, I on a stool.

"The fever rises. Govind is now delirious. Ma, he says, looking at me. Ma. I hold his hand. He sighs. Stay here, he says. Yes yes, my heart says, yes. I stroke his face. The man moves about the room. It is almost four o'clock. Skipper will soon be here and I a woman. I rise, pick up my handbag. Govind turns over. Ma, he says, Amma, don't leave. The man looks at me. Amma! Govind is scared, desperate. The man looks at me, pleading. His eyes are red with coal dust. His shirt is specked with coal dust. His bone-coloured drill trousers are streaked with coal dust. He has come a long way in a train. In third class. I open my handbag. For several days I have been carrying my examination fees but not paid it. The cashier's desk always has a long queue of examinees. I hesitantly take out the crisp pack of five-rupee notes. I dare not look at the man. Will he throw it back at me? I look at him humbly, I who plead now. 'Please send for his mother,' I say, stretching my hand with the money, 'Please.' I take out the ones as well. I plead. He hesitates, looks at me, takes the money. 'You are very kind,' he says. I turn away. 'Your books, Miss Venkatesan,' he hands my pile of notebooks to me, each with my name neatly written with a calligraphic pen. 'You are very kind,' he says again. I do not know whether he is angry, malicious, or grateful. I still do not know."

Jaya stopped. After a spell of silence, she rose and walked away, towards her mother's house.

"She is my sister," Mira said, with pride.

Mayura did not say anything.

Mira continued, with unwonted spite, "You are jealous. You don't have even three hours to look back upon."

Mayura did not say anything.

"You are jealous." There was a note of glee.

Mayura raised her eyebrows in scorn, now in control of herself. "You are so very right, my dear cousin, so very right. I do envy her life in the quiet boonies back of the beyond, with a tobacco-chewing man and a houseful of dirty children." She looked at the adolescent by her side. Mira scooped a handful of water from the tank and flung it on Mayura's face. "I hate you, I hate you," she sobbed and rushed away.

Neera

IT CAN'T BE, MAYURA said to herself. And yet . . . Never had it been delayed
so long. A day, at most two days. She examined herself carefully as though
seeking some proof that it was not so. She knew her body would have
nothing to reveal but she looked again and again for some sign that would
dispel the fear that had been gnawing within her for these three days. Early
every morning, twice at mealtimes, once in the middle of the night, she
had felt the familiar stab of cramps, welcome so welcome, but nothing
had happened. Self induced and imaginary. It can't be, she said to herself.
And yet . . . never before. Never. Twenty-seven days for nine years, she was
proud of her record whenever she read Manimoy Dutt's weekly articles
and advice in Femistree magazine. Manimoy Dutt, she thought, feeling
bitter against the innocuous trivia of the question-and-answer columns
that floated by in her mind's eye. Dear Manimoy: Is it true that a strong
dose of castor oil after a very hot bath will . . . Dear wrongdoer: No, the
old belief that heating the body or eating tea leaves . . . So many remedies
suggested by so many hopefuls turned down by Manimoy, always saying
there was no easy way out, no safe way. No way, she thought furiously, no
way out of this bestial condition. But there must be. Pills, hormones, there
must be.

When Mayura came out of the bathroom, her mother asked her, "Is
something wrong?"

She peevishly replied, "Of course not. What would be?"

"You've been running to that room so often today, I wondered if you
had an upset stomach," were her mother's words but her look of curiosity
revealed her thoughts.

Mayura walked away. Parvati sent a quick prayer upward. From the day Mayura returned, she had been praying that the girl be pregnant. She made a pact with all the goddesses in her pantheon. A hundred coconuts every Friday in November to Sreedevi, mother of earth, goddess of fertility; an offering of brocade sari in person to Meenakshi at her Madurai shrine; feeding of Brahmins at the temple every Tuesday through December; libations to life giving Ganga if she animated the speck within Mayura as she had animated the sixty thousand sons of Sagara; the list grew longer day by day and Parvati, in an ecstasy of faith shut herself to the fact that the matter was already beyond the deities' control. If Mayura were pregnant all the problems would be solved automatically; this she believed, and so she watched her daughter and prayed to all the goddesses in her pantheon. Now she added two minor deities to her list and walked downstairs emanating jubilation.

Mayura shut herself in her room, breast constricted with shame and pain.

An hour later she came down. "I am going to see a friend," she addressed her mother's back as she walked through the living room to the front veranda.

"Who?" Parvati wheeled round and hastened after her. Mayura stared at her mother, who halted her advance before the onslaught of cold contempt. Hastily Parvati added, "It is just that I'd like to know when you'll be back. maybe I could send the car after Appa returns if you'd tell me where to send it. It might rain. I have asked the tailor to come this evening."

She was seldom nervous but when she was, she had a compulsive urge to keep talking, anything at all would do, till she regained her composure. Parvati did not want her daughter out of sight. There was too much talk already. And the girl did the most unheard of things. Last evening she had gone to the beach alone. Alone! to Mylapore beach which had become a loafers' playground. It was not the same place it had been when the children were children, and could walk there and back in safety. Parvati was near tears with suspicion and suspense.

"Heck, just to see a girl friend," Mayura shouted, reading her mother's fears, "Neera Mehta, if that puts at rest your sneaky suspecting mind."

Parvati smiled broadly, not heeding the jab. "Ah, Dr Mala's daughter!" Her voice lilted with relief. Dr Mala's Maternity Clinic was where Saveri's second child had been born. Dr Mala had a lucky touch. "Neera has been shuttling between Madras and Bangalore ever since she was married. Did you phone to make sure she's here and not in Bangalore? She comes and goes any time she wants, now that the highway has been made so good."

"Of course, I have, she's here. Bye."

Neera had been pleasantly surprised to get Mayura's call. Mayura visiting of her own accord! How long it was since she had done that! And now, when she has walked out, so they said, on her husband! Perhaps she was changed now, or rather she was once again what she had been in their Sacred Heart Convent days before she had grown to her proud aloofness.

She ran up to her room to change into something more decent than the kaftan she was lounging in. She stood at the window for a moment before closing the curtain. It stuck halfway. A shiver ran down her spine. Then she made herself smile. These were new curtains that her mother had made for the room after the wedding. She smiled because it was still a dark blue. That was Mamma. Everything in the house had been exactly the same as far as she could remember.

By pulling the chair close to the wall, Neera could clamber on to the windowsill and look out. She could see the top of the garage on one side and she could see the garden below her and the road beyond the low compound wall of the house. Her ayah, against whose ample bosom Neera had been nurtured since infancy, never allowed her to play outside in the afternoons, and so Neera often knelt or stood on the windowsill and watched the cars and buses roll by, honking their horns. Sometimes hawkers stood at the gate with coloured balloons flying upward from their push-carts. Sometimes women came with baskets of vegetables or fruit on their head. Sometimes beggars came asking for money or rice. There was one beggar who came very often and cried in a bass voice that cracked towards the end, "Ammmaaa!" The gardener always sent every one of these people away.

Neera liked her room. All her friends were there, some pushed under the bed, some pasted on the light blue walls, some on picture blocks, some in her books. She particularly liked the big, coloured procession that marched up from the foot of her bed. There were drummers and trumpeteers and children and grownups and horses. Very near the pillow was a gold caparisoned elephant with a princess in a red howdah. The name of the princess was Suvarnalata. Neera called her Lata. She also called her Tinky, Asha, Mayura or Kitty, depending which of these four friends she liked best at the moment.

Neera disliked her room by night. It was so dismal and dark. Every night, before going away to her corner of the veranda outside Neera's room, Ayah drew the curtains and switched off the light. From her bed, Neera could see only part of the window where, because of a faulty curtain ring, the two halves of the curtain could never meet unless carefully pulled tight. The rest of the window was hidden by heavy dark blue curtains printed with darker blue flowers, each the size of a pumpkin. She hated Ayah for many things, but most of all for drawing the curtains each night and making the room dark and dismal. Ayah was not a careful woman in anything except in caring for her charge. Every night Neera stared at the friendly chink of brightness till she fell asleep. This concentration on the line of light kept the hobgoblins away because they hated brightness, she knew. She wished she could have some of the starry sky shining on her bed. It was so lonely and frightening to be shut away from the sky.

One night, while the ayah had gone downstairs to get Neera's nightly glass of milk, Neera tried pulling the strings of the curtain. The curtains drew closer together, shutting out even the thin streak of sky. But before she could try anything else, Ayah returned and Neera had to drink the milk, rinse her mouth, and jump into bed. Ayah patted her cheeks, tucked in the mosquito net, took her mat, bedsheet and pillow, switched off the light and went to her corner under the stairway to the terrace. Neera stared at the place where the chink should have been. Hobgoblins came out of the cupboard. They stood outside the netting and made ugly faces at her. She stared hard at the dark blue curtain with the darker blue flowers that could not be seen but were there, each the size of a pumpkin. She tried to remember how the fairy godmother had made a coach and six for Cinderella with a pumpkin. But the ugly hobgoblins stood on, and Neera yelled till Ayah came in and scolded her and rocked her against her bosom till she slept.

Another night, Neera pulled both strings of the curtain but nothing happened. In a way she was glad that nothing had happened, that the curtains still had that chink of light.

Neera tried to remember to watch how Ayah pulled open the curtains in the morning. But every day she forgot, for once it was morning and daylight who could remember about darkness and curtains? And so every night she remembered that she had forgotten and decided she would not forget next morning.

Another night she pulled again and again at the curtain itself, knowing Ayah had gone down and would not be back until she had talked a long time with the cook. Something snapped and half the curtain hung loose. Ayah came in and scolded her, and said the dark blue flowers would punish her for pulling them down, and did she know there were flowers that swallowed naughty children like the cat lapped up the milk? But that night, Neera did not care what the ayah said. She had the brightness she loved. Later, a little star came in and sat on her bed and told her all about his life in the sky.

The next morning, Neera told the gardener about her new friend, the star. He laughed so loudly, Ayah came out of the house and wanted to know what was happening. When he told her, she swooped down, caught the girl in her fat arms, and pressed her fingers down the girl's face and knocked her closed fists against her temples to cast out the evil eye. She wailed, "Oh, I hope the churel hasn't cast her evil eye on my precious lamb. How often I have told Doctoramma I don't like this tamarind tree growing so close to my darling's window. Oh oh."

"What is that?" Neera asked the gardener. "That word chura that Ayah uses so often?"

He only laughed, and told her not to worry. Ayah was a good woman but ever so superstitious. "Don't listen to the old drum. Come, help me carry these flowers inside."

That evening, when Neera refused to eat spinach, which she hated, Ayah rolled spinach with rice and forced the little ball into her mouth. Neera spat it out.

"If you don't eat this, the churel will come for you."

"They won't, churels are my friends," Neera said, "I love them."

At which Ayah shook her, and said, "Never say that. Never. A churel is the ghost of a woman who dies with her newborn child, and so she comes to carry away little girls, especially naughty girls who don't eat their food."

Neera's mother came in just then and rebuked Ayah, "Don't feed the child such stupid ideas. There are no such things as churels."

Neera smiled. She would never be afraid of churels again. Mamma said they did not exist, and Mamma knew. Mamma knew everything.

Neera loved her mother. She loved every bit of her. She loved her starched white sari and crisp white blouse, and her neat knot of hair, and her wrist watch that tick-ticked ever so softly with the long red dial rushing round and round. She loved her long gentle fingers and her beautiful beautiful face. She loved her because she was Mamma and not Ayah, had nothing in common with fat, loud Ayah who wore coloured shiny silk saris and had a paan-smelling mouth.

Neera loved her mother's rooms, her big table and fat books that had stupid black pictures; she loved her mother's sweet smelling almirahs where saris and blouses hung neatly from coloured hangers. There were only two things she hated in that room—the white coat and the stetho-scope. Mamma always carried them with her, and Neera was jealous of them.

But Neera hated something even more, and that was the telephone, the little black monster that always took her mother away. The driver too was to blame because he drove the car that took her away every morning. But the driver took her, Neera, to the park and to the shops where Mamma allowed her to buy chocolate and toys. So he was not so bad. But the tele-phone was wicked. It was even more wicked than Ayah, for at least she cooked nice things for Mamma when Mamma returned in the evening, and because she was always around to take care of her.

Neera hated the telephone the most because she feared it. Whenever it rang, Mamma rushed away. And often it rang at night.

Neera seldom heard the phone itself at night. But the hustle-bustle that followed it woke her most times: Ayah's heavy thud thud up and down the stairs, opening and shutting of doors, the creaking of the garage door, the shutting of the front door, the banging of the car door—one or the other would wake the girl, and she would start crying, and Ayah would come and soothe her or scold her according to her mood, saying Doctor-amma had to go because the telephone had called her. Then Neera would cry even louder, and Mamma would come in and kiss her and pat her and say, "Now sleep like a good little girl, my darling. I'll see you at breakfast." And Mamma would go away, coat and stethoscope in hand, and the car door would bang shut, and Ayah would come in. Sometimes, she would soothe her and tell her a story; sometimes she would sit on the bed and complain loudly; most often she would take Neera in her arms and rock her violently, as though she would rather slap her, and often she would say, "Unless you stop crying, your mother won't come back. Why should she come back when all you do is cry cry cry?"

"Sometimes Neera would say, "She WILL come back, this is where she lives. So there." And she would stick her tongue out at Ayah. Sometimes she would stop crying, paralyzed by the sheer force in Ayah's voice. But most often, she cried louder than before, terrified that Ayah was confirming something that she always feared anyhow, that Mamma would not come back. The ayah was wrong, she would sob. Hadn't Mamma said she would see her at breakfast? How could she see her if she did not return? But black-tongued Ayah's words came after Mamma's and so had the ring of finality and authority.

One morning, Ayah came to the garden where Neera was helping the gardener by watering plants with her toy watering-can while he weeded the zinnia bed. "My poor sister is dying. Oh, poor woman. I hope I see her alive. Doctoramma said I could go at once, and she has even told Driver to take me to the station. O, I must go get ready."

"Where are we going?" Neera was excited. Ayah never went anywhere without her, of course.

Ayah gathered her to her breast and kissed her many times over. "My precious lambkin, I have to go without you. But I'll come back soon, very soon." And she spoke for fifteen minutes without stopping. Neera did not understand a word of what she said, though the gardener seemed to understand every word and clucked sympathetically.

Neera cried all the way to the station and back. Mamma, who had stayed home, assured her Ayah would return soon, that she had gone to see her sister who was ill, that she would come back very soon, but Neera wanted her "now." Mamma took over Ayah's work. She fed Neera, washed her up, took her to the Clinic and let her play in her office room while she attended to patients. That evening, she had a cot brought into Neera's room and made her bed next to the child's. She held Neera in her arms and told her a beautiful story about Suvarnalata, which even Ayah had never told her, and Neera was happier than Suvarnalata could ever be in spite of sitting on a gold-caparisoned elephant in a red howdah. Mamma, moreover, kept the curtains open. Neera could see the sky outside, and next to her was her own lovely Mamma.

Neera saw more of her mother in the next few days than she usually saw in a month. Mamma ate with her, spent all the evenings with her. Whenever Neera cried, or was about to cry, Mamma kissed her and said, "No, no, my darling is too old to cry," or "Mamma doesn't like to see big girls crying."

One night, Neera was wakened by some sound. She opened her eyes and whimpered, as a prelude to crying. But the moonlight came in reassuringly, and she could see Mamma reaching out to the telephone. Mamma had brought the dirty monster along with her cot. Its black cord trailed all the way from Neera's room to Mamma's. Neera wanted to cry, but she did not. Her mother, standing at the phone, seemed to say, Mamma's big little girl must not cry.

"Time the contractions with a watch, Thimma, how many times to tell you that? I'll be there in a few minutes." Mamma left the room. Neera strained her eyes towards the door; she saw the light on the veranda, she heard her mother coming out of her room, she smelt the starch on a new sari. Tears rolled down Neera's face. She sat up, her throat parched, her arms limp, her eyes burning; Mamma will come now, surely she'll come and kiss her and say as she always did, "Now go to sleep like a good little girl, my darling. I'll see you at breakfast." Surely, surely she will. She always did, always.

The car doors slammed shut, and the car carried her mother away.

Neera ran out to the taxi and eagerly embraced Mayura who responded warmly despite herself, saying, "Neera, I am so glad to see you." As though to counteract her moment of weakness, she added with impersonal enthusiasm, "Such ages since we met. And you look bright and lively as ever."

"Do I?" Neera was genuinely astonished. Could she really look bright and lively ever again? She led her friend to the drawing room and they sat on a long sofa. Mayura looked around and said, "This room has been exactly like this as far back as I can remember."

"Mother likes it that way."

"As ordered and in place as the instruments on her surgical tray."

Neera felt slightly uncomfortable. She never knew whether Mayura was being sarcastic or sincere.

"And how is your mother?" Mayura continued.

"Fine, thank you. Busy as ever. Never returns before eight o'clock now that she has gone back to working at the hospital."

Mayura looked at her watch. It was not yet five. Disappointed, she continued the conversation without interest. "What happened to the Clinic?"

"That is prospering too. Mamma has employed two doctors to take care of that. Of course, she is there every morning just to help out."

Their small talk continued endlessly. They had chaklis and lemonade, exchanged opinions on the current movies and dance concerts, were soon bored with each other and with themselves. Once or twice the conversation verged on something personal but veered away as imperceptibly. Mayura wondered why she had come to this bovine creature. Neera had always been a lump of good nature, with soft, non-descript features and clear complexion. Neera broke into her thoughts as she looked her over. "Tell me, Mayu, have I changed? I mean I know I have, but I wonder if it shows."

Mayura looked over her coolly and said, "Plumper, of course, but considering you people often double your weight after marriage, you haven't done too badly." Neera smarted under the condescension in Mayura's voice. There was another chasm of silence.

Mayura, with a bored sigh, took out a nail file from her handbag and started shaping the moons of her fingernails. She was annoyed with herself. The whole idea of asking Dr Mala for help was preposterously impractical. All that she could do was to get it confirmed, which would be better than this agony of not knowing. But that could be done just as easily with all due publicity by her mother calling for an appointment etcetera etcetera. She might as well leave right away instead of continuing this inane conversation.

Neera looked pensively at her friend. How eagerly they had embraced each other! Gone the moment of contact. If they could talk, just talk about themselves. Why did Mayu come away from her husband? Is that what women do, is that what a woman should do if she found out her husband enjoyed two beds? If only they could talk! Mayu was just as arrogant and cold now as she had been these many years. But over the phone, and as she got off the taxi, how warm she had been. She was unhappy, that was obvious. Two unhappy women. If they could talk, just talk about themselves. Gone the moment of contact.

Neera extracted from the glass bookcase an album of her wedding photographs. Mayura smiled wryly. The album. Inevitable and inescapable, the wedding album. As inevitable and inescapable as chaklis and lemonade. Neera did not notice her expression. She moved closer to Mayura and opened the album. A straw to bridge the chasm. She said, "Actually, you should be showing your album. You are the new bride. Maybe you've seen these already. I recall Mamma saying your mother had come in person to give your wedding invitation. I wasn't here then. Do you want to see?"

"Oh, of course. An excellent conversation piece, these wedding albums."

It has come to this, Neera thought, the straw disappearing downstream.

On the first page was the elaborate wedding invitation, with a procession and drummers and musicians, bridegroom on horseback. Dr Dinesh Mehta MBBS (Madras) MD (London)—all the details were there—names and job titles of parents, grandparents. Mayura shook her head at the ornateness of the card. "Like my Suvarnalata, do you remember her?" Neera tried another straw, linking them to their childhood bonds.

Mayura did not bite. "Rather dashing, isn't he?"

"Yes, my husband is handsome."

"And a reputed obstetrician to boot!"

Sarcasm? Flippancy? Neera was wary. "Yes, a very good surgeon, yes," she said slowly.

"You sound rather sorry he is so handsome and honoured."

"No, no, of course I am proud, very proud of him."

Never could take a joke. A dumb girl, always has been. Pretty, some would say. Her husband probably thought her ravishing. MD, London. Lucky girl. Aloud, she said, "Isn't life as a midwife's wife quite a pain in the neck?"

"One has to make oneself as happy as one can, no matter what one's husband is or is not."

Trying to slip in some advice, the bitch.

Neera went on earnestly, "Don't you think so?"

"Oh, quit that."

"But what else can one do? If one is married, that's it. One has to accept many facts, however unpleasant . . ."

"Heck, chuck all that Manimoy stuff to the lovelorn and the deserted."

Neera's face flushed with passion. "Why do you think it was something personal about you? You think everyone you meet is thinking only of you all the time. I didn't say your husband was after another woman . . . is he?"

Mayura was taken aback. She had never thought that people might be thinking so. "Of course not," she said haughtily.

"What are you huffing about then?"

". . . and even if he were, it is none of your bitchy business."

"No." The blood drained out of Neera's face. She said, "No, it is none of my business. Each for herself. Each an island entire unto herself. I am sorry, Mayura, I'm sorry."

"Oh, heck, you make me sick with your overpoliteness. Owning up when you are not even to blame. No wonder your husband dotes on you." She jabbed at a candid shot where Dinesh was looking at Neera, who was talking to someone else. The photographer had caught an expression of frank adoration and placed it in front of the world.

Neera took the album from Mayura's lap. "You will excuse me," she said quietly, "there need be no conversation piece between us, and no conversation." She replaced the album in the glass case. "And if you intend on waiting for Mother—in which case congratulations—make yourself comfortable and wait. You can always call for Ayah to get you a cup of tea, if you wish." She walked out of the room slowly, leashing every muscle to prevent herself from rushing out.

Neera had risen, in a moment, to superb majesty. Mayura wanted to kneel down and worship her. Aloud, she was sarcastic. "You have unplumbed histrionic talents, Neera, that momentous exit could have gone straight into *Gone with the Wind*." All of Neera's friends knew she had seen that film seven times.

There was no reply from Neera, who was sitting on the divan in the next room and reaching out to the rack for a magazine. Mayura moved towards the other room, hesitated, turned back, took her handbag and left. It was ten minutes past six o'clock.

Neera heard her leave. The house was silent. Neera walked up the stairs to her room and curled up on the bed. Dinesh will soon be home from the hospital, she thought, and he'll call me tonight because he didn't yesterday. And if I tell him I have my reservation on Saturday's Brindavan Express, he'll kiss the mouthpiece and say it was the happiest news he had heard in centuries and I'll believe him. I suppose I should not, I know I should not, but I will, I don't know why, but I will. I know about Yamuna, I know they've been as much man and wife as any two can be, for years. I know I am the intruder in the triangle and I know he loves her but I can't believe he doesn't love me. Maybe men can love two women at the same time, maybe some men can.

She looked at the curtains, and even though this was perhaps the fourth set of curtains since her childhood she could see the darker blue flowers each the size of a pumpkin, just as she had seen them on either side of the chink of light between the doors of the bathroom the night before she had come away.

From the bed, she could see him at the washbasin, sloshing water on his face. The fragrance of Mysore Sandal Soap floated out to her.

He came out, took his comb from the dresser and went in again. She watched him comb his hair. He thrust his face nearer the mirror and felt his chin. He seemed satisfied. He shaved this evening, she thought, and I thought it was for me.

He came out without switching off the light so he could see his dress rack. He pulled out a hanger that neatly held a pair of trousers and shirt that she had matched and placed there from the dhobi's bundle of ironed clothes. He dressed. He then picked up his shoes and socks. He took the socks to the beam of light to make sure he had not taken an odd pair. He then came to the bed and, sitting on the edge, started putting on his socks.

Neera reached out and placed her hand on his leg.

"Awake, sweetie?" he asked, patting her cheek. "I took the phone on the very first ring, but I guess not soon enough not to disturb your beauty sleep."

She did not answer.

"It is that poor woman I told you about. We were hoping she would be able to carry through for another week; each week makes the chances so much better at this stage. But I guess it is not to be. Tough on her, and on us, eh?" He tied his shoelaces. "I hope I don't wake you when I come back. Sleep well, sweetie. See you in the morning." He kissed her on her forehead and left, switching off the bathroom light on his way out. She heard the car door shut softly. He was careful with his car. She heard the car roll down the driveway.

Neera looked at the stethoscope that he had not bothered to take. He will not need it, she thought dully. What more natural than that a doctor, especially an obstetrician, should rush off after a phone call? Babies were being born all the time, day and night. She, a doctor's daughter and a doctor's wife, should know that. The white coat and stethoscope had become familiar over the years. So had the telephone. Long ago she had accepted their role in her life. And that was why she had never recalled her childhood fears all these years. Till tonight. Till tonight when the sound of the phone ringing had taken her back to her room with the dark blue curtains and the darker blue flowers each the size of a pumpkin.

The terror and the tears subsided. A mounting certainty clawed at her heart. So it was true! Not that there was any room for hoping otherwise, and yet . . .

Why had she not seen it before this? Why had she not been told? They had told her, she realized now. Some said it regretfully, some with malice, some as a joke.

"Neera thinks the world of Dinesh. She can't do without him even for a day." "She is not the only one as we know."

"Neera has a gift for being happy." "For being blind, you mean."

During the last two days Neera had lived over the past fifteen months again and again, sifting out facts, phrases, actions, gossip. She had held each piece of evidence as objectively as she could. The truth was obvious, incontrovertible. For three nights she had lain awake wondering, waiting for the phone to ring. Dinesh had made love to her and had gone to sleep, his hand on her bare breast. She had lain awake wondering if the phone would ring. It had, and he had gone. Neera had taken the afternoon train to Madras, leaving a message with his receptionist that her mother wanted her. On arriving, she had said some similar lie to her mother.

Neera rose, opened wide the curtains, and looked down at the garden with its symmetrical bed of flowers, at the sultry sky with stray sultry clouds waiting for the sea breeze to blow them across the sky, at her mangalsutra that had got twisted as she lay, and she sighed. When Mayura's voice had come over the phone, she had been excited, hopeful that her childhood friend would give her the courage to do what she herself had done, if the gossips were right about Mayura's return. Neera could not say why or how or what but only that Mayura had provided her with an answer whose implications she did not know yet. She only knew that if Mayura, with her pride and poise, could not hide that deep well of loneliness in which she was, hers was not the answer for Neera. She thought about Dinesh, his effusive words and acts of admiration for her, as though every new detail he found about her tastes or idiosyncrasies delighted him, his unfailing enthusiasm for the sari and jewellery she chose for each party, his daily dozen little notes and phone calls . . .

He treats me like his mistress, she thought with sudden clarity. Yamuna was his wife, but she was his mistress. She smiled. But men changed mistresses, never their wives. She sighed. She would cross that bridge when she came to it.

She went to the phone to tell Jivan, her mother's man of all work, to buy her a ticket on Saturday's Brindavan Express.

Suhas and Devika

SATURDAY WAS ONE OF those days that start sultry and stay sultry. Gray clouds sagged from the sky, pendulous and barren like the breasts of a fat old woman. Ceiling fans desultorily swirled the same hot humid air over and over again around the same rooms. Underclothes clung to itchy bodies wet with sweat. People walked around with greasy faces and frayed tempers.

"Why doesn't your mother use clay water pitchers to cool and contain large quantities of water instead of depending on unhealthy ice cubes? And with so many growing children in the house, how far can a tray of ice cubes take you? Stupid, inefficient fools, no sense of what is good for the body . . . a houseful of youngsters with sore throats, that's what she'll have to handle. Our age-old custom of cooling boiled water in baked clay pitchers is too low-class for your uppity mother, eh?"

Gita, tray in hand, cowered under her grandfather's tirade. That morning, the ice trays in their own refrigerator had been emptied twice already, and now Parvati urgently needed ice for the buttermilk to be offered to some VIPs who had dropped by to see Jagannathan. It was just bad luck that Aunt Chandra and family had gone away to a wedding in Adyar. The only other refrigerator in Hari Vilas was a small GEC that the judge kept in his dining room. It was filled with bottles and vials of his medicine, and every morning the ice trays were cleaned and filled with water that was never used but had to be there in case of emergency. A cold compress was one of the answers the judge had for all kinds of ailments, and every morning he supervised while Munisamy cleaned the ice tray and put it back.

Gita secretly cursed her mother for having sent her to the lion's den, and escaped from the old man's tirade as soon as she dared.

Being the second Saturday of the month, everyone was at home, but the customary cheerfulness of holidays evaporated into the air already saturated with sullen humidity. Even Venkatesan lost his temper that morning. "How many times have I told you not to dismember the newspaper?" His sons grumblingly turned their rooms inside out searching for the sheet of last Wednesday's newspaper that had reported in microscopic detail some insignificant work carried out in some obscure field by one of Venkatesan's former students. "Who but an incorrigible fool would insert a research item in the Sports section," Venkatesan fumed. The boys grumbled and mumbled while Venkatesan fumed in bursts of ill-humour.

Mayura sat in her room, hating herself and the rest of the world. Downstairs, the VIP guests had left but Aunt Alamu had dropped by. Parvati was telling Aunt Alamu how her mother instinct had told her of Mayura's pregnant condition the moment she saw her alighting from the taxi cab. Mayura clenched her fists in helpless anger. She flung away *Sense and Sensibility* in disgust. What a colossal bore of a book. An over-rated novelist who knew neither people nor life. She picked up *Peyton Place* to see if it would distract her from her broodings. Silly retailing from a warehouse of pseudoexcitement custom-made for immature teenagers, she thought, flinging that away also. She started oiling her hair, massaging in steady motions. Why did it always feel so good if someone else did it? When she was a child, Aunt Lakshmi was the one she ran to when getting ready for school. Aunt Lakshmi always had time for her, unlike her mother who oiled, combed and braided her hair in two minutes flat. Aunt Lakshmi would part her hair, a little at a time, and place a drop or two of oil, at each spot. Then she would massage the oil into the scalp, first with the tips of her fingers and then with the palm of her hand. Oh, how good it felt. Why did it feel good only when some-one did it? Mayura remembered Raghu's hands on her hair. It was a ritual they had—to massage each other's shoulders, neck and then he needed more—he wanted his back and legs massaged. She asked for equal time, and for the first time felt how tingly blissful it was to lie on one's stomach and be massaged. Raghu was a sensualist, exulting in his body, proud of his muscles, and his raring penis. Was that so wrong? Mayura lay down and imagined his hands moving over her breasts. But then she thought of his

conversations with his friends, and how he bragged about his perform-
ance, as he called it, and she hated him and herself. Good riddance.

As the morning wore on, tempers cooled. It was still sultry, but one
expected lunch hours to be sultry and so took it in stride. Chander
had dropped by and kept them engaged with his stories of Canada.
He spoke with his Canadian accent, which he could turn on and off
depending on who his listeners were. This morning he had brought
a small replica of what he called the Gold-Headed Cane. "It is a ritual
that goes back to about 1840, eh, and celebrates the end of the annual
winter hibernation from mid-December to mid-April when no ships
could enter the Montreal harbour because of the ice on St Lawrence
river."
    "A harbour on a river?" Jayaram said, incredulously.
    "Yeah, Montreal is a thousand miles inland eh, but the harbour is a bee-
hive. You've got to imagine yourself in 1840 eh, when the only trade
Canada had was with Europe, and so it was like being cut off from civilization for six months because the river was frozen or had ice floes and
the sea was pretty rough too, eh? So they had this trophy for the captain
of the first ship to arrive each spring. At first, the trophy was a top hat,
but around 1880, it became the gold-headed cane. See this, the real one
is about five times longer, about seventy-eight centimetres, and with a
fourteen-karat gold head that was about four centimetres high and as
much in diameter at its widest, but this is a good replica. You can see the
Canadian coat of arms coloured with inlaid enamel. Neat eh?" Madhavan
took the souvenir, and ran his fingers over the embossed coat of arms with
obvious appreciation. "Would be a shame to tote it back all the way, don't
you think?" he said.
    "Not a chance," his brother said, "he has brought it for his lady-love,
not for you."
    Ever since Chander had arrived from Canada, he had been teased about
his eligibility as a bachelor waiting to be baited by those of his parents'
friends who had marriageable daughters or nieces, and who phoned or
dropped in, with mangoes or apples or laddus which they had just "happened" to have bought or made the previous day.
    "Whoe'er she be, the not impossible she," Madhavan sang.

*

After lunch, Jayaraman's friends came by, and everyone excitedly started on the Kasur episode of the war.

"There is no way to know what is actually taking place. Our newspapers merely lap up government releases and spew them out without bothering to edit even typographical errors. The journalists have no push, no courage to go to the frontlines; and even if someone has enough enterprise to get the inside scoop on some story, his editor will blue-pencil it for fear of government boycott of ads. Slaves of vested interests, bah. I bet the readers of the *New York Times* get to read a lot more details than we do."

"Oh pipe down, Jay, everyone knows those bastards out west are for Pakistan," Rama Rao interrupted.

Raju said, "And so would you if you had poured one-and-a-half billion dollars to equip their army. You wouldn't care to report that the forty-five-ton Patton tanks you gave had been blasted off the scene by the Indian army."

"Wonder what the Paks will do now that America has withdrawn military aid."

"And so have the Brits halted arms movement to us."

"Who needs these superjets anyway? We'll soon run out of petrol to fuel them."

"And so will the enemy."

"Then both sides will be on their own, without foreign aid, and our superiority will come out beyond question."

Jayaram drily said, "Without petrol, there can be no modern warfare. We'll have to have buffaloes pulling their abandoned tanks to our side of the line, and claiming high and mighty feats. Modern warfare . . ."

"Oh, shut up. Who needs modern warfare? Look at Viet Nam. The Viet Cong with their homemade bombs . . ."

"Homemade, bah. The Chinks are loading them."

"Bastards. Whetting their knives to strike us on the back while we are busy lambasting the Paks."

"Let them strike," Jayaram shouted. "If I had my way, I'd lure them into striking now even if it means getting a couple of hundred of our guys butchered by them."

"Gosh, how callous!"

"A callousness that will pay high dividends. We'll have the powers rushing over to our side if the Chinese attack us. Like the Brits provoked the Germans into sinking the Cunard liner, I forget the name, just to bait America into the war."

Jagannathan looked up from his newspaper to say, "That is a rather unjustified accusation. The Court of Inquiry ruled . . ."

"Cut it out, Dad, you are so damned loyal to the Union Jack, you'd swear even Jallianwala Bagh was justified," Madhavan interrupted his father.

"Divide and rule, divide and leave. The secret behind the building up of the Empire . . ."

"Coupled with unscrupulousness and cunning . . ."

"More than anything, our own foolhardiness. Any invader who steps into India gets to grab the whole land thanks to traitors in our own ranks. From Harshavardhan on . . ."

"Why only Harsha on? Start with the *Mahabharata*. There's a book of despicable traitors. Looks like the decadence of the Hindu society started two thousand years ago."

"Decrying India is the only thing most of us do most of the time," Madhavan jumped in defense. "Let us talk of now, not of the past. Men of a decadent nation would not be shooting down F-86 Sabre jets from little Gnats."

"Right, kid. Every day, every moment, a hero is coming into his own out there."

"The hour produces the men."

"The Great Awakening, bah. Mass hysteria," Jayaram shouted. "The way we rose as one man when the Chinese attacked, one would have thought we'd build Ram Rajya in a trice. What happened when they left? We went back to our internecine squabbles."

". . . and empty coffers, thanks to the same hysteria that made individuals put their gold into government hands that promptly sent it down the drain or into private pockets."

"We'll rise again. We rose under Gandhi. Stands to reason we can rise once more. We are licking those Paks as we speak."

Conversation wove in and out but always returned to the war. Suddenly one of them said, "To hell with Kasur, let's go to Shanti Theatre."

"I vote for Eskimo Cafe. Who wants to sit through a three-hour film? Much better to sit over Cassata ice cream for an hour."

"I don't care where we go, as long as it is air-conditioned."

The group disappeared in a minute, and the veranda was empty.

Mayura, who had been raptly attentive, watched them leave. Boys are so disconcertingly fickle, she thought. They were not interested in the subject, only in whipping themselves into a state of intoxicated excitement or aggressiveness. The war, James Bond, cricket tests, space feats, girls, politics, all seemed to carry the same weight.

And some never grew up. Raghu and his cronies were as carried away even by less significant matters than these boys. They sat for hours dissecting Krishnan's Wimbledon debacle as though it mattered, as though . . . Mayura impatiently rose. If she went into the house, she'd have to pass through the living room, and one or other of the chattering females there would follow her with over-solicitous enquiries.

Mayura walked to Maitreyi Nivas instead, and took the back stairs to her cousin's room.

Suhas turned from the mirror and put down the bottle of vermilion paste she had just used for her forehead. She then changed her mind, and rubbed it off with a swab of cotton wool. From the row of small, white plastic jars she selected one that held purple-coloured powder. She planned to wear a white cotton sari that had a mauve border. In the middle of her forehead, she put a dab of vaseline as base, and carefully shaped a round spot of powder on it.

She held up the mauve choli and said, "I love this delicate shade but I'm afraid it doesn't go with my complexion."

Mayura, from her perch on the windowsill, replied in that maddeningly superior tone of hers, "Your fears are quite justified, I assure you."

Suhas was a cute, small-made girl of nineteen. Her face was an even chocolate brown, smooth, like whipped butter. The white of her eyes was pale blue, as in infants, and her pupils were a dark depthless black, and seemed to shine brighter by contrast. There was a perky expression about her full dark lips, as though she was about to play a practical joke. She had a habit of stretching out her rather long neck, and it gave her small upturned head the balance of a bird about to dart through the air. From her father, Krishnan, she inherited the crookedness of her nose; from her mother Mukta, she inherited gregariousness. She was popular in her college, and had the reputation of being one of the best-dressed girls. She flushed now at her cousin's remark. The dark hue of her face did not reveal the blood that rushed up her cheeks, but a vein throbbed on her dark slim neck like a caged bird flapping its wings.

Mayura turned her face to the window. "Saveri and her brood. Not a single absentee at Hari Vilas today."

Suhas desperately thought, Why doesn't she go away?

"I couldn't stand it any more. So much cackling. I see you are going out . . ."

"Yes, Devika and I plan to go to Midland for the matinee." Suhas reluctantly revealed her plan for the afternoon. Now that it was told, she felt she ought to invite Mayura. She took a deep breath, collecting her will-power for the great effort at cordiality.

". . . because it would be great if I could use your room all afternoon," Mayura completed her sentence.

Suhas sighed with relief.

Mayura continued, "I think I'll be safe here. Only Periyappa saw me coming here and he isn't likely to tell anyone."

"Yes, I am sure it wouldn't strike him to."

"So I can have some peace. I need it."

"Sure."

"The way they've been celebrating . . ."

"Good reason to. First grandchild and all . . ."

"Heck, what hasty conclusions people draw. I am only a few days over-due but Mother has broadcast it with megaphone and buntings. It makes me sick."

"The baby?"

"Ha ha, what a joke!" With that single sarcastic cut, Mayura made her-self the victor of the moment.

Suhas picked up the sari and choli she had let drop on the chair. She decided to be fully dressed so that they could leave as soon as Devika arrived. Devika was her mother's niece, vivacious and gregarious like herself. But Devika was going through a bad spate of depression. Vijay Balaram, her young uncle and Mayura's, to whom Devika was engaged, was away at the Front, a Flight Lieutenant in the Air Force. Devika had been prey to fits of depression ever since the war began. During the week, college and studies carried her through, but the weekend hit her hard. Knowing this, Suhas had proposed a matinee. She quickly changed into the mauve choli and wrapped the sari around her. She did not want Devika to be subjected to Mayura's venom. Mayura was worse than thoughts of the war because she was so inescapably nearer and so unmistakably real. When one's imagination was at work, the war was terribly frightening. But to be depressed by Mayura needed no imagination. Mayura was very much there, unhappy, arrogant, sadistically slinging poisoned shafts at everyone around her.

Mayura moodily watched her cousin neatly pleating her starched sari into place.

"Before one gets married, one has many dreams about the ecstasy of the body."

Suhas slipped a pleat in her astonishment. Mayura confiding in her? Fast upon curiosity came an unaccountable fear—whatever it was that Mayura wanted to tell her, Suhas did not want to hear. Whoever touched this proud, unhappy woman suffered. She carried a deadly infectious vindictiveness in herself.

Suhas diverted any confidence Mayura was about to tell her by lightly saying, "I've heard that Queen Victoria loved her time with Prince Albert so much they spent most of the first six months of their marriage in bed."

Mayura continued, "In actuality, it is plainly revolting. Cigarette-smelling mouths and lipstick patches clamming together, stinking of sweat and secretions."

"No, it isn't so," Suhas cried out unthinkingly. For a moment Mayura turned her cool eyes on Suhas, who shrank from the contempt in them. Then Mayura turned away, "You won't understand."

Suhas looked at the long, slim figure in front of her. Her gaze lingered on the straight line of thin lips. How can you know anything about love and its exaltation? I pity the poor man who had to kiss those bloodless lips of yours, she thought, and ran her tongue over her own full lips, curved like Rama's bow, as he described them. Visveswaran, her own Vish. She smiled triumphantly. She, Suhas, was dark and homely but she had lips that could be kissed. There can be no desecration where one loves and is willing to be loved.

Mayura looked at her again, the same cold look of supreme contempt. Suhas's thoughts cracked into a spiderweb of lacerations spreading out from one central point of recent remembrance.

Suhas came out of the bathroom, still singing at the top of her voice. She threw the towel back on its rack, and passed through a spare room on her way back to her own. Venkatesh Periyappa intercepted her there and said, "In high spirits, seems."

She laughed happily.

"Any reason in particular? Party? Aced your exam?"

"I got a letter from Amma," she sang her glib lie.

Her uncle stood at the door and watched her reflection where her left hand vigorously combed her thick black curls. He caught her good humour, but there was a sad enviousness in his voice when he said, "How happy a letter from your mother makes you! Happier than anything we give . . ."

"O, Perippa! what do you mean?"

"Nothing, Su, just that I am jealous of my brother for having such a vivacious daughter."

"Flatterer!"

"Gladly we give a parent's love but ask no rights. We don't know where you go, who your friends are . . ."

"Sit down, Perippa, and I'll tell you everything about everyone in my classes," she reeled off a dozen names with one or other detail about each one's looks or habits or opinions.

Her uncle laughed with her, and left.

Suhas braided her long wavy hair. She pulled out a biscuit coloured sari. Vish's favourite. He loved those dark blue teardrops on the body of the sari. She studied her own reflection. Why do you think me beautiful, my darling. For your sake, I wish I were.

She put on her slippers and ran downstairs. "Perima, I am going out!"

"Be back before it gets dark, Su. The sun is almost setting already," Lakshmi called out her usual injunction.

Suhas smiled to herself.

Once outside the gate, she quickened her pace and entered the old park three blocks behind the Hari Vilas wall. It was not maintained as a park. From time to time plans were made by the residents of the area to clean up and bring the park to a usable condition. Newspapers vociferously spouted readers' views in intermittent spates of civic consciousness. Nothing happened and nobody really expected anything to happen. Huge trees and untrimmed hedges, bushes sprawling anyhow, small pink flowers and zinnias wildly peeping through wilder and taller weeds, fear of snakes and scorpions, all these effectively made the park desolate and unwanted by all but young pairs of lovers. This made the park notorious and out-of-bounds for self-righteous "decent" people, who avoided all but the path that ran diagonally through it, providing a short cut from the residential locality to the shopping centre on the other side.

Vish was already there, under a peepul tree.

"Absolutely ravishing," he greeted her. "Here," he gave her a rose. "No, wait," he plunged into a nearby hedge and came out with a wild flower, royal blue, like a small bluebell. She put it in her hair, and held the rose in her hand.

"You are always here first," she pouted. "I wanted to surprise you by being first today."

He laughed fondly. "Fibber. You purposely come late so you can have me thinking up the most naughty thoughts." He took her hand.

"Oh no, you mustn't," she said, making no move to withdraw it.

They exchanged inconsequential gossip about college and friends. She told him how the history professor had walked out in anger; he told her how the zoology guy had pounced a test on them, the mean geezer. She described Madhu's new lace sari; he promised she'd have more saris in her wardrobe than Madhu ever had or will. She asked him about his tennis; he narrated how Bhaskar's father, the coach, had slapped Bhaskar in front of everyone when the boy came out of the court after losing the match. On and on, they laughed over trifles, and gently teased each other with words and fingers.

"It is late, I've got to go." She moved suddenly.

He pulled her to the ground and leaned her against himself. The first touch. At last he had dared, at last she had allowed him, after all these weeks. He ran his forefinger down her cheeks and neck, and she did not resist. And they sat on, silent.

This is love, she thought.

"I love you, Su, I love you."

How strong he is, how gentle!

"I feel like Apollo and Hercules in one."

My sweet love.

"Or Arjun and Bhima, or Majnun and who?"

"I must go."

They rose together, and walked hand in hand to the wicket.

"So soon?"

"I must."

"Couldn't we stay here forever?"

"Soon, let us hope."

"Tomorrow?"

"Maybe."

"Must, say you will."

"My darling." It took her all her courage to say it aloud. He gasped at the unexpected endearment. Intoxicated and totally oblivious of the street lamp nearby, they embraced each other. Steps behind them made them spring apart. She retreated into the shadow. He walked back into the park.

Two ladies, shopping baskets in hand, squeezed their baskets and themselves through the wicket.

"Did you see them?"

"Didn't I? Who is the girl?"

"Why? do you know the boy?"

"Oh no. But the girl, who is she?" They whispered loudly, as women do when gossiping. "Is it Leela's daughter?"

"No no. Mukta Krishnan's. The girl has been at her uncle's since Mukta's husband was transferred last November. I forget her name. North Indianish it is. But she is Mukta's daughter all right."

"No wonder, no wonder at all. Like mother, like daughter. However strictly you bring them up, it comes in the blood, the wantonness of the mother."

The women went their way.

The girl stood stunned. Then she started crying—silent sobs so deep the sound never reached the air—that the beauty, the purity, the sublimity of her first embrace was thus shattered by the casual words of a passerby, desecrated and cheapened forever.

That evening was weeks behind her. Since then there had been other evenings, other ecstasies but Suhas remembered only that single shattering moment as she watched Mayura's long slender fingers interlocked around her left knee as she sat on the window sill.

The silence was broken by Mayura. "I see your cousin at the gate."

"Devika?"

"Why else would I bring an arrival to your attention? Neela went in a little while ago, but I didn't think she was worth disturbing your thoughts for."

Suhas thought, I wish Devika would go away. I wish I had hung a branch of neem leaves outside my window to warn her that smallpox is ensconced here.

Devika bounded up the stairs and entered the room like a whirlwind. "Oh Su, I am awfully late, but we can still make it if we take a taxi. Why, is anything wrong? You look like you've been robbed."

Almond-complexioned, with several perennial but shifting pimples, narrow forehead, dark brown hair tied in a pony tail, dark brown eyes set wide on either side of a nose that had no bridge but assumed sudden aquilinity further down, a mobile mouth with one chipped tooth, Devika was known as a tornado of energy. She was neither stout nor slim, but she was one of those who lost or gained weight almost perceptibly. She had two sets of cholis, she claimed, one for her Krishnapaksham and one for her Shuklapaksham, the waning and waxing cycles of the moon. And her temper was like Coca Cola, as she put it, full of fizz when fizzing, and doggoneawful flat otherwise.

Devika went straight to the dressing table and dabbed some talc on her perspiring neck. In the mirror, she saw Mayura. She sharply swivelled around and went up to her. "Hello Mayura! Is it true you are pregnant?"

Mayura flushed darkly.

Devika turned to Suhas with tears in her eyes. She emptied a palmful of talc into the air and pulled the dresser ottoman next to Suhas. "I hope she isn't, Su. I'll never forgive myself if she is, never."

Suhas looked at her, puzzled.

"I didn't know it was so easy to get pregnant. If I had known, I'd have married Vij. He wanted so much that we get married, so much to leave me pregnant." Tears rolled down her cheeks.

Suhas leaned forward and touched her cousin's knee. "Devika, please, please." Devika buried her head in her hands and cried soundlessly. Suhas continued, "Devi, please don't cry. You know the war will be over soon."

"But he might die before that. He said he had nothing to live for."

"Hush, of course he will return, and you will get married and have a cricket team of children," Suhas tried to joke, but her voice was full of pain.

Devika's voice was only a whisper, almost a whimper, "I didn't know it was so easy to conceive."

"It isn't, it really isn't. There are only a few hours each month, thirty-six or something, it really is a miracle each time . . ."

"Four hundred million sperms at each ejection," Mayura said drily. "One doesn't have much chance withstanding four hundred million."

"Our child could have been two months on his way," Devika said wistfully. "That's what he wanted, that I should spend these months waiting with a positive attitude for something positive, those were his words, thinking of life not death, fulfilment not hunger, actuality not abstractions."

Suhas looked at her cousin's tearstained face. Think of the future, she wanted to say. But what did the future hold? The war might continue for a long time. Newspapers celebrated our soldiers' heroic deeds—Patton tanks captured, jets shot down, villages won—but victories took their toll of blood, young blood and shattered hopes. What could she say to her cousin?

"The first time he asked me not to delay the wedding was that evening in June when he heard about the imminent war," Devika said. "We were returning after dinner at Buhari's. We were just a few yards inside our gate when a scooter screeched to a halt at the gate and someone yelled out his name. Vij ran back. It was Lieutenant Mani. They spoke excitedly for a couple of minutes and then Mani rushed off on his scooter. Vij ran to me.

"'It is war,' he cried jubilantly. 'It is going to be war, no more pussyfooting around the negotiating table.' He swept me into his arms and kissed me square on the lips. It was our first kiss, and I was intensely conscious that it was my very first. I strained myself towards him to prolong it. I tried to draw that moment to eternity, at least to make him conscious it was our first kiss, but he drew away and pecked me all over my face in wild excitement. I realized that to him it was only an expression of joy at something else, that he only needed to do something fast and wild. He waltzed me across the lawn saying all kinds of mad things, like, It is going to be war! Boy we'll show them! We'll shoot their pants off them. Great that the government has woken up at last . . . we'll scare the daylights out of those buggers . . .

"'How do you know?' I said. 'You are insane.'

"'We know,' he answered smugly, 'it has been coming a long time, and now we know it is near, very near.' And then he got excited again and boasted and defied imaginary enemies. Suddenly he embraced me, and asked, 'And when shall we get married, love? Friday?' It was a Wednesday. I laughed.

"'Let's get married soon, love, so that I can have a son. And we'll call him Ajit, the invincible. General Ajit Balaram, Chief of Army Staff, that's what he'll be, sounds good, what?' He spoke of this and that, but wouldn't come into the house, and rushed off on his scooter.

"The next week followed a pattern. He would come around noon, and take me to Captain Varma's at the Mount Headquarters. Mani would be there, and Mohan Malhotra and Kesavan Nair. They would talk war, plan war, act war. Captain Varma had a military map of the countries, and they would pore over it, sticking pins, planning strategies, deducing enemy movement and strength and casualties. Hour after hour they would argue and shout and often abuse each other in their zealous wargame. Vij would make me sit beside him, and throw his arms around me sometimes, or just hold my hand or keep his hand on my knee. He seldom spoke to me but I was happy just to be there by his side. On the third day, Mohan said, 'This isn't much by way of entertainment for Devika,' and Vij said, 'She understands. She is born to be a soldier's wife,' and Nair said, 'You are a lucky chap, the girls I take out wouldn't stand a minute of all this. They don't allow me even to mention the W word.'

"'Except in the past tense,' Captain Varma added, 'that thrills them for sure, anything we have done in the past.'

"Mohan said, 'Well, some guys get all the luck, and Vijay has been a lucky bounder all along.'

"I felt so thrilled, so flattered.

"When I wasn't with him, I used to realize how pointless the whole thing was. They were like boys fascinated by a new game, not caring about the reality, which of course was that they had no say at all in the matter. I knew the meaninglessness of this make-believe. Yet, when I was with them, it was not infantile any more. And I too was sure the war was coming.

"We'd return around six, and Vij would stay for dinner and talk to Appa and so on. He asked me not to delay the wedding. He had only three weeks of leave left. He even asked Appa, and Appa was quite willing. Mother even more so, because she was so worried about the hours we kept; often he and I would go to the late-night cinema, or sit in the garden till eleven at night, and she poor thing was worried out of her mind, as though we would ever do anything wrong, poor thing. It was I who hesitated. I told Appa the war was coming, but he didn't believe it. No one did. But I knew, and I was afraid. I tell you I was scared that Vij would go back after his leave and never return. I know it is mean and cowardly but I didn't want to be a widow. I didn't tell him so but one day he asked me if I was afraid he would die. And I did not reply, and so he knew. He tilted my chin up and laughed into my eyes. 'Once I have a wife and son waiting for me, do you think I can be killed? Not even if Yama himself came with his black noose. No, my love, I will die only if you say no now.'

"And I said No, I said it, and oh god, god, he's gone to die."

Devika burst into renewed weeping. Suhas looked at her compassionately. Mayura sat immobile on the window sill as though she was not listening.

Devika continued, "Two days later, he spoke to me again about it. Why do you withhold yourself? he asked, why don't you give me at least a few nights of memories to live on?

"Next day he was more lighthearted, and I told him I'd rather be a virgin than a grass widow, and he said, 'Why, love, you'll be too busy preparing to be a mother to even miss me,' and I said it wasn't possible, not with less than four weeks left, and he said, 'Shall we bet on that? Just give me a chance. She who gives me a child, to her feet I shall bring the world's love and luxuries unending.' But then he became more serious, and said all would be well, and only a few died, and I was born to be a soldier's wife. He told me of how the fishermen believe that the love and loyalty of their wives is what kept the storms from swallowing them, and that is why they could go out day after day on the treacherous sea. I shall never forget that night. He spoke, not joking or teasing any more but pleading, begging me to marry him so he would have the will to live, that I might bear his seed so he would have something to live for, or dying, leave a part of him alive. I hated him then, oh how I hated him for wanting to use me and ruin me. And because I could not put my accusation into words, I burst out crying.

"Next morning, he came to me and apologized for his selfishness. 'When one is young, one never thinks of death,' he said, 'one feels that death is something that strikes others, not oneself, but there are risks. I won't mouth the cliche that more people die crossing the street than in a war.' He was very tender, very humble, but very distant too. I could feel it. And then he said he was cancelling the remaining days of his leave and returning to Delhi immediately. 'Give me time,' I wanted to say, 'just a day, half a day to think.' Aloud I said, 'Let us get married before you leave.' He smiled, a sad smile, one corner of his mouth lower than the other. 'I'll see you in the evening. My train is not till eleven.' And I knew he was going to leave no matter what anyone said. I loved him more at that moment than I ever had loved him or anyone else in the world. Oh Su . . ." she dropped on her knees and buried her head in the pillow. Suhas gently stroked her hair.

"He left at once, before I knew he was going, he was gone. And I followed him here. I reached before he did for I met him coming in from the rear gate. I came to tell him we would, should, will get married right away."

"Knowing he was going away no matter what anyone said," Mayura repeated with a faint jeer.

Devika did not hear her. She said, "And he said, No."

"Just as you wanted," Mayura said.

Devika turned. "What? I couldn't hear you."

Mayura shrugged.

There was a pause. Then Devika burst out, "Why didn't he agree? I begged him. I tried to seduce him, and still he said No. I threatened hysterically, but he was so gentle, so sad, so gentle with me. When I swore I'd join the Ramakrishna-Nivedita Mission, that's when he got angry. He pulled me and shook me and said, 'Don't you ever do that, don't you dare even to think of such a thing.' I was scared at his anger, and he saw I was scared, and he said softly, 'This body of yours must enjoy and be enjoyed. These marble thighs, these firm breasts cupped by passionate hands,' and I almost said, 'You undress me with your words, Vij,' but I am glad I didn't because he was talking about something else. He said, 'All human bodies are the same, male and female; they seek the same thing, fulfilment. Not just the writhing and surging, culminating in the release, mind you that is necessary, as necessary as pissing but as inconsequential. I mean the yearning, wanting, wondering, waiting for a more lasting fulfilment, a feeling of godlikeness. This is I, and I am God. A great yearning for becoming more than yourself. To see and feel the beauty inherent in the most basic actions we go through. One may rationalize about hormones and sperms and ova and mammals and urges, but the wonder remains, the wonder of being part of creation, part of another human being who makes one whole.'

"'Let us get married,' I said.

"'No,' he said, 'Not now. We must wait.'

"'Let us make that whole together,' I said.

"'In time, if god wills,' he said.

"'Don't leave me,' I pleaded.

"And he smiled more cheerfully and said, 'Sweetest love I do not go for weariness of thee, nor in hope the world can show a truer love for me. Our country needs me, Devika. The sooner I go the better.'"

Devika paused. She ended quietly, "So he left. And when war was declared, everyone was glad we had not got married, and now I am torn with guilt and remorse and longing."

"Pining for martyrdom is the pastime of the secure."

Devika looked at her uncomprehendingly. Suhas's eyes filled with tears, knowing that Mayura's words would slowly penetrate into her cousin's understanding, making her brood over them for days. She lashed out at Mayura, "And deserting one's husband is, no doubt, your idea of reaching martyrdom. What a great achievement for one who isn't woman enough to be a wife." Mayura dropped her gaze, and Suhas, knowing she had scored, could not resist a further jab. "Now you can watch your burgeoning belly and feel more martyred than ever."

Devika looked at her reproachfully. "Oh, Su, don't be so rude!" She moved toward Mayura, as though apologizing for her cousin. Her eyes, still luminescent with tears, lingered gently on Mayura, and Mayura, unable to bear that compassion hastened out of the room, her self-confidence and superior smile vapouring into the afternoon air.

Here to Stay

SO IT IS HERE to stay.

Mayura was still in bed though it was past eight. Sunshine poured into the room. Bright diagonal beams revealed white specks of lazily floating dust. The sight made her sick. Each speck looked like the head of a sperm swimming endlessly up her womb.

Twice in the early hours, her bladder had driven her to the toilet but it had hardly been worth the effort. The third visit had been at five o'clock, and then she had slept for two hours. For an hour now she had been awake in a dull stupor. Soon she was wide awake and acutely conscious of the itchy burning sensation. But she decided not to go. Once she left the room, her mother would surely race upstairs to find out about her condition, and no doubt promise all the goddesses in the universe a hundred-and-eight coconuts if her condition remained unchanged.

So it was here to stay.

It was lodging itself more securely every hour, a tiny tumour that could with a scrape of a scalpel be removed and thrown away. But every hour gave it more strength. Tentacles were being formed, a cord thrown out slowly but inexorably establishing its position while the rest of the body struggled to oust the alien. Nausea rose within her in a giant spurt from the very pit of her stomach as though with one mighty effort it was trying to throw out the monster. She held her breath and it stopped its climb. She swallowed the stale spit in her mouth. It added to the nausea; she felt filthy, with unwashed mouth and bursting bladder. She reached out for one of the tiny packets of scented supari she had secreted from the paan-daan the previous day. As she chewed the betelnuts, the stale smell in her mouth vanished. The strain on her bladder miraculously disappeared.

She stretched herself straight and yawned. She knew all this was not genuine, that one did not get nausea or overburdened bladder within the first month. This wasn't genuine, but . . .

But there was no avoiding the fact. It was here to stay. It was growing, unceasingly, relentlessly increasing in size like a decomposed body at the bottom of the river. Bigger and bigger, from embryo to fetus to child, a pink jelly squeezing itself into a different shape, throwing out arms and legs, clinging sucking feeding. And there was nothing she could do about it. Her blood was being diverted to feed an unwanted mass that could with a scrape of a scalpel be scooped out and thrown away. That was the most anguishing thought, the ease with which the cancer could be rid, the utter impossibility of doing so.

Begot in brutish passion, conceived in resentment, what future could he have? He would grow up knowing he was unwanted; if he was insensitive like his father it would not matter. But if he were sensitive, like Uncle Venkatesh?

Mayura realized that all of a sudden it had become he. He is my son, she thought. Then she said it aloud, "He is my son." An onrush of sadness engulfed her breast. This was not what she had hoped for him, not this at all. Undefined hopes and desires passed in and out of her mind. What had she wanted? what had she hoped for him? She could not answer, but it was not this, not this at all. Her firstborn, whom she had had since she was woman. Watched the virgin waste waiting to be blessed that it may bloom. Blessed with bridal flowers.

From resentment to pity to guilt. She had wronged him. And she would continue to wrong him. There was nothing she could do about it. She resented him now and she would regret his coming. He was begot in brutish passion.

But what does it matter, she burst out in self-defense. The whole process was purely biological. Love had nothing to do with it. An unwanted child was no worse off than a child of many prayers. If a sperm travelled long enough and was strong enough, a child was conceived. Nor had love anything to do with a child's future, for the future depended on himself and his genes. A child inherits as much whether begot in love or lust. Why then are Jaya's children so different? so obviously lacking in something? Environment. Jaya did not live in Madras but in the boondocks. But her own son would live here in the city. He'd be born in Hari Vilas and there-fore well endowed with environmental advantages. He was her son, and therefore well endowed in every way. He would have the surroundings and love and money that she had grown up with.

But she was not conceived in resentment.

Or was she? Who knows? She'll never know. Had she been conceived in love? Her father and her mother, so practical, so worldly wise, in what moment of workaday lovemaking was she begot? And for that matter, all those around her, in what moment of workaday lovemaking had they been conceived?

With cold deliberation, Mayura visualized her parents in bed; ferreting, seeking achievement and seeming success, her mother moaning in volup-tuous pleasure or, rather, pretending voluptuous pleasure. Aunt Chandra and Uncle Murti, plump, smug, bovine. Mukta and Uncle Krishnan, one sensuously seeking new stimuli, the other taciturn, his large frame heaving lazily, trying to get it over and done with. Uncle Venkatesh and Aunt Lakshmi, both gentle, love without passion as their daughter's was passion without love. All ludicrous old people in ludicrous animal postures, even Saveri and Sripati, over whose forms she lingered because they were perfect—Saveri, beautiful, gentle, refined, and Sripati, all that one could wish a man to be, a scholar and idealist. Perfect complements. The perfection or imperfection of the parents came through in the children, as had the intolerable crudeness of Jaya and her tobacco-chewing husband.

So it came to this, children did show the relationship between their parents. Her son then? What chance did he have? None at all? She had wronged him. She was guilty.

But who knew in what moment of workaday lovemaking she had been conceived, and all those around her animated in a moment of senseless skyward kicking of legs? Who could know what her father had felt for his wife that night almost twenty-three years ago? Those two years in London, what was he then? What unworded accusation, what silent guilt passed invisible yet palpable between those two men who were soon to be related? Who could know? Who could know what these men and women had been twenty years ago? for that matter who could know what she would be like twenty years from now? Embittered, like Jaya? regretting lost youth, like Aunt Kamakshi? masculine and slightly moustached, like Mother? No man grows to be like his mother. That's his misfortune. Every woman does, that's hers.

What had Raghu's mother been like? And his father? Those figures were not even shadows to him they had brought into the world. He had never referred to them; he didn't even possess a photograph of them; or if he did, it was nowhere in sight. How would such a son react to being a father? Mayura bit her lip. She knew exactly what his immediate reaction would be. He'd kiss her on the navel or worse, and then he'd rush off to the phone. Double quick work, what? Didn't I tell you I'd do it, fellows? Bull's eye second month. Would have made it first time around if that bed had come on time. The old one used to creak, jangles a sensitive chap like me, you know . . . come along fellows, let's celebrate!

Mayura pushed him away, preferring to listen to the bubbles in her abdomen.

And all the time it was growing, gnawing its niche in her womb, putting out a thousand tentacles to stealthily suck at her blood and grow like a balloon, a twist here, a stretch there, into a human body, complete with eyes, heart, brain, genitals. The wonder, the glory of it! A wondrous process was taking place within her. Her son, her flesh and blood transformed into a living breathing being, the glory, the wondrousness of it!

Orgasm over, Mayura turned limply sideward. Undefined hopes of years vapoured away, leaving her burning all over. Then her skin cooled slowly, like a Kashmir lake giving up its heat in winter. One point of itchy burning remained. Not this, not this at all.

The moment was gone. It had been an overpowering moment, but the wave had receded, throwing her on the pebbly sand, a mollusc on its back, vulnerably soft and helpless.

That is all it resolves to, Vij.

She lay still. The beam of sunlight had vanished from her room. She could hear the usual sounds of the morning—the maidservant drawing water from the well, breakfast things being cleared away, car engines being revved up, children shouting goodbye.

The sounds faded as she lay gazing into the glare of the mid-morning sun.

It must have seeped in gradually for she felt no change, no overwhelming revelation awakening her into despair, just a knowledge that was there as though it had always been there. It must have taken her over imperceptibly for she had felt no sudden illumination blinding her, just a brightening as though the morning glare had gone inward and laid open to view the end of the forked road.

The road forked here, but no matter which path she took, the way would be long, dreary, wearying. The fork would fork again, there would be fork after fork after fork, but no matter what fork she took, it would be the same. Child or no child, husband or no husband, the way would be long and dreary, with occasional lightning flashes that left her world a little darker for a little while.

Saveri

SAVERI MOMENTARILY HESITATED at the steps of her brother's house as the sound of voices raised in excitement warned her that one of the all-too-frequent bouts between Parvati and Mayura was in progress. There was something infinitely pathetic and at the same time incredibly admirable about the way Mayura was fighting her war, back to the wall, hemmed in by parents and relatives who parried and thrust at all times, irrelevantly breaking into peaceful conversations with drawn daggers. Mayura was giving way, Saveri could see that. During the first two weeks, Mayura had only rarely sallied forth from her formidable tower of silence, and always talked back in triumph after single encounters. But now, after her latest victory anointed in blood which, to Saveri, seemed brought about by will power, Mayura, instead of becoming more powerful had become more vulnerable. She was now fighting on their terms, on their home ground, with words. She would start an argument, inviting an attack; then suddenly she would retreat, with regal disdain true, but retreat nevertheless. Saveri wanted openly and unequivocally to support Mayura in her decision not to return. But her instinct of self-survival restrained her. Being trained to defer the whispers of instincts to the demands of reason, she knew the only way she could save herself was by not coming to Hari Vilas. But the children loved the hustle-bustle of Hari Vilas, and they had to have their weekend visits. Now, listening to the voices, she felt herself about to take up Mayura's defense, and knowing that, she wanted to flee for her own safety. She thought of going to her father's house but Vichu and Sita had already run to Mayura, who had come out of the house. Without any preliminaries Mayura burst out, "Saveri, do me a favour, please, please."

"Of course. Any time. Would you care to come to the beach? The children have been pestering me all week. How about you and Gita joining us?" Saveri spoke louder than usual in her haste to keep Mayura from making her request, whatever it was, because she sensed danger.

"Saveri, may I spend a couple of days with you? I need a change. I'll go mad listening to Amma. Everyone treats me as though I am a leper, and Amma never stops talking. Please let me come with you, please."

Say no, the warning bell screamed, say no. But her answer came, a reflex, "You are always welcome. You don't have to beg and plead. You've always been welcome."

"People change all too quickly."

"All that is mine is thine," Saveri added lightly, but her heart was heavy with fear. She wanted to run away, as though by running away she could have Mayura unsay her request. "I have to pick up a book," she lied. "Forgot it last time, I'll be back in a couple of minutes, and then we'll go to the beach."

She hastened to the solitude of her father's library. She went to the hallway dark with law journals bound in bleak brown, and she leaned against one of the ceiling-high teak shelves.

Why did Mayura have to invite herself, oh gods, why? She did not ask herself why she had agreed. There was nothing else she could have done. Proffering hospitality and help was a reflex, spontaneously, automatically extended. But why did Mayura have to invite herself? oh gods, what was she to do now?

Mayura's return had gashed open her own wound, and she bled each time she saw or thought of the girl. Don't go back to him if you've started like this, she wanted to cry out. Don't drift into a fate similar to mine. But Saveri restrained herself. A marriage was a holy sacrament, after all, though it had turned out so badly for herself. Perhaps Mayu's marriage could be saved. But Saveri had a nagging anxiety that her silence might wreck Mayura's life. If she told Mayura that compromises don't really work, that patching up led only to a blind end, that the sooner one cut off the rotting limb the better off one would be, then Mayura perhaps could do something worthwhile with her life instead of being helpless, dependent, lonely like herself.

She might be able to save Mayura. But what about herself? With hypocrisy and scheming and skimping, Saveri had built up the facade of a happy marriage for herself. Nobody knew, nobody even suspected, that anything was wrong, that Sripati had no intention of returning home, that their marriage had long been a threadbare rag. As the world saw it, Sripati like scores of young men had gone to America for a PhD and like them he would return to wife and homeland in due time. If she could scheme a visit to America for next year, however short, the succeeding few years would be taken care of as far as gossip was concerned. He'd comply, he himself did not care what people said, but he'd comply, she knew he would, if she planned it carefully. Nobody knew the truth, and nobody would know, unless she babbled it out. And Mayura's presence brought her to the brink of confession. Don't go back. Learn from me, she wanted to shout each time she heard them cajoling, threatening, exhorting Mayura to go back to her husband. In the loneliness of her home, she had gone through agonies of reassessment. Was the facade worth all this? Would it not be better to be open like Mayura about the failure? Was the facade worth this—the heartbreak of solitude and silence, the strain of sustained hypocrisy that was sapping her vitality, slowly eating into her nerves, gradually nibbling at her sanity. Hypocrisy—piling up typed letters purportedly from Sripati to the children who in turn wrote letters that were never posted; carefully building up a consistent picture of Sripati's work and movements to be mentioned as though in passing to the family members; buying toys from Spencer's so the children, and through them the others, would think he had sent them; this daily torture of fibbing and camouflaging, was it worthwhile? It was easy to be honest and forthright, but to continue this routine of deception taxed her beyond endurance. Oh gods, whereto was she bound, and wherefore?

But after the reassessment came a vehement affirmative—yes, it was worthwhile. The children were happy, secure in a world she had built for them. And she could live one day at a time, though planning for days and weeks at a time. Soon deception would become a habit, perhaps it might even become reflexive.

Saveri walked up and down the library, trying to compose herself. If Mayura were to stay for several days in her house, night and day—Mayura whom she had always loved more than the others because of the bond between the girl and Sripati—would her secret defended with hypocrisy and skimping and scheming through two years remain a secret?

Saveri stopped and picked out a volume at random and opened it. "When Arjuna, with razor-faced shaft, struck off Karna's head adorned with a face beautiful as the Moon, then O King, loud cries of Oh and Alas were heard of creatures in heaven, in the welkin, and on the Earth." In novels, when people open the Scripture at random, they come upon something very relevant and rewarding, she said aloud. Talking aloud was a habit she had developed of late. During the long afternoons, while Sita spoke to ants or flowers or her dolls, Saveri spoke to the child about her thoughts, and the di-monologue was comforting. Saveri realized that Sita was not there, and she felt embarrassed. She searched out Kalidasa's *Kumara Sambhavam* because she had read it recently and so could talk about it in case someone started discussing it when she returned it a few days later. Her mind had become accustomed to working out minute details to cope with exigencies, however remote and improbable.

"Enter it in the register," her father said as she was about to walk out. She was startled, not having noticed that he was in his reclining chair on the veranda. Ramakrishna Iyer, with characteristic orderliness, had a ledger where those who borrowed books were supposed to enter their names, the date, and title of the volumes. People seldom did, and whenever he discovered that a book had been moved, he collared the first person he met and declaimed on the necessity of discipline and order.

Saveri smiled at his voice and words. Dear disciplinarian father, with his authoritative and reassuring bark. She made the required entry in the blue-lined heavy ledger.

"On your way to somewhere?" he asked. Her smile vapoured at the loneliness in his voice. She grew painfully conscious of the desolate solitude in her own existence, which like his was surrounded by loving people who were kept at a distance by oneself, fate, what you will. She wanted to run up to him and kneeling by his side, push her head under the arm of his chair and into his lap as she had so often done in her childhood when she'd got the worst of a quarrel with Raja. Saveri stood still, with tears spurting up her lonely heart. Then she swallowed her tears. He was not lonely. There had been no loneliness in his voice. She was transferring her own loneliness to him. He was not lonely. He was never lonely. He had his books and his plans and his thoughts.

Saveri said, "Yes, we are on our way to the beach," and without daring to clear her choked throat she slowly walked away.

"I will carry it."

"No, I."

"I asked first."

"I took it first."

Vichu and Sita fought over Mayura's overnight bag as they walked toward the beach. Mayura mediated and worked out a compromise. Saveri followed, listening silently to the ceaseless chatter of her children that was interspersed with fragmentary sentences from Mayura. Once on the beach, Mayura challenged them to a race and the three sped away after leaving their sandals and bag in her charge. Mayura purposely trailed behind Sita, who was duly thrilled at getting second place.

While the three built a fortress and moat, Saveri sat apart and mused silently. Mayura was never very friendly with youngsters when adults were around, but she was a different person when alone with them. They were always excited when she looked after them in their parents' absence. Often they came to their mothers with some fantastic make-believe or fairy tale not found in any book, and the source could usually be traced to Mayura.

Saveri bemusedly watched Vichu's efforts to impress Mayura. That again was one of her uncanny charms; children, especially boys, were inclined to show off in her presence and wanted her attention and approval. Mayura was building a shoe next to the castle and telling them about the huge shoe in Kamala Nehru Park where the old woman of the nursery rhyme lived. Sita trilled out the lines proudly while Vichu looked apologetically at Mayura, ashamed of his sister's shrill singing. As though to make up for her loudness, he asked softly if there was a fountain at that park with coloured water. Proudly he added, "My daddy's park does."

Sita broke in even more boastfully, "Do you live in the sky? My daddy does."

"Skyscraper, stupid."

"And do you have an es es . . ."

"Eslator, like in Daddy's shop?"

"It is a . . ." Sita fumbled for words and failing, added, "My daddy has an eslator in his shop."

Vichu said, "Daddy's shop is called Marshall Field and there are ten thousand toy aeroplanes that really fly, and ten thousand toy cars that run on battery!"

"Like your train?"

"Daddy sent a toy train for my birthday. I'll show you when we get home."

Saveri sighed. Daddy, Daddy's shop, Daddy's fountain. Always it is Daddy. It has to be. She had never stopped to think why she had started and continued to build up this colossus. There was no reason, only some driving force that said it must be so. One must hero-worship one's father, nobody else. Yes, she had learnt that. But she had also learned that hero worship had no part at all in that tensile relationship between the woman in a woman and the man in her husband. It could spin a gossamer thread between the earth and the stars but could not connect the woman in a woman to a man. Which is why though the woman in her had long lost contact with the man who was her husband, she still hero-worshipped him as she had the first day she saw him.

Early in her first year of college, a girl friend had dragged her to hear an inter-college debate. The topic—compulsory military training for college students—was a stale one, and the room was stuffy with the odour of human beings. Saveri looked forward only to the end of a boring afternoon. That is probably why she was so impressed with Sripati who, when the moderator pressed the bell at the end of eight minutes allotted to each speaker, broke off midway a sentence and with a polite "Thank you" sat down. It was such a contrast to the others' desperate rush to finish their prepared orations even after the bell, that Saveri mentioned it with amused admiration to her friend, who immediately launched on a panegyric of Sripati, the best student of chemistry Presidency College could boast of in the last fifty years. Saveri said he looked very handsome, and her friend laughed so loudly that someone behind them shushed them.

Saveri scrutinised him more closely. He was tallish, thinnish, with sinewy arms and huge hands that seemed out of proportion with the rest of his body. He had a sallow face, thin lips, and an Adam's apple that bobbed spasmodically. He sat there, a head above the others, looking at some point above the audience, his intense eyes altogether too protuberant for his thin face. Yes, he was powerfully, magnetically handsome, he was like (Saveri mentally ran through the gamut of mythological figures) like Siva burning Kamadeva to cinders. No, not Siva for there was something hungry and demonic in his expression. Then of a sudden it came to her— he was like Jokanaan, yes Oscar Wilde's Jokanaan.

"And did he have a tuft too?"

"Yes, a tuft so long that he used it as a whip." Mayura was improvising a Tenali Rama tale and when Sita asked this question, they digressed to list the uses to which a long tuft could be put.

"To sweep the floor!"

"To use as a skipping rope!"

"To pull a cart!"

Alternately Vichu and Sita voiced their suggestions, which became more and more imaginative as they ran out of plausible ideas. Just then a tufted peanut vendor passed by and the children doubled over with laughter. "He looks like Vaithi Iyer," Vichu said. The vendor had little in common with Vaithi Iyer except for his thick tuft that was looped into a knot behind his head, but it was enough to give a new turn to their game; it was easier to concoct uses now that the hypothetical tuft had become invested with a familiar name and personality.

Vaithi Iyer was a friend, or rather a dependant, of the judge. He was in effect an odd-job man, but he was treated as a family friend. His achievements ranged from getting sugar and coffee seeds in the black market to being general supervisor at all family celebrations. Whenever there was talk of arranging a marriage, he became a self-appointed marriage broker. Vaithi Iyer scurried to and fro more often, bringing turmeric-edged horoscopes scrolled up in his waistband, giving long resumés of prospective grooms and their antecedents. Except for Saveri's, not one of the marriages at Hari Vilas till then had owed anything to his efforts, but whenever there was a marriage to be arranged, he gave himself a promotion, and invited himself more often to meals and tiffin through the simple strategy of staying on through lunch hours and tea time.

Saveri found his visits entertaining. He had amusing mannerisms that she liked to watch unseen by him. When he had something to say that he considered very important, he would walk to the veranda and spit out tobacco juice (much to Munisami's chagrin), shake loose his tuft knot and tie it up again. Then he would return to the room, stuffing a pinch of snuff into his nose, and start speaking in a confidential whisper with many gestures and pauses. Everything about him wreaked of his profession of professionlessness—his hush-hush voice, his alacrity at changing his tone and theme to please his listener, his unquenchable thirst for coffee, his undue deference offset by his occasional I-know-all-about-you look, the many turmeric-edged horoscopes wrapped untidily in a bundle, and a whole lot of addresses and family histories bundled in his head.

After one of his visits, Saveri entered her father's study. "Come, tell me all the news," she said in an intimately casual tone that few dared adopt with him, "how many Prince Charmings has Vaithi Iyer lined up for me?"

"Hardly one, it seems," her father replied, and ticked off names on the list he had made. "A zamindar from Tanjore district, age and antecedents are satisfactory, but I must check on his character . . ."

"Wonderful. Tell me more about him. Do you suspect he has a harem tucked away somewhere?"

"Don't be facetious, he has no job and I don't believe in . . ."

"The idle rich?" she completed for him.

"And here is the son of a man I knew once."

"That is disqualification enough," she laughed.

"This one is no good, a widower."

"Aren't you a stickler for experience?"

"And this Subrahmanian . . ."

"Oh no, never a list without a Subrahmanian. Is there a Venkataraman too?"

"Good brahmin names. You youngsters are enamoured of north-Indianish contractions. Look at this—Suresh! Terrible. As a matter of fact, there is a Venkataraman, a fine young engineer posted in Pilani."

"I'm sure he is myopic with all that desert sand in his eyes."

"That should be qualification enough," her father came back at her and laughed loudly, enormously pleased with his own joke. His laughter typhooned into a heavy rumble, endearing in its uninhibited boyish hilarity. Saveri marvelled at his charming naivete that made him enjoy absurdly simple witticisms. He laughed on, pointing to a framed reproduction from a painting from the Tate Gallery, that occupied an incongruous place between two stacks of old files. Saveri did not have to look at it to know what it was—a young woman in pink looking into a mirror, with the caption reading:

> If no one ever marries me!
> And I don't see why they should,
> As Dad says I am not pretty,
> And I am seldom very good.

They laughed together.

"Tell me about the others."

Her father read down the list: Gopinath, Ramesh, Sripati . . ."

"That is a pleasant name. Let us have the details, height, weight, size, shape . . ."

"Twenty-four, matriculated from Tiruchi, first-class first in Chemistry . . ."

"From Presidency?"

"I suppose so. Just says Madras."

"I wonder if it is the same . . ."

"Know him? Invited to Ceylon for a conference, gold medal for ranking first in the university . . ."

"The same! A brilliant brain," she gestured her admiration. Saveri had not heard him recently, but those first two years of her college education, she had gone to every debate since that first one. She vividly recalled his intense eyes, his large hands that could with a sweep crumple and throw away opponents' arguments, his wiry frame, his half-starved expression, and her own secret admiration, hoarded, nurtured and treasured as only first untold love can be. "A brilliant scholar," she repeated.

"I can believe it, his school and college careers seem replete with honours. But no, he is out. He is teaching in a hole of a private college. No money, no prospects."

"You can't look down on a man merely because he is poor."

"Poor? Who is talking of poverty, Savitri?" The judge always called her

Savitri, the name Maitreyi had chosen and that had got thrown out along the way. "I reject him because he is wasting his brilliant brain as you call it. What has he done since his MSc? Just been stagnant as a cesspool instead of taking up research and working his way to academic laurels."

"Just two years . . ."

"A young man who wastes the precious years of his youth is not likely to go far. More likely to waste his whole life in a bog of contentment. A private college no one has heard of. Pah."

"Maybe he needed the money. Maybe he has sisters and brothers to support."

"If so, I'd sympathize with him. More, I'd respect him. However," he shrugged off the topic, "here is a lawyer, fine family, been to England too, but I've never heard of him. Poor as a churchmouse, probably."

"See, you are obsessed with the idea of money." She was still thinking of Sripati, remembering again how she had held him as a star in her heart. Suddenly he was now magically transformed into an accessible, male human being.

Her father was saying, ". . . and if a man is not making money, he is incompetent, right?"

"No. In some professions, one never makes money. One studies and teaches, one works because one likes the work." Her father looked at her quizzically. "Like our Venkatesh," she added.

"That is different. He chose his life. But this lawyer, the only reason to be in Law is to win your cases. Okay, if he is idealistic, he can take pro bono cases, there are hundreds of poor clients who need help. Mind you, if you choose someone who is poor, I shall certainly welcome him. I flatter myself that I have influenced your taste. I trust your choice, Savitri, but when I am doing the choosing, I shall try to place you either in money or in prospective wealth. I have trained all of you to take hardships in your stride in case your future holds misfortune, but that is no reason deliberately to choose poverty or misfortune for one's children. Yes, I have always insisted on training all of you to weather rough patches. You wouldn't remember, but I made Venkatesh and Jagannathan walk to and from school, two miles each way, the Ford standing idle in the portico all day. The gossipmongers called me stingy, inconsiderate, silly, cruel. Did I care? I wanted self-discipline. But only blabber-mouthed pseudo-idealists court privation." He paused. "But later," he ran his left hand back of his head, a mannerism he had when tired, "perhaps I grew more selfish . . . I spent less time on the younger children's education . . . I don't know . . . anyway, the point has always been that each of you will have to adjust your life according to your material fortune, however meagre maybe your lot."

"Oh, Father, you have enough for all of us."

"I have money, Savitri, yes. But expect nothing from me once you are married, especially if your destiny takes you to a lower station. If I come in with my money then, it will be an intrusion on your private life, and to thrust my head between husband and wife is utterly revolting to me. A woman must make do with whatever her husband earns. It is the primary requisite of a self-respecting man's married life. And if she doesn't, it is entirely between them. Mind you, you will have money of your own, just as you have now. But not for everyday use."

Saveri did not understand or care at the time. She did not know what it was to be rich until she was married to a poor man. .

Sita's shrieks of pleasure brought her back. Starting from two feet apart, Vichu and Sita had dug a tunnel and were now shaking hands inside it. Now the shrieks became louder as Mayura's fingers met theirs from a side tunnel.

How and why Ramakrishna Iyer reversed his verdict on Sripati, Saveri never came to know. It merely happened that she, her father, or the other party rejected every alliance proposed in the next six months. When in March of the following year, her father asked her if he could invite Sripati on a formal visit, her heart leaped. She knew with superstitious faith that this was the beginning of a life to which all her days and nights had led her; she was as her namesake of old, wedded at first sight. In my heart I have wed him and a woman weds but once.

Her father mentioned that he was now in the faculty of the best engineering college in the city, that he came from a family that was not rich but his money was his own . . . Trivialities, she was marrying the man, not his family.

When Saveri went with her husband to his father's house in Tiruchi she realized how mistaken she was. One does, indeed, marry a family, joins it as inescapably as though one were wed to it. As soon as she stepped into the long narrow house in the agraharam, shut in from both sides by common walls between houses, so typical of the Brahmin quarter near the Rock temple, she knew how different her background was from his. For the first few hours, she felt a nostalgic surge of emotional attachment to her heritage, the pristine asceticism of her ancestors in the spotlessly clean house totally bare of westernised furniture except for the chairs on the front veranda, on which women never sat anyway. This was her ascetic heritage where there were no servants to demean themselves and their masters, where women were most scrupulous in their service, putting children and menfolk before themselves. But the glamour wore off all too soon; the facts remained. Musty wet clothes hung from wires strung across the dark rooms when there was a wealth of sunlight behind the house. The garbage vat in front of the house was full of plantain leaves from which the remains of meals were pecked and licked off by birds and cows and flies. The house jutted into the narrow street that was crowded all day with people. Worst of all were the neighbours. They came in groups of twos and threes to congratulate her mother-in-law on the high connection she had made. Ensconcing themselves on the mats spread for them, they partook sumptuously of the delicacies prepared for the marriage at Hari Vilas, and wondered aloud why the ghee used for the sweetmeats did not smell quite as pure as their village ghee. Critically examining Saveri's form and features, they passed a string of personal comments on "the judge's daughter." Next came a scrutiny of the dowry and jewellery. "The diamonds on the earrings are rather small, aren't they?" "Hollow bangles! Is the judge skimping on his last child?" "No silver water pot? Well what are wedding customs coming to?" "This nose stud is just ruby, not diamond . . . why, it isn't even ruby, just some cheap stone set in fake gold!" Saveri had bought that stud long ago for her part in a school drama, and she was surprised to see it there. Her nose had never been pierced, a detail that the neighbours very quickly noticed, with disapproval.

Their conduct seemed in shocking bad taste. Was it envy that incited them to these comments? Or just habit?

Nobody bothered that she was right there, in their presence. Nobody saw her as a person. She was the judge's daughter, to be stared at, held in awe by the youngsters, whispered about by teenagers, teased by sisters-in-law and their sisters-in-law. They assumed she was totally ignorant of household chores and teased her accordingly. "Let me sweep the floor. Poor rich girl, you wouldn't know which end of the broom to hold."

"Here is a mat. Poor rich girl, you'd be used only to silk mats, not plain floors."

At first, Saveri was deeply hurt but as days passed she knew that though the jibe was obvious, they meant well and held no grudge against her. She particularly recalled her mother-in-law's remark, "Our new daughter-in-law is very ignorant but very innocently so." Sripati's father worked in a government office in the accounts section. His was a low-paid job, but the women in the house had more saris and jewels than Saveri had ever owned until her marriage. She mentioned this as they were dressing for a shopping excursion. Sripati's younger sister laughed. She said, "People who go in cars can afford to wear rags. You have only to step out of a car and the shop manager comes running out with a red carpet. Not for us! Only if we wear gold-bordered saris and diamond earrings will any of the salesmen deign to attend on us." She said it matter-of-factly, without any bitterness. That was the way of the world, and one had to adapt oneself accordingly, she seemed to say. But Saveri was genuinely surprised and expressed her astonishment, which is when her mother-in-law said she was ignorant but innocently so.

She slowly became aware of the subtle stratifications in society which are borne and perpetuated by the victims themselves. She got brief glimpses of why those around her were the way they were, and because of the glimpses she could blend into the life of the family and the agraharam into which she had married. But not Sripati. He stood apart from them, a god immersed in contemplation, a giant intellect surrounded by petty-minded pigmies. In those early days, she wanted to withdraw herself from the family lest she become like them and thus unworthy of Sripati. He stood alone, in aloof silence, never participating in family hours which revolved around jokes and teasing at the expense of the newlyweds. He shut himself in a room or went out after lunch and returned only at dinner time. He was so irritable and introspective that Saveri was afraid of him. Even in the privacy of their room he did not emerge from his clamlike silence. She was married to the family but not yet to the man. One day, when he told her why, her love burst into brighter flame. "Yes, I have been out all day every day. I feel claustrophobic here, helplessly watching them making an exhibit of you. I thought I'd brought home a wife. Turns out I've brought home a judge's daughter, a judge's daughter," he muttered the phrase over and over again.

"Only a few days more, and we'll be on our own."

The few days passed by and the year, then a second year. But she remained a judge's daughter. And then it did not matter any more.

"Oh Amma, look!" Sita fell on her, laughing. They had covered her feet with sand and she had not felt it. It became a game for Sita to play and replay untiringly. Where are your feet? Has the crow carried them away? Ah, here they are! Heaping sand, questioning, wiggling the toes out of the sand with exclamations. They played at it for fifteen minutes, and then the children went off to pick shells.

"They are such darlings, Saveri, and so intelligent!"

"Oh, are they?" she said, noncommittally.

"Vichu knows so much about places and people, planes and ships and what have you. All learnt from his father's letters, I suppose."

"Yes, yes, he's quick to grasp and memorize."

"His dad must be writing long letters! If it is so full of lessons, I wonder how the little ones can take a letter. I mean, I never could read through *A Father's Letters to His Daughter*. I bet Indira Priyadarshini didn't either!"

"She would have if she worshipped Nehru as Vichu worships his father. Both look forward to his letters. They'd be broken-hearted if they didn't get a letter every Friday. I read it to them after dinner." The words slipped off the tongue easily, casually. So, she need not be afraid of Mayura after all.

Mayura said enviously, "Lucky you to have such bright children. Lucky children to have such a brainy father."

Saveri did not say anything. Mayura continued, slowly, "I envy you. I've always admired academics. And here I end up with someone who doesn't read, the only books in the house are National Geographics, doesn't know anything, no classics, no languages, no music . . ."

"It isn't what a man knows but what he is that's . . ."

"And a man is what he knows. It is the intellect that matters."

"A woman can't live with an abstraction."

"I can. That's what I've always wanted in a man. The only thing I've wanted in a man. If a man does not have brains I can't respect him and I can't love a man I can't respect."

"But . . ."

"And don't tell me I must. I can't. I can't."

"But intellect alone . . ."

"Is enough for me. If I had married a scientist, I'd gladly spend my life serving him, however eccentric, egocentric, crazy he might be. You are so lucky, Saveri. Sripati is such a scholar, he even looks like one, receding hair, long sallow face, so sloppy in his dress, so distinguished. And he'll come back with academic distinctions," she said dreamily, "and he'll have his colleagues and students coming home, a coterie of workers engrossed in research, discussing their theories, their experiments, it doesn't matter if you don't understand a word of what they say, it would be heaven to have them there, scientists and thinkers, and he at the centre . . ."

Wistfully Saveri said, "You almost make me believe it will happen."

"But of course it will. How can it not?"

"Oh," Saveri floundered, "there may not be a job for him here."

"No job? For a Chicago PhD? With universities and IITs sprouting up all over the country?"

Saveri continued to scoop up sand and run it through her fingers. Yes, there had been a super-brainy group discussing far into the night, but not anything academic. They were a close-knit group, all teaching in colleges, all young, all Brahmins, all bitter. Their discussions ranged from politics to education to their own lives but it always slid into the same theme— their future in Madras.

They grew more bitter once Narayanan, a physics lecturer, joined their group. Narayanan had just lost his job in a private college because the nephew of one of the trustees had just graduated, and the position was being reserved for him. Narayanan had only been a stop-gap appointment until the fellow got his Master's. Narayanan knew that now, but at the time had turned down a better-paying job in another town so he could live in the city and have access to the latest journals in the University Library. But all too soon he was disillusioned. Narayanan's refrain was, A Brahmin is always the last to be recruited, the first to be sacked. If there was no other person for the job or if he had far higher qualifications than the job needed, he might get hired, but take it from me, the moment they get one of their own, the Brahmin is thrown out on his ear. Only as an accounts clerk was his job safe because no one else could get mathematics into their clay-filled heads. The arguments ran the same route, varying in slight details but always on the same track.

"It cannot be," Saveri would burst out, "it can't be all that bad."

One or other would narrate yet another specific incident, complete with the names of the victim and oppressor. It was common knowledge that colleges had for years systematically been cutting down Brahmin recruitments in all departments, and that one couldn't even get admission into professional colleges any more, leave alone get to be a professor. And if they could not oust those who were already there, they insulted them at every turn; after all, wasn't Saveri's brother one of the unfortunate singled out for persecution?

Saveri had no answer for that. But she did not give up. "We ought not be bitter. We ought not encourage and foster feelings of animosity within us."

"Why not?" Narayanan would flare. "It is because of passive spinelessness that we have been driven from corner to corner."

"But we have not been. Only some of us, a small minority."

"A small minority! You want statistics, I've brought you numbers and charts, but you don't want to accept them." There would be more examples of discrimination.

"But there are Brahmins at the top level in every office."

"The more misfortune for us. Traitors, bootlicking Brahmins willing to do anything to keep their petty positions in the hierarchy."

"There are a few bad men, a few weak men everywhere, but the system is still fair."

"Oh, Saveri, you don't know anything about the world. You've lived a sheltered life in a family of decent people who marry other decent people and live happily ever after. You don't know life."

"I know this—we ought not be bitter."

"You are foolish or childish or both."

"Hatred, even of baseness / Distorts the features / Anger even at injustice / Makes the voice grow hoarse."

"Yes, anger distorts features, but we too like Brecht must go on prefer-ring to be ugly and hoarse to being passively servile."

Once Saveri broached the subject of going north for a job. There were more job prospects in the northern parts of the country, but all of them were so bound to the south, and to Madras, to be more specific.

Saveri remembered Narayanan's outburst: "You naïve innocent. There is no place for us anywhere. In the north we are Madrasis and therefore outcasts. In the south we are Brahmins and therefore pariahs. There is no place for us anywhere unless we are willing to bear injustice and perse-cution."

"No place anywhere in our own, our native land, our own our Mother India," Visvanathan sang to a popular tune, " here, jis desh mein Ganga behti hai."

Soon the group grew smaller. Gopalan was the first to leave, Columbia University, New York. Then Visvanathan, Iowa State University, Ames. Then Ramani, York University, Toronto. More joined the group. More left. Narayanan went to the Punjab, and a year later to UCLA, Los Angeles. Then Hariharan, St Catherine's, Oxford. Rangan, University of Texas, Dallas. Radhakrishnan, UMich, Ann Arbor. Krishnamurti, Michigan State, East Lansing. Then everyone in Physics left for UCLA, and Saveri could imagine them meeting every evening at Narayanan's, and arguing, discussing, trying to cook sambhar and aviyal. Sripati was almost the last of the group to leave. He left a month after Sita's second birthday. And six months after he left, Swaminathan came to bid good-bye, University of British Columbia, Vancouver. The most vociferous of the lot, he was still aggressively optimistic. We will return one day, he said, and build a centre of research that will produce Ramanujans and Ramans in every field.

"Scattered like desert sand," Saveri said. Mayura turned and asked, "What?"

Saveri sighed. "Time to go home." She rose and dragged away the unwilling children from the sound of the sea that lashed ceaselessly against the sand. Sita monopolized Mayura's hand and attention all the way home. Vichu gave Mayu the most beautiful shell he had picked, a broad, flat, translucent-white shell with a brilliant ocellus at one end streaking a riotous purple all the way to the edge.

Once home, Saveri hastily started preparing dinner. Mayura helped and the children spread their shells on the floor to sort out and clean.

"This house is such a lovely place," Mayura said, washing the potatoes at the sink. "Remember the hovel you first had?"

"Can I forget?"

"That really was sordid. I can even now hear Lakshmi Athai's sobs the first day we called on you. She didn't say a word in the taxi, and then the moment we entered the house she started weeping, buckets and buckets. Everyone did, one way or another. Father was so wretchedly miserable for days, and Raja was just about ready to strangle Sripati. Oh, that was a week of passions all right."

When they returned to Madras from Tiruchi, Sripati and Saveri set up house in Sripati's one-room flat in Triplicane. It was in an alley three blocks from Bell Road; a narrow opening in a continuous row of shops led straight up a flight of stairs which ended in a wall with a door on either side. The door to the right was theirs. They had a room and a kitchen to themselves. They shared a bathroom and a lavatory with the family next door. There was a tap in the courtyard below that was shared by those in the tailor's and grocer's shops and two other families. Actually, it was one of the better flats in the locality. Between the two flats on either side of the staircase there was a patch of terrace, and their flat had a window each on three sides, a luxury in the eyes of the neighbours. Sripati had poached upon a piece of the terrace and put up a room six feet by nine with a roof of corrugated iron sheets and walls of woven bamboo. The landlord started a wrangle which ended with the rent being raised.

There was little furniture and no room for any. Sripati was stubbornly puritanical and saw no need for any chairs. Very grudgingly he allowed her to bring a comfortable cane chair and a wall mirror and chest of drawers from Hari Vilas, where her room was half-stacked with her wedding gifts and dowry.

People from Hari Vilas visited them in small groups. They did not betray their dismay while with her. Back at Hari Vilas, they released their appalled reaction. Some cried, some were furious, some incredulous. They described the flat to Ramakrishna Iyer, who alone did not visit Saveri. He listened without emotion, and said, "She will get used to it." Once he broke up a group that was lamenting Saveri's plight and his heartlessness with a thunderous call to Jagannathan. When his son hastened to him, he said, "No one is to interfere in Savitri's life."

No one dared. For another thing, Saveri herself seemed totally unaware of the squalor of her surroundings. She was married to a man she adored, and now at last they were on their own.

Mayura was saying, "Strangely enough I couldn't understand what all the fuss was about. I admit I felt queasy walking through those streets, alongside that mosque and cemetery with its deathlike smell and dirty spitting people and all that. But, heck, you were so obviously glowing with happiness, I didn't see why everyone was so weepy. You were happy, weren't you?"

"Yes, very."

The first three months were heavenly. Then Sripati's elder sister came from Tiruchi and ended their honeymoon. The neighbours came to know that the quiet girl they had ignored was Justice Ramakrishna Iyer's daughter. Curious, helpful, inquisitive, they trickled in. News spread. She could not go anywhere without someone telling someone that she was a judge's daughter. And of course there was the further question, Why? The wealthy always married into wealth. Why this alliance? They searched for past gossip but found no story tagged to her college days. They concluded she had been born under a wretched star with Saturn predominating. A girl with a wretched horoscope should consider herself lucky to get such an upright, studious young man like our Sripati. One day, soon after his sister left, Saveri regretted aloud that his sister's visit had made her "the judge's daughter" all over again. Sripati smiled strangely. "You were lucky to have three months of freedom," he said.

He had enjoyed no such freedom. No matter whom he met, he was greeted with envious congratulation or some snide remark. "Our Sripati is a judge's son-in-law now."

"He won't look at the likes of us now on." "Hey, rich man's boy, how about giving us a ride in your car? Just ask the old man for one."

When college had reopened, so had the barrage of quips and sarcasms. They predicted he would soon move into the judge's house and live there in luxury as a kept son-in-law.

Saveri came to know all this in bits and pieces. She learnt to recognize Sripati's moods; gentle probing would bring out a particular jibe that had hurt him that particular day. Her heart went out to him and she felt as mortified as he.

"It is enough to emasculate any man," he shouted out one day. She did not tell him not to be so sensitive, not to brood over passing remarks. Those were months of ecstatic pain.

One day, ten months after her wedding, Saveri woke to the realization that her husband resented her. She did not know how long he had been thus. Now that her consciousness had been slapped awake, she noticed words and actions that she had not before. She saw the poisoned barbs he aimed at her, caught his piqued expressions, noticed how easily he took umbrage. In his love-making he was more aggressive, and when he let her go, it was with secret triumph. It will pass, she thought. She curtailed her visits to Hari Vilas, and when she did go she took the bus both ways, refusing her brother's car. She stopped bringing sweetmeats from Hari Vilas. She refrained from speaking about her visits. She even consciously restrained herself from referring to her childhood or her relatives.

She thought Sripati had got over his resentment. She thought they were going to be happy. And then he grew more vindictive. He shot his darts with studied vituperance. She fled to Hari Vilas for comfort. She went there almost every afternoon and though she did not complain, her unhappiness was evident to all there. On the rare visits that Sripati a accompanied her, he was formidably correct in his behaviour. The judge and he got along very well. Between the others and Sripati there was a veil which neither side wanted to lift. Only the judge could have counselled Sripati but he seemed to have no such inclination.

The more optimistic among them were sure that things would change once Saveri became pregnant. She did, in the second year. Ten weeks before the baby was due she went to Hari Vilas. Home, people, friendly chatter, comfort, attendants. And then the baby, beautiful, helpless, adorable. The change in Saveri took place then, suddenly as so many changes in her life. She thought back on the two-and-a-half years of unrewarding passiveness, of never-fulfilled hopes, of unreciprocated love. It made her more bitter and resentful than Sripati had ever been. And to her personal relationship she added the material discomforts she had borne in that wretched squalor. She thought back on it, appalled at how she could have lived there. Staying at Hari Vilas drove home the contrast that even frequent visits had not. She was born in aristocratic Mylapore, of rich parents, educated in the best school and college in the metropolis, surrounded by comfort and love, steeped in wealth. Why should she give up these luxuries, she who was born to and entitled to them? And her son was heir to the heritage of Hari Vilas. She would not rob him, she vowed, she would give her son everything she had enjoyed, and more, mother love that had been deprived her. Nothing but the best for the cherub at her breast.

She returned to her husband's house in the backstreets of Triplicane with resentment bottled up to the point of explosion, not only waiting but looking for a catalyst to make it boil over and explode. But fate had decreed differently. Sripati was delighted to have her home. He crooned endlessly over the cradle, suffused with pleasure and pride. She was still the judge's daughter, but the child was his son. One day he came to the kitchen and said, "We've got to move out of here. My son must have more room, he'll soon start crawling and this place is filthy."

"It has been good enough for us," she said sarcastically.

"But Savi, we are adults, we can bear hardships. But our son must have better things than we have had. Isn't that so, my son?"

Half afraid he would change his mind, she rushed off to her father next morning.

"Where would you want it?" her father asked.

"Not on a main road but close to the bus route to college and here," she answered promptly.

"And what would you be willing to pay?"

She hesitated. "Seventy-five? Eighty?"

Two days later her father gave her three addresses. One was a two-room flat in a block, one was the upper floor of a house, one was a small but independent house. All three were luxurious compared to her flat, all were just off the main road, all were occupied by families who had no intention of moving out. Saveri came and told her father as much.

"They are available," he said, "have your choice. I'd choose the independent house, if I were you."

"For eighty rupees? Just eighty rupees?"

"It is a rather small one, isn't it?"

"Small? It is a palace. Has a good-sized living room and three other rooms besides a large kitchen, bath and all that."

"Oh, I forgot to tell you. The landlord wants to keep one of the rooms. He's a decent fellow and all he wants is a decent tenant who'll quit without giving any trouble whenever he wants to move in."

"But the man you sent with me said the people living there now were the owners!"

Her father's eyes smiled shamefacedly.

Saveri looked keenly at him. "What is the story for the other two?"

"Same, with a few variations."

She smiled and then sighed. "He'll see through it."

Sripati did not. He came to see the judge. "It is a fine house," he said dubiously, "I can't believe it is renting for eighty rupees."

Ramakrishna Iyer went through the same story about the room to be retained by the landlord and about quitting without giving trouble, which as Sripati should know is a landlord's greatest nightmare with all the new regulations about tenants' rights. It was just luck, he said, that Vaithi Iyer had come to know about the house, a very capable man, Vaithi Iyer . . .

He continued, "I suggest that you change and add a few things before you move in, like an electric pump for the well and maybe a sink in the kitchen."

"When I have the money, I certainly will," Sripati replied politely, but Saveri felt him bristling.

The judge said, "Oh, I don't mean you should pay for it yourself. No sane tenant should. Comfort is a prerequisite for a happy life, and one should always try to get the most out of an honest deal. The owner is quite a rich fellow and I think he could be persuaded to invest in improvements, what? After all he hopes to live there after his retirement. He's up in the north somewhere. My man knows the details."

That was how Saveri had got this lovely little house. The corner room that was locked up, and opened once or twice a year by a man from the landlord up north was, she suspected, furnished with junk bought by Vaithi Iyer with her father's money from some second-hand shop. In those months of recovered harmony she often almost blurted out the truth about the landlord up north but fortunately had not. And then came a time when nothing mattered any more.

Saveri woke to the smell of potatoes getting burnt. She had been cooking almost unawares and dinner was ready. The children ate without fussing because the deal was that they could play at trains only if they ate well and quickly.

Saveri poured milk into two glasses and mixed sugar in each. She took the glasses, and closing the kitchen for the night went to the bedroom. Vichu was assembling the rails for his train. Sita sat next to him on the floor, her button mouth alternating between a pout and a plea. "Let me do something," she implored. Vichu shook his head, allowing her only to hold the carriages. He had his father's straight mouth, which, as he bent over his rails in concentration, had the same streak of cruelty that Saveri had recalled time and again these last few hours.

"Please."

"No, you don't know anything about tracks and engines. Girls never do. Go play with your dolls."

He placed the engine on the track and switched on the battery circuit. Sit a held her breath in excitement. Along the oval track rolled the engine, sleek shining black. Mayura clucked her admiration, and Vichu was immensely gratified by her interest. He stepped up his showmanship, trailing an extra carriage behind the engine, building bridges of books and tunnels with newspaper. Mayura was relaxed, happy, almost gentle because she was laughing then. When she laughed, her whole face sparkled, like Ramakrishna Iyer's when he smiled. It was a long time since Saveri had seen this expression on the younger woman's face. She was glad for Mayu, still fearful for herself. Mayu's presence had broken her frail thermometer of bitter memories and the mercury scurried across time in shimmering pain.

Saveri went to the bathroom to have a wash. There had been no time earlier for anything but rinsing of hands because Vichu, like his father, ate well only if he got his meals within half an hour of returning from anywhere. How many days during that first year Sripati had refused dinner because it was not ready on his return from his evening visits with friends. Her arms were still sticky with the salt beach air. She decided to have a shower. The water was warm and the spray pricked her clean of salt and dust. A man who has not indulged in the pleasure of a shower before going to bed has missed out a chunk of life, her father had told Sripati at a time when he was less prone to bristling up. A new shower had been installed before they moved into the house, and Sripati often referred to the pleasure of a shower, especially when there were two to enjoy it. Each individual prick roused a nerve centre and set it pulsing sensuously. She could feel the long fingers of his large hand running down her spine awakening to life a thousand nerve ends that danced in insatiable pleasure. As she wiped herself dry, she looked at the long mirror on the back of the door. Her face and arms were darker than the even brown of her body. Strands of hair broke loose from her knot and fell down her back in black waves. As she twisted her hair back into a coil, she noticed a small patch of soap lather on the dark fuzz of her underarm. She wet the edge of the towel at the tap and wiped it off. Her feet got wet when she opened the tap and so she wiped them dry again. She went nearer the mirror and scrutinized herself. Her unhappiness had not touched her body. Her full breasts were firm and virgin-looking except for the thickened nipples. She had chiselled hips and a flat abdomen. Only the inner edges of her thighs had a pad of superfluous fat. It did not matter. Nothing mattered any more. Saveri wore a loose blouse for the night, and a soft cotton sari so old the print on it had faded. Comb in hand she went back to the bedroom. The children were still playing. Mayu was sitting on a bed that had been made for her along-side the other beds. She had an old issue of *The Illustrated Weekly* in her hand. When Saveri entered, she turned a few pages and held up the "News in Pictures" page. "This fellow reminds me of Swaminathan," she said, "do you remember him?"

"What a coincidence! I was thinking about him on the beach today."

"You've been thinking so much this evening I guessed everyone you've ever known must have passed through your mind, and not very pleas-antly either."

So her face gave away her thoughts! She had to be careful.

Mayu continued, "I remember him so well. A short dark man with a perennial torrent of words. Talking of building a new society, a Platonic republic of brahmins. You know what? I was in love with him. At that time I was in love with everyone in that group by turn."

"Hm."

"Starting of course with Sripati who was my first and longest crush. I fell for him in your marriage pandal. Of course at the time I was in love with you already. You were my first star of the evening. I guess I outgrew that crush but my crush on Sripati went on." Mayura spoke slowly, relishing each memory before releasing it. "And then this group. The most wonderful two months in all my teens. Vichu was a baby then and you had just had a miscarriage. I came to help you through the first week and I stayed on and on for weeks and cried buckets in secret when Appa took me away back home. It was the most wonderful time of my life. They would come here almost everyday and talk and talk. And you were a pale goddess moving amongst men," Mayu laughed, "replenishing their coffee and groundnuts. It was such fun, the groundnuts were so delicious, soft and fresh boiled in salt-water within the shells. And they would throw the empty shells at each other. Narayan chewed even the shells, he liked the salt softness of the insides of the shells . . . and their jokes were so witty and sometimes so silly, remember the silliest Baldev Singh jokes, like the one where he was told no one was talking to him because of the stink of his socks, and being surprised when people kept away even after he changed his socks and put the old ones in his pocket . . . so ridiculously silly but how we laughed! And you laughed so much you choked and had to be smacked on the back to get the coffee out of your windpipe," Mayura laughed at the memory.

Saveri stopped combing her hair. Mayura was recalling those very evenings she had relived that evening. But so differently! In a low slow anguished whisper she turned to Mayura. "I was thinking of just those days on the beach. But not the laughter, only the frustration, the rebelliousness, the brimming bitterness . . ." She stretched her hand involuntarily. "Have I been doing that all along? Recalling only the resentment and not the laughter? Hoarding bitterness instead of distilling out the happiest moments to treasure and re-live?"

Mayura kneeled forward to clasp the extended hand. "Oh, Saveri, he's been away so long you've given way to depression," she said tenderly.

Saveri felt a flood of need rising within her, the need to talk, to touch, to share. The need to hope. But no, she would not go through all that again, days of lonely hope, nights of prayer and expectation. No, she had suffered too much to build that façade to now raze it in favour of yet another trip to the foot of the rainbow; she had borne too much alone to find any comfort in sharing. And yet, to hope again! Her temples throbbed with anticipation, to hope and dream and desire!

Saveri sharply withdrew her hand and turned away. No, she should not indulge in that delusion, infinitely pleasurable though it was. There was no basis for hope, not the remotest. Not a single letter had mentioned anything even remotely personal, not a phrase or word with overtones of love. He sent a money order once every few months, with short non-committal letters, a line about his work, sometimes mentioning a conference or seminar he had attended, a paragraph about the weather. She both resented and welcomed the money orders. It meant he still cared, or maybe that he just hated her and felt he had to throw money at her as a debt he had to repay. She put his money in a separate bank account, and spent the money that her father deposited into her account every month. He had started it the month after Sripati left for the United States, and had simply mentioned that a similar amount would be deposited into the joint account they had started when she was in college. They had never talked about it again.

During the second year she had posted several of Vichu's letters to Sripati, with her own voice between the lines. Vichu's letters were briefly acknowledged, her voice ignored. On Vichu's sixth birthday she bought an American toy from the smugglers' stalls along harbour street. It ran on battery and had a red blinking light when in motion. The next morning, Vichu gave her a letter that he had written entirely on his own, about how he loved the toy his father had sent; on reading it, she was moved into a new spate of hope, and she posted it. His reply came very promptly. "If you want to bring up your children on illusions, that is your business. Both, the illusions and the children, are yours, and since you have the money to pamper yourself, why not?"

Saveri steeled herself into consciousness. Carefully controlling her voice, she said, "It's been a long day. I am so tired I could just lie down . . ."

"... like a tired child and weep away this life of care which I have borne and yet must bear," Mayura added softly.

To dream, to desire, to hope! Saveri took a deep breath. As lightly as she could, she said, "It is time to put to bed the little bundles of care that I have borne. Come Situ, time for bed Vichu."

It took another ten minutes to persuade them to leave the train. Vichu drank his milk, changed into his nightclothes, washed his mouth, went to the toilet and bounced into bed.

"Thank you for the shell, Vichu, it is the most beautiful shell I have ever seen," Mayura said. He smiled proudly. Sita sat on, entranced by the black engine trailing red and blue carriages on the oval tracks. Saveri sat next to her, milk tumbler in hand.

That letter too is a part, only a small part of memory, one side of her intoned, only a small ugly part. Not small, the other side cried out, it fills everything, there hasn't been anything else, nothing, nothing at all.

"Come Situ, good girl, let's see if you can drink this by the time I count to ten. One," Saveri paused a few moments, "two ..."

Lying on her bed, Mayura was thinking, "Have I been doing that all along? Noticing, remembering, hoarding only my own bitterness, not his laughter? Raghu had a madcap charm that could be captivating. He made up nonsensical little jingles extempore, vulgar but spontaneous and light. One evening she was dressing for a party. She was at the mirror in her petticoat, making her coiffure before wearing her sari. He was sitting on the bed, putting on his shoes. He leaned forward and pulled the string of her petticoat, which fell to the ground. She let go of her hair and stooped to retrieve her fallen garment. He patted her behind and blew it a kiss. "In all this world so fair I've had the best of luck, Of all the world's fair dears Mine has the best ..." He stopped. "Give me a word that rhymes with luck, other than you know what."

She told him a Baldev Singh joke—how he complimented Lady Mountbatten on her duck pond using the Hindi word because he didn't know the English word for ducks.

Raghu slapped his thighs and roared. "Oh that's a good one, Madam your badaks are lovely, I must tell it to the boys. By the way, I thought the word for duck was hans."

"Hans is for swan," she said, "you should know better, you are the Bombaywala."

"My little ugly duckling, once she puts on her bras, is the dearest daintiest hansling that there ever was."

Raghu was vulgar, ill-bred, boorish, but he had an inexhaustible capacity for laughter. Mayura grudgingly granted that. It is not enough, she told herself, it does not wipe away his lusts.

Sita held out her empty tumbler triumphantly. Her mother took down her nightdress from the rack.

"We have to change my Dolly first." She took out her favourite doll from the doll crib in the corner. It was a big one. Of pink celluloid, it had soft brown hair, and blue eyes that closed when it was laid down. Sita stripped her of her blue nylon dress of frills and lace. She slipped on a pink muslin nightgown. As her mother unbuttoned her dress, she patted the doll's cheek.

"Ma, isn't she the most darling dolly you have seen?"

"Yes, lift your arm."

"I like her best of all. I love her more than all the others. Lila has a red dress for her doll, ma, will you make me one for mine?"

"Sure, dear, lift your other arm now."

"When she grows a little older, we'll celebrate her wedding."

"Yes."

"We'll marry her to Lila's soldier doll. Ma, have you seen her new soldier?"

"No, I'll ask her to show him to me tomorrow. Don't shake so much."

"He is brown, and he has black eyes and white dress and a white cap and a blue tie."

"He is a sailor then."

"What is a sailor?"

"One who goes in ships."

"Daddy went in an aeroplane."

Saveri led the child to her bed. "Now close your eyes."

"Ma, are you really going to buy Vichu a bike?"

"Yes."

"When?"

"For his birthday. That's months away. Now close your eyes."

"Ma, can I go on the bike?"

"We'll see. You have to grow up a little more. Keep your eyes closed."

"Can my dolly go on the bike?"

"Yes, we'll see."

Sita suddenly jumped out of bed and went to the doll crib. "I'll take you all on the bike, but only if you are good." She patted each of her dolls, calling them by name, and put them to bed.

Soon after Sita's first birthday, Saveri bought her a big cloth doll.

"Oh, I knew it would start one of these days. Dolls, Pah, dolls. I don't want my daughter playing all the time with dolls. My stomach turns when I see eight- and ten-year-olds still doll-crazy."

Saveri watched Sita as she came back with her Dolly, and lay down. "Situ, have you soosooed?" The child pretended to sleep, closing her eyes so hard they puckered. Saveri gently pulled her out of bed. "Go, little princess, it will take just a minute. That's my darling."

Sita went to the bathroom, doll in hand. Then she ran back. Saveri, stooping to disassemble the train, heard the doll fall and looked up. Sita accidentally stepped on it.

For a moment, there was absolute silence. Then the child started crying loudly. She looked at the doll, she took off its dress, looked again and cried, tears streaming down her cheeks. The doll was cracked from neck to waist. She looked at her mother and cried.

Saveri sat on the floor and drew the child to her lap. The cries quietened down after a long time. Little sobs vibrated the child's body against her mother's breast.

"Why did I have to break it, Ma?" she said between sobs. "Why did I have to break the most beautiful doll in the whole world myself?"

"Sshh. I will fix it tomorrow. No one will know it ever broke."

"Why did I have to break it, Ma? My own doll, the most lovely dollie in the whole world. Mine."

"My darling, everyone breaks the most beautiful things, step by step, friendships," Saveri sighed, "and marriage sometimes. And it is always ourselves."

Mayura, staring at the ceiling, felt the remark was for her. But she did not flare up. She moved her hand from under her head to her side. Her bed creaked. Her thoughts shot off to the bed in Bombay. One afternoon, about two weeks after their arrival in Bombay, three men brought in and assembled a breathtakingly huge bed, a four-poster of the old zamana complete with carved legs and mirrored headboard. Then came a Dunlopillo mattress and quilted satin pillows. Mayura stood staring at it long after the men left.

"It is so monstrously big," she exclaimed as soon as Raghu came home from work. "The bed! Has it been assembled already?" He rushed off to the bedroom and bounced on it with boyish delight.

"Come on, darling, what do you think it is for?" His suddenness swept her off her feet.

"Wasn't it wonderful, my chickety chick." She was reluctant to admit it was.

"So colossally huge," she said lying back.

"It should be. After all it is the most important thing in life right now, isn't it?"

"I'd be ashamed to be seen . . ."

"Nobody except me is going to see you on it, or so I hope," he laughed. "Luxury what? Not for us those thin mattresses on narrow wooden cots. I am an artist, sensitive, my body open and alive to pleasures," he chuckled, "of the bed, my present field of specialization, and I make no bones about it."

Spontaneity, another of Raghu's charms. She smiled now thinking about it. But the smile drained away as she remembered the sequel. "I must tell the boys. They've been asking about it." He rushed off to the phone. "A beauty . . . come down and have a look at it, just billows all across the room, a foam of luxury . . . of course I've tried it, what else do you think I've been doing for the last hour, it has been tested and proven the world's best bed . . . yeah thanks, promptness is my second name . . ."

She had recalled this part with anguished shame ever since, and had never admitted the pleasure that had preceded it. To distill out the happiest moments, the laughter, not the resentment. Mayura tossed about. She had to think, she had to be alone to sort out and see what really happened and what really mattered.

Saveri had carried Sita who was sobbing in her sleep and gently placed her on her own side of the bed that she shared with her daughter. The child reached out to her convulsively and the mother bent down. "Ma, where is she?" Saveri handed her the broken doll. The child held the doll in the crook of her arm and curled herself, still sobbing. Saveri lay down beside her and encircled both child and doll with her arm.

Mayura turned on her side and watched the figures next to her. She looked at Saveri's back and the childhand on her cheek. She was moved into the orbit and rhythm of the child's sobs and the mother's gentle rocking. Her firstborn should be a daughter, she mused, because he loved girls. Girls were charming because they cried, he said, it was such a pleasure coaxing them back into laughter. Sadist, she had thought then. She had not once cried in his presence, too proud too hurt to give way to tears. But tears did not mean triumph or defeat as she had supposed. It meant this, this rhythm of closeness. Her breast throbbed with vicarious ecstasy. Raghu was at heart a romantic but he exaggerated his emotions so much that they became caricatures. But deep down he was a romantic who waxed lyrical over the image of a nightingale pressing its throat against a thorn to sing. One Sunday morning three of his friends had dropped in uninvited and as always were invited by Raghu to stay on for the next meal. At lunch, one of them suggested they go to a matinee. They perused the newspaper columns for the films playing in the city.

"How about *Sangam*?"

"No way, seen it twice already."

"*Mughal-e-Azam*? I was abroad when it was first released and believe it or not, I haven't seen it yet."

"You didn't miss much. Since any film we choose is going to be a repeat for someone or other, how about seeing a real classic, *Tansen*?"

"Hey, Raghu, I knew you were older than me but didn't know you were that antediluvian!"

Raghu started defending his choice, interspersing his narration with songs from the film. ". . . And then Emperor Akbar exiles Tansen's beloved from his court so that from his heartbreak and loneliness, Tansen would pour forth such exquisite sadness as would delight his royal listener into

melancholy. And of course that is what happens. He sings terrific lyrics
. . . and then there is the scene where the princess is dying and cannot be
saved unless the lamp she believes to be her life symbol gets lighted on its
own. And Tansen sings 'Diya Jalao'and the princess is saved." He sang a
few lines of the song. "And then our hero wanders through the kingdom,
consumed by the fire he had generated within him to light the lamp in
that superhuman effort. I was ready to sob my heart out the first time I
saw it."

They went to *Tansen*. As Tansen lay dying of the fire within him that
could not be quenched except by rain that has been called down by the
power of music, his beloved found him and started singing "Barasare" and
clouds slowly floated into the blue sky. At this point, Raghu's clasp on her
hand tightened in remembered pleasure. Mayura very deliberately said,
"Look at the pimples showing on her face! Our make-up artists have come
a long way since then." Raghu's fingers released hers.

Mayura pressed her forehead against the pillow. I am sorry, Raghu, I am
sorry. She opened her eyes. Saveri and Sita were asleep. The light was still
on. Mayura stared at the the curve of Saveri's hip, that appeared larger
than it was because she was lying on her side. Mayura substituted Sripati's
hand for Sita's and eyed them.

How could she have worked herself into any feeling of love or apology
over Raghu? She hated herself.

A few minutes later, Saveri rose, and kneeling on the bed, lifted the child
to the other side of the bed. Then she pushed the train track under the
bed, switched off the light and lay down.

Mayura turned on her back and said, "Everyone was desperately hoping
I'd be pregnant."

"Hm."

"They were so disappointed when it turned out otherwise they've been
rather bitchy ever since."

"Hm."

"I don't blame them. I was more bitchy then than they are now."

"So I gathered."

"I didn't want a child."

"I am glad for you that it turned out as it did."

"Nobody else is glad, I assure you."

"They had their reasons, or hopes I should say."

"Didn't they though! Everyone was so sure I'd go back if a child was on its way."

"Most of us do expect a child to work miracles."

"I wouldn't have let that change matters."

"I am glad for you that you aren't expecting. You are at more liberty this way to make your decision."

"I've already made it, thanks." The chilly words got out despite herself. She felt suddenly bitter. "He would have been happy, no, not happy but boastful in his perverted way. One more proof of his prowess, a corollary to all his jactitations, to be instantly broadcast to all his friends."

Bitterness evoked greater bitterness. "Better that than total disregard, as was my fate."

Mayura asked unbelievingly, "You mean Sripati didn't want a child?"

"He didn't care either way. If I were superstitious, why, poor Vichu would have withered within me that very evening . . . we were in Triplicane at the time."

She paused in a vain effort to control herself. Then the story came out in slow low flashbacks.

I run up the first flight of stairs, two steps at a time. I halt on the landing. I look at the locked door and smile. My eyes linger on the vanishing black ink that spells his name. Home. I open the door. I take off my slippers and place my handbag on the windowsill. I go to the bathroom and wash my hands, feet and face. Some day I will have a wash basin so I can have a wash without splashing water on my sari border. How the spiders do work. I must clean up. The flat must be spotless and perfect today. I sweep the floor of the front room. Next the kitchen. The broom is so used up it is short and thin, I have to bend way down to sweep the floor. But it is done soon. I put the sugar tin back in its place. I arrange the four sparkling bell-metal tumblers in a row. I smile. I see a little tumbler at the end of the row. It will be of silver.

I go out to the terrace. I have to go to the terrace to enter our bedroom, a bamboo-walled room built on floor space encroached from the terrace. This room is so small if you enter the room at night, you step on the bed.

Now the mattresses are rolled and pushed to a corner. I decide to change the pillow covers. I pull them out, and taking his I bury my face in the smell of Vaseline hair tonic. Don't be silly, there's work to be done. I reroll the mattresses and take the covers with me.

I have to bring water from the ground floor if I wish to mop the floor. I do want to and so I go down and carry up two buckets of water. I like mopping the floor. The red polished surface shines like glass and I wash my hands happily. As I stand for a minute admiring my own work, the sparrows twitter. Oh my god, birds! Why don't they go to trees, but then where are the trees in this built-up neighbourhood? I look up. There hadn't been much straw and strings today. Does that mean they have finished building their nest? How many times I have driven them off so they wouldn't start their nest here. I gave up several days ago. And now their nest was ready. I hope there aren't any . . . yet . . . two sparrows fly in.

I look around. If I could have some heavy curtains the room wouldn't get so hot. But he does not like curtains or furniture. Totally uncalled for luxuries, he says, that we can't afford right now. I agree. We are still young, I am in no hurry. After all Father didn't get rich overnight either. And just because I was born into wealth is no reason I should expect to continue in that style. There's truth in what Sri says though he is too bitter about it. Poor Sri, he'll be back in half an hour and tiffin is not yet ready.

I hurry. I cut the onions, slice the potatoes. I mix the gram flour with water and salt. I light the Primus. I place the skillet and pour oil. In my haste, I overbrown the first lot of bajjis and the smell of oil fills the flat. I lower the flame and fry the rest. Everything is ready. And not a minute too soon either.

He comes in. "What news at the college today?" I ask him.

"Why do you ask every day? Nothing happened. What can happen? I'll tell you myself if anything of interest ever happens."

"Just a casual question, a habit."

"Fine, my shouting too is just a habit. Ha ha." He laughs mockingly. I retreat. I place the plate of bajjis and chutney on the table.

"I told you to take away this nest. Look what they've done to my new pair of trousers. A judge's daughter may have a hundred saris but a lecturer can afford only two pairs of trousers . . ."

"I'll wipe it off with a wet cloth. It won't show at all. Won't take a minute. Have your tiffin. I'll get you your coffee." But even as I say it I know I should attend to the trousers first and so I take a hand towel and wipe the white speck off his brown pair that is on the hanger and dust the chalk off his grey pair that he has just pulled off in favour of a veshti. I go back to the kitchen, talking over my shoulder. "There wasn't much rubbish on the floor today. I think they've finished their nest. Strange creatures, why do they live in the city instead of out there. They won't have housing shortage there, and why do they persist in trying to build on a precarious corner of the wall? How can a nest rest securely on that right angle with just an inch and a half of wireboard as base? I do hope the whole thing doesn't fall off."

I take the coffee and come back to the room, looking at myself as I pass the wall mirror. The heat was already making my face a grease pan. And why was he so out of mood today of all days?

"Sparrows, nests, sobstuff. You women! Weep your head off now. There, there."

I place the tumbler of coffee on the table. I wince as a small feather strikes my cheek and flies out as though to rejoin the nest that is now on the terrace. I look out. Another lonely feather is floating away.

"It was a very sweet nest," I say tonelessly, "they've been working at it for two weeks now. God knows from where they get the energy to fly in and out all day, bringing a piece of string, a straw each time. God knows how they get the small soft feathers that line the inside of their seemingly crude nest. Such long and careful preparation. Unfatherly father, to destroy that hard-built nest when you do not have the patience to drive a hook for a hammock or the money to buy a cradle for your coming child."

"Is that so?" he says, "oh well, it had to happen some time I suppose."

Saveri stopped. Bitterness slowly oozed from the lulling monotone of her voice and the air was mucky in the ensuing silence.

Maurya stretched her hand and sought the other's. She did not find it. Passionately she burst out, "It was only one day, one unfortunate day, only one unfortunate hour of the thousands you have spent together. There were other hours, happy heavenly moments, there were, there were, Saveri." Mayura was calling for reassurance, desperately wanting to be told there had been and there would be happier hours in Saveri's life and her own.

Her anguish came through to Saveri who now laid her own hand on hers. Mayura gratefully drew that token of reassurance across her lips and cheek. "There were and will be," she whispered. Saveri trembled at the touch. To touch, to hope, to desire. She returned the pressure and repeated, "There were and will be."

Saveri bit her lips. She had said too much. Just as she had feared. She must not speak. Never let down her guard, never. The silence was broken. Mayura was quietly sobbing. Saveri sighed, and then sighed again. She who had been so desperate to be held and comforted was now called upon to comfort and hold. She pulled the edge of her sari from under her sleeping child who had rolled close to her, and slid on to the other bed, cradling Mayura's head against herself. There were and will be, she said soothingly. There were and will be.

Chandramati

18 IX. An audible sigh of relief ripples through Hari Vilas. No more is the air brittle as spun-sugar threads. People are extricating themselves from the strangulating love-hate filaments that she throws wherever she goes. Overnight, people have become as of old.

Should one draw the obvious inference that all will reconcile themselves to her desertion of her husband if she would but take herself out of their sight? It is too early to draw any conclusion.

⌒

Relief was tinged with resentment. Mayura had reopened old wounds; not only that, had made each articulate out loud memories never expressed till then, memories best forgotten. The words had come uncontrolled, uncontrollable, because something within them was driving the memories upward and outward, as though this would somehow make things easier for the young woman. And because memories had been dredged up and outward into words, there was a deep resentment made more bitter by the young woman's hauteur.

But after resentment came reassessment. Now that her sympathy-repelling personality was withdrawn, people remembered another Mayura.

A rosy baby, dimpled cheeks and dimpled bottom, never crying except when hungry. Kamakshi sighed with reminiscent pleasure, sweet Cuticura-powder smell of baby bottom and fresh diapers brought in from the sun.

Chandra thought of the many evenings Mayura had babysat the children in those early years, when Murti would drag her off to the Club. "Don't worry, Chandra Athai, go enjoy. They'll be asleep most of the time, and you know I love reading." Mayura was an avid reader in her teens, always reading voraciously, often quite indiscriminately, devouring comic strips and Sexton Blakes, Shaw and Sophocles, with the same concentration. Proud, in order to hide her shyness. Sharp-tongued for the same reason. But generous-hearted, ready to share everything she had, even the large box of Reeves watercolours her father had specially got from someone in England. Suhas remembered how Mayura had allowed her to waste the colours that afternoon ten years ago; she remembered because her father had caught her at it and had slapped her for mixing the colours anyhow, royal blue on ochre on green; her father who never touched anyone in anger had slapped, and Mayura had intervened with, "That's okay, Periyappa, I should have been here to teach her the right way," and the next day Suhas had done the same unforgivable wasting, and still Mayura had not given her away. An insignificant incident, but Suhas recalled it now. Mayura was unhappy, who wouldn't be with such a man?

And so it went on, their attitude swinging to the other extreme from total resentment to total sympathy, but soon finding a balance somewhere in the area of, Who wouldn't be unhappy with such a man.

And they remembered other things. Not about Mayura alone. But others as well.

That Sunday morning, Murti coughed as Chandra passed by his cane recliner. It was an age-old signal by men to draw their wife's attention. Chandra came back to the veranda. He laid aside the newspaper and said, "Always in a hurry. Why don't you sit down?"

Another signal. Chandra drew up a chair and sat down.

"I noticed a few minutes ago that Nataraj is engrossed in drawing. Copying some Gothic arches."

"He'd be better off spending that time at his science texts."

"I wondered if you would go up and spend a few minutes with him. He seems to have some talent but seems ignorant of basic rules, like perspective for instance."

"Oh, they'll teach that at school."

"In the one hour per week that they have drawing class?"

Chandra gestured with her hands. "Now? On a Sunday morning? with the house in a mess, the washerman at the door, rice and dal to be cleaned and soaked for tomorrow's idli . . ."

"Just a few minutes, in the evening, maybe."

"Me teach anyone? It is years since I did anything with the pencil except write accounts. Who has the time? You and your impractical suggestions." Chandra rose impatiently, and left.

Murti sadly hid his face behind *The Hindu*. Tables turned. Once, she had been enthusiastic about drawing and painting, and she would cajole him into taking her to various shows at the Art Centre. And he had smothered her interest more effectively and cruelly than men who snubbed their wives with rudeness and contempt. He had laughed it off with his good-humoured laugh. Earnestly she had often spoken about taking afternoon lessons, and he had laughed it off. If you have talent, it can be cultivated at home, he said, and bought a whole lot of paints and paper and easel. I sadly fear, my mistress dear, that you might not have all that talent after all, he'd said after a few months of seeing the easel unused.

Even after the children started coming, she had persisted. Maybe she could get someone to come home and teach her, while the children had their afternoon nap. And he had laughed it away. Sure, just find one. Snatching moments here and there to pick peepul leaves, soak them in water two days . . . and after returning from the Club late in the evening, she would sit at the water tray and pick out a leaf and wipe it with a brush till the veins alone remained. And he, how often he had made her leave it midway. "All day you are busy dabbing powder on baby bottoms, and now at night you are dabbing paint over your leaf. You never have any time for me." Gently she would remonstrate, "But I've been with you all evening." "That's different. I want you to talk to me now." "This doesn't stop me from talking and listening." "But it isn't the same as talking here," and he would pull her to bed. With laughter and love he had pushed her paints out of her life. And now he wanted to make amends. Their son's passing flirtation with Gothic arches was only an excuse to get Chandra back to her easel.

Murti sighed. We kill our dream children without meaning to. And yet, it might be that with persuasion, now that the children were grown, she could be led back to her talent.

Home Not Home

MAYURA RETURNED EARLY MONDAY morning. She hoped no one would notice her in the bustle of Monday morning, but everyone did. They greeted her with warmth, took time off to relate something or other of interest that had happened in her absence.

"Hurray," Tara yelled out, seeing her. "Just the person who can help us out." Maya came out on her balcony to see what the shouting was about, recognized Mayura, waved out and went back in. Tara's younger sister, Gayatri, rushed up from her house, still chewing a mouthful, and asked, "Hey, Mayu, would you run up to Safire and reserve seats for YTT. Someone or other has exams all week starting Wednesday, and so we have to see it this evening. Please?"

"Sure," Mayura said.

"Five tickets, assuming you are coming, of course." Gayatri rushed off. Not a minute to waste. Monday morning.

Mayura felt tears of gratitude rising up her throat. Gayatri's spontaneous request had confirmed what others' greetings had implied. It was like old times. The nightmare of sixteen weeks was over as though it had never been. Home was home again. She, Mayura, was Mayu, sister, daughter, cousin, not a stranger whose presence petrified laughter and stultified conversation. It was good to be home again.

Her father dropped her off at Spencer's on his way to his office. She walked around the store, bought herself a bottle of Anne French cleansing cream, and then walked out and into Victoria Technical Institute, where she wandered through the show rooms for almost an hour. Then she took a taxi to Safire, and was there five minutes before the box office opened. She laughed happily at the billboards, Sophia Loren as the ever-pregnant woman, flowers, fishes, gesticulating Italians. She bought five tickets for the evening show of *Yesterday, Today and Tomorrow*, and took a taxi home. The cook was clearing the table. Mayura took a second helping of the cucumber-lentil salad she had wanted in the morning, but could not get to because of the bustle of Monday morning. Then she went to her room.

The silence of noon hour stretched like a gossamer awning from one end of Hari Vilas to the other. It is good to be home again, Mayura told herself deliberately. But there was no answering gladness within her. She looked around and the sight of the room that had given her so much pleasure in the morning now deadened her. The divan, which had been moved in after the wedding, had been moved back to its old room. Her study table, which Gita had taken after Mayura had left for Bombay, was back here. Her books, stored away in a wall cupboard these sixteen weeks were back on the shelves. There was something terribly final about having the articles of furniture back where they had been for years. Dire finality too in the casual way people had treated her all morning, accepting the fact that she was here to stay.

There had been no letter for her. To nip off the hope within her that daily waited for the postman, she had repeatedly told herself that she did not expect any. Which did not prevent her from expecting. The dire finality of it all.

Mayura tossed about on her bed, and smothered her cheek in the pillow. She wanted Saveri. The pillow was no substitute for Saveri's wordless warmth, nor her own hands clutching her aching breast for Saveri's silent strength. She wanted Saveri. Mayura trembled as she relived the wordless giving and taking that had bound them. Together they had built a universe, a universe of exquisite hope, had felt the movement of the stars, each a steady pin of hope shining in the firmament.

It was over now. They had torn themselves apart from their world of pain. "I dare not talk to you any more," Saveri had said the previous afternoon, and she had not asked why. She too had sensed the fear within herself. She dared not talk because the new set of memories of her weeks in Bombay that had risen were too personal, too too tender for her to own up to anybody, even herself. She needed time to think, to sort out the extremes, to find out where she really stood. She had to get away from the hope that had been transmitted between them, There were and will be.

Mayura ran her fingers over the edge of the pillow. Raghu, Raghu, my husband, my love. There was no response within her. She whipped herself into the hopes and memories she had experienced when with Saveri. No response. No response.

So, was this where she really stood? Where was the assurance, promise, oath, given by Saveri in that world of wordless strength, There were and will be?

Mayura was sweating from every pore in her effort to wake the dead self within her. She bit into her knuckles to keep from howling her anguish. She clung to the sides of the bed; she beat her head against the pillow; she bit her lips until they bled; she wished for long nails so she could dig them into her breasts. Dead, dead, dead.

She lay face down on the cool floor. Dead dead dead.

Raghu, husband, come in. Dead dead dead.

A simple thrust to rend the you the me that it maybe the you in me.

Pain, she was a universe in herself, a universe of pain.

Limply she rested on Saveri's cool breast till sleep washed over her.

"Hey, Mayu, got the tickets?"

Mayura rose and smoothed out her dress. It was only 3:30, but Gayatri was already back. "Sure," Mayura came out of her room. "How come you're back so early?"

"Ask no questions and you'll get no fibs. I'm famished. Hope Ma has made something good."

Parvati came to the steps of the staircase and said, "Have your tiffin here. I have your favourite today, vermicelli and morkuzhambu."

"You bet, Maami," Gayatri pushed Mayura ahead of her and they went down to the dining room and sat there an hour, while one by one, others came home and joined them.

Jayaram fumed when he heard of their evening plans. "Mean cats, you girls, why couldn't you buy tickets for all of us. Of course we want to see Sophia Loren."

Mukundan joined them, and went on and on about the set of tennis he had won, and the girls slipped out.

I don't make them ill at ease any more, Mayura thought, and winced at the finality it implied. They have accepted my fate; I too will soon get used to it.

The Patriarch Moves to Action

"IS THERE ANYONE AROUND who can spend an hour helping me?"

The booming voice, as always, neutralized the wheel of time, and then set it in centripetal motion around itself. Lakshmi dropped the food in her hand and rose from her lunch. Chandra, who had come to Parvati's on an errand, cut short her sentence and hastened to the door. Munisami, lying in the shade of the flight of steps, jumped up and quickly spat out the forbidden wad of tobacco. To Mayura, the call was of telepathic import, an answer to her half hour brooding at the dark outside of the stained glass window, getting up her courage to go to her grandfather for distraction. She flew down, and was on her grandfather's veranda before Munisami's parabola of tobacco juice hit the flowerbed.

"I want to check through this almirah of books," Ramakrishna Iyer said, walking into his library. Mayura followed him. "Here, stand on this stool . . . carefully . . ." he roared as the three legged stool wobbled ever so slightly, "check if the title I call out is on the shelf, and stop me if you can't locate the volume." He started reading off a list of titles. They were in complete sets—Dickens, red leather binding and thin snow-white pages; complete Thackeray, with dust cover torn at the edges; Hardy, volumes of blue clothbound, thick pages, bold type; complete Meredith, *Boswell's Life of Johnson* in two volumes; three copies of *The Vicar of Wakefield*; complete Stevenson, complete Scott with gilt-edged pages; Galsworthy, Wilde, Barrie, Wodehouse. Mayura's eyes squinted as they roved along, up, down the shelves. Whenever she reported a missing title, the old man growled against the particular person who had borrowed it, or declaimed in general against borrowers, or about the history of that particular volume, when it had been bought, where it had been for years, how often he had replaced *Tess* and *Oliver Twist* . . . and all the time he kept reading out titles and she tried to keep up.

"That will be all," he said, "unless you'd care to copy all these cards on to foolscap."

"Oh, sure." She took the cards.

"It doesn't have to be done. The College librarian can do it himself, if there is a librarian, that is."

Mayura looked at him in dismay. Librarian?

"They'll be here next Wednesday. I think I'll give them the steel-shelved almirah instead of this teak."

He was giving them away! Mayura did not dare ask him. Was he giving them away?

"Oh," she said, weakly.

"The youngsters of this generation don't read, that's the trouble, they don't read," her grandfather shouted angrily. "Loafing on street corners. We had to read by the light of kerosene lanterns in our days, but we read, oh yes, we read. Didn't blind ourselves either. Look at today's youngsters, all myopic or half blind seeing films, wide screen, 75 mm Technicolor, huh," he repeated the screaming banners of billboards.

"Everyone in this house has read most of these," she waved the cards, "not much else, maybe, but these for sure."

"And why did you read them? Because they are here. Because I spent money buying books. Whereas today nobody buys any book but the bare texts necessary for examinations. And bazaar notes, oh yes, *Calculus at Your Fingertips*, and *Malik Notes on English Poetry*. No sense of values. They'd rather buy terylene shirts and saris. Huh. Let us hope the students read these masterpieces once they are placed in their library. Modern generation . . . lazy dunces with no taste or culture . . ."

"Are they going to a college?" she asked, afraid to ask, yet impelled out of dismay.

"Yes, yes, of course."

"Oh."

"To Chandrayya Arts College."

"Oh no," she broke out, "it is a pigeonhole of an undergraduate college, hardly 300 students . . ."

"And an extra four hundred volumes from this week on."

"So backward the boys wouldn't know any of these names."

"Greater then their need to have them placed in front of them."

"Why, they probably don't even have a separate room for the library. Only stupid students who want a degree, not an education."

"It's so everywhere. Why only Chandrayya's? How much do the bigger colleges spend on their libraries? on literature classics I mean. Nil." The old man walked up and down impatiently. "Education. We don't have public education any more. The responsibility has devolved on parents, and parents are too busy shopping or playing bridge at the Gymkhana Club. Hah." He stopped walking and thumped on the table. "I'll tell you why I am giving this to Chandrayya's. Mind you, I'd have preferred a women's college. I still have faith in our women, though some of them are damnedly asinine when they emerge into public fields. I phoned two women's colleges this morning between 10:30 and 10:45, and in neither was the Principal in. I expect the Principal to be in at 10:29 every day. If they are not disciplined, how can they command any discipline in the students? Then I phoned two of the bigger colleges. Same story. So I decided I'd had enough of bigger colleges, who as you say have a separate room for the library. Then I phoned Chandrayya, and he had been there since ten in the morning, he said. So he gets it. I am glad it turned out that way because I know Chandrayya. Completely unbalanced mentally, but he is a good fellow, as honest as a businessman can ever be. And yes, a good fellow, to sink his business profits into a college."

Mayura pressed the rich padded leather of Little Dorrit. "Giving it away, just like that," she said slowly. How could he? They belonged here. "It will be a personal loss."

"Ah, yes." He took the book from her and ran his finger along the gilt edge. "That is why I had to use the surgeon's knife, sudden, swift."

"Where was the hurry?" she was almost crying.

"Ah, just what everyone says about anything I do. Where's the hurry, they say. Why don't you put it in your will? I don't want anyone to wait for my death, that is why. I am late as it is. Possession is the bane of mortals ... I must look into the rest of these books soon, very soon, all these Law volumes." He ran his fingers through his white hair. "I wish I could give them all away to a single institution instead of donating them piecemeal. So difficult to find colleges untouched by nepotism and inefficiency. So much, so much to be done," he started pacing more impatiently. "And so little time."

"You have a long time ahead," she said softly.

"Young woman, I am seventy-six years old. Mind you, I am very fit for my age, more so than most men of fifty. But the heart is a treacherous thing. It betrayed me eight years ago, and I know it will betray me to death one of these days. One has to be ready. One has to set one's house in order. But I have no time. Sometimes I feel I have no time at all to die." He laughed one of his hearty wave-upon-wave laughs.

Mayura placed the edge of her sari on the tears that had fallen on the quilt-soft cover of *Little Dorrit*.

"Yes," he said, looking away from her, "It is difficult. Books have been my life. More faithful than dogs, and more rewarding." He gesticulated as he spoke. "Books, beautiful books, profound books, amusing books, a world of books, my world of my books. Bought with my money, read with my eyes, appreciated with my mind. Mine, and therefore to be given away." He ran his hands across the air, denuding the shelves of books. His eyes winced.

"Mine, and therefore to be given away," he repeated firmly.

Mayura pressed the infant-soft foam between thumb and fingers, and held it close as though to save it and all the rest from ravage. "You are giving them away to get some horrible masochistic satisfaction," she said sibilantly, carried away by her sense of loss. She then held her breath and looked furtively at her grandfather.

The old man's scintillating eyes stared on at the denuded shelves. He said, "Strong words, young woman, strong words indeed. maybe it is. An act of bravado or conscience or what you will, a Rhett Butlerian fling for a lost cause. Mind you, I realize it is too late to mean much. A sacrifice made when one is so near one's bamboo bed is not much of a sacrifice ... I've never consciously earned any moral coronets. Most of my renunciations have been thrust on me. I've never been called upon to make sacrifices. Sacrifices have been made for me. I did not give up pleasures of the palate, my ulcerous stomach did that for me. When I reached the age at which, our scriptures say, one should detach oneself from the life of a householder, my wife was taken away from me. And then, when the scriptures say we should detach ourselves from human bonds, friends and children severed themselves from me. But this disciplining, or masochistic orgy as you call it, is going to be self-inflicted. All this stripped to the very walls," he swept the books into nothingness, "no books, no lamp-holding maidens of bronze, no Venus rising from the foam, no Old Masters on the walls, nothing, nothing at all except this vast empty hall, and I watching my brilliant stained-glass window till the sun goes down."

Ramakrishna Iyer turned away and looked at the stained-glass window. "It is time for my afternoon rest. You may go now." He walked out of the room, dragging his slippers with his feet, arms hanging straight down, palms back.

Mayura took the foolscap sheets and copied out a page of titles like an automaton. She then rose and placed *Little Dorrit* on the shelf. She walked around, touching books, looking at pictures, running her hands over bronze figurines. The man is mad, she whispered proudly, he has always been mad but more so now than ever before. In between framed lithographs were framed photographs, every one of them of himself. She walked from one photograph to the next, watched him grow from a turbaned, full-faced junior at the Bar to a judge in full regalia. His face had grown bigger very gradually, his sharp nose acquired flesh at the end, his lips became thinner, eyes smaller and brighter, cheeks fleshier and bigger. There were no lines on his face till much later in life, except for the three parallel lines on his forehead that appeared early in the 1930s. The dedicated determination of youth was transformed into a steely sternness, it was difficult to say when, but one was very clearly present in the 20s and the other in the 40s. There were only two photographs after 1950. Mayura wandered around again, touching books, staring at art reproductions, running her fingers over bronze figurines.

He is mad, she said, and came back to the table and copied some more titles. The fountain pen ran out of ink. She knew that all stationery needs were kept in one of the Godrej almirahs, the second from the left. There was no key on the table, only scribbled sheafs of paper under ivory inlaid paperweights. There were several pencils, and an old-fashioned nib holder in an inkstand that was dry. She picked up one of the pencils, but decided against using it. She rose from her chair and stepped across to the working side of the table. She did not sit on the old man's huge revolving chair. The drawers to the left were locked. She opened the top drawer on the other side and put her fingers under several notebooks to search for the key. She found a bunch of keys, and was about to close the drawer when she noticed her name on one of the notebooks. She picked it up, realized what she was doing, and put it back; she noticed that the notebook on which she placed it had Vij's name on it. Furtively, she picked up the first notebook again and flipped it open. A loose sheet fell out. There were several loose sheets, but most of them were affixed to a page with paper clips. She opened the first page. "It is almost a week since Mayura's dramatic arrival. Her case has already been considerably wrecked. Everyone knows she should go back. Unfortunately everyone has said as much."

She closed the book and leaned her hand on the table while tears spurted from her eyes unchecked. After a few moments, she resolutely wiped her eyes. He is mad, and I have become a sissy. She noiselessly shut the drawer after replacing the notebook, and she left the library.

She went back to her room. She sat at the window and stared again at the black circle of glass so brilliant from inside, so bleak from here she wanted to throw a stone and shatter it to fragments. She wished she could throw a spear that would shatter the circular window and enter her grand-father's heart. She hated him for not saying a word to her about her return, and sneaking it on paper for his amusement. She was a guinea pig studied closely and written about. He found it amusing no doubt, to carry out this observation and to record all the data. And then he would burn it. She had seen his periodical bonfires, scores of scribbled-upon sheets thrown into the pit at the end of the coconut grove, and set aflame. He was mad, and she was a sissy who could not stop crying.

Perhaps tomorrow would bring a letter. What was she to do if days went by without any letter from him? Why didn't her father force her back to Bombay? It was wrong for a man to keep his daughter once she was married. But everyone had accepted that she was here to stay. She could not live with a vulgar brute.

Mayura turned away from the window. People would not start coming back from schools and offices for another three hours. Once they did, she could get someone to accompany her to the beach. That was one place she could forget herself. But it was not possible to go there alone. Loafers with wolf calls and offensive remarks were everywhere nowadays. She could go to Radha's and talk to her great-uncle. He too was mad, but he was more quietly mad. Maybe she could help him with something. He'd be back from the Museum by now because he worked only in the mornings. Maybe Radha would be home, she sometimes had afternoons off. But she had become a stranger, one could not talk to her any more, she fled away on some pretext or other. Well, so had others at first, maybe Radha too had come around. The terrifying finality of it all! Mayura went downstairs. Her mother was mending a split seam in a choli; there were several cholis by her side. Worries about her children notwithstanding, her mother continued to get stouter, not pleasantly plump like Aunt Chandra but a seam-splitting, uncomfortable stoutness. Mayura sat by her mother and helped her sew. Her mother spoke ramblingly about menus and dinners.

At 3:45, as always, her grandfather went out, umbrella in hand; his shoulder cloth had a gold border, which meant that he was going to some select seminar or study group. Mayura waited till he was out of the main gate. Then she went to the library, passing Munisami the watchdog who also had waited till the Master was out of the gate before taking out his tobacco pouch as he sat on his haunches, leaning on the portico wall. She took out the notebook with her name on the cover and closed the drawer. She carried a stool to the far corner of the hall and started reading.

2 IX 65. It is almost a week since Mayura's dramatic arrival. Her case has already been considerably wrecked. Everyone knows she should go back. Unfortunately everyone has said as much.

It pays in a court of law to say what you have to say in forthright and forceful terms. But not in human crises. The truth couched in words becomes meaningless. Hence the "Ineffable Name," "Yahveh," "Om."

4 IX. Each man for himself must decide.

By coercion and anger, persuasion and tears, we only distort his vision. An intelligent person, endowed with reason, brought up with a good sense of values, will see the right path for himself.

Interference only brings out the mule in man.

In my generation, women earned their freedom. Today's woman demands it.

5 IX. Collective guilt is far worse than individual guilt. One can speak about the latter, one can get counsel and consolation; it lightens when it is shared; it purifies, at worst, it wrecks one's life. Collective guilt emasculates the community; members move with stealth, seeking to avoid each other, for meeting another is like looking into a mirror when your face is smitten with pus-filled boils.

6 IX 65. She is like a beggar at the door who does not beg, who does not speak, but will not go away. He does not even look at you but the guilty ever feel his eyes and the world's on themselves.

What master mind-readers beggars are! They sit outside our temples, begging bowls in front of them. One who goes to the temple to thank, throws them a coin in the gratitude of his heart; one who goes to ask, throws them two because being himself a supplicant he needs must be assured of the words, Ask and it shall be given.

Beggars exploit not our sense of compassion but our sense of guilt. And if we pass them by without giving, the more wretched we.

7 IX. Am I evading my responsibility? Non-interference, faith in individual maturity, silent disapproval . . . are these only excuses to justify my inaction?

Inarticulation is the plague that prostrates the middle class.

I inarticulate? Words I have always had at my command. What then restrains me? What restrains everyone here? Why don't people talk of pertinent matters instead of delivering mandates from the podium?

8 IX. I find some have been conversing. They have retreated, blanched by her contempt.

10 IX. Medusa turned men to stone. Circe transformed men into swine. Here is one who twists healthy people into bundles of bleeding sores.

The young are often callous. The unhappy young more often so and more deliberately so.

Blanched to the bone.

*

This morning I was reading the *Express* at Venkatesan's and he was correcting student papers.

"How can you bear a lifetime of teaching the same things?" she asked, coming to us. A common enough question that started a common enough conversation. But she went on to provoke Venkatesan. He, mild man, only smiled and grunted acquiescence from time to time, as one would humour a child. Along the way he said without being even aware that the words could hold anything personal, "We have this consolation that in science we get all the thrill of emotional experience without its heartbreaks." Cruelty took visible shape in the downward drooping of her bloodless lips. "A heck of a thrill, I am sure, cooped up in a pea-sized college. A tripos Cantabrian rotting in a nameless 'sanctum of higher learning,' swallowing all the toady insults panned out to him . . ." She went on, referring to the humiliation meted out to him by the blackguards who govern our university, and this at a time when he is still smarting from their latest shot excluding him from research committees on the pretext that his publications don't add up, scraps of paper that even morons can get nowadays as a matter of course if they plod at some thesis, however outdated, long enough . . .

12 IX. Mayura feels raped. Does he feel that he has raped? One may see a rape in an act which is not so to the other. She taught me that, put me right on what I had thought, my Maitreyi.

Remorse-ridden for the pain I had caused her, the long travail that sucked away her body sap and made her a martyred skeleton, I hid from her I had loved as a child but now hardly knew despite three children I had begotten on her, perhaps not in love, perhaps not even in need, perhaps through mere habit.

I was at my table, not working, for I could not concentrate those days. I never have been able to work when my conscience is troubled. She came in.

"I wish you wouldn't be so solicitous about the hours I keep, about my meals, my dress, my sleep. This is worse than nagging," I told her irritatedly. She came and stood at my table. She ran her fingers over the pincushion and quietly asked, "Why do you feel you have raped me?" At first I could not believe I had heard aright. I did not look up, wishing to spare her the embarrassment of words that she was surely regretting even then. I thought she would go away and that we could pretend she had never said anything or that I had not heard what she said. But she did not go. She stood there, her fingers feeling the pinheads, and she said, "You felt so the first night and you have felt so ever since. Why do you think I am only a vessel for your passion and that the passion is itself vile?" She sat down.

We talked then. I expressed many silly thoughts in pompous language. I said she was glorifying the bestial because the beast within her was starving. Because she sat there on the edge of the chair, as my clients sat, words came to me, fluent, vitriolic, insubstantial, drowning her softspoken phrases in oratorical bombast. Not for long.

That night was our nuptial night.

13 IX. Once I used to think that these daily jottings, which are stacked in the locked almirahs around me are nuclei of profundities. Perhaps they are merely the rantings of an old man who must talk, even if it is only in an artificial medium to an inanimate listener. Why say even it is only? One can speak more fluently and more intimately with one's pen than with one's tongue. But to what effect? For what end? Some write diaries in order to recall and relive the past. Fools. The quickest way to forget an experience is to write it out. Self-conducted therapy then? Have I been evading my responsibility by talking to an inanimate listener in an artificial medium?

14 IX. Self-pride will pull her through, I hope, if what I hear is indeed true. The months of waiting are not going to be easy, but self-pride will pull her through. Vanquish self-pride say the Selfless ones. And yet pride is a virtue in that it strengthens self-control and weakens self-pity. It helps a sensitive mind to stem over the hurt, the laceration which, if one were to love oneself a little less or others a little more, would leave too deep a scar for the immediate future to remove or ordinary love to forgive.

16 IX. Mayura feels raped. The agony and the relief have changed nothing, perhaps only increased resentment. I pity her. I am also afraid—of her and for her. I pity her for her ill-focused idealism. Snobbishness they call

it. She has got it from me, they say, egotism, snobbishness, obstinacy, all from me.

Savitri was here this evening. I saw her being waylaid, so to say, by Parvati to take part in an argument in progress, no uncommon occurrence since this girl's return. It was Parvati who did most of the talking, no uncommon feature this either; and out came the inevitable charge, "She is her grandfather all over—egocentric and arrogant, insisting that her rabbit has but three legs, stubbornness incarnate." And Savitri retorted with unexpected vehemence, "Why don't you list the other qualities she has inherited from him—intelligence, integrity, above all sensitivity?"

Savitri stands by me though I have done all too little for her. To be born to old parents is a boon, people think. In a way, yes. Money and love are lavished by doting parents grateful for this proof of their virility. Yet . . . I feel I have not done right by her. Sometimes when I look at her when she thinks she is alone, I wonder if all is well between her and that eccentric husband of hers. I feel guilty.

Oh Hari! Why should I feel guilty about all of them? I am weak. I admire Cain now. What irony that Yahveh punished Cain for reaching that state of detachment for which yogis strive! It wasn't detachment alone I know, I know this isn't a correct parallel, but I do envy Cain now . . .

17 IX. I am troubled, guilt-ridden. How my mind wanders of a sudden! I work at my book through sheer willpower. If I let myself relax, I succumb to long hours of mental peregrination. I am my brother's keeper. I must talk to her. She is unhappy, lost. And I who have not lifted a finger for those sprung of my loins, not for Venkatesh wasting his life in a well, not for Savitri, not even for my Raja, feel impelled to do something for her.

Irony! At last the stone Ganesha, as our saying goes, moved from his inertia, but to no avail. What a wall of inarticulation there is between us! I have long reconciled myself to a certain loneliness. I know they think of me as a discipinarian, an iron-handed patriarch. But I did not know the wall was so insurmountably high.

I looked for her half an hour ago, knowing she spends a lot of time here in the library. I broached the subject lightly. She merely looked at me, and

I had to fight off the feeling that she had Kumar's eyes, just a little baleful when he did not know how to approach an algebra problem; I'd give him the first step and he'd find the solution in a trice, and smile with his anemic lips.

Well, feeling like a nervous actor who must have a cue, I said, "No doubt you think old fogies are not qualified to discuss matters of the heart, eh? Ah, but the things we could tell you about ourselves!" I did not want that tone, but that was the only one I could call upon. Bantering is yet another way in which inarticulation seeks relief. She looked at me with Kumar's eyes. Thank god she blinked and Kumar vanished. I came away.

Once again I assayed out and once again I am back without having said what I set out to say. Once again my tone was light, bantering, and once again she looked at me. But this time I saw differently. I ought to be very ashamed of myself but I am flattered too and consequently deeply pained. Vij once said, "Children demand nothing less than perfection from their parents. They do not see them as a man and a woman but as an idealised unit." I wonder at what battlefront of this insane war he is. Admirable boy, I have come to love his company as I have loved only Raja's.

There is no greater hurt than the realization that your hero is made of clay. Consequently no contempt greater than that heaped on a hero turned clay.

18 IX. An audible sigh of relief ripples through Hari Vilas. No more is the air brittle as spunsugar threads. People are extricating themselves from the strangulating love-hate filaments she throws wherever she goes. Overnight, people have become as of old.

Should one draw the obvious inference that all will reconcile themselves to her desertion of her husband if she would but take herself out of their presence? Out of sight, out of conscience? It is too early to draw any fair conclusion. Once she returns from Savitri's we might know more.

20 IX. Mayura is looking for a face-saving straw. Everyone has been moving towards an acceptance of her decision. One cannot hear unfavourable reports about a stranger from a friend without tending to believe the friend to the stranger's detriment. Meanwhile Mayura has been moving towards another acceptance.

All she wants now is to save face. Too proud to apologize she wants him to make the first move. She waits all morning for a letter from him. But he, who would have thought from her reports that he was a man, has said nothing. After the first two telegrams of the first week, there has been silence.

To humble oneself is not easy. I know that only too well. Therefore did our sages advocate self-mortification, therefore do devotees walk on their knees up the steps of Mater Dolorosa, therefore is the newly-initiated brahmachari made to go begging, "Bhavati, Bhiksham dehi."

Why do you wait when you know what you want? To get what you want, strive all you can. And may you never desire ought but the right.

Forgive me, I have erred. Say it, woman, say it. For lesser faults have many suffered heavier punishment. For mistaking Shravana's pitcher gurgle, for unwittingly killing a deer in copulation were Dasaratha and Pandu bereft of son and sex.

Humble yourself, no one else can do it for you. Rather, others can but your future is yours only if you do it yourself. Or? Intercession. Perhaps Christianity makes it easier than our Karma.

There is no truth in the belief that one can pray for another's soul. Anything I do for you, I do for myself, to absolve myself to some degree, infinitesimal though it be, of my past sins of omission, for my part in Raja being what he is, in Savitri's loneliness, in . . . O God why have you opened my eyes so late in life? Lord of the world I was as I walked through the pathless woods. The winds denuded the trees and left me open to the thundering rain and I realized I was lost. And I fell on my knees that had not bent in seventy years. A flash of lightning showed me where the shelter was. It also seared my legs from under me.

Mayura turned back the pages at random and started reading and found herself reading to the very end. And again opening at random, she was carried all the way to the end. She went through the sheafs several times.

Tearing a slip of paper from the half sheets of paper tied to the leg of the table, she wrote, Forgive me, I have erred. She stared at it in disgust, tore it into minute bits and buried them beneath the crumpled balls that lay in the wastepaper basket. She replaced the notebook in the drawer. She noticed that her grandfather had added several titles from the bundle of cards to the foolscap. A half-empty ink bottle was on the table and there were three other fountain pens as well as the one she had used in the afternoon. She smiled sadly, visualizing how irritatedly he would have shaken the empty pen and then opened the almirah with an impatient bang and filled that and several other pens to avoid such a disgusting inter-ruption for the next week or two. She was alternately choked with anger and love for her grandfather. She drew out the notebook and read parts of it once again, and then she replaced it. She left the library. She skirted Maitreyi Nivas, under the gooseberry tree, into the coconut grove. Snatches of sentences slapped her as she passed under low-foliaged mango trees. She walked till the birds loudly protested her intrusion. Then she went home for dinner.

She did not come down next morning till nine. People were rushing around, getting ready for school, college, office. She drew a deck chair to the front veranda and sank into it with an old *Reader's Digest*.

School, college, office, life went on as always. It sometimes left some persons behind, like a shell thrown ashore; there were myriad beautiful shells on the shore. They were dead. Had they been alive with ugly smelly creatures that spelt life for them, they would not have been washed ashore perhaps.

"Has the post come, Mayu?" Lakshmi called out from a balcony.

"I don't know," Mayura carelessly replied, "I don't know."

The postman had not yet come. From the beginning of time she had sat there behind the pillar from where she could see the gate. At last he came. He wheeled his bicycle into the gate and stood it against a palm tree; he placed his khaki cap on his head as though he had to be in full uniform when delivering letters; then he went to her grandfather's veranda. He took another eon at Lakshmi's and then went back for his cycle. He came to the steps near her, leaned his cycle against himself and held out several letters. She stood up and took them from him. None of the four letters was for her. She went in, placed the letters on the dining table and returned to her chair. Eon after eon she would wait. There were myriad beautiful shells on the shore, so beautiful, so dead.

A few minutes later she heard her grandfather's slip-slip steps. She fretted at his habit of dragging his slippers instead of lifting them.

He cleared his throat apologetically. She turned and looked at him. "I just wanted to tell you that two days ago I . . ." he stopped, staring at her in a mildly hypnotized way. "Oh well, nothing," he said, and slip-slip his steps receded. She watched his back. His spotless white veshti was, as usual, too short at the back, and his shoulder cloth hung way back as though it would drop behind him in a moment. The leonine majesty of his figure was accentuated by the clumsiness of his attire. Mayura purposely concentrated on the shortness of his veshti and his simian gait because she wanted to hate him. He will make another entry now, of how her look reminded him of Kumar's.

What had be come to say? What a wall of inarticulation there is between us.

Mayura went up to her room and sat at her table, that had been brought back from Gita's room. The dire finality of it all.

She pulled out a sheet of drawing paper, and with painstaking care copied sketches from a *Mother Goose* volume left behind by Sita. The mouse that ran down the clock looked more like a mongoose. She erased it and drew it over again. And meanwhile the clock was ticking.

She took out her letter pad; it was of polished leather, dyed green, with intricate Shanti Niketan work on it. A wedding gift from one of Appa's friends. Dear Raghuraman, she started. It sounded much too formal. She tore the sheet into minute bits and threw them into the basket.

My dear Raghu, she started and wrote two pages without stopping. She read it over and was appalled at what she had written. It brimmed over with philosophic and literary spurts. She could imagine what he'd do. He could not appreciate words, he had no feeling for the subtle or sublime. He could lavish trite clichés and extravagant endearments but there was no tenderness in him, only a hulking crudeness. Night after night he had taken her, not with insistent haste which she could have borne because it left her alone, chaste, untouched, but with slow wheedling movements that roused her without her volition and twisted her into a form, a being, a state of existence not her own. He would laugh uproariously on reading this letter and, as always, share it with his friends. "An iceberg on top, but boy, what a firebrand within," he had said the morning after their arrival in Bombay.

She would not return to such a man. She could not live a lifetime with such a man. She ought not. She tore the letter into shreds and, sweeping them off the table, she buried her face in the crook of her arm and cried.

It was dark when she woke. Another day was over.

She had a wash and she joined the family at dinner. Her father and mother spoke about her grandfather's latest madness of giving away his books. Her brother and Ramani were boisterous as usual, her sister easily teased. They laughed, they grumbled, they grabbed. The dire finality of it all.

As the clock struck nine, all conversation stopped. "This is All India Radio giving you the news . . ." Ceasefire had been declared. The voice of the news-reader, bass and steady, continued sonorously, in sharp contrast to the boys' war-cries of frustration. "Chavan is an ass." "God, what bounders! To stop when we could have licked them flat to the ground." Cousins dropped in to join the postmortem while adults moved to Chandra's to have their own panel discussion. Devika, appearing of a sudden, rushed about, embracing one and all in a delirium of joy. She had her arms around Mayura before she realized it was Mayura. There was a fraction of a second when the younger woman's arms instinctively slackened but Mayura was far too carried away to be hurt. She said, "I am so happy for you, so happy for you." Devika's mad whirling stopped in a tight embrace and then she careened away to someone else. Mayura thought, I want to cry, I wish I could cry for sheer joy.

The instant passed. It will come now, she thought, the jealousy and the pain.

Devika was now running to Ramakrishna Iyer. Mayura could not imagine the old man embracing anyone or anyone daring to embrace him, but Devika was wild enough now to do even that. "Admirable boy, I have come to love his company as I have loved only Raja's." She felt a razor-sharp shaft of jealousy not only because Devika was in love but because she was with the old man at this moment.

Mayura climbed slowly up the stairs. Somewhere there was a letter pad which she had to open. And a pen which her hand had to hold.

"Forgive me, I have erred." What superhuman strength it needed to utter those five words.

She was a superior mind, even her grandfather admitted that. But she was bound to Raghu, with his trite humour, his complete lack of dignity. "But he, who would have thought from her reports that he was a man..." Night after night not with insistent haste ... "Why do you think I am only a vessel for your passion and that the passion is itself vile?"

"Humble yourself . . . Say it woman, say it." I can't, I can't. Her vitals churned with the nausea of travail. Do it for me, she begged, he had written that he could do it for her. Just this one time, just once and she would never ask him or anyone for anything else ever again. Just this once.

Mayura doodled on the back of the drawing sheet. Seven castles with seven moats took shape in the clouds. The clock struck one. The mouse ran down. The clock struck two. The you in me, the I in you. The clock struck three. The clock had gone berserk. It did not allow seconds to tick by. There were sixty seconds to a minute, thirty minutes to a half-hour. And the clock ought strike only once every half hour. It was middle of the night and she was sitting at the table that had been taken but returned because she was here to stay. Forever and forever the clock would strike, which is what it was doing, striking instead of ticking, strike one strike two. One plus one made two but one times one remained one and that is why one might see rape in an act that is not so to the other. But one taken away from one made zero and zero was cipher, nought, nothing, and a woman ought not cipher herself out of existence just because she sees rape in an act that is not so to the other. But one divided by one remained one and that was the secret of this arithmetic. Now she had the answer. One divided by one remained one and so she could stay here where home was home. But the awful finality of it all, ah that was another matter, especially when the clock insisted on striking instead of ticking and the mouse, the mouse did not run any more because it was time all good girls were in bed, alone, oh sweetheart that is a real good one I must tell it to the boys, the boys were there, always there, drooling over their bed the gorgeous bed with quilted satin and carved ebony legs that rocket skyward to the tentacles of agony or of ecstasy why why why couldn't it be both but how could that be when one sees rape in an act that is not so to the other?

Your future is yours only if you do it yourself. Of course, that is what she was doing, she was wresting the future for herself though her arm was dead with the weight of her head taking rest. A brief rest before the final effort, a rest with legs stretched, head on pillow, a good rest a last good rest with no fear of hungry hands groping, probing, and who knows but the world may end tonight.

Say it woman, say it. But of course, Thatha, I am about to say it. It is not easy, as you know. But you are right. Mine and therefore to be given away. Come then, let us say it. A deep breath, here I close my eyes and when I count ten, one two the I in you . . . so far away . . . yet it will be so because it must be so because one into one is one and that is the reason why one ought not see rape in an act that is not so to the other.

Forgive me, I have erred. What superhuman strength it needs . . . yes I must sleep so I can collect all my superhuman strength, and who knows but the world might end tonight.

Dawn, how early it comes! Aurora, cymbals in hand, coming to wake gods and men, while I, I go out to meet my hairy hulking lord and husband, but who knows the beast might turn into a prince and I queen of the seven castles.

The milkman had come and gone. The postman will soon be here. One could wait and see. Five hours will not make much difference. But no, if it were done when tis done, then 'twere well it were done quickly. What a joyous epithalamion!

One times one was also one. Mayura awoke and looked around. When they next come, the divan should be placed against the wall under the window. He was a fresh air fiend, one of those who took skipping rope and dumbbells to the terrace every morning. Next summer, we'll make love under the open sky and meanwhile let us now while Orion looks in on our window . . . He would like the divan under the window.

She started composing the letter in her head. Deleting, changing, adding, rephrasing. It was done. The day had begun. The last but one day. Gita could have the table. The plane for Bombay left at two o'clock. Her letter would go by that flight today and she by the same flight Saturday. The phone call would come tomorrow. The last day but one.

Mayura brushed her teeth, went downstairs, had a cup of coffee, ended her morning ablutions with a shower. She dressed herself in a crisp cotton sari. Feeling clean and fresh, she returned to her room and wrote the letter. It read well. She did not take the entire blame but the feeling of regret was certainly there, and overtones of apology. Please ask me to come and I shall come she had said, but not in those words.

The post box at the corner was not cleared till eight and it was hardly seven, but her steps were hurried as she walked, letter discreetly tucked between the folds of her sari. As she entered the gate after speeding the letter Bombayward, she saw her grandfather on his veranda. She went up to him and said, "I know now why people bathe before going to the temple."

"Approach the day as you would a temple. Purity of spirit will develop naturally," he said.

"I also know why some people keep quoting the scriptures. The words take on an intimate relevancy, however farfetched it may seem to others."

The old man's raised eyebrows asked her for further explanation of her cryptogram. She said, "I have just posted a letter."

"Well well, who would have thought there was anything but feather in that head of yours?"

Mayura was stung. But she remembered. "Bantering is yet another way in which inarticulation seeks relief."

Uncle Venkatesh was returning from his morning walk to the beach. He passed her on his way to his father. Mayura caught her breath and cursed herself. She ought not have told him of the letter. What if there was no reply or a rude one? What if he did not want her back? She felt limp. Now everyone would know she had written a letter and everyone would wait for a reply and the reply might never come or come rudely. She waited in torment as her uncle walked up to her grandfather. The old man spoke to his son but made no mention of the letter. Mayura sighed with relief. She knew that her grandfather either made announcements immediately on hearing a piece of news, or never. But the freshness was gone out of the morning. In her pride, she had not once thought of rejection. What if it was too late? What if he had taken or gone back to another woman? Maya had said men like Raghu and his friends only talked about conquests, conquests they had never made. But Maya could be wrong. Who knows anything about anyone, least of all about the man one marries? "A flash of lightning showed me where the shelter was. It also seared my legs from under me."

*

"I was so relieved when she was up early and so cheerful and brisk. Look at her now. She's been in her room seven hours. Refuses lunch, refuses to open her door. Whatever am I to do with such a daughter? O what sins I must have committed in my last birth!" Parvati poured out her plaints to Lakshmi. "Why! There's the postman coming a second time! Must be a telegram."

The postman came up. "Express delivery for Mayura Raghuraman."

Parvati rushed her weight up the stairs, breathlessly shouting for Mayura. She knocked on Mayura's door. "Hurry child, hurry. The postman is waiting." Mayura came out and followed her mother down. Lakshmi had already signed for the letter. "It is from Bombay," she said, her voice scarcely concealing her curiosity.

"It must be from our son-in-law, open it quickly, child. Are you a pillar? As unmoved as a rock. Pah, open it quickly."

"You needn't get excited, Mother, heck, how inquisitive people are!" Mayura's voice was cold. It was easy to be icy when someone was behaving as agitated as her mother. She did not open the envelope. She had to be alone, absolutely alone. There was only one place her mother wouldn't dare follow her to—the judge's rooms. With great effort, Mayura put on an air of non-chalance and walked into the hallway of the library. She knew he would not hear her, he'd be on the veranda in his easy-chair, reading *The Hindu*.

She tremblingly leaned against an almirah. The blue velvet-finish envelope was so light she was sure it held only a slip of paper. "Go to hell," he could well have written his favourite slang, "I can do without you." Why had she to post a letter that morning of all mornings? If she had waited another day as she had waited eons . . .

It was terrifying that an envelope should hold so much. She slit it with a hairpin and opened the sheet of vellum paper.

Dear Love,

I do not know what unhappiness has driven you from my arms. I woke up last night to the fragrance of your hair. It was only the jasmine bush below our window.

I cannot imagine of what crime I have been arraigned and condemned in your mind's awful Hague. I can understand now what Santanu would have felt, poor blighter, when his wife threw baby after baby into the river. Wives are a dumbfounding breed, a breed quite different from other women, it seems. One should not even try to fathom them, I've concluded. But it so happens that a spouse is not a commodity you can fling out the window. We've got it in the neck for better for worse. Let's make it for better.

Raghu

Mayura waved the letter like a victory pennant. She went to her grandfather and held it out. "It's from him," she said, tittering somewhat hysterically in her embarrassment and joy.

"Less than three days! Why that's a prompt reply!" he said.

"But it isn't a reply! I posted my letter only this morning, remember? Isn't that a wonderful coincidence? Just read it, it's so funny."

He read it. The scene was different from the one she had imagined when she stretched it out to him. But she wasn't Devika.

He returned the letter. "Starts off rather romantically. Changed his mind midway, apparently."

"Oh, the anticlimactic touch is intentional, you know."

His eyes smiled along a hundred marvellous wrinkles. "It is so difficult for us to be uninhibited. Writing poetry is easy enough compared to writing love letters, eh? Never the twain shall meet."

"We can't all be Keats." Suddenly she wasn't ashamed or shy about defending Raghu. She wished he would say something disparaging about Raghu so she could align herself openly with the man she was wedded to. But her grandfather only said, "Youngsters tend to overrate that immature sufferer of synaesthetic diarrhea." He put his reading glasses into the spectacle case. "Mind you, I've always wondered how the Brownings wrote their letters. We couldn't, any more than you could take the night train to Bombay."

"Do you think I should?" she asked eagerly, but quickly added, "Oh well, where's the hurry?"

His smile spread to his mouth.

Mayura put the letter back in its velvet-finish envelope. She would leave on Sunday afternoon; seventy hours was a proper period of time.

Ramakrishna Iyer composed himself for his afternoon siesta. It was gratifying to see youngsters, featherheaded though they be, happy. But the fact remained—he was selfishness incarnate. Anything I do for you, I do for myself, to absolve myself to some degree, infinitesimal though it be . . .

Lessons from Our Children

A Tribute to the Wisdom of Kids

Joan Aho Ryan

Health Communications, Inc.
Deerfield Beach, Florida

www.hci-online.com

We would like to acknowledge the following publishers and individuals for permission to reprint the following material. (Note: The material that was penned anonymously, that is in the public domain or that was written by Joan Aho Ryan is not included in this listing.)

The Hare(s) and the Tortoise. Reprinted with permission of Mary L. Crain. ©1999 Mary L. Crain.

Doctorcito. Reprinted with permission of Allen A. Bennett. ©1999 Allen A. Bennett.

Baubles and Bibles. Reprinted with permission of JoAnn Blake. ©1999 JoAnn Blake.

Looking Inside. Reprinted with permission of Pat M. Costner. ©1999 Pat M. Costner.

"It's the Only Face I've Got" and *Rainbow Eyes.* Reprinted with permission of Janice Anthony. ©1999 Janice Anthony.

Anything Is Possible. Reprinted with permission of Vickie McGrory. ©1999 Vickie McGrory.

Ode to My Grandma. Reprinted with permission of Jon Mikel Emery and Helen Emery. ©1999 Jon Mikel Emery and Helen Emery.

The Real Meaning of Love. Reprinted with permission of Melissa Sutinen. ©1999 Melissa Sutinen.

We Caretakers. Reprinted with permission of Edward P. Stephani. ©1999 Edward P. Stephani.

(permissions continued on page 203)

Library of Congress Cataloging-in-Publication Data

Ryan, Joan Aho, date.
    Lessons from our children : a tribute to the wisdom of kids / Joan Aho Ryan.
        p.   cm.
    ISBN 1-55874-691-9 (trade pbk.)
    1. Children Anecdotes.   2. Parent and child Anecdotes.   I. Title.
HQ767.9.R93 1999   99-31723
305.23—dc21   CIP

Publisher: Health Communications, Inc.
                3201 S.W. 15th Street
                Deerfield Beach, Florida 33442-8190

Cover design by Lisa Camp
Inside book design by Lawna Patterson Oldfield

There is a wisdom of the head,
and . . . a wisdom of the heart.

—Charles Dickens

Contents

Foreword

One day four years ago, when I was getting ready for school, I reached for the comic section of the daily newspaper—just to have my laugh for the day. On the front page, I saw a photograph of a young boy wearing a red vest, raising his fist high in the air. The headline read: "Battled Child Labor, Boy, 12, Murdered!"

I guess it was because I also was twelve years old at the time that the story attracted my interest. The article was about a young boy from Pakistan who, for sixteen dollars, had been sold into slavery as a carpet weaver and had spoken out against child labor in defense of his peers.

I had never heard of child labor, but I was amazed that someone so young could be such a great hero. I did some research and discovered that there are 250 million child laborers in the world—many working in slave-like conditions. Reading this story inspired me and motivated me to take action. I gathered a group of friends and we formed the organization called Free the Children—which has since become an international network of children helping children.

I was very pleased when Joan Aho Ryan asked me to write the foreword to her book, *Lessons from Our Children: A Tribute to the Wisdom of Kids,* because I realize from my own experience the power that stories of children's courage and bravery can have, and how much they can inspire others.

Over the past three years, in my travels for Free the Children, I have had the opportunity to meet many children. Children like eight-year-old Jeffrey in Manila, who spends his days sifting through garbage dump searching for plastics and other items to sell in order to help his family survive. Children like Munillal, who had been sold into slavery as a carpet weaver, but never lost

hope that he would see his mother again one day. Children like
the girls I met in India, who carried their friend from place to
place because she had no legs. Children like the students of St.
Joan of Arc School in St. Clair Shores, Michigan, who sold their
toys and did odd jobs to raise money to build a Free the Children
school in Nicaragua.

Jose, a street child in Brazil, was another of these children. I
met Jose in the streets of San Salvador, where he lived with a
group of street children, all of whom were between the ages of
eight and fourteen. Jose and his friends showed me where they
slept at night—in an old abandoned bus shelter under cardboard
boxes. They had to be careful, he said, because the police might
beat them if they found their secret hideout. I spent the day playing soccer on the streets with Jose and friends. An old plastic
bottle that they had found in the garbage served as the soccer ball
because the street children are too poor to own a real soccer
ball. We had a lot of fun until one of the kids fell on the bottle,
breaking it into several pieces.

It was getting late anyway and time for me to leave. Jose knew
that I was returning to Canada and wanted to give me a gift—but
he had nothing. He had no home, no toys, no books. He had
nothing to give except the clothes he was wearing. So, he took
the shirt off his back and handed it to me. Jose didn't stop to
think that he had no other shirt to wear or that he would be cold
that night. He gave me his most precious possession—the soccer
shirt of his favorite team. Of course, I told Jose that I could never
take his shirt, but he insisted. So, I took off the plain white T-shirt
I was wearing and gave it to Jose. Although Jose's shirt was dirty
and had a couple of small holes, it was a colorful soccer shirt and
certainly much nicer than mine. Jose grinned from ear to ear
when I put it on.

I will never forget Jose because he taught me more about sharing that day than anyone I had ever known. He may have been
a poor street child, but I saw more goodness in him than in all
the world leaders I had met. I realized that if everyone in this
world shared like Jose there would be no more hunger or loneliness and much less pain in the world.

When we first started Free the Children, we were just a group of friends—all of us twelve years old. Today, there are tens of thousands of young people in more than twenty countries around the world who have become involved in Free the Children activities: building schools, putting together school and health kits, buying land for poor families and speaking out in defense of their poor or marginalized peers.

Often, when we are young, adults will say that we are not old enough or smart enough or skilled enough to do anything about the suffering we see in the world. You must never believe this. Children are not simply empty vessels to be filled. They are people with ideas, talents, opinions and dreams.

Children believe that there is nothing to stop their dreams from coming true. Some may call this wishful thinking and may think it too idealistic—as if it were a stage children needed to out-grow—but I think that this world could do with more idealism and dreamers. Remember, it was the dreamers who thought that one day the Berlin Wall would fall, apartheid in South Africa would end and a human being would walk on the moon.

Mahatma Gandhi once said that if there is to be peace in the world it must begin with children. When you read *Lessons from Our Children,* I am sure you will agree.

Hats off to Joan Aho Ryan for believing in young people!

Craig Kielburger
founder, Free the Children

Acknowledgments

One of the real pleasures of compiling and editing this collection was having the opportunity to keep in touch with some of the contributors to my two previous books, *Lessons from Mom* and *Lessons from Dad.* I was delighted to find them eager to participate in *Lessons from Our Children* and want to acknowledge the talented writers who are now represented in all three books: Betsy Bee, Mary Ledford, Margaret McDonald, Dot Reese and Laurel Turner. Their enthusiastic support of all these projects is much appreciated. Thanks, too, to Virginea Cooper and Leigh Muller, whose work has appeared in two of the three books in this series.

I am also grateful to all those who are making their debut in *Lessons from Our Children,* from Sally Brungart who, at eighty-five years of age, is the most senior contributor, to the youngest, eleven-year-old Jon Emery. From Maine to California and every state in between, these wonderful stories, poems, essays and anecdotes came from people eager to share their thoughts and feelings about the wisdom of kids. It was an exhilarating experience to be the recipient of so much generosity and goodwill, and I am thankful to every single individual whose work became part of the collection.

My husband Jack provided invaluable guidance on this project. I have no doubt it's a far better book because of his insights. Thanks, Toots. My daughter, Diana, and her husband, Randy, inspired me in ways they cannot imagine and I am grateful to them for that inspiration, and for teaching me a few lessons that could probably fill another book. I am most appreciative of the efforts of my sister, Pat, who made the time in her busy life to encourage her friends and colleagues to participate in this project. Her support has meant a great deal to me.

I am grateful to Craig Kielburger, the sixteen-year-old founder of Free the Children, for providing a foreword that perfectly complements the tone of this book. Through the efforts of the international organization he established four years ago (at the age of twelve!), he has raised awareness of the worldwide abuse of children used in child labor, built schools in developing countries, distributed health kits, and initiated many other humanitarian projects to break the cycle of poverty and ignorance that inflicts suffering on so many children. This movement, founded by a child and built by thousands of other children, is a splendid testimonial to the power of children to change the world.

Special thanks to Peter Vegso, President of Health Communications, for his continuing support, and the good advice that helped me set goals and make some tough decisions. I also want to acknowledge the members of the HCI team who were professional, responsive and most helpful to me throughout the process: Christine Belleris, editorial codirector; Lisa Drucker, associate editor; Kim Weiss, director of public relations, and the public relations department; Teri Peluso, executive assistant; Terry Burke, vice president of sales and marketing, and his sales team; and Kelly Maragni, director of marketing, and the marketing department.

My heartfelt thanks to Jack Canfield, coauthor of the *Chicken Soup for the Soul* books, who has generously given me his endorsement. I am proud to have his name on the cover of this book.

Finally, I want to acknowledge the hundreds of folks across America who sent me stories and other material I was unable to use. Not having space for all the many worthwhile contributions that deserved to be published was the only negative aspect to conceiving and producing this book. However, somewhere down the road all these voices may be heard in a new book that may well be *More Lessons from Our Children*. Based on the response I've received, it's evident there are still many more stories to be told about what we can learn from our children.

Introduction

The playwright James M. Barrie is reputed to have said, "I am not young enough to know everything." Since many parents have ample evidence that their kids still have a lot to learn, this undoubtedly seems a bit of a stretch. In fact, I can hear the voices in protest at this humble statement, as we adults grapple with the unruly children in our lives—whether our own, our grand-children, nephews, nieces, students, the kids next door or any young person who we wish would just grow up already. It's an undeniable fact that they misbehave, defy us and need to be disciplined, taught and guided for what seems an endless period of childhood and youth. But it's also clear to me that we can learn from our children; often, in unexpected ways.

Lessons from Our Children grew out of this conviction. When I began collecting material for the book, I felt strongly that, with just a little prompting, many people would respond to this idea and would want to tell a story about a child who opened their hearts and minds and, in the process, taught them a lesson that was never forgotten. To my great surprise, little prompting was necessary. Instead, the moment I described the project, people would begin to recount some experience in their own lives, and there was a great outpouring of admiration, love and respect for a child who had made an indelible impression.

The result is this book. It's been a great learning experience for me, too, as I've gotten to know about children whose actions not only touch the lives of those around them, but have far-reaching consequences for the world we live in. As an example, there is a story about a thirteen-year-old boy who began a local beach clean-up drive that grew to a national movement involving one hundred volunteer groups across the country. And there are countless other youngsters you will meet in these pages who, through word and deed, demonstrate all the qualities we hope to instill in them until one day, to our great joy, we see that the seeds we planted have taken root and blossomed.

Of course, this is what we strive for in raising our children. We dedicate ourselves to teaching them how to do unto others, how to make a difference in the world, and behave in accordance with high moral and ethical standards. What parent hasn't wondered if, despite all his or her best efforts, the lessons would not be heeded, or some other negative influences would take hold? What parent hasn't breathed a sigh of relief when the terrible two, the poor student or rebellious teenager evolves from stage to stage and, finally, is an adult who has turned out just fine?

We've all had those anxious moments about our kids. And we've all had those glorious moments when they exceeded all our expectations and made us realize how precious—and wise—they can be.

Lessons from Our Children is about these moments, like the little boy who cheers up his despondent mother by telling her that she's "famous for her love." What a wonderful idea! You'll laugh and maybe shed a tear or two, when you read about these kids who inspire, encourage, love and teach us about ourselves and deepen the connection we have to each other and the world we live in.

I hope this book will be as enjoyable and enriching for you as it has been for me to put it all together.

The Hare(s) and the Tortoise

*Nothing can be done at once
hastily and prudently.*

—Publilius Syrus

My son, Mark, was four years old and this was his first Easter egg hunt. All the children were massed behind the starting line, a yellow ribbon, waiting to begin. When the ribbon was cut they all started running, except for Mark.

"Run," I hollered, "run, Mark, hurry." But he paid no attention to me. He was about one hundred feet behind the rest of the kids who were racing madly, to and fro, looking for the hidden eggs. "Oh, he won't get a thing," I said to my sister who was standing beside me. Her son, Danny, was one of the first of the children to go tearing off.

Then I saw Mark bend over and it looked like he had found an egg. Then once more he picked up something. Within five minutes, all the eggs had been claimed and the little ones were heading back to the starting line to show their "mommies" what they had found. Some had one egg, some had two and a few even had three.

Then I saw Mark heading my way. His bag was full! When we unpacked them, I counted twelve eggs! All the other children, in their haste, had run right past these eggs. But not Mark. He had just slowly moseyed along picking up the eggs the other children

1

had run past. Sometimes, I learned then, our kids do better when we don't push them too hard, if we can only learn to just let them go at their own pace.

Mary L. Crain

Doctorcito

Little doctor, full of hope,
A wonder with a stethoscope.
Checks the pulse of teddy bear,
Cat and dolly—has to care
About the health of one and all.
Peeks in ears and eyes and nose,
to be sure—as I suppose,
Like all good doctors should—
That every vital sign is good.
With all the loving care he'll give,
Everything is bound to live.
In spite of poverty or wealth,
Doctorcito brings them health.
For every symptom, every ill,
He prescribes a sugar pill.

I wrote this poem, "Doctorcito," for my son, Dr. Andrew Bennett of Arlington, Washington when he was six years old. He is now in a family practice with his pal from medical school days, Dr. James Fletcher. Andy was a little doctor almost from the start and the compassion he showed so early is now a guiding principle in his life.

Allen A. Bennett

3

Baubles and Bibles

*W*ho steals my purse steals trash;
'tis something, nothing . . .

—William Shakespeare

The brutal wind played an eerie tune as it pushed against the car door. I tried to exit, but it seemed to fight me, as if to keep me inside and safe from the cold. We were experiencing a bone-chilling week, and I looked forward to the warmth of my comfortable home. The sight of smoke rising from the chimney told me I would soon have my wish.

My twelve-year-old son and I were returning home after a trip to the golden arches. When we entered the side door leading to the kitchen, I immediately knew that something was wrong. Before I could turn on the light, I realized that the house was incredibly cold, and I could feel the same wind I thought I'd escaped. One flip of the light switch would confuse me even further. The window above the sink was broken, and hundreds of pieces of glass formed a mosaic on my kitchen floor. Still unsure of what had happened, I began moving farther into the room. I was startled when my son grabbed my arm and pulled me back outside. "Someone broke in and might still be inside," he said. We ran to a neighbor's and called the police.

When they arrived, we re-entered the house and immediately realized that, indeed, the burglars had been present when we ran

4

for help. The patio doors were now opened, and they were closed when we first discovered the crime. I shivered at the thought of what might have happened if we hadn't fled. As we moved from room to room assessing the damage and trying to determine what had been taken, it suddenly hit me. What if they had found my jewelry?

I ran to the bedroom. None of the drawers seemed to be disturbed, but I wasn't ready to allow myself to breathe a sigh of relief. As I slid my hand beneath the clothes and felt for the smooth velvet pouch, I felt only the roughness of the wood. The diamonds, the gold—all of it gone. I tried to ignore the tightness in my throat, but I knew the tears were inevitable.

Before the first tear formed, I was startled by the sound of my son's voice. "Mom, mom," he yelled, "come in here—hurry!" I ran to the den, new fear overtaking me. *What now,* I wondered. What other treasure did they take from me?

He was standing there, eyes glistening and a smile as wide as a seascape. Clutched in his hands was the family Bible. "They didn't take our Bible," he joyfully announced. For a few seconds, I was unable to speak. Thankfully, the disappointment in myself was overshadowed by the pride I felt in him. While I was feeling despondent over some shiny trinkets, he was celebrating what is truly valuable. A parent's duty is to teach his children well, but God allows those roles to be reversed when necessary. That was more than twenty years ago, and I remain extremely grateful for his timely intervention. There is nothing more priceless than a valuable lesson.

JoAnn Blake

Looking Inside

*Beware, as long as you live, of judging
people by appearances.*

—Jean de La Fontaine

Born to God-fearing Southern Baptist parents, I thought for
forty-one years that I looked at others on the inside and never
based my opinions on what people looked like on the outside.
My seventeen-year-old son, Max, taught me a lesson that I will
never forget.

I had been divorced from my son's father for six years and was
in love with a wonderful man, Dennis, whom I decided to marry.
We wanted our children to be a part of the small ceremony that
we planned with family and close friends. I asked my son to walk
with me down the aisle at the chapel to "give me away" as is the
custom in the South. However, although I knew that he loved his
hair long, I insisted that he cut it to be in the wedding. Being the
independent child that I had taught him to be, he refused.
Through tears, I told him that he could not be in the wedding.
Max's sister, Holly, and his stepsister, April, were both part of the
ceremony but I was firm in my belief that Max would just not
make a good impression and could not escort me down the aisle.
My son, not showing any anger toward me, came to the wedding
and expressed his happiness for Dennis and me.

After a short while, I realized that it should not have mattered if my son had short or long hair. I began to understand that I did not always see people inside: only on the surface. Max is now a man of twenty-five with long hair. He is a beautiful person. He is quiet and unassuming, yet is passionate in his beliefs.

Max has always shown great respect for his stepfather and me. He also treats women fairly and honestly, which I cannot say about some of the men I know who have short haircuts. I am sure that occasionally when others look at him and see only the long hair, his jeans and his baseball cap, they assume he's rough and tough. These people are making the same mistake I made, they do not look *inside*.

I went to the Baptist church all my life, but it took my son to teach me what's important about people. I deeply regret that I kept my son from participating in one of the most important events of my life. I realize now that I did this because I was raised in a community where people worried about what others might say about them if their children did not look "normal" according to the accepted community definition. Unfortunately, most people do not take the time to get to know other individuals if their outside appearance does not conform to the norms of the community.

I have apologized to my son and told him how sorry I am for what I did. I am very proud of Max—proud to be with him anytime, anyplace. To me, he is more acceptable and loving than most men will ever be.

Thank you, Max, for teaching me the importance of what is inside. I strive every day to remember this during my daily contact with others.

Pat M. Costner

"It's the Only Face I've Got"

*One loses so many laughs by
not laughing at oneself.*

—Sara Jeannette Duncan

My son John, always the strong-willed child, was a particular trial at the age of five when virtually everything he did brought me to the limits of my patience, and his father's, too.

On one particular day, John had been into one activity after another with nine out of ten of these activities being beyond the rules we expected to be maintained in our home. Finally, near the end of the day, John once again fractured a rule and was caught red-handed by his dad.

Very sternly, John was called "front and center" to receive the deserved tongue-lashing and the inevitable banishment to his room. John reluctantly obeyed the call to attention and slowly presented himself to his dad, who instantly proceeded to unleash his frustration at John's inability to remember and follow rules.

After about five minutes of this lecture, John began to think of other things, which was apparent to his father and me because his face was unable to hide his thoughts. Smiles formed on his lips, eyebrows raised and lowered, eyes batted; even his ears began to wiggle. This continued for several moments until his father admonished him sternly, "John, wipe that look off your face!"

John's face instantly went still and a look of concentration changed his features. Finally, very innocently and very seriously, he looked at his dad and said, "But Dad, it's the only face I've got!" The tongue-lashing came to an abrupt halt as his father burst into gales of laughter and put his arm around his son. In loving tones, he then reassured John that, indeed, he only had one face and we both loved it just as it was.

Janice Anthony

Anything Is Possible

Ask many of us who are disabled what we would like in life and you would be surprised how few would say, "Not to be disabled."
We accept our limitations.

—Itzhak Perlman

On October 18, 1991, my oldest daughter, Amanda, became suddenly paralyzed one morning. It was the worst day of my life, and undoubtedly hers. Amanda was five years old at the time, and had just started kindergarten and learned to ride a two-wheel bicycle.

After numerous tests, her doctors determined that a virus of unknown origin had caused this tragedy. Throughout her three-month hospital stay, Amanda relearned how to sit, among other things, and also learned how to propel a wheelchair.

I remember the thoughts I had at the time, dwelling most of all on the things she was not then able to do and reviewing constantly in my mind all the things she would miss in her young life. Amanda did not think this way. She tackled every obstacle that came her way and never once complained about anything. In fact, she has not once—to this day—ever complained about her paralysis or the fact that she has lost the use of her legs.

One day I asked her if she would like to have a hand cycle, a bicycle propelled with the hands rather than the feet, and she

10

replied, "Mom, you don't ride a bike so I don't really need to either."

Her determination and independence have grown incredibly over the past few years! She now has a hand cycle which she uses for exercise. She plays wheelchair basketball, golfs and she has participated in the Junior National Wheelchair Championships during the past two summers. This year, she returned from the competitions in Seattle with four silver and two bronze medals.

Amanda has taught me, and many others, that it is not how much you have, but what you do with what you *do* have—regardless of the obstacles. With Amanda as my example, I now believe that anything is possible.

Vickie McGrory

Ode to My Grandma

She is gentle, affectionate and my number one
friend in the world.
She takes care of me and takes me places.
She's taught me things I wouldn't have known,
and tells me how much I have grown.
She compliments me for almost everything.
She makes me feel bright and sunny inside.
She reads to me, helps me with homework
and always makes sure I'm having a wonderful time.
In return, I care for her when she is sick or hurt,
Even if it means millions of trips up and down the stairs.
You could refer to her as all of these things,
but I just call her, GRANDMA!

Jon Mikel Emery, sixth grade

The Real Meaning of Love

Love conquers all things;
let us too surrender to Love.

—Virgil

April 22, 1997. It is the day our lives changed forever. It is the day our beloved son, Uriah, tragically died at the age of sixteen. This is his story, a story that relates how he taught us the real meaning of love.

Uriah was born to us on September 22, 1980. He was a beautiful child with dark curly hair, sparkling eyes and a smile that lit up his whole face.

My husband Bruce and I were young and poor, but we had each other and Uriah. He was our only child and was the center of our world. We loved him dearly.

Uriah did the usual things any boy growing up did. He attended school, played hockey and went to Sunday school.

He always had a hug for me and his dad and would tell me, "I love you, more!" each night before he went to sleep.

All too soon came his teen years. He started high school. He dated, still played hockey and joined the J.V. football team. Once a week, Uriah attended confirmation class at church. We were happy and we still had hugs and "I love you, more!" each night.

Everything seemed to be going well until his sophomore year at high school. He started hanging around with a different group of kids. Uriah was popular and had many friends while growing up, so we didn't think much of this.

Soon after meeting his new friends, he began to stay out late and dressed differently. We suspected he was experimenting with drugs and alcohol.

One day I received a call from the high school secretary. She informed me that our son hadn't been attending school and had missed so many days that he would not pass his sophomore year.

I confronted him with the news. He refused to hear what I had to say and ran away.

My husband and I searched for him for several agonizing days. We finally found him at a local restaurant with a friend.

We were so happy to see him! I told him to come home and he did. We talked, cried and hugged. We told him we loved him no matter what he did. Uriah could not believe that we did not punish him for what he'd done. That evening he wrote this poem to us:

Uriah's Poem of Thanks and Love

Loving, caring, looking out for their little one
Teaching their flesh and blood to grow and understand
Not to make mistakes of what they made in the past
Watching their own from birth to death.

Helping their own through the harsh and easy times
Memories and experiences you'll never forget
Trying to say "Thanks" for so much they've done
There's no way to repay the "thanks" except to say, "I love
you."

You love them for so much they have done
The best you can do is listen and obey
Sometimes it's hard to do but try your best and be honest
And see what happens in the end.

But all I have to say is thanks.
You helped me and taught me.

The way I can repay is to say,
THANKS AND I LOVE YOU!

Uriah Sutinen
March 20, 1997

Things seemed to get better and we were trying to help him.
Uriah was in the process of getting transferred to another school
for the remainder of the year. He still went to hockey and still
liked confirmation class. He liked "Pastor Al."

At the last confirmation class Uriah attended, the topic was
about unconditional love. He asked Pastor Al, "Does anyone
really love like that?"

Then he began to see his old friends again and started to stay
out late. A few days later, our boy was dead. His friends
pressured him to get high from inhaling a can of air freshener. It's
called "huffing." He had an arrhythmia.

We were devastated. Our world had collapsed. Our only child
was gone.

Without the love of family and friends, I don't know how we
could have made it through the early days of our loss. Though he
may be gone from us physically, Uriah lives on through the love
we share with each other and with family and friends.

Uriah taught us how precious life and love is. He taught many
about love. Pastor Al talks to couples planning to marry about
Uriah and the love he once so deeply questioned.

We miss our son terribly. Not a day passes that he is not in our
thoughts. But I know Uriah is watching over us and his new
brother now. We were blessed with the birth of Isaiah fifteen
months later.

Melissa Sutinen

We Caretakers

A robin redbreast in a cage
Sets all heaven in a rage.

—William Blake

Come with me to lovely Escanaba, on the shores of Little Bay De Noc, on the upper arm of Lake Michigan. Escanaba has a quiet island park, where ducks, geese and seagulls make their home in the summer. My son Steve and I shared many summer Saturdays in that park.

Almost like yesterday, I recall telling Steve how important it is for everyone to keep our park clean and safe. Even if it is an extra struggle to lift the lid on a waste receptacle, the smallest candy wrapper should be tossed there.

Steve and I have fond memories of having observed the antics of all the creatures that make their homes in the park. Above all, we learned to appreciate the graceful seagulls who are the caretakers of the park. Not surprising then that young Steve would notice something was not right with one of the seagulls.

This gull had a long, matted string of monofilament line tightly wrapped around its webbed feet. Perhaps some fisherman had cut the twisted line from his fishing pole, and thoughtlessly discarded it on the rocks where the gulls search for food. But now, that line would mean slow death for one unfortunate feathered caretaker.

"That seagull is in bad trouble, Dad," Steve commented. "We have to do something to help it." But what could we do? Have you ever tried to catch a seagull?

Had I been alone, I would have walked away feeling sad for the gull. But seven-year-old Steve insisted that even the lowliest creature deserves our assistance if it is in trouble. How could I argue with this point of view?

We had some hamburger buns with us. Steve tried feeding the starving gull, tossing torn bits of the buns toward the bird, luring him closer and closer. Each time Steve got close, he lunged for the fishing line, only to have the gull fly for several yards out of his reach. I could read the disappointment in my young son's eyes as he said, "What are you going to do, Dad?" Maybe he knew there was no chance his plea would fall on deaf ears.

"Find me a branch as tall and straight as you are," I told Steve, "we'll catch him." He came back with a willow limb, about five feet long. We trimmed the limb with my pocketknife.

I placed the stick straight out in front of me, flat on the grass. Steve and I crouched low, and stayed very still. Now he threw out pieces of the bun just beyond the end of the stick. Cautiously, the trusting gull crash landed. Hop-flying, he inched ever closer as he gobbled up our bait. When his position was just right, I raised the stick slightly. Then, quickly and firmly, I placed it down on the grass, right between his tangled legs. He spread his wings. A swirl of air could be felt as he attempted to lift himself skyward. He was pinned to the ground.

Steve held the stick in place while I gently folded in the gull's wings. We laid him on his side. Steve used the pocketknife to cut away the entangled fishing line. A few minutes later, our feathered friend was free. As we backed away, he stood up, not knowing what to do next. Then he did a little appreciation dance. Maybe he was thanking us. Moments later he was airborne with the other gulls.

What a happy moment that experience was in our life! There were lessons for both of us. But my son taught me we are morally obligated to save even the lowliest living creature.

Edward P. Stephani

"You Can't Get Lost, Mom"

Ask, and it shall be given to you;
seek, and ye shall find . . .

—Matthew 7:7

Unlike me, my eldest son must have been born with both a sense of direction and one of purpose. While he was starting his last year at Shawnee State Community College, I had just enrolled. I would have had more confidence tagging along with my youngest son who was just entering first grade. At least I could recite the alphabet, solve simple math problems and was a fair speller.

However, here I was contending with young adults in a vast building, Massie Hall, which thoroughly intimidated me. "Don't worry, Mom, you can't get lost," my eldest said. He then proceeded to give me a guided tour, from the basement snack room to the ground floor, where the college library was housed in one huge room. From there, we went up and down stairways and through a maze of corridors. Afterwards, regardless of my eldest son's assurances, I frequently lost my way.

I felt safe with books, so under a work-study program being offered I applied for, and received, a job in the college library. My eldest continued helping me complete the forms to apply for grants, and, when he couldn't, the application forms were crusted with opaque correction fluid.

18

Several years after graduating, I landed a job as a braider machine operator for the world's largest producer of shoe lace. The building housing the production facility dwarfed Massie Hall and although my eldest son wasn't with me when I arrived on my first day of work I could, nevertheless, hear his quiet reassurance, "You won't get lost, Mom."

I had never operated anything more complicated than home appliances, and the challenge of operating the complex braiding machines is, for me, just that—a challenge. From the beginning there were many times when I arrived home in a worried state because of the complexity of my job. True to form, my eldest son would offer his words of encouragement: "You can do it, Mom."

Ten years have passed, and I'm still employed by the same company while, concurrently, attempting to get established in the intimidating world of writers. In this new endeavor, my greatest fear is that of becoming a wanderer, like Moses. Even in this, my eldest son still offers encouragement, still helps me to find direction.

It has slowly dawned on me that this is the son who, at age sixteen, checked borrowed trotlines from a borrowed rowboat. He oared through murky waters where alligators thrived with only a hand-held flashlight to see by. He didn't do this for the sport of it, but for our food.

When my life's cycle on this Earth nears completion, and I must journey on alone, I hope he is by my bedside, holding my hand, quietly reassuring me, "It's okay, Mom, you can't get lost."

Charlotte A. Thomas

The Daring Young Man

*To conquer without risk is to
triumph without glory.*

—Pierre Corneille

It has been so long since my children were training me to be
a mother I have nearly forgotten their childhood. My oldest child
will be fifty this year. I certainly remember learning patience
from them, but what mother has not learned that lesson from her
children? We may teach our children and inspire them, but by
manipulation they train us to be their slaves, until we finally
learn how to be parents.

Watching my grandchildren grow up reminds me of lessons I
learned from my children. When I see my four-year-old grand-
daughter throw a temper tantrum, I laugh. Her father held the
record for holding his breath in a fit of temper until she came
along. His temper eventually turned into rebellion as a teenage
child of the seventies. I spent many sleepless nights wondering
where he was during those years. He dropped out of college and
left home to live the hippie life of those other flower children his
age. I despaired of his ever getting an education and having a
family.

Well, I was wrong. The drive that sent him into temper tantrums
and rebellion has served him well, once he learned to control it to
his advantage. During his years of rebellion, he literally had to

take a job digging ditches in order to support himself since we would no longer give him money nor shelter. I am sure I suffered more than he. For he did so well digging ditches, the foreman of the construction company where he worked promoted him to driving the forklift. He soon learned to read blueprints as required by his job and gained confidence in his abilities.

So the prodigal returned home and asked our help in returning to college to study architecture. He completed his education and is now vice president and partner in his architectural firm.

I learned two lessons from this child. First, never give up on your children *for it's not where they start, but where they finish.* And secondly, unbridled emotions can be harnessed and work for good for those who are ready to take control of their lives.

My other child has taught me that patience and self-control and a kindness of heart will see you through many difficult times. She has proven that in her life, which has not always been easy. She is now a speech therapist dealing with children who have speech problems. How lucky they are to have this kind and gentle teacher! In a facetious moment, I remarked that she is so kind and adaptable that she could live on an island with a gorilla and be happy. She was not amused.

But the lesson I have learned in my old age that has brought me the most joy I learned from my grandson. He is sixteen now, but last year, before he could obtain his driver's license, he had to be accompanied by an adult when he drove. For a few brief months, he loved being with me as long as he was driving my new car that had lots of features he liked. Of course, speed is the greatest delight of the teenager, and I grew a few more gray hairs as we sped around corners and screeched to a halt at stop lights.

One day, when I had had just about all the excitement I could stand, I yelled at him to slow down. He did so reluctantly. We were on the way back to his house and I suggested we take the route less traveled, the one that had less traffic. I said to him, "Will, this route is the safest way home."

In response, he called me by the name he gave me as a child. "Baba," he said, "you'll never have any fun if you always do the safest thing. *Sometimes, you just have to be daring.*"

How true those words are, particularly for the senior citizen I am and the conservative lifestyle I have fallen into. Since that day, I have learned to take the more dangerous route sometimes, in order to prove to myself that I can still do it. I make decisions now that to me seem daring, but really aren't. They just make me feel younger and freer, even in the smallest of everyday decisions.

For example, as I stood at the bread counter at the grocery store the other day, agonizing over whether to buy the whole-grain bread without much fat (the safe choice) or the cinnamon nut swirl (the one I really like), I remembered Will's words. Unhesitatingly, I tossed the cinnamon nut swirl into my cart. This may not be my grandson's idea of daring—but it sure felt good!

Betsy Bee

Life Is Precious

*T*he greatest reverence is due the young.

—Decimus Junius Juvenal

Some people want to be different; some, on the other hand, *just want to be like everyone else*. My son was one of the latter.

So many people take life for granted. They complain, they blame, they make no effort to establish a positive outlook on life. Then there are the children who are born "different." Perhaps they are missing a limb. Perhaps their heart wasn't fully formed. Perhaps they have no control over their body or its functions. Or perhaps it is because of a syndrome or disorder. Whatever the reason, these are the children I am writing about.

They want to play. They want to read. They want to run. They want to be around other children—away from the doctors, the therapists, the hospitals, the operations. Away from the stares and the name calling. *They want to be accepted.*

It is from these children that we all can learn. I did.

Before he was two years old, my son had nine operations. Each operation took us to a specialty children's hospital. Then we went home—something that many of the children we met don't often get to do.

Yet it is these children, our most frail, our most priceless resource—our future—who *long* for tomorrow. They are fighters. They are fighters from the day they are born. They are fighters

23

until the day they die, and some of them do so much too early. But, until that dreadful day, they give, much more than many of us notice and much greater than most of us realize.

They push, they strive, they work. Harder than you. More than I. *They live.* They live their life, they live to the fullest. Just look into the eyes of a child struggling to be "just like everyone else" and you will see the message loud and clear: *Life is precious.*

Terri-Gayl Hoshell

Zack and the Ducks

The first law of ecology is that everything is related to everything else.

—Barry Commoner

The sun set a splendid azure vermilion. Evening stars appeared eastward, as fish strikes radiated the lake's surface. Insects dodged hungry bass in flitting arches while my son, Zachary, skipped stones across the water's surface.

Zack has blessed me as a parent and a human being.

He is a happy fellow, social, energetic, a bit of a jailhouse lawyer. He loves baseball, cartoons, books and just cast aside his training wheels.

Like his Daddy, he questions everything. (I hope his answers come more easily.)

Here is a portrait of Zachary at the lake:

> Dusk falls as do the breezes,
> The lake calms.
> A pair of ducks with young,
> visit our shoreline.
> Zack dashes from the house,
> hot dog rolls banging his knee,
> in time with sprinter's strides.
> His time.

He bounds to the dock,
fearless of swooping bats,
all quacks and giggles.
Morsels splash, bag empties,
and gorged, departing,
the family flaps thanks,
as Zack sweetly says,
"Go on ducks, go on duckies,
I'll see you another time.
Go home and don't get hurt.
It was so fun. (tears)
I had the best time of my life."
And Daddy holds him,
reassuring his boydom,
knowing ducklings, as promised,
will fly.

If we adults nurtured fellow beings as Zack did his guests; if we caressed each day as the best of our lives, and had fun without pretense, we'd not have time to argue differences, or ponder our neighbors' shortcomings.

Zachary feeding the ducks was an awakening for us both. He experienced kindness, and I was reborn.

Zachary recalls a flower's bloom, an easy smile and the rarity of rainbows.

I love him, ideally.

Rich Fiegelman

Reflection

Children make you want to start life over.

—Muhammad Ali

With grandchildren, you can finally relax and have fun, because you're not so busy raising them." Invariably, I hear this same comment from people I encounter in my job. Their eyes shine with a special light, but it goes much further than the wonderment of creation.

Love for a grandchild is like no other love. I discovered that truth when my granddaughter, Brooke, was born and have experienced it twice more since then with the birth of my grandsons, Jacob and Cy.

When I look at my grandchildren, I see flashes of days gone by, little nuances of the children my daughters once were. As a single mother, bringing up two kids, I was as busy as could be, owning a business and continually educating myself in my profession, plus trying to spend time with my children and have a social life besides. The years went by in a flurry.

Time is still spinning by, evidenced by the fact that, seemingly overnight, Brooke is two-and-a-half years old. Recently, she and her six-month-old brother came for a visit.

The first order of the day was to tape the door locks. There would be no danger of privacy during the next two weeks or of a two-and-a-half year old being locked in a room by herself.

27

Talk about busy. Brooke gives a whole new meaning to the word. Between her chasing my cat, grinding Cheerios into my carpet, "helping" take care of baby brother, playing on the beach, pitching a fit when leaving the beach, "reading" books, doing puzzles, bathtime, mealtime . . . Whew! I was numb by the time they left.

Afterward, I sat down on the sofa and surveyed the wreckage of my apartment. On the mirrored wall in my living room, I noticed two little handprints side by side. I could see Brooke jumping on the sofa cushions, her blond curls bouncing up and down as she watched herself in the mirror.

"You might fall," I remember saying gently.

Brooke had stood for a second, hands pressed against the glass, and looked at me, blue eyes dancing mischievously.

In the old days, I would have yelled at my children, "Don't jump on the couch and don't put your hands on the mirror."

Instead, I grabbed Brooke's hand and held on. She giggled and started jumping again, wilder than ever in the security of my grasp.

The memory of her antics lit up my face as I glanced in the mirror. Suddenly I missed all my offspring. I got up and busied myself with the cleanup of my apartment. First, I attacked the smudged glass on the doors to the balcony. It looked as if fifty toddlers had been there instead of just one. Oatmeal on the walls and the sticky glue left on the doors by the masking tape were a real pain to get off. Finally, when all the Cheerios were vacuumed up, I sat down again.

The place was spic-and-span, and empty. The evening sun shone all along my sparkling mirrored wall except in one spot where two tiny handprints remained, reminding me of second chances, and more special than all the perfect sunsets I will ever see.

Patricia K. Deaton

Thoughts of an Old Grandmother

*Children are made of eyes and ears,
and nothing,
however minute, escapes their
microscopic observation.*

—Frances Anne Kemble

The moon was full last night, my Trisha. When I saw it, I thought of you. You make us aware of the moon's presence, even in the daytime, as you point it out to us.

We think of you often since you returned home. Life with you is like an adventure. You help us see things we never noticed before; like the butterfly whose wings are moved by the wind. You do not know that the butterfly is already dead, so you place it softly on the grass. "I don't want to hurt him," you whisper in my ear.

When I hear the trains, it reminds me of your excitement while standing on the bridge, with the train rushing beneath us. When I see the river, I am reminded of your joy at the glimpse of a boat skipping along on the water. You help us become aware of the sound of tree frogs in the evening, and of the chirping bird calls when the night is dark and still.

You are so quick to use the magic words: *I love you, thank you, you're welcome, please* and *I'm sorry,* at the times when they are needed most.

We love to hear you call, "Sweet dreams," and "Good night God" as we prepare for bed at night. You remind us to share our pillow with you, by your words, "Granny, you have to share you know."

When we hear the fire siren, we remember your concerned remark, "Somebody needs help!" You are such a caring person. You add spice to our life. Don't allow the years to wipe away your wonder in life. Come back to visit us again, Trisha, because life can be pretty dull for Papaw and me without our little four-year-old around.

Garnet (Jackson) Piatt

An Open Letter to Jackie

*Courage is rightly esteemed the
first of human qualities
because it is the quality which
guarantees all others.*

—Winston Churchill

Your daddy didn't know, Jackie. He didn't know that when he threw the ignited can of gasoline away from himself that you were standing behind him and your little six-year-old body would be the direct target of that inferno of hell.

I was a nineteen-year-old student nurse that Saturday morning in the summer of 1954, doing my assigned tour of duty in the emergency room. When you and your daddy were brought in, your daddy was conscious—not burned nearly as badly as you.

You lay there on the stretcher with the entire upper part of your small body—face, ears, neck, eyes, chest and arms—seared. Your body's protective cover seared. You moaned softly and your entire body shivered in the worst pain imaginable to mankind. The doctor immediately ordered morphine for you but I don't think it helped.

Jackie, I prayed silently, as I worked with the quickly assembled team of doctors and nurses, that God had blessed you with unconsciousness. And I have prayed that same prayer for you many times in the years since.

31

Somehow, you lived. I next saw you when I was assigned my tour of duty in surgery. Your body was ready for debridement—the removal of scar tissue under the most sterile conditions. But, unfortunately, you stopped breathing under anesthesia and the twice-a-week debridements had to be done with you wide awake, with only a shot of pain medication to help you endure the agony.

At first, you begged not to have the debridements done but you soon realized the procedure was inevitable and you started to pray. And you didn't pray just for yourself. You prayed for others. Once you prayed for "My little sister who had the mumps and I'm afraid they're going to fall on her."

This prayer nearly evoked a smile from the three of us—the surgeon, the operating room nurse and me—who were working rapidly with sterile efficiency to make your time of agony as short as possible. But we couldn't afford to smile and we only spoke the words necessary to get each debridement over with. You see, Jackie, a smile or a word might have burst the dam of tears each of us had built in our chest and our eyes would have flooded with the tears of sympathy we felt for you. So we had to keep our eyes dry. For your sake, we could not afford the luxury of tears.

But you lived, Jackie, and you loved us and we loved you and you prayed, and you prayed, and you prayed and your sweet and loving nature permeated the soul of each of us.

After a few months of healing you were flown to a burn center in Texas for grafts and the building of eyelids and nose and ears. When I visited with you just before that trip, I did not see scar tissue and eyes without lids and missing ears. I saw only beauty. The beauty that only suffering, endurance and patience can produce. I could finally put my arms around you very gently and kiss you and run to find a private place where I could let the dam in my chest burst, as I finally shed the myriad of tears that had accumulated there for you.

I next saw you when you were nearly twenty and I was a wife and mother. We passed in the hospital corridor and I recognized your beautiful face. A face sculpted by pain and prayer, patience and perseverance. My effusive words of joy and my hugs didn't seem to embarrass you. You were now a man. A man of high moral character and gentle countenance, with a sweet, sincere smile. A happy young man.

I haven't seen you since, although I would love to. I did hear that you had become a respiratory therapist, had married a pretty girl who worked in the hospital pharmacy and had moved to Virginia.

I always think of you when I read Romans 5:3-5, ". . . rejoice in suffering, because we know that suffering produces persever- ance; perseverance, character; and character, hope. And hope does not disappoint us . . ."

Thank you, Jackie, for teaching me when we were both so young the truth and dependability of this biblical lesson. God bless you, Jackie, wherever you are. I love you.

Mary B. Ledford

A Child's Pain Is
Parent's Pain

*Nobody has ever measured, even poets,
how much a heart can hold.*

—Zelda Fitzgerald

When my wife and I were getting ready to have our first child, all the parents we knew—including our own—took the liberty of telling us what it would be like to have kids.

They told us being parents was going to be a big responsibility, but that it also would be rewarding, fulfilling, even fun. And they were right.

They also said having children would tax our nerves, try our patience and steal our freedom. They told us it would be expensive, but worth every penny. They said we would have to make sacrifices, but we would receive much more in return. And they were right about all that, too.

With all the advice we got, however, nobody told us how much it was going to hurt. And nobody told us it was going to keep hurting, even when you are fortunate enough to have relatively healthy, happy and successful kids, as we do. So for the benefit of you fledgling parents, I'm going to lay it out for you.

It starts in infancy, usually with teething. They are in pain and there isn't much you can do but hold them, rock them and share their pain. It doesn't occur to you then that you will be sharing their pain for the rest of your life. But you will.

Every time they scrape a knee or bruise an elbow, you will feel it, probably more than they do. Every time they come home crying because some jerk has made fun of them or called them a name, your pain will be exceeded only by your rage.

At times, your parental responsibilities will force you to be a party to their pain. Even though you know the shot they're getting from the doctor is going to help them, you feel as if you're betraying them when you carry them, crying and writhing, into the examining room or the dentist's office.

When my daughter was a tot, she cut herself deeply on a broken soda bottle. We took her to the emergency room for stitches. The doctor requested that either my wife or I help keep Laura as calm as possible. Tina volunteered me.

So I found myself holding her arm down while the doctor put stitches in her hand. And the entire time, she sobbed, "Daddy, make them stop! Please, Daddy, it hurts! Make them stop!" It broke my heart.

Fortunately, it was over quickly. And that was the last time I had to deal with such a situation. But it was not the last time I would hurt for one of them. As the years flew by, they graduated from scraped knees to broken hearts.

And when that happens, you long for the days when they could be healed with a few stitches or a Band-Aid. Because our two younger kids were active in band, these hurts usually took the form of a disappointing audition for some honors band or another. If it wasn't that they didn't make it, it was that they didn't make first or second chair.

And just when you think they are mature enough to handle life's little valleys, along come broken romances. Although you know they will survive, and find another boyfriend or girlfriend, you can't tell them that because they won't believe it anymore than you would have when you were their age.

Your helplessness, in fact, makes you feel their sorrow more than if it was your own heart that was broken. After all, you've spent their whole life making things better for them. So, once again, all you can do is hold them, rock them and share their pain.

And the strangest thing of all is that you wouldn't have it any other way.

Ray Recchi
columnist, Sun-Sentinel, *Fort Lauderdale, Florida*

Laughter's Magic

Children aren't happy with nothing to ignore,
And that's what parents were created for.

—Ogden Nash

Loud static from the alarm launched me into the day, waking me from one of those drowning dreams. You know, the kind when you can't scream and everyone who you thought loved you is standing around watching as you descend. It was 5:30 A.M. A gerbil about to get on board her wheel, I rolled out of bed and into the shower. By the time I get to Annie and Abbey's room to wake them up for school, my journey on the wheel is in full gear. The girls try desperately to open their eyes, murmuring questions like, "Mom, why do you do this to us?"

It's just me, my two daughters—Abbey, nine and Annie, eleven—and my female golden retriever. I run my business, my household and my life with little reprieve. I often find my mind in one place and my body in another. While I had my mother's full attention growing up, my girls have to share my energy with everything else going on in our lives. This nineties preoccupation with keeping things going (life on the wheel), makes one forget how to stop and laugh at the stupid things.

It was a typical day on the wheel; my deadlines were unreasonable, the pressure was mounting, I had writer's block and the kids were home (where I work) in the afternoon. They have an unspoken respect for Mom's work: Keep quiet as possible and interrupt her as little as possible.

But that day—whether the planets were out of alignment or the moon full—the kids were bouncing off the walls. The girls were supposed to be doing their homework in the room next to my office, but they kept singing the song from the television show, *Candid Camera*. They sang in harmony, repeating the familiar tune over and over.

It sounded good, but at the time all I could think about was my work. "Stop singing and do your homework!" I yelled. "Okay, Mom," Annie said. Still humming, the younger daughter enticed my older daughter to chime in. Before I knew it, we had another full-blown jam session.

"You must do your homework!" I barked. I could feel my body temperature rising to unnatural degrees. "School is important. Do you want to lose your playtime? You will, you know. I'm serious." I separated them and sent them to their respective rooms. The walls between them did nothing to stop the merriment. Before I knew it, they were back at it, although in their separate rooms. My threats had done nothing to put a lid on their high spirits.

I was livid. By then, I had convinced myself that we'd have to relinquish the house due to the income I was losing wasting time disciplining them. I pulled one of those scary parent things when you make loud noises getting up as a warning that you're coming and ready to do serious battle. With bulging neck veins and a face as red as a beet, I flung open Abbey's door with every intention of exploding with anger. Abbey looked up at me, all innocence, and said, "I can't help it, Mom, I just want to have fun." Her voice was sweet and pleading.

I was powerless to resist that face, and, as Annie came tentatively into the room, I started laughing. We laughed a hearty laugh—the uncontrollable kind—and I reached down to hug them close to me. My mind became clear. We weren't going to lose the house. The kids just wanted to have fun. It was a good day, and I realized I was blessed with two adorable, happy children.

Now, we make it a point to be stupid at least once a week.

Don't get me wrong, I still lose my mind and my patience. But thanks to Annie and Abbey, I haven't lost sight of what's really important. I know how to get off that wheel.

Lisette Hilton

Growing People

*Children are our most valuable
natural resource.*

—Herbert C. Hoover

During my first spring at Lost Valley, I was working in the garden with two interns when my inquisitive three-year-old daughter came along. Having just finished prepping a bed, we began to sow while engaged in discussion about something lofty and ponderous. I acknowledged Ariel's presence by stroking her head full of curls.

She stood at my side for a few minutes looking pensive before she inquired, "Hey, Mama, why you are planting seeds?"

In a teaching/work mode, I blurted in reply, "Ariel, we're planting seeds because it's time to sow our spring crops. We've just finished sheet mulching this bed and we're planting seeds into the sifted compost layer on top."

"But why, Mama?" asked Ariel.

"Well, because we want to grow our own food. We want to be more self-reliant . . ."

Ariel interrupted, now rather frustrated, "But why you are planting seeds, Mama?"

"Ariel, we're planting mountain spinach, calendula, borage and . . ."

"But why?" Ariel pleaded.

"But why *what*, Ariel?" I exclaimed.

Ariel persisted, "Why you are planting seeds?"

This exchange continued a few more times, with me searching seriously for a suitable answer, while trying to maintain my composure. Finally, throwing my arms into the air, I said, "Ariel, we're planting seeds because we like to plant seeds!"

"Oh!" exclaimed Ariel with great relief, and she ran off.

One morning the next spring, I was transplanting brassicas. My plan was to finish out four flats before moving on to the rest of the ten things I had on my list and intended to finish that day. Along came Ariel.

"Can I help?" she asked.

"Sure," I responded, trying to hide my slight reluctance, knowing that help from a four-year-old isn't always conducive to productivity. Nonetheless, Ariel gleefully picked up a trowel and plunged it wholeheartedly into the soil. I showed her how to place a kale plant firmly into the ground, so that it stood up straight, and then water it in. She proceeded to attempt transplanting as I tried to keep my gasps and instructions to a minimum.

After a few minutes, she sat contentedly singing to and petting the "babies" she'd planted. Then, looking up at me, she noted my pace and reprimanded me for my haste. "Mom, be gentle with the babies, you have to sing to each one and touch them like this," she demonstrated. I felt my resistance and agitation rise. Sighing, I envisioned things on my list being transferred to the next day—surrender is sweet, but painful.

"You're right, Ariel," and I joined her impromptu song, letting her lead. "And thesu-un brings you-u light, a-a—and ke-eps you warm, fairies dancing all a-a-round . . .," we sang off-key in operatic style. Pretty soon we were alternating making up each line; then it became a rhyming game and the verses got more and more absurd until we were both making up nonsense and laughing hysterically.

All of a sudden, Ariel stood up, ran over and jumped on my back, knocking me over from a squatting position, and we both tumbled into the path, laughing. Ariel flung her arms around me, kissed my cheek and proclaimed, "I love you, Mommy!" and promptly got up and ran off to find her buddy, Matthew.

I went back to planting, singing to each "baby" kale, collard and broccoli as I worked. The words of Wendell Berry came to mind, "We're not growing food, we're growing people."

Julianne Tilt

Just in Time

*Ah, that such sweet things should be fleet,
Such fleet things sweet.*

—Algernon Charles Swinburne

My definition of success has undergone a complete transformation since my son was born. I used to think success was, in large part, based on whether I had met my schedule for the day. Placing great emphasis on meeting deadlines, I raced through each day, happy only if I was able to check off every item on my "things to do" list that traveled with me everywhere. If I didn't see a row of checkmarks by the day's end, in my eyes the day was a failure. I'd agonize about adding the items to the ensuing day's list and go to bed with an uneasy feeling, resolving to get an early start in the morning to attain every goal I had planned for myself.

My son has other plans and, thankfully, he's shared them with me. In his big brown eyes and beaming smile, he's asking me, "What's the rush, Mom?" It took me awhile to even ponder that question. In fact, in the first few months after he was born, I would feel myself becoming more anxious by the minute when his afternoon feedings took longer than I had anticipated. I had, generously, I assumed, allotted twenty minutes and he wasn't even halfway finished in thirty! "This is going to throw a wrench in the rest of my day. I've got to get him on a better schedule," I'd say to myself as the ticking of the clock taunted me. But, I found, one of the most wonderful things about babies is they get you off your schedule. For me, it couldn't have come at a better time.

Why does everything have to get done today, anyway? My son challenges me to ask myself that question whenever he takes his time eating or insists that we play a little longer. Before he was born, I was a prisoner to my schedule. I assumed everything had to get done at the assigned time. But I've learned, thanks to Griffin, that it doesn't. One of the most extraordinary lessons he's taught me is to slow down and appreciate life for what it's really about: living. He's shown me that schedules and "to do" lists, while helpful, aren't to be followed to the letter—that they're just not that important in the big scheme of things. This tiny human being, who's barely two feet tall, has skillfully rearranged my priorities, helping me to see things for what they really are.

And it goes well beyond merely spending time with him. I've learned to behold each moment, to see things I never would have noticed before. There's a lake near our house surrounded by a path used by everyone from joggers to moms strolling their little ones. My husband and I walked our dog (at lightning speed, of course) around the lake at least a hundred times before Griffin was born, and yet never once did I take the time to notice that there's a beautiful family of swans living among the bounty of ducks and geese. And never did I notice that at a certain time of the day, sunlight reflecting off the ripples of the water looks like a sea of glittering diamonds. Maybe I never would have noticed these things. But thanks to my son, I've stopped to sit down— literally—and enjoy these simple, yet special, gifts.

Thanks to him, I have changed my definition of success. Success is making him smile and laugh. It's being blessed with the ability to be a work-at-home mom and to be there to watch him make new discoveries. It's singing to him and feeling him nuzzle up to my chest as he drifts off to sleep in my arms. It's providing him with a stable environment sustained by a strong marriage. It's the freedom I've gained from the realization that my purpose in life is not to make sure the house is spotless each and every day or to attempt to be "perfect" in everything I do, or to keep to a schedule that dictates every facet of my life.

Recently, Griffin gave me a big scare. He was gagging to the point where his face turned bright red and I had to call 911. I was terrified. What could be happening? He couldn't have anything stuck in his throat, I thought, since my husband and I are so careful not to leave small objects lying around. By the time the paramedics arrived, he seemed fine—the gagging had pretty much subsided and he was alert and happy. (I, on the other hand, was so upset I could barely speak.) The paramedics told me his airway was clear, but that I should take him to his pediatrician just to be safe.

Minutes after they left, the gagging started up again. As we pulled into the parking lot at his doctor's office, it was nonstop and far worse than it had been at home. I rushed him into the office in a frenzy and blurted out the situation to the first person I saw. But before we could get him into an examination room, he let out a big cough and a small piece of a candy wrapper flew out of his mouth. How he got hold of it, I still don't know.

Although the doctor proclaimed him to be "fine" after a thorough examination, I was far from fine. All I could think about was what *could* have happened. What if the wrapper had become lodged in his throat? What if he had gotten hold of something bigger that he couldn't cough up? What if???

I couldn't stop shaking and couldn't control the thoughts racing through my mind. In one instant, my life could have changed forever. I don't know what I would do if anything ever happened to him.

The incident made me realize that the time I have with Griffin is a precious gift that I have to take advantage of every day. After all, he's not *always* going to love snuggling and spending all of his time with me. He's not *always* going to have a soft, fuzzy head I can rub my cheek against or chubby little fingers that can barely wrap around my thumb. He won't *always* light up the moment he sees me or giggle whenever I tickle the sides of his belly. He won't *always* look at everything around him with wonder and amazement. He won't *always* depend on me to take care of him.

I once thought the best part of being a parent came when the days of diapers, bottles and highchairs were long gone. Now I get teary-eyed with the thought of him learning how to walk and the day he won't be content to sit in my lap and drift off to sleep as we listen to our favorite lullaby tape. I wish I could bottle up this time and make it last forever. Since I can't, I don't intend to waste one moment of it. I'm not about to let one of the most precious seasons of my life pass me by.

Lisa M. Horan

Curiosity

This child, learning about her world,
Asks "Why?" a thousand times.
I think about her questions,
Sort through the pockets of my mind,
Feel around for the right words, the best words,
For my answer.
She listens to me, adding to her inventory of answers.

And I wonder,
When was the last time I asked "Why"?
No matter how old we are,
We must, like the child,
Ask questions,
Seek information,
Learn new things,
Restock the pockets of our minds.

Virginea Dunn Cooper

Dedicated to Brittany Virginea Dunn, age eleven.

Now That's Funny

*Laughter is the shortest distance
between two people.*

—Victor Borge

I'll never forget the day I got the first real, genuine laugh out of my son. I don't remember anything in my life feeling that good. It was just so intoxicating and heartwarming that I'd like to have that laugh bottled and put into an I.V. that drips into me endlessly.

When he hadn't laughed for the first few months, I just decided I wasn't funny. It must be my fault; I'm trying to make him laugh, he's not laughing, it's me. It never dawned on me that he just wasn't ready.

For the first few months, you get nothing. Then you get smiles. Actually, not "smiles" per se, but little cheek spasms that *look* like smiles and in fact are him wincing as a pocket of gas rockets through his torso. Sometimes it's not even that; they're just arbitrary, uncontrolled twitches that, when you're hoping for a smile, you decide are "close enough."

Then, after a while, you start to get actual smiles, and you learn the difference. You get a real smile and you can't believe your good fortune. I'm not sure why it's such a big deal. I'd hate to think I'm really that desperate for approval. What it is, I've decided, is the first sign that you're actually getting through; that this is not just two interplanetary beings staring at each other. With that smile, you know that *they* know you're out there.

But it becomes addictive. In no time, that smile is no longer enough. You need more. You need—the Laugh. And you'll do anything to get it. You make faces, funny noises. You animate dolls and produce entire one-act plays around them. You talk high, you talk low. You mock the child's mother in her presence, hoping to parlay one laugh into two. There is nothing you won't try.

Ironically, the first laugh I got came from doing something that I had been doing for months: a simple raspberry on the belly. This has different names in different families: Slurpies, Bloweys, Churtles, Normans—all basically an intense compression of air from the lips-of-an-adult against the stomach-of-a-child, resulting in the amusingly loud, disruptive, faux-fart effect.

At first, I didn't know for sure I was getting the laugh. I was holding the kid up in the air, showing off for company, my face implanted deep into his rib cage to make sure the raspberry was registering. The noise was so loud and forceful that to my ears, it was drowning out the laugh. Everyone else in the room had a clear view and was having a ball. I would hear them laugh in response to his laugh, pull my head up to see, but by the time I got there, the laugh was over. It was a little unfair, actually, seeing as how I was the one doing all the work. I would "raspberry" faster and shorter, trying to get back up in time to catch the laugh. But I kept missing it. Sort of like standing up to get a good look at your lap: It's gone before you get there.

But then it happened—the monumental and glorious breakthrough. I coaxed from my son a sustained laugh, saw it and heard it with my own eyes and ears, and—I just wanted to dive in and spend my entire lifetime in the fluffy cloud of that moment.

And I couldn't help wondering why this wasn't funny to him the first few thousand times I did it. Why now? Why wasn't it amusing January through May? I decided that in the beginning, it doesn't matter how amusing anything is; if you're three days old, you're just not in the mood to laugh. The machinery is there. The wiring that will let you laugh is installed at birth, but it's sort of like cable; someone has to turn it on. It needs to be initialized and activated and then, hopefully, it should keep working forever.

Of course some people grow up and *stop* laughing, and it's entirely possible that if you lift up their shirts and give them a raspberry, they'll start laughing, too. However, I don't know these people, and I don't really feel it's my place to blow on their bellies.

Paul Reiser

Personality

My seven-year-old daughter and I were sitting on the sofa one evening talking about our new golden retriever puppy, Jake. I remarked to her that I thought the dog had a very sweet personality.

Adrianna immediately piped up, "He's not a person so he can't have a personality. He has a doganality."

Intrigued by her train of thought, I asked her about our cat, Sniff. "What about Sniff? Does he have a personality?"

"No," she replied, "he has a catanality."

Marjorie L. Lundgren

Charlie

*This is my beloved Son, in whom
I am well pleased.*

—Matthew 3:17

I am back in the cool amber shadows of the Chiricahua Mountains in southern Arizona after having spent three days and two nights in Tucson, taking him back and forth to specialists for more tests. I am taking apart an old John Deere tractor. I have just baled five acres of alfalfa with two of my farm hands—Hector and Jesus. I am afraid to stop working, or to go inside and settle down with Wilhelmina for the evening. I am afraid to go to sleep. I am afraid of the telephone ringing and the doctors in Tucson saying his cancer's back. I am afraid of the cells in my son's brain exploding or bubbling up right now as he hands me a hammer and screwdriver.

He smiles broadly, pats me on the shoulder, and then seeks my right hand to shake. "You're smiling at me so nicely, Dad. I hope our meal tonight is so delicious." He says those types of things now, all the time, without retention, as if each time he makes the same statement it's the first time. But we have heard the same routine over and over and over since he got several islands of his brain back. My son has little ability to initiate activities on his own. I have to remind him of his hygienic duties. He can't tell the difference between spaghetti and mashed potatoes, or an orange slice from an apple, because he can't recall and associate those words. Almost all words and associations have vanished from my son's brain.

For all intents and purposes, my son is brain-injured, as if he had been slammed head first into a wall going fifty miles an hour on a motorcycle. No scars on the outside, except for a missing testicle where the germ cancer cell permeated its pathogen into him.

My son is big and healthy—five years cancer-free. He is a ward of his parents, and he has little to do with his two sons because his wife just went and packed up one day and they vanished into thin air. There is a divorce coming down the pike—she's been filing papers from Las Vegas, New Mexico. Her pain is understandable, because when the doctors were hooking him up to bags of caustic concoctions, and when his brain cells danced and heaved and jumbled and soared for the Apache mountains of his father and grandfather's home, he denied that six-year marriage, denied the four-year-old son, denied the fetus forming inside her as his.

The sun is low in the sky, and there is snow on the peaks of the Dragoon Mountains. It is November, the month of my son's birth forty-one years ago. I hear coyotes in an arroyo some two or three miles away. There are Cooper's hawks and brown eagles in the sky. My son smiles each morning at the half acre of pumpkins in front, and he pats the heads of several squash, wishing them a good day.

On our two hundred acres, we have a stream and a ponding area where I like to take my son in his shrinking state of recall. We have an apple orchard. Charlie likes going down there and picking apples. Either Hector or his mother usually accompany him because there's no telling where he'd wander off to.

My son smiles, and his round, pink-skinned head is like a bald beacon in the evening. He looks tired around the eyes, as if a tortoise's wrinkled skin just crept up there overnight. He's paunchy, and his muscles are reluctant to bend. He gets cold easily, and he has to be barked at to assist him to follow through on a simple job like sweeping the front porch or hanging up laundry. He looks perfectly healthy, except he's a bit exaggeratedly stiff. But, anyone new to his company figures out that something isn't just right with him. The way he looks at people directly in the eyes.

The overacting when it comes to weather and food and smiles. He's always grabbing people's hands for a shake. There's no mistaking that he is different.

But he always smiles, and if one looks closely, his pupils sort of pulsate and vibrate when he looks at something deep in his depth of vision. This is because of all the chemo eating away at his brain and the roaring microbes which suffocated large areas of his brain. He has virtually no short-term immediate memory, and his long-term memory is mostly rehearsed as he goes on and on about birth dates and weddings and his favorite vacation spots and his grade point averages all the way back to elementary school. He has portions of his memory tucked away in a black leather fanny pack which his mother gave to him three years ago for his thirty-ninth birthday.

He spends most of his time with me in the fields, or with his mother cleaning up the house. But he is virtually useless as a worker. He has to be motivated and supervised. I've caught him wandering away, sneaking a conversation with someone riding his horse down the road. Or worse, with some tourist asking directions to the winery, or some camper looking for directions to the national park entrance.

My son is a prisoner in his world of no recall. He knows no boundaries, no limits of social courtesy, no beneficial or dangerous signals from the natural world I helped raise him in. I have to lead him around my farm, and my wife leads him through the same tasks of clearing off our supper table and putting his folded clothes away.

"Dad, when will I be done? What's your favorite food, Dad? Mine is steak, then, number two, cheesed hamburger, and, then, well, third is some kind of fish meal. Are we almost finished, Dad? Do you know what we're having for supper?"

The night my son lost his memory, he was two months into his chemotherapy. It was two nights after Christmas. We were up from Saint David and stayed in a trailer park near the Arizona Cancer Center in Tucson. I was ready to go home and let his mother stay with him while Charlie went through the pain of the chemicals eating away at his cells.

The day before, he had received two copies of his article for his doctorate project on microbiology. Some journal in England had printed it: "The Incidence of Viral Growth in Genetically Altered Organisms Using Second Generational Antibiotic Intrusions." He talked all day about the research, about his last class before receiving his doctorate. My son's hands, the skin so soft, so sure, dignified, precise. His fingers are nimble. He spent so many years looking at cells, working cultures in petri dishes, writing reports, searching the guts of libraries for his answers.

My hands have broken earth, twisted the metal of farming implements, cracked under the elements of sun and cold. I've got a bit of palsy. My heart isn't so sharp anymore. I'm solid gray. I look five years beyond my sixty-four. My son's disease dredged more age deep inside where I don't let many look. I will have to keep working this land, and Wilhelmina will have to continue as a nurse.

I buried my son five years ago. He left us. This strapping, athletic, sharp-minded almost-Ph.D., who was the best husband and father, vanished in a cloud of chemicals and drugs and boiling cells.

I have reconciled myself with this new person in my midst. I'm not always patient with him, and I forget that the disease and chemicals ate his brain, that all this repetition and questioning isn't his fault. I have helped to remake this man, who was stripped of language, who had to be taught how to eat, who had to relearn the milestones—thumbtack flags—of his family.

But this fellow has taught me so much more. And I am remade because of his daily ritual of planting his feet deep in our family's earth; his thumbs up when he sees the horses and chickens.

My sick son has taught me about the life still left inside his soul even though he has the shell of a tortoise as his intellect. The one great fear a parent can have until he or she slips off this Earth came true for me. Oh, the loss of a child for a parent is the worst pain in life, and the real Charlie is gone. I've had my words with my God. I've had my own rituals in the middle of the mountains—Apache style, no less. But this son of mine has taught me so much about life, because he is that—LIFE—even with the miasma eating at his memories, even though he seems like an idiot savant to most, on the surface.

It has been six, going on seven years since he was first diagnosed. And the roller coaster called life has taken me and my wife and the whole Wesson clan through some bumps and into some major wrecks.

The chemo. The radiation. The days we thought the cancer had taken him. The meningitis, the encephalitis. The ranting and raving in his early days after the bacteria ran through his brain. All the knowledge gone. Down the drain. He forgot me, his mother, his wife and son.

"Choreo-carcinoma," that's what his oncologist called it. Something like a raging cancer which dances through the body. Charlie, of all people, falling to this rampant demon. He worked so hard to get his doctorate. He was healthy. He knew the ins and outs of cells as a top-notch microbiologist.

My son's hands are soft, and as I hold his hand with the soil between us, I am glad I sheltered his hands from the work I do in the fields, pulling piston heads from tractors and bringing in the alfalfa. I wanted so much more for my only son, not the harsh sun of a southern Arizona farm, not the burning skin, not the back-breaking lifting and hoeing.

Before he got enmeshed in this entanglement of cancer and meningitis, I was a bitter man in some ways. I had taken for granted the soil as something sacred. I had begun to look at the crops as a commodity, the elements as my nemesis. My son Charlie, who has slipped away into a mental maze, has taught me to smile again. He says the damnedest things, and he goes up to waitresses and mechanics and spreads a kind of joy to them because he asks them about themselves, finds their responses so remarkable that he records bits and pieces of what they say in one of his notebooks.

Those people, even the passerby in some truck stop on his way to California, well, they take something spiritual from that boy . . . a glowing essence of what it is to be simple and pure and good.

I have seen how fragile death is, how far a man's heart can vanish into the endless toil of work. I see Charlie patting the pumpkins and talking to dogs in a field and shaking the hand of a scarecrow and then fake punching his head in a laughing grimace. My son. And I hold all my feelings as a man left in this world naked, in my hand.

I could fall to my knees and ask forgiveness each day for my transgressions, but I see the ray of hope—life—coursing through my life from the roots of Charlie's soul. I am sure again of why I have been set into this land, and I am honored to be able to help this man, this partially realized man who was so good and honest and smart.

"Did I ever tell you about my bowling record . . . my favorite thing in the world to do?" Charlie rattles on and on to Sam Snyder who ranches cattle and is our neighbor and who has heard Charlie's limited tales time and time again.

"First, when I use to live in Austin, Texas, where I received my undergraduate degree—which, by the way, I received with a 3.6 G.P.A.—my bowling average was 180. My highest game was 220. And, then in Tucson, when I was working on my master's in microbiology, which I received with a 4.0 G.P.A., I . . ."

Sam smiles and winks and pats my boy on the back and shows him a new game booklet, the words all hidden in a jumble of letters horizontal, diagonal and backwards. Snyder is a softer man since Charlie came back to the farm, since Charlie captured the soul of this valley, these mountains, this big sky southeastern Arizona. Everyone in this valley who has run into my son, they all have something changeable inside.

Charlie is the emissary of hope, the will of human life to overcome the primitive routing of our bodies.

Because of this boy, this big, dome-headed man, I am alive again, as deep into the blood of my roots which have worked this land. I still have the power to make something out of the chaos, and view that magnificent slant on life which Charlie calls, "This good living farm in the middle of our apple valley."

Paul K. Haeder

Lessons from a Three-Year-Old

*Children have more need of models
than of critics.*

—Joseph Joubert

I'm talking to someone, making a point. My hands move though the air expressively. The person I'm talking with notices my fingernails. My fingers curl into the palms of my hands, recoiling like the witch's feet in *The Wizard of Oz* when a house falls in Munchkinland.

This doesn't happen anymore, though. Not since having to explain myself to my three-year-old daughter.

I had always wondered what, if anything, would make me stop picking at and biting my nails. At age thirty-nine, maybe I didn't want fingernails badly enough. No big deal, really. Unattractive, but who was hurting? Plus it was soothing to pick, pick, pick under the table during a boring meeting or at dinner with someone who made me uncomfortable.

Everything changed when Katie started imitating me. I didn't want her to be teased about this or scolded. I wanted her to spend lazy afternoons at the beach, polishing fingernails and toenails and doing other things young girls do. And I didn't want to get blamed for her bad habit. But most importantly, I couldn't ask her to not take on a habit I hadn't yet broken myself. It wouldn't have been fair.

Now my nails are long and polished. It seems everything has become a reminder of my newfound femininity. Dialing a telephone, working on the computer, even picking up a fork is an opportunity to feel good about myself. A habit was broken; integrity preserved.

That's not all I'm learning from Katie.

Want to know what empathy is? Try shedding a few tears in front of a preschooler. It doesn't matter that she has nothing to do with the reason you're upset. Any attempts to explain that are futile. You feel badly, so does she. And she won't feel better until you do. Husbands and wives who wonder how they can better relate don't need to look any further than into the eyes of their child.

I recently worked as a reporter and frequently took Katie with me on trips to the courthouse where I was getting news on, well, the bad guys. Sometimes we'd share an elevator with them as they were on their way to a court appearance in their handcuffs and bright orange coveralls. Katie beamed at them, smiled, started chatting them up. Like they were every bit as much human beings as the rest of us.

Katie's not much into analyzing. Ask her "Why?" in reference to anything and she says it just *is*. She may have a point.

Katie would challenge anyone who says looks don't matter. She has red hair, with curls that would make Julia Louis-Dreyfus swoon. Elderly women stop me at the grocery store to ask if they can touch it. Younger women tell me she should be in commercials. Katie gets more attention than the almost-bald toddlers who wear headbands so you know they're girls. If you think she's oblivious, you haven't seen the movie star smile she flashes for the camera.

I'm not wild for fruits and vegetables, but I eat a lot of them because it's the right thing to do. Katie's as likely to want a cucumber or a carrot as a piece of candy. I didn't understand until I realized she thinks that because Mommy's eating this stuff it must be good.

This much clout is fleeting, but it could save her a lifetime of worries about her weight. In exercising that clout, I've dropped thirty pounds. All that rhetoric about teaching by example finally clicked: I don't have to study up on how to be a good parent, I just have to be a good person.

My husband and I have our own business, and it's based at home. We take turns working and playing with Katie. When she's with relatives for the weekend and it's bedtime, she cries for both of us. Try telling *her* dads don't matter as much as moms.

Katie can't go to sleep without the following: a story, prayers and something we call "a report on the day." Kids learn early: it's not cool to have long talks with Mom or Dad. But a child trying to delay bedtime is a captive audience. So we take stock of the day's events: what happened, what made us happy or sad, what we'll dream about that night, and what we want to do when we wake up. At age three, sometimes the most she can think of to dream about is "waking up."

Katie can be talked out of the umpteenth glass of milk before drifting off. Deny her the report, however, and there is hell—I mean, heck—to pay. She knows already that it's not so much whether you've won or lost by the time your head hits the pillow, it's the story.

But kids get help from more than their parents with that story.

Not long ago, Katie built a toy machine gun out of inter-locking—and, ironically, pastel—blocks. She climbed up on the coffee table, pointed the "gun" at us and announced, "I'm gonna give you to the count of ten to get your ugly, yellow, no-good keister off my property before I pump your guts full of lead." Turns out it was a scene from a movie in the movie, *Home Alone,* that she had been watching earlier.

Maybe there's still time to sign up for a parenting class after all.

Maureen Anderson

A Boy and a Fish

*Man is a complex being; he makes
deserts bloom and lakes die.*

—Gil Stern

As parents sometimes do, I look for small glimpses of humanity in my fifteen-year-old son, Mike. I search for evidence that all I have striven to teach him has somehow taken root in this contrary, argumentative creature known as "the dreaded adolescent."

The apple of my eye is as exasperating and uncivilized as any teenager has the audacity to be. His arrogance and apparent lack of sensitivity often leave his father and me shaking our heads and throwing up our hands in frustration. We frequently doubt that there is even a remote possibility that this baggy-panted, baseball-capped boy could ever grow up to resemble anything close to a human being.

But, sometimes, small hope glimmers in the strangest of places and experiences. In our case, it came disguised as a fish.

We were staying at our favorite country inn on a small lake outside Kingston, New York. While I soaked up some of the countryside, Mike and his dad fished the still and steamy waters of Williams Lake. Just before dark, I returned to our room to find a large fish in the bathroom sink. *Wow,* I thought, *somebody caught something!* Knowing that all catches were promptly returned to the water, I had to wonder: *What was so special about* this *fish?*

61

My curiosity and I stood on the dock as the two great fishermen silently dipped their oars toward shore. Upon docking, Mike leapt from the boat. The face that came toward me was not one of excitement, but of anguish. "Mom—did you see it? I didn't mean to, Mom. It was an accident. I killed it. I just wanted to have my picture taken with it, but my camera was back in the room and it just took too long. Mom, I tried to throw him back—I really tried hard, but it was too late."

And so it went, all night long. "I can't believe I killed him, Mom. Why'd I have to take a stupid picture? Lots of other people should be catching that pickerel and throwing him back. He should be swimming around right now, Mom. You know, they stock this lake with bass and trout, but *not* pickerel. It takes a long time for a pickerel to get that big and there really aren't many pickerel *in* the lake."

Nothing we said could console him. The "it was only a fish" rationale proved meaningless as his conscience held him hostage using only a dead pickerel. Some would surely have had a chuckle over such a big deal being made over a measly fish, but I couldn't have been more proud. Clearly, his values were alive and well, his head was firmly on his shoulders, and his heart was definitely in the right place.

As we drove back to the lake later that same evening, I considered Mike's thoughtful silence in the back seat. That night, I forgave him his small inconsiderations and large arrogances, as the humanity I searched for emerged in small tortured pieces.

I've no doubt that the road to Mike's manhood will be long and littered with large and small traumas. But, as we closed our eyes that night, in the dark and quiet of our room, I was secretly thanking the fish who unwittingly sacrificed himself to reveal my son's true colors.

As he slipped away into the lake of dreams, Mike added a single footnote to the day's experience, assuring me that this boy would indeed grow up to be a fine human being.

"Mom—did you see how beautiful he was?"

Michele Pace Hofbauer

The Tender Heart

Children and dogs are as necessary
to the welfare of this country as
Wall Street and the railroads.

—Harry S. Truman

I was twenty-one at the time. My little brother, Wade, was only seven. Our family was struggling in those days, as were many of our neighbors. Often, there was no food in the house. Many times we didn't even have lunch to take to school. As you can imagine, childhood toys and treats were few and far between.

One very hot summer day as I was returning from my job, I saw Wade in the backyard. He was standing next to a very pathetic, sickly-looking stray dog who, I learned later, had wandered into our neighborhood. One look at the poor animal and I knew there was only one thing that could be done—that *had* to be done. The only merciful solution was that he had to be put to sleep.

Even as I explained the situation, little Wade wanted nothing to do with it. With giant tears in his innocent eyes, he said, hopefully, "I know what we can do, Rob. We can take him to a vet. I've saved up ten whole dollars." Wade used his money (saved from occasional allowance money) to help put the poor little dog out of his misery. Never once did he consider that he might have gotten a little toy or game for himself—something I know he

63

longed for. He showed no hesitation about wanting to give all he had to help the suffering animal.

That summer day, so long ago, my little brother taught me a lesson of love and compassion that I have never forgotten. All these years later, I sometimes wonder: *What was it that led the poor little dog into our yard?* Perhaps he knew where he would find a caring heart.

Robin Czombos

Famous for Your Love

*Fame usually comes to those who are
thinking about something else.*

—Oliver Wendell Holmes, Jr.

Last year, I suffered from depression because I wanted so badly to take care of my mother in my home. I was certain that it would help my mother and that, with the assistance of a live-in caregiver, I could do it. However, my two older brothers would not allow it! They felt she needed to be in a nursing home to be watched on a twenty-four hour basis. I fought and fought, trying to convince them of the benefits Mom would receive by being always around loved ones. But they would not give in, and I was denied my wish.

She smiles when her grandchildren sit on her lap. She laughs when I wear my torn jeans, telling me I look like a slob. She strokes my hair with such love. I miss her very much.

My mom has dementia as a result of strokes she has suffered, and she is bound to a wheelchair. She can't carry on long conversations, but if you communicate in short phrases, as you do with a toddler, she is able to respond. Since I had just raised three children through their toddler stages, I felt fully prepared—and willing—to take care of another child: my mother.

I was aware that this would change our family life, but my husband and three children were willing to accommodate my desire.

After losing the battle with my brothers, I broke down crying in front of the children. Kerry, my ten-year-old, asked what was wrong. I told her I wished I was rich and famous like Michael Jordan, because then my brothers couldn't stop me from having my mother in our home.

Kerry looked up at me and said, "But you *are* famous, Mom. You're famous for your love."

My eight-year-old, Allison, chimed right in and said I shouldn't feel bad because I had tried to fight for my mom, and six-year-old Neal added that it would have been fun to have Grandma at our house "Because she's funny and says silly things to us and makes cute faces."

Kerry and Allison comforted me and made me laugh at a time when I thought life was bleak and I was in despair. How wonderful it is, after all, to be famous for your love. I could not ask for a greater gift.

Theresa A. Anderson

Laura Takes to the Water

*A child is a quicksilver fountain, spilling over
with tomorrows and tomorrows,
And that is why she is richer than you and I.*

—Mayor Tom Bradley

She took to the water like a dolphin, keen to learn. Supported by water wings, she struck out, while I circled around her, protecting her as she struggled to learn.

We were almost there. A few sessions later, she didn't need anything to keep her afloat and could make two or three swiping strokes before I caught her and stopped her from going under.

The breakthrough came in London during an exceptionally hot summer, and I took the girls to the Serpentine, the swimming lake in the middle of Hyde Park. I led Laura by the hand into the water while her big sister, Susannah, who was a seasoned swimmer at eleven, watched from the side. Carefully, I lifted her with her chin just above the water and placed my hand under her eight-year-old tummy.

Her arms and legs made desperate frog movements and then . . . I let go . . . and she was swimming!

Only two, three, four, maybe five frantic strokes, but she was swimming.

From then on, we were swimming together—she with quick, mousy strokes, while I circled around her. We graduated to the deep end. Her strokes lengthened and grew stronger and the circle grew wider. No matter how well she swam, I circled her. I didn't know then that she was ready to swim out of the circle.

I should have realized this. Years before, she'd shown me how independent she was meant to become when, with her tiny hand enclosed in mine, I'd taken her to school for the first time. At the school gate, she politely unfastened my hand and walked into her world.

Some of our best times were swimming times, and the best of those times were during our last holiday together on one of the bleak Western Isles of Scotland. Protected from the sea at low tide by massive black rocks was a magical dark, deep pool. We sat around it all day, and when the sun had warmed the top six inches of the surface we went in. In all that splashing delight, the cold scarcely mattered.

Our last swim was the iciest and the best. Overlooking the sea on the Island of Mull, a waterfall crashed down on a round pool which, in its turn, slipped the water over its lip to splash down into the sea. Even at the height of summer—which, in Scotland is never very hot—the water descending from the sparse mountain top brings the chill down with it.

I sat on a branch hanging over the water, sometimes dipping my toe into the swirling thirty-two degrees.

"I'm not saying I'm *going* to swim," I said, "but I *might* swim."

The afternoon made the rock pool sparkle. I sat on the branch in the sun for half an hour. Soon it would be too late: The murky shadows of the mountain would block out the sun's rays.

Still I hesitated.

"I didn't say I *was* going to swim. I only said I *might*."

And then I went in.

It was as I'd expected: icy cold but exhilarating. And all at once, there was Laura splashing beside me. Then I felt a tingle as my body found its own warmth in the water. We were two swirling dolphins, circling round each other, swimming as one—communicating and laughing through our brash, joyful strokes while we gulped down the clearest, sweetest water we had ever tasted. Sometimes we let the waterfall gush over our heads and wash over our faces while we bubbled with laughter underneath. The tingling warmth got to us, and we stayed and stayed until the dank shadow of the mountain began to darken the pool. Then we got out to wrap into thick towels, aching as the blood returned to our bodies in the raw, late afternoon sunlight.

The heartlifting joy of that swim still tingles in my memory like the ice-cold water.

I didn't know then that she was destined to go out of my life forever, and I would have to learn to live without her, rather than she without me. I'd taught her how to swim, but in that cold, gurgling pool, she'd taught me how to let go.

No one can ever recover from the grief of a daughter lost long before her time. I feel as I did when the small girl went through the school gate, leaving me behind. But I also see her warm and loving as ever—but independent and free. She walks boldly into the waves and starts to swim with strong, confident strokes. She swims onward and outward, pacing herself, never tiring. And her head is well above water.

Peter Hawkins

[EDITORS' NOTE: *Laura was killed in an automobile accident at the age of eighteen.*]

From a Distance

*All things are subject to change,
and we change with them.*

—Anonymous

Quite some time ago, I had an experience involving my children that I will never forget. It carried a sad, but very powerful, lesson in how to love.

At the time, I was in a very bad relationship and did not have enough sense to see it. I had to learn the hard way and, unfortunately, so did the children. One night, they were placed in the custody of the state as a direct result of the relationship problem I was going through.

As time progressed, I came to realize that I did not have the openness and the understanding that raising healthy children required. It became clear to me that these children needed a loving, caring home that I was not then able to provide. After some deep soul-searching, I made the decision to put my children up for adoption. They were to be placed with the foster families that were providing them with the love and affection that they so deserved.

As a result of this choice, I was allowed to see them one last time for a tearful goodbye. As I watched the two youngest leave with their new mother, I felt a sense of calm and a new hope for the future. Then it was time to say good-bye to the oldest of my

70

three children. My daughter and I sat in a room with a counselor and I told her of the decision I had made—trying to explain my reasons. To this day, it still makes me cry when I think about that moment.

About eight years later, I got to see my oldest—from a distance. Looking at her, I knew that I had made the right decision, not just for her and the two youngest, but for me.

Looking back, I realize that I was totally unprepared to raise children at that point in my life. The decision to let them go certainly gave them a more *normal* life than they would have had—but it also helped me to help myself. I was able to remove myself from the relationship and, by learning to accept my shortcomings, I learned to love openly and freely. Most of all, I learned how to love myself and all who care about me.

I now have a healthy five-year-old daughter, and recently married a wonderful man. We are expecting a baby this Christmas. I have survived all of the bad and all of the wrong of my life, and the heart-wrenching decision I made years ago proved to be the right one. Even though my children have not lived with me, and know nothing of how they have helped me, I want to thank them, from the bottom of my heart.

Beckey Kite

For Nikki

Hope is the thing with feathers—
That perches in the soul—
And sings the tune without words—
And never stops, at all.

—Emily Dickinson

We were just an ordinary family with ordinary problems until March, 1992, when I was diagnosed with bone cancer. Needless to say, our lives have never been the same.

At age thirty-two, I found myself facing aggressive chemotherapy, radiation therapy and radical surgery, none of which could guarantee my survival. It was a time of physical pain, emotional depression and bottomless fear.

As a single parent with an uncertain future, my greatest concern was for my only child, Nicole. At that time, Nikki was only nine years old, a third-grade honor student faced with the prospect of losing the only parent she had ever known. While this disease could rob me of my life, it would rob her of the innocence of childhood. While most children her age concerned themselves with toys and playtime, she carried a burden that no child should ever have to bear. Even though I tried to maintain a brave exterior, my heart ached when I looked into those huge brown eyes. I was more afraid for her than for myself. What kind of life would she have without a mother? Who would love her and care for her as only a mother could?

I chose to be honest with her in respect to my illness. She was told that I had cancer and that I might die. I wanted her to be prepared. I wanted her to know that I would love her forever, whether on earth or from heaven. I wanted her to know that she would be raised by people who would love her and take good care of her. I wanted her to know that she would not be alone.

While these larger issues were agonizing, a more immediate problem surfaced. How would she react when I lost my hair due to chemotherapy? Would she be afraid of me? This fear grew as my hair thinned. I knew the time was fast approaching when I would become completely bald.

Three weeks after my first chemo treatment, I had showered and was sitting on my bed. After putting on my nightgown, I unwrapped the towel from around my head. I gingerly ran the towel through my hair. I could feel tufts of hair gently hitting my shoulders and floating onto the bed and floor. I looked at the blond wisps, horrified. (No matter what they tell you, you're never quite prepared for this moment.) I struggled to choke back tears and regain my composure. Just then, Nikki wandered into the bedroom. My horror quickly turned to panic. She walked over to the bed and reached up with her small hand to touch my head.

She looked at me and said, "Mom, guess what? Your hair is falling out!"

And then she started to laugh. And as she laughed, I heard myself laughing. My panic was quickly turning to relief.

"Look in the mirror, Mom," she said. And we laughed even harder. We laughed until we cried.

It was the first of many lessons from my daughter.

During my illness, Nikki was always there beside me. She held a pan for me when I was sick from chemotherapy. She learned to give me daily injections when the insurance company would no longer pay for nurses' visits. She helped me learn to walk again after my surgery. She never once complained or showed the fear that must have been in her heart.

It was her strength that gave me strength. It was her laughter that kept me laughing. It was her faith and perseverance that gave me faith and perseverance. Looking into her eyes, I found the inspiration to fight for my life—and win.

Karen Augustine

Mango Memories

He has the gift of quiet.

—John Le Carré

I met him at a bookstore. He was ten years old and he was from India. He was a poet, like me. I wanted to do a reading to share my deepest feelings with the world, and he was there for the same reason.

Mangos were his favorite fruit. They were sweet and the color of the sunset. I met his mom and dad the same day, and his little sister, Rachel, as well. Later, I learned that he had the use of only one arm. I noticed it because he had to sign his name to a list of the participants involved in the poetry readings. One arm was normal, and the other, the one he used to sign, was curled up.

What a gift to the world! He wrote some of the most beautiful poems I have ever read. The thoughts he expressed in those poems transformed me, and made me feel different in many ways.

We became friends. I went to his home whenever I could—usually once a week—to help him with his poetry writing. Sometimes his mom would make *samosas*. Their home always smelled spicy and wonderful aromas filled the air.

I believe George helped me as well. Sitting with him in his family's kitchen, with pen and paper, poised to write, he seemed to slow down my thought processes. I became less concerned with pleasing the world through my words, and began to want to please myself.

Although words can be extremely effective, I learned that silence can be even more so. As I sat by his side, George wrote a poem about India. In the poem, he described why he loved mangos, and he revealed his feeling about the closeness of his family. Although he was just a child, to me he was older and wiser than many adults. His words of wisdom stay with me even now as I look within, quietly, for answers George knew could not be found in the world outside.

Paula Timpson

Thoughts About My Daughter

To My Daughter

Don't ever let
me hear you say
you've failed
for lack of nerve.
With fingers small
And scissors blunt
You cut the paper first,
Then proved yourself
and left behind
a trail of golden curls.

Rehearsal

She scurries by with spoon in hand
to dig a rich supply of dirt.
He stoops to fill a plastic pail
And gathers water from a ditch.
Together they build a house of mud,
The first one like it on the street.
Today's improvisators.
Tomorrow's innovators.

To Baby, Before Your Birth

The thought of this household guest
Has thrilled me.
I've even gone so far
As to prepare for your coming.
A long wait for me,
But well worth the time spent.
Man's calculations tell me
You're due in eleven days,
But man's agenda is unlike God's.
I stand empty-armed,
But full in body and spirit,
As I wait.

Sandra Ervin Adams

One Small Step for Mom

*One of the advantages of being disorderly
is that one is constantly making
exciting discoveries.*

—A. A. Milne

I walked into the kitchen at around 4:30 P.M., all set to prepare
my thirteen-year-old's favorite birthday dinner, only to see the
whole place teeming with little girls. It wasn't just my three, but
their friends as well. It was clear their pretzel-making enterprise
had gotten out of hand. All I could see was the stretch of dark,
brick-look, vinyl floor spread with ethereal powdery footprints
and my smooth white counter encrusted with dehydrating, over-
worked dough. My sparkling kitchen looked for all the world like
the uninhabitable surface of the moon.

Like a rocket off of a launch pad, I exploded. "WHAT IN THE
WORLD IS GOING ON HERE?"

In the moment of stillness that followed, the moon dust settled
gently on the children's magazine from the day's mail, lying open
to the enticing pretzel recipe they'd found, its brightly colored
green and yellow ink dulled under a layer of flour. It had also
settled on the cookie sheet laden with globby masterpieces: an
elephant, a bear, a turtle and a cat on a pillow. It had also settled
on the small, downcast figures in aprons rolled up at the waist,
their doughy hands dropped to their sides.

Too late I realized I had blundered into their fragile atmosphere without my protective space suit on. Too late I realized what I had failed to see: a half-dozen little girls hopping about, defying gravity in the enthusiasm of creation, their faces dusted equally with flour and joy.

But maybe it wasn't too late. With an arm around the nearest girl I exclaimed at the imaginative pretzel animals. I tasted the amazing dough. I hugged the would-be cooks in turn. I smiled, and like magic their enthusiasm returned. Once again, the room buzzed with happiness as we cleaned up the mess together.

You'd think that after two decades of mothering I'd have the inherent compromises that come with the job down to a science. After all, I've lived through light years of finger-paintings plastering kitchen counters, traveled through galaxies of family room quilt forts, and cleaned around eons of sprouting carrot tops in bowls.

For years I've put up with unknown matter in my freezer and fridge, unidentified flying objects captured in fruit jars on the dining table, and wriggling aliens in my bathtub. I've had bathroom towel magic carpets circumnavigate my house, mud pies like meteors land in my oven, and Magic Marker orbit my upholstery.

I've unearthed bologna from my red high-heel shoes, puttylike material fused to the insides of jeans pockets and burn marks of unknown origin on the carpet. I've tramped through heaps of dress-up clothes and stepped carefully over innumerable paper cup castles. My life is a nebula of home-crushed snow cones, sticky sugar-water tea parties and floating puzzle pieces. You'd think I'd know by now that children at work discovering their universe is worth a kitchen being temporarily transformed into *The Outer Limits*.

Their pretzels turned out fine even though they were on the thick side and had to bake quite a while. But it was a little inconvenient that they didn't grease the cooking sheet. I've been scrubbing at scorched dough on aluminum on and off for two days now, thinking of it as a sort of penance. I think of it this way: If Neil Armstrong can take one small step on the moon, a mom can take one small step toward merely allowing their children's exploration of our own home planet.

But it sure takes a world of patience.

Janice Graham

You Were Right

*There is a road from the eye to the heart
that does not go through the intellect.*

—G. K. Chesterton

A child brings so much into a life that the changes are hardly noticed until they have become overwhelming. People often find that they have changed, and that they have become different, without remembering what caused this change.

While I do not remember what led up to it, I certainly remember when I noticed the change—and was surprised by it. Steven was the cause of that change.

Steven was four years old, and I had been taking care of him since he was born. Although he was not my child, I loved him as if he was, and still do. Before Steven came along, I had always said that I did not ever want to have children, and that the only good thing about kids was that you could give them back to their parents when they got dirty or noisy.

Before Steven was born I was working full-time at a job I loved and going to school pursuing a degree in a field I liked. After he was born, I realized that daycare was not the wonderful thing I had always thought it to be. I felt that he was withering from a lack of attention, and I knew that they could not cherish him as I could. So I left my job and quit school. I decided to stay home with my aunt's child.

82

I loved him tremendously, but every now and then a doubt would surface as to whether or not I should let him go back to daycare/school so that I could go back to work.

Being out of work meant that I had no money and no way of making any. That was a tough spot to be in, regardless of my feelings, but I seldom thought that I had not made the right decision. The night I fully realized I had made the right decision, and accepted and was actually thrilled by it, was the night that changed my life.

That night I was working on something in my room, and Steven was in there with me playing. He had a few cars and blocks on the floor, but they were not sufficient to hold his interest. Nothing in my room holds his interest for long except, of course, my things. He is so fascinated by these "things" that he calls my room the "treasure room."

In all honesty, I love my room and would have to admit that it is a bit of a treasure. I am a collector, and pick up stuff wherever I go. Not junk, though. I never buy a souvenir nor do I own one. I find things that touch my heart, whether a rock on the lakeside near my father's home, or a feather that I found at the zoo. Some things are bought, some are found, but all are treasured.

As we entered my room that evening, Steven's eyes immediately began wandering in search of some new gem to admire and touch. He spotted it just in front of some of my prized books. He walked over and picked up a blue ceramic box and began turning it over and over in his hands. Even though I knew it was a lovely box, and great fun to look at, I cautioned him to be careful and asked him to put it down since I was concerned that it would open and the contents would come spilling out. "Oh no," he said, "I won't open it, Momma Gail, I promise." I was not convinced.

"Put it down, Steven," I said. "You may look with your eyes, but please don't touch the box. Here, how about my teddy bear? Or maybe these seashells. Aren't they pretty? Come play with them." All to no avail.

I knew that my attempts to distract him were futile, but still I tried. I became a bit exasperated, as I really wanted him to put the box down. I did not want the contents all over the floor. He was having no part of it.

He squatted down and hunched over, turning the box round and round. "Look, Momma Gail, look how pretty."

"Yes, baby, I know. Put it down now, and let's go play with your toys." And then it happened. The box lid tumbled off, and the potpourri poured out all over the carpet.

The vanilla scent drifted up to my nostrils, which were flaring. I was upset that after telling him so many times he had completely ignored what I had said, and then it happened, just as I had predicted. As that sweet angelic face turned up to look at me, I realized I had to control my temper.

"See, Momma Gail, you were right," he said. "It *would* spill. You were right! I'm going to pick it up now, okay?"

He bent his little head to the task, and began picking up the potpourri piece by piece with great concentration. My heart overflowed with love at his recognition that he had a job to do in cleaning up, and that everything would then be all right. How wise, and how uncomplicated!

His calmness made me realize how ridiculous anger would have been as a response to such a small incident. I knew in that moment that I had made the right decision, and that my heart had always known.

It was just a matter of the head accepting what my heart knew. Although I had not created him with my body, I had shaped him through raising him.

I knew then that Steven was just as much my child as if I had given birth to him. I gave birth from my heart, rather than from my womb.

Gail E. Rigby

Blessed Events

*Children are vari-colored tea, coffee,
chocolate, mocha, honey . . . but the shades
of color now count for nothing.*

—James Baldwin

I retired at sixty-five from years of factory work to become a babysitter for my grandchildren: a beautiful little girl, followed eight years later by a charming little boy. I loved taking care of them, but often wondered if I were doing the job correctly. It seems so easy to overlook discipline when you are dealing with grandchildren.

When Heather was a teenager, she became enamored with the basketball team of a local high school. The majority of the players were black. We didn't want our child becoming too deeply involved with any one player, so when she graduated and chose to go to a college out of town, we were relieved, at least for a while. When my son's family came home after dropping her off at college, her brother came running down to me and said, "Guess what, Gram? Heather's roommate is a black girl."

Angie was a lovely girl and Heather brought her with her during several weekend visits. She was quiet and very well-mannered. Her parents were professional people, but still Heather was not invited for a return visit. This upset me and convinced me that all prejudice isn't from white to black. I worried about Heather

85

because I knew that due to her friendship with Angie, she would have more contact with black people.

I felt this situation would lead to problems. And, sure enough, that is what happened. During her third year of college, she became pregnant, and the father was a black man. It was a heartbreaking time for all of us. Heather had decided she would give the baby up for adoption when it was born. But when the time came, she could not do it. She left college and came to our hometown to have her baby. We told her that we would help her raise her child.

When she brought the baby home for the first time, I thought I had never seen such a beautiful creature. She was very lightskinned, but it was the eyes that astonished me. They were brown, almost black, but the whites had a bluish tint that gave her eyes a look of mystery. When you looked into her eyes, you had the feeling that this child knew things you had no knowledge of. We accepted her into our family and adored her. Heather got a part-time job and started taking courses at the local college.

Then she got a job with a firm in Maryland. After living with us for three-and-a-half years, they moved away. It was a difficult and anxious time for us. We worried about her living so far away. She rented a small house, and after several months, she told us a person was moving in with her to share the expenses. He was a black man, she told us, divorced and with two children to support. The idea was to share expenses and babysitting chores since one worked days and the other worked at night. It seemed to be an ideal arrangement.

Heather and Karrelle, my great granddaughter, would come home for weekend visits every few months. After Richard, the divorced man, had lived with her for a year, Heather began hinting about bringing him home with her. I had mixed feelings about the situation. On one hand, she would have someone to share the driving on the long journey. On the other, I dreaded the impact it might have on our neighbors. We have lived in this house and the area for over fifty years, and there has never been a black person around. But I couldn't tell her she could not bring him along. The next holiday was Memorial Day, so we made arrangements for them to visit that weekend. I consoled myself by thinking that if Richard were as light-skinned as Karrelle, it wouldn't be such a big deal.

The day finally came. I was sitting in my chair waiting for them to arrive. Suddenly I heard the back door open, and footsteps running into the living room. There she was, jumping on my lap, with hugs and kisses. "Oh, Gram," Karrelle cried, "I have such a nice surprise for you. I brought my little sister with me, and she is so beautiful."

I sensed a movement at the side of my chair, and when I looked, there stood the blackest little girl I had ever seen. She was so black it was startling. I could sense that she was a little confused and shy. My eyes filled with tears as I pulled her onto my lap, and into the embrace with Karrelle and me. So, there we sat, black, white and "mixed up," as my little one calls herself. I thanked God as I realized that I was part of a miracle. This event took place so I would understand color does not matter. It is not important what my neighbors think or how they react. Because I know that love is color blind, and a little child shall lead them.

Sally Brungart

Kids Say the Darndest Things

*W*hen talking to kids, you've
got to pretend that you don't know much—
and a few seconds later you realize
you're not pretending.

—**Bill Cosby**

In the beginning, there was Art Linkletter, and God saw that Art was good and God said that Art *is* good. A few years after the beginning, there was Cosby, who never argued with God. Cosby knew that Art was an adult with a remarkable hobby: He actually listened to children. He knew that mankind's silliest saying was not *Do not remove this tag from mattress under penalty of law,* but *Children should be seen and not heard,* a tough rule to follow on a television show.

Art knew that adults are just kids who've lost their way, just kids who owe money and who've stopped saying what they really think. And so, Art preferred the wonderfully honest talk of kids, who guilelessly say exactly what's on their minds, even if they don't know what they're saying. Moreover, Art knew a happy truth I also have learned: that the greatest wits who ever lived, from Cyrano de Bergerac to Fat Albert, could never have invented the kind of delightful originality that endlessly bubbles from kids.

"My dad yells at my older brother a lot," a six-year-old girl once told me.

"Why does he have to do that"? I asked her.

"Oh, you know," she said. "He's a *boy*."

"Yes, most brothers are. But why does your dad have to yell at him?"

"Oh, *you* know how *boys* are."

"No, how are they?"

"Stupid."

"And when they become men?"

"Stupider."

Just as I don't argue with God, I don't argue with six-year-old girls because both know more than I do. I just know that the candor of such children is always surprising, sometimes unnerving, and frequently to be treasured.

Moreover, the logic of kids goes far beyond the tiny brain of an adult.

"Mr. Cosby," a six-year-old once said to me. "I know your wife's name."

"Really," I replied. "What is it?"

"Mrs. Cosby."

Could I have argued with *him?* That kid would have known who is buried in Grant's Tomb. Grant and *Mrs.* Grant. And their son, Cary.

Kids blend logic and creativity into a magnificent mix. For example, I once heard an eight-year-old boy recite this particularly moving passage from the Lord's Prayer: ". . . And lead us not into Penn Station and deliver us from eagles . . ."

Did *Aristotle* have more wisdom? Which of us truly wants to be led into Penn Station, even when the rush hour is over? And would any of us want to be FedExed to eagles, which might deliver *us* somewhere?

By now you're aware that there is a difference between children and old people that has nothing to do with the size of their portfolios. The difference—it's the one big thing Dr. Spock missed—is that kids like to keep their hands in their pockets and old people want you to take them out. When I was five, at least once a day an old person told me to take my hands out of my pockets. You see, in those medieval days, any old person could hit you.

"I brought you into this world," my father used to tell me, "and I can take you out."

Children are as creative with songs as they are with reasons why their hands should stay in their pockets, why they have to put peas in their noses, and why they didn't do it and couldn't have done it and don't know what you're talking about anyway. Who but a child could have collaborated with Stephen Foster to produce the unforgettable new blend of travel and medicine I heard when a five-year-old boy sang to me, "Oh, I come from Alabama with a Band-Aid on my knee."

And he's goin' to Louisiana, his fractured love to see.

The updated version of the Lord's Prayer was the kind of genius I keep hearing from America's shortest wits on my CBS show, *Kids Say the Darndest Things,* the kind that Art Linkletter heard from more than 27,000 kids while running his wondrous *House Party* on radio and TV from 1945 to 1969. The kids I've loved and listened to and laughed with on my show are the grandchildren of the ones who lit up Art Linkletter forty years ago. They're a bit more knowledgeable than Art's. They know that radioactivity isn't a lot of broadcasting, that a free agent isn't a spy on parole, and that a stork who delivered babies would have to bring them through the vaginal canal.

Moreover, most of the kids today, especially, the four-year-olds, would probably tell me, "Cosby, don't you realize that kids are now saying the *damndest* things? However, no matter what you call them, the things that kids are saying today are still every bit as funny and original and wise and ridiculous and absolutely enchanting as ever. Just listen . . .

Bill Cosby

More Than Dirt

Speak to the earth, and it shall teach thee.

—Job 12:8

He crept out into the crisp morning air after getting up early just to spend a little time alone. Wandering around the yard just before dawn, he hoped to catch the first glimpse of the morning as it rambled down the runway of the day, pushing aside the residue of violet and blue left from the starry night just past. Reed relished the stillness, even though he could hear the sounds of cars on the road below, and a lone cricket completing its symphony of sound in a nearby bush. He was glad to be alive and thought himself a lucky man as he considered the babies tucked in bed and his wife deep in slumber back inside the house.

He thought about his busy days, how every moment was planned in advance, each item methodically recorded and checked, his whole life executed for efficiency. That was partly why moments like this were so important. It seemed like the only way to balance the busyness. His mind shifted to the overgrown grass and the grapevines along the far fence begging to be pruned. October days were sliding into November, and that meant icy storms followed by drifts of snow upon the ground where he now stood.

Figuring it to be nearing 6 A.M., he focused his mind and began to plan the day. If he got started soon, he would easily have time to cut the grass, prune the grapes and maybe even plant the bulbs he had bought at the nursery the week before. Deciding to do the more tedious tasks first, he turned to tackle the grapes and then, he mused, he would move on to the lawn. That left his most favored chore for the last, as a sort of reward for finishing the other two. Making fairly good time, he moved from grapes to grass.

Just as he was about to begin planting the bulbs, the children flooded into the yard. They had finished dressing and little Laura had the evidence of breakfast still on her face. Positioning himself upon his knees on the cool, moist earth, he thrust his spade into the milk chocolate soil. Heaving a shovelful upward, he marveled as tiny clumps tumbled down from the too-full load. Making several cup-shaped holes, he plopped a sandy colored bulb into each. Soon he became aware of his four-year-old son, Sam, standing next to him. He turned slightly and glanced at Sam's face. It was full of emotion and a strange nervousness. As their eyes locked he wondered what could be wrong with his blond-haired boy. As his field of vision widened, he could see a bat in one hand and a ball in the other. The reason became clear: Sam had an agenda of his own on this Saturday morning.

At first, he tried to convince the boy of the virtues of what he was doing. He reassured him of the importance of planting, and how much Mommy wanted flowers in the spring. He told him about how the wee blossoms would sprout from the bulbs, much the same as a butterfly emerges from a cocoon. He told him about how snow covers the bulb in the winter, but that never stops it from coming through in the spring.

Sam didn't say a word. Pleading only with his eyes, all three feet of him stood upright and firm. Finally, the boy spoke, his voice faint yet determined. "Daddy, what's more important, me or the dirt?" Sam's words sent a chill through his father. Reed kept his eyes fixed on his child and thought about how precious this miniature version of himself was. Nothing could be more important right now than the look on Sam's face. His question was a valid one. He needed his father's reassurance.

"Oh Sam," Reed responded, taking his small son in his arms. "You are. I'd rather play ball with you than do anything else." Sam's face glowed with happiness as he handed his father the bat.

Mary Ann Swenson

The Trouble with Rearview Mirror Living

*Make it a rule of life never to
regret and never look back. Regret is
an appalling waste of energy; you can't build
on it; it's good only for wallowing in.*

—Katherine Mansfield

The year was 1983, and it wasn't a very good one. Picking up the pieces strewn about by divorce was tough, and at times it was easier to just sweep them under the rug.

The problem with that approach, though, was I continued to stumble over the bumps I came to know as compulsive self-doubt. With my head screwed on backward during those years, I constantly tripped over masked anger and bitter disappointment at the loss of the "happy family" dream to which I had always aspired. I was now a statistic, and so was my son.

One day, as I was half-heartedly playing a popular children's game with my three-year-old son, I learned a lesson I'll never forget.

"Mommy, your little guy is facing backwards!" Neil exclaimed. "He can't see where he's going!" *No wonder this character kept getting sent back to the beginning—time after time.*

Could that be it? I began to see a parallel here with my own life. Looking back and dwelling on all the past hurts and losses was keeping me from moving forward. I should have known that.

Neil knew it, and I took his advice. Soon, I had new goals, and my eyes never looked in the rearview mirror. They were fixed straight ahead.

Carole Williams Pore

Homemade from the Heart

What comes from the heart, goes to the heart.

—Samuel Taylor Coleridge

My husband and I quit our full-time jobs and recently moved across the state to be closer to our families. This is something we had planned for some time. My husband had also decided to make a career change that involved returning to college.

I became the only wage earner, and as a consequence our lifestyle took a decidedly different economic turn. We looked for every way we could to save money, and we slowly instilled these restraints into our two children. No more weekends at the movies, no more having lunch or dinner out, no more designer clothing or shoes. Our family outings became trips to the local library to check out movies or books, and walks down to the school to play baseball or football. Our motto became "Use it up, make it do or do without."

When we moved, our nine-year-old daughter, Amanda, had a hard time leaving one of her closest friends, Breann. They had been in the habit of calling each other nearly every day and spent most of their free time at one another's home. After we moved, there simply weren't funds for long-distance phone calls, so they began writing letters.

Breann's birthday was coming up in a month. Amanda worried over what she could give her. At first we thought about buying

95

something she might like, without spending a lot. After a while, I forgot about the birthday but apparently Amanda had not. She put a lot of thought into what would be a nice gift.

Little did I realize the impact of our newly adopted lifestyle. One day, she asked me to sit with her and look over some papers she said were meant for Breann's birthday. What she showed me tugged at my heart and made me realize that even a nine-year-old can have insight into what is really important.

Amanda had prepared and collected several papers with activities for Breann to do on each one. These activities included coloring pictures she had drawn, a dot-to-dot she had created, a "What's wrong with this picture?" activity she had made, and blank sheets of paper inscribed at the top, in Amanda's handwriting, "Draw Your Own Dreams on These Pages."

I was amazed at the type and variety of activities she had prepared. What also touched me was the birthday card she had handmade for Breann. She drew two girls holding hands. The note inside the card read, "Breann—Happy Birthday! This might not be what you wanted, but the best thing you can get is homemade from the heart."

After her birthday, Breann sent a "thank you" letter saying the gift she received from Amanda really meant a lot to her.

JoAnn Townsend

Mad Dad

*Anything which parents have
not learned from experience they can
now learn from their children.*

—Anonymous

My husband and I have three boys: Kevin who is now twenty-three, Joe who is seventeen and Rory who is fifteen. Over the years I have learned many lessons from the three of them, and some of the best were also the simplest. For instance, they taught me the benefits of swinging on the swing set once a day (it really relaxes) as well as the advantages of cutting peanut butter-and-jelly sandwiches into triangles (making it easy to avoid crusts). They also taught me that it is much more fun to take a nap in a makeshift tent in the living room than in your "boring old bedroom."

To this day I'm a firm believer that a daily dose of these "kid" rituals contributes not only to diversity but to the maintenance of your sanity. They also educated me in more pragmatic areas, such as how to fill a water balloon without spraying water all over the kitchen, and which eye to close when you're aiming at the bad guys. However, I never did learn to play video games without waving the controller around in the air. Frankly, I think they didn't want me to learn because it's so funny to watch me flailing the thing around. But they did teach me one lesson, years ago, which changed my perspective, and probably added years to my life.

It must have been summertime, because the boys were all in grade school but I had been home with them all day. They were engaged in their usual raucous fun. When they were that age, they were constantly on the move and we basically had our home decorated in a NerfBall motif. Don't get me wrong, they weren't bad boys, they were just *very* active.

Well, when my husband got home after a long day, I told the boys to quiet down. My husband was in our room changing his clothes and I was starting dinner. The boys were not close to quieting down, and although I didn't even know how my husband was feeling, I insisted that they end their running and playing even though it truly wasn't bothering me at all.

You see, I have made kind of an art out of "buffering" people from one another. I don't want anyone I care about doing anything that might bother, anger or hurt anyone else I care about. In the meantime, the only person who gets stressed out about all this is the one person I *am* responsible for—me.

Convinced that my husband would soon emerge from our room wanting to read the paper undisturbed, and that the boys' rough-housing would disturb him, I became even more agitated. So with my teeth clenched firmly together I went in and said to them, "Listen, if you don't stop running around in here you're going to make Dad mad. And if you make Dad mad, that's going to make me mad." They all stopped in their tracks and looked at me with the same puzzled expression and the same wrinkled-up, freckled noses. And then one of them spoke for them all, saying very deliberately, "But Mom, if Dad was at work and he got mad, you wouldn't get mad."

I ran this through my stressed-out brain. "If Dad was at work and he got mad (pausing here to reflect) you wouldn't get mad." I pondered this for a moment and then realized how irrational I was. Getting mad simply because someone else was getting mad was, well—ridiculous. They nailed it. This was logic I couldn't argue with. This was advice people pay hundreds, maybe thousands, of dollars to hear from a trained professional. Not only was it exactly what I needed to hear, it was phrased in one succinct statement. They said in one sentence what could fill an entire book, and they said it in the clearest of terms.

"You're absolutely right," I said, and returned to the kitchen. I then proceeded to remove myself so far from the situation that I don't remember if they got in trouble with their Dad on that occasion or not.

I realize I tend to be a bit stubborn (especially when it comes to having someone point out that I may be wrong and that it might be time for a change), but I embraced this new attitude with enthusiasm—shedding responsibility (as best as I could) for the foul temper and disagreeability of anyone else.

My boys *and* my husband would hasten to tell you that I am not completely cured of my "buffer-itis" even now. But whenever I barge in where I'm not needed and get that look that says "Butt out, Mom" I think back to that day and the lesson I learned from my three little men. And the nicest part of all is that, even though I am reminded to leave well enough alone during unhappy times, I am invited with open arms to share the times of joy. And there have been *many* joyful times. Thanks, guys!

Laurel Turner

My Hero

Success is not the result of spontaneous combustion. You must set yourself on fire.

—Reggie Leach

Heroes come from all walks of life. Talented athletes, combat-ready soldiers, brave police officers, fire fighters, and even teachers—all of these people are heroes and are often honored with awards, or media recognition. My hero is not like that; he's just an ordinary student with an *extraordinary* spirit. He will never receive a medal, or awards, but he should, for he faced a formidable enemy and his spirit triumphed.

My hero was born a healthy, attractive baby with loving parents who recorded his every move for posterity. Each small accomplishment like sitting up, talking, and crawling was met with applause, oohs and ahs. This was my hero's life, and it was *good* until he started school.

My hero had trouble initially with the letters of the alphabet. It was hard for him to distinguish Ns and Hs. His spirit was shattered when his first grade teacher asked him to read. The words seemed obvious to his peers, but not to him.

A rush of emotions filled him. My hero became embarrassed. His cheeks were red and hot, and fear gripped his throat. He could not breathe. He felt dizzy and only vaguely aware of the name-calling around him. He just wanted to die. He hid in the womb of his closet to avoid the harsh new world. His spirit was low.

Luckily his caring mother noted the sudden changes in his personality, talked to him and had him tested.

Little did he know that he was part of a group of elite people like Sir Winston Churchill, Franklin D. Roosevelt, Mark Twain and Albert Einstein who all suffered from this same handicap. They were all learning disabled.

Almost 2.5 million American school children have some type of learning disability. My hero's particular problem is dyslexia. My hero's mother read everything she could about dyslexia and shared it with her son. "Dyslexia is not a disease, and it doesn't mean you're stupid," she told him. "It just means that your brain is miswired, but with the help of multisensory lessons from a trained tutor, you can learn to read." My hero's spirit was buoyed.

My young hero enjoyed the special attention from his tutor and began to slowly piece together the puzzle; however, in the wisdom of the school district, the following year he was placed in a segregated class with other "special" children. My hero's spirit hit bottom then because he said, "Why don't they just put a dunce cap on my head and write 'stupid' across my forehead?" His anger increased when he realized he was reading a first-grade picture book in the fourth grade—*how degrading!* He had to learn baby rhymes like, "Across the heaven and down makes seven." *How childish!* I witnessed his complete frustration when I saw him digging into a pad of paper with a pen when he became upset with his limitations.

His parents interceded again, taking their son to a counselor who helped him to channel his energy. He decided to face his enemy—dyslexia—with great fervor. He prepared for his battles with hours of relentless mental calisthenics. Flash cards, word games, color-coded charts and tables all helped hone my hero into a fighting machine. He prepared his body. At first, he trained with the cross-country team as a release for his anger, but soon found that the running helped him develop stamina.

His spirit prevailed. My hero could have given in to the dark side of his enemy by quitting school, being illiterate or becoming a juvenile delinquent, but he would not allow that to happen. I'm proud to say that my hero, my nephew, graduated from high school with an A/B average and is now attending college.

He is, and always will be, my hero—because he never gave up.

Jeanine Turpie

The Perfect Little Tour Guide

*To see a world in a grain of
sand and heaven in a wild flower,
Hold infinity in the palm of your
hand and eternity in an hour.*

—William Blake

I have often marveled as people recount the profound things that children say, and have laughed at the profundity and humor when kids do and "say the darndest things." But until my little son was born, I had no idea how profound simply their *being* was!

I have watched countless new mothers and fathers bustle about; exhausted, thrilled and overwhelmed at parenthood. I was following in the same tradition. I had read all the books, worked on the nursery, had plans and intentions for a daily walk. I also planned to keep TV to a minimum, listen to classical music and "read stories" constantly. Life was getting planned well.

Then, somewhere between reality and pure zombie-dom, I was snatched away into a delightful, beautiful realm of existence called "new." This "new" world is beautiful! Did you know there are a zillion shades of green, depending on how the light hits it? Did you know that blankets aren't just warm, but they have all kinds of texture, holes and "fuzzies" that stick out (and they're fascinating)?

To go on a walk *with* a baby is an overload experience for the senses. There are hundreds of sounds, from the different birds

103

and the air moving the leaves to the rhythmic gravel crunching under the stroller wheels. His ears are new—he's never heard these sounds before and it is wondrous! So it is with each of the senses. There is so much detail those bright eyes pick up, and so many textures to touch. We once spent an entire afternoon just feeling the trunks of trees. I never knew how entertaining banging a rock on a drainpipe can be, and that the sound changes depending on the size and shape of the rock.

Have you ever looked at life through a child's eyes? I mean *really* looked? Can you look at the letter T for the first time? Be entranced by a piece of dust floating through a sunbeam? Want to brush your teeth all night long? Love cleaning so much you want to sleep with your broom? Or how about eating macaroni and cheese? It's a firm, slimy, cheesy, slippery, experience. I always just gulped it down, it wasn't worth savoring like an hors d'oeuvre of fresh paté—until now.

When my little cousin was about two years old, he got the coordination of his body together and learned to jump. Well, he jumped and jumped and jumped all day long. He jumped and hopped everywhere, his face radiating pure glee. It was as if he just couldn't believe how neat this little body of his was! Why is it that we grown-ups take shortcuts whenever we can in order to exert the least possible energy from these glorious bodies?

Then there was my baby and unlit candles. Somehow he learned (probably from watching me) that some candles smell good. Well, now he has to smell every candle he sees, wherever we are. He smells flowers, my cheek and even leaves, and he has to share the experience. I have learned that some leaves smell very good! (I don't think I ever would have thought of smelling a leaf.)

Carpet is a great hiding place of small things and pumpkins are wonderful. Bottles of perfume in the department store's glass cases are the sparkliest and rain is a miracle. Letters of the alphabet don't always look the same, cracks in the sidewalk are fascinating, just like light switches; shadows are a mystery. There is so much to learn, experience and accomplish in this world of "new." It's no wonder these little ones have such a hard time giving up the day when night and slumber roll in!

There will come a time as he grows older when he will become more accustomed to this old world of ours. I only hope I have been a good enough student that I might be able to remind and teach him that, although things will begin to seem ordinary and even boring, a little tour guide through life once made me realize that really *nothing* is.

There is so much we take for granted as part of our existence—things we don't ignore, because we never noticed them in the first place. It is as if my awareness had become gray or out of focus. I used to only notice the big or important things. But joy, I am being taught, is found in the sharpness of the detail. I may have *given* life to my little boy, but he *showed* it to me.

Erin K. Smith-Day

The Quiz

*The simplest questions are
the hardest to answer.*

—Northrop Frye

How do you answer the question: "Where is God and why can't you see him?" when it comes from a three-year-old? As my three-year-old daughter and I were discussing how her day went in school, we passed a church. The conversation about school stopped and an entirely new focus began:

"Mommy, is church open?"

"Well, I don't see any cars in the parking lot. Maybe it's closed," I responded.

"You know, Mommy," (in a matter-of-fact tone and nodding her little head) Kaylyn says, "God is in church!"

"Yes I know, baby."

"If he is in church, why can't you see him?" she persisted.

"Because he is a spirit," I answered.

"What is a spirit?" my inquisitive little one asked.

Thinking hard and trying to put it in a way the child could best understand, I said, "A spirit is invisible, and when something is invisible it means that it's there even if you can't see it."

Still not satisfied, my daughter persisted: "People live in their house and they are there in their rooms, so why isn't God in his room in the church?" She folded her arms, waiting for my answer.

106

Now exhausted from seeking answers to her questions, I responded, "Kaylyn, God lives in everyone's heart. That's where he lives."

Eyebrows raised, and with a small smile as if delighted by the answer, she asked, "Does God live in my heart?"

I assured her that God surely lived in her heart. By her widening smile, and the cessation of questions, I knew that I had satisfied the curiosity of a little girl who really asks tough questions.

Sarah Fernandez

The Ice-Cream Cone

*Pretty much all the honest truthtelling there is
in the world is done by children.*

—Anonymous

Raising children is a learning process for a parent. For instance, if you give a flip, top-of-the-head answer to a child's innocent question, it may later be crammed down your throat. A young daughter contributed significantly to my learning process.

My wife and I followed the advice of Dr. Spock most of the time. Then, one night at the dinner table, I told my four-year-old daughter to stop talking and eat or I'd pour my glass of water on her head.

"You do, and I'll tell Dr. Spook."

"Spock. His name is 'Spock'"

"You call him 'Spook.'"

"That's different. I'm older."

Our home was in the rolling hills of southern Pennsylvania, at least ten miles from the closest village. One hot Saturday afternoon I decided to go into town for some cigars. When I got in the car, there were two young daughters, ages four and eight, firmly enthroned in the back seat.

"We're going, too," they announced simultaneously.

Upon arrival at the only drugstore open in the small village, I told the girls I would be back in a minute and to stay in the car.

"How 'bout an ice-cream cone, Daddy?" The backseat vibrated with bouncing bodies.

"I don't have any money," I said. It was a statement I came to regret.

When I returned with a pack of Philly cigars, I extracted one from the pack and proceeded to light it. As I took a long-awaited puff, I heard the plaintive voice of the four-year-old.

"Dad, how come you have money for cigars, but not for ice cream?"

The question rolled around in my head as I fingered the cigar. The guilt was overwhelming, made even worse when I glanced in the mirror and saw two forlorn faces waiting for my response.

"You are wrong. I do have money for ice-cream cones. What flavors?"

"Chocolate," the older daughter yelled excitedly.

"Strawberry, two dips," the four-year-old screamed.

When I returned with the two ice-cream cones I spit out the cigar. It had the taste of gall.

And you know what? I never smoked another one.

Sam G. Higgins

Listening for a Volkswagen

Keep your fears to yourself,
but share your courage.

—Robert Louis Stevenson

I did not begin to worry until the digital numbers on the electric clock across the bedroom (I had to squint tightly to see them clearly without my glasses) read 12:30. I had actually slept for forty-five minutes or so until then, and when I woke and saw the time I told myself that the hour had no special significance. He would be home shortly. I would wait. I listened for the sound of a Volkswagen "bug" vibrating up the street.

I remembered the many times I had returned home late from parties and high school football games and let myself in with my key, tiptoeing into the bathroom trying not to wake my parents, only to hear one of them ask, as if they had not yet slept, "Did you have a nice time, Son?" They would ask if we won the game, or how many kids were at the party, and I would tell them and go on to bed. They showed interest but did not pry.

The clock read 12:32. I thought more time had passed. A car swished by on Greenbrier, the reflection of its lights moving briefly on the wall behind me, but it was not a Volkswagen. I knew the sound of his car intimately. It had been my prized new possession in 1974, my first new car in ten years. African Red and a new car smell that slowly faded over the next decade. Ellen,

110

my wife, called it "Rosy." She has named all our cars.

The year after I bought it, he and I had made a long summer trip together to Florida to visit his grandparents, and to Tennessee, where my brother lived. The thing rode like a Cadillac, I bragged to Ellen, but he had slept on his blanket spread out on the down-turned rear seatback most of the road trip. At age six, he seemed glad to get home again to his own bed and his toys.

I gave the car to Erik after his sixteenth birthday. I bought a new Chrysler, and he cleaned and restored some of the luster of Rosy and proudly drove it to school the next Monday to show to his friends. Three months later, he and his best buddy bought tickets to a music concert and asked permission to drive the car to downtown Atlanta on a Friday evening.

I could not believe that the clock read only 12:35. I got up to find my glasses. I put them on and walked to the door that opened into the carport. He would come in that door. I lifted up on my toes to peek through the window at the top and surveyed the empty driveway and the lamp-lit street beyond. Emily, our dog, slept soundly half in and half out of her Snoopy doghouse in the back yard. No sign of my son.

When I passed the bedroom door a second time, Ellen said, "Why are you up?"

"I can't sleep," I said.

"You might as well," she responded, sounding frayed. "Staying awake won't bring him home any quicker."

"He should be here any minute." I stood at the door, wanting to accept her good advice but unable to abandon my vigil. "The concert ended at 11:30. He should have been home by now."

The clock read 12:50. I walked outside and stood under the carport in the dark. Emily got up and stood watching me for a time, her ears on alert. When I did not retreat inside, she came over and sat down next to the gate and listened with me for his car.

I had agreed to let him drive the Volkswagen into town for the concert. My heart said no, but my head intervened. Too much violence in the center city, my heart said. Random, crazy things go wrong. "Come straight home," I told him.

"You can't go with him everywhere," Ellen advised, hiding her own anxiety. "He has to learn some things on his own."

"He shouldn't have to risk his life to learn," I said. "Go on back to bed. You're tired."

When he had whimpered in the night as an infant, I usually heard him first and got up to check. I once found him sitting in the open windowsill of our second floor apartment, watching traffic on the street fifty yards away. He was two-and-a-half. I urged him back to bed, closed the window, and braced it to prevent his opening it again.

At one o'clock, I dressed and searched for my car keys.

"Where are you going?" Ellen inquired sleepily.

"I'm going to find him."

"In downtown Atlanta at this hour? You're crazy. He could be anywhere."

"I'm going to find him."

Emily watched as I backed the Chrysler out of the carport and turned onto Greenbrier. I switched on a popular Atlanta radio station for local news, just in case. At the end of the street, I turned left, and just as I did, a familiar Volkswagen with a scrawny teenage driver turned into the street coming toward me. I let it pass, but glimpsed the wide-eyed surprise of the kid as he spotted my car. I turned around and followed him back to the house.

"How was the concert?" I asked with supreme control.

"Great, Dad. How come you're up?"

Emily wagged her body at us from the other side of the gate. "I thought you might have had car trouble," I lied.

"No," he said. "The parking lot had closed when we got back to the car. I had to find a policeman to get someone to come and open it up so we could get out."

"No trouble?"

"No."

Ellen let us in the door.

"I told you," she said as I undressed a second time for bed.

"He parked in the wrong lot," I said, defensively.

"But he found a solution all by himself."

"Yes." I had to admit my surprise. Erik had always been a

surprise to me, from the beginning. In spite of our careful planning for his birth, it took him ten months to arrive. His behavior as he grew up seemed often either too old for his age or too immature. He would get himself into a squeak and get out by himself, usually undamaged. I rarely arrived in time for a rescue. Ellen accused me of deliberately timing business trips to avoid his worst escapades. Somehow, he survived without any immediate help from his father.

"I don't think I can live long enough for him to grow up," I sighed as I got into bed, failing once again to learn the lesson my child was teaching me. I closed my eyes and tried to go limp. "It's like an old-time movie. Always teetering on the edge. I feel like I'm living on the railroad tracks."

"And you wanted three kids," Ellen reminded me.

Wm. Richard Dempsey

Incidental Teachers

Child of God, therefore children of God,
therefore brothers.

—Eric Gill

Nine years and four children after our first was born, we adopted a sixth child. Patrick was an infant when he came to us. Of mixed black and white parentage, he had dark eyes, curly brown hair and a café au lait complexion.

He was not a child we went looking for, but rather one who found us. A foster child in my sister's home, I fell in love with this "special angel" and wanted him for my own. Never think that I adopted him for any altruistic motive, because that is not true. I wanted him, only him, and would never have considered taking another child in his place.

He was accepted into our family as easily as the others had been before him. Oh, there were a few "it must be nice to be special around here," or "Mom, Pat's got my book," and "you mean I have to let him play with my friends?" Not that I would have labeled these outbursts problems, they were just common, everyday family squabbles that occurred with the arrival of each new addition.

My love for this special child was so intense and the bonding so strong that, like the ignorant ostrich who puts its head in the sand, I assumed that others would undoubtedly share my feelings.

It is only now, though, as I consider the lessons I learned from my children that the real truth is brought home to me.

Chuck, my second oldest son, taught me one of my first "lessons." Pat had not been with us long, only a matter of weeks as I recall, when Chuck came banging through the back door. With tears washing down his cheeks, he stuttered over the words, "They said I had a dirty nigger for a brother."

My heart broke for both the brown-haired special angel and my red-headed second son. I knew who "they" were. "They" were the other children in the neighborhood—once friends and now enemies. Brushing at the tears that kept flowing, I asked, "And what did you say?"

"I told them he was a Kiger (our family name), and not a nigger, and that he wasn't dirty because you gave him a bath every day."

The second memorable lesson came several years later. I learned this from Jim, our third son and fifth child. It seems, as the story was told, that Jim, being sixteen, had the job of driving himself and his younger brother to school. After having dropped Pat off in front of the building, he parked his car in the lot. Here he was accosted by another boy who demanded to know why "that" was in his car. A hooked thumb indicated Pat, who stood waiting by the front entrance.

"That," Jim explained, "is my brother."

I saw love in the tears that flowed from a young boy's eyes in the parking lot confrontation. There was honor in the words "he's a Kiger" and "'that' is my brother." I sensed a response to duty in the way two very young men defended their own. Trapped by the memory, I shed a few tears of my own.

I loved Pat and therefore accepted him. My sons accepted Pat and therefore loved him. Mine was a selfish love, one that fed my ego and met my needs. Their love met the needs of their brother. It was a lesson long in coming, but one I will never forget.

Barbara A. Kiger

Training a Tiger

*A child must learn early to
believe that he is somebody worthwhile
and that he can do many
praiseworthy things.*

—Anonymous

You as a parent have a lot of learning to do yourself, not only about your child but about yourself. I have found that in my life when I gave to and shared with others, I almost always ended up helping myself. I got a better understanding of who I was, and my life improved as a result.

Things don't always go smoothly. You must allow room for disagreement. In fact, I always encouraged Tiger to question what I was saying and, if he found me in error, to let me know so I could learn, too. In this way, parents can learn from their children as well. Not many children are afforded that opportunity because most parents don't want to make themselves vulnerable like that.

You could never be laid more bare than I was with Tiger during some of our first golf outings. He was eighteen months old, couldn't count to five, but he intuitively knew a par-5 from a par-4 and a par-3. He would keep score of not only his strokes but mine, too. He'd say, "Daddy, you got a double bogey." Now, that was six strokes and he couldn't count to five. It was amazing. He was watching how many strokes it took to get to the green and how many putts you took. Evidently, he added all this up in his head and came out with a phrase or number. And it wasn't six or seven, it was double bogey or triple bogey. So you see, I couldn't "massage" my golf scores, not around Tiger.

Earl Woods

Indian Summer

*We cannot command nature
except by obeying her.*

—Francis Bacon

It was a perfect Indian summer Sunday afternoon. The leaves were just beginning to change from a moss green to a Macintosh apple red.

Our family had gathered together for a surprise birthday celebration. After the last piece of coconut cake was devoured, we set out for a walk. We strolled together enjoying the last remnants of a too-short summer. Four-year-old Savanah skipped happily between us.

It was fun being in the company of the little golden-tressed charmer. She stopped to examine leaves on the sidewalk, bending over to select the more colorful ones; turning each one in her hands, marveling at the splashes of color, mesmerized by the rich hues.

By the time we arrived at our destination, the park, the bouquet was complete. Leaves of maple and oak, feathers of blue jay and crow. A floral designer could not have duplicated the work of the little hands; her eye for color could not be outdone by the finest artist.

Savanah swung, she scaled and slid. Her laughter filled our day. She ran, trusting and secure, into the arms of the wind. The sun was beginning to make an exit. Dusk was making an entrance, like an unwanted visitor.

We walked home, exhausted. Savanah's hair framed her face in moist ringlets. I carried her in my arms when she complained that she was too tired to walk. I talked to her of autumn, of pumpkin pie and frosty cold cider. I talked about Halloween and ghosts and goblins. We talked about the "Great Pumpkin" and how he descends each Halloween into the hearts of children of all ages. Savanah's dark eyes danced with excitement. "Isn't it all wonderful," she laughed breathlessly.

Yes, Savanah, sometimes it takes a little one with golden hair to remind us all of the magic of the seasons, the beauty of the day and the magnificence of the moment. There will always be problems in our lives—death, divorce, addictions, illness and financial woes—but the magic days of autumn are few.

We must enjoy the simple moments and cherish them.

Oh, yes, Savanah, "It is all wonderful." Thanks for the reminder.

Rita Nearhood

Rainbow Eyes

Children and fools cannot lie.

—John Heywood

I was twenty-seven years old and living in Oklahoma City. I was married at the time but I had no children of my own. However, my life for years had always been surrounded by the beautiful bright eyes of children.

At that time, I was attending college full-time to complete my teaching degree in elementary education and working part-time at a childcare facility. I had been at this job for about a year and dearly loved the children.

Well, tragedy struck my life one day on the way to work. Living in the country, I was commuting in just before sunrise to open the daycare center. I was driving, my husband in the passenger seat, when I crested a hill to find a cow laying in my lane. I reacted quickly but still lost control of the car. I sailed through the barbed wire into a telephone pole and landed sideways off in a field. My husband had been thrown from the car and was later found to have severely twisted several vertebrae in his back and also many loose teeth. I survived with minor bumps and bruises but was badly shaken. We were both transported to the hospital where I was released, but my husband remained for almost a week.

I, of course, didn't make it to the daycare center that day but was back at work early the next morning. At this point I was

120

starting to feel a little sore and the bruises were coloring well, especially the one at the corner of my eye where I had made contact with the rearview mirror. Very self-conscious of my appearance, but needing to be busy, I proceeded to work and began to rehash the story as parents entered the center to drop off their children for the day.

About mid-morning, one of my favorite friends arrived. Elizabeth was four years old, redheaded and extremely bubbly. This particular morning, Elizabeth bounded into class as usual and ran over to give me a hug. She stopped just short of where I was standing and planted both feet. I was preparing myself for some sort of rejection because of the condition of my face when Elizabeth burst into a smile and said, "Ms. Jan, you have a rainbow on your face!"

And yes indeed, I did. It had rained the day before and we had been so lucky to have survived the accident. I suddenly realized that a rainbow full of bright colors and sunshine was present in my life. It took a four-year-old child to help me see the sun behind the clouds.

Janice Anthony

WWJD?
(What Would Jesus Do?)

*Unto whomsoever much is given,
of him shall much be required.*

—Luke 12:48

There is a popular "novelty" based on this premise these days, but there's nothing simplistic about the idea. It's a small, colored nylon bracelet with the letters WWJD on them. Those letters stand for "What would Jesus do?" And while the idea might sound simple, the implications can be life-changing.

Recently, my two daughters—Candace, age eleven, and Caitlin, age seven—wanted a few of these bracelets we had stocked in our books, gifts and supplies store here in Athens, Alabama. They asked for, and received, a few additional bracelets to give to their friends at school. We talked a little about the bracelets after they put them on. Both girls could readily tell us what WWJD stood for, but we talked to them about how everything they do should reflect that thought and how that question should be a guide for how we live our lives.

The next day during supper, Caitlin was telling us about playing during recess at school. As she talked, I realized that she was actually telling us about a situation where most of the children in her classroom were "ganging up" on a less-popular classmate. I asked her to explain what she was talking about and my suspicions were confirmed.

I then asked her, "Caitlin, let me ask you something . . ." but she interrupted me and said, "I know—what would Jesus do?" As we talked about it, she began to cry and said if she was "friends" with this other child then no one would like her. I tried to explain to her that if her other friends were *real* friends, then they wouldn't stop liking her just because she was friendly with this other child.

That evening, she telephoned one of her best friends (one of those to whom she had given the WWJD bracelet) and told her that Jesus wouldn't want them to be mean to this little boy, and that she thought they should be nice to him. Her friend replied that she wanted to do what the Bible said, and she'd do just that.

What would Jesus do? It's a good question, and Caitlin came up with the right answer.

Scott Tidwell

As Young as I Used to Be

*All that we see or seem
Is but a dream within a dream.*

—Edgar Allan Poe

It had been a long hard day, perhaps a bit more hectic than most. Even though our two older boys had left the nest and were happily seeking higher education, Alan, at sixteen, still kept me pretty busy, though not as busy as did his two younger brothers, Billy and Kenny, the eight-year-old twins. I was attending college part-time myself, holding down a job, running the household, serving our community as a member of the Planning Commission and rehearsing in a community theater play. A busy schedule indeed. Nothing had prepared me for such harried middle-age years.

The day wasn't over yet. I had just returned from work, had homework to do before rushing off to a rehearsal and I was in the middle of preparing dinner. That was when Alan asked me to do yet another thing.

I sighed. I felt I had a right to be tired. "Alan, I'm sorry, but I just can't. You know, I'm not as young as I used to be."

Alan was not unsympathetic. He looked at me with kindness and love and said, "You never were."

That brought me up short. Of course I'm not as young as I used to be. Of course I never was. *No one* is as young as he used to be, not even a newborn baby.

124

When I had stopped chuckling, I reflected on the wisdom of my young son, who turned a cliché on its ear, pointing out how silly it is to rely on tired old excuses.

Florence Esten Kaufman

Making a Difference

*Hurt not the earth, neither the sea,
nor the trees.*

—Revelation 7:3

Living near Lake Erie most of my life, I have spent many years with my husband volunteering in the fight against pollution and the dumping of toxins into the Great Lakes. Working full-time and raising three children, sometimes it gets pretty hopeless and discouraging.

In the late 1980s, we noticed an increase in the medical waste along the shoreline; specifically, syringes and peritoneal dialysis bags. Local authorities told me the syringes were from diabetics and the bags were most likely from home dialysis use. Basically, no one seemed to want to help.

Working in the urology clinic of a hospital, I knew home dialysis patients were more responsible than that. I also knew the dangers of contaminated fluid in the bags. In the spring of 1988, my family had picked up nineteen dialysis bags that had washed up on the beach.

On that Easter Sunday, I was walking along the shoreline with my thirteen-year-old son, Jim, when we came upon the twentieth bag. I was frustrated and furious. I was fuming as I muttered and kicked the bag into Lake Erie like some deranged football player kicking a deflated pigskin wide and right.

Jim stopped dead in his tracks and said, "Mom, what are you doing?" I ranted and raved about people being slobs and ended with: "Jim, why bother? No one cares." He looked at me with tears in those big brown eyes and simply said: "But *we* care."

For one split second, everything made sense to me: the world, nature, children. I got the connection. I knew people *did* care and we needed to keep spreading the message. This adolescent, this kid who barely spoke to anyone over sixteen (who I couldn't believe was even walking with me, much less paying attention to my environmental work), actually knew the importance of our water! I did it, I caused someone to care! I hugged him as hard as I could and we both traipsed into the lake to retrieve the bag.

The next day in front of my aghast coworkers, I threw the bag onto the copy machine and made twenty-five copies. I sent them to everyone from the local health department to the FBI. I've never been a radical, but I had a mission! I logged the lot numbers and expiration dates and sent them along with the copies. I knew if the government could track down tampered-with aspirin bottles which had been found in stores, I could do the same.

Within a month, I received a call from the Center for Marine Conservation in Washington, D.C. They were starting an International Coastal Cleanup project and wanted representation on Lake Erie. They asked if I would recruit volunteers to clean and log trash that had washed up on a section of the New York State shoreline. Was this my kismet?

The project has since grown and grown. The International Cleanup has become the largest volunteer environmental project in the world. My "Great Lakes Beach Sweep" grew from ninety-five volunteers to over two thousand who faithfully log and remove tons of debris from our beautiful lake every September. Jim was one of the most dedicated of these volunteers.

When people ask me why I spend countless hours lecturing about the dangers of marine pollution and the ways we can help our Earth, I look them straight in the eye and truthfully say, "Because one child cared."

Sharen Trembath

It's Only a Word

*The love of truth lies at the
root of much humour.*

—Robertson Davies

Words are the tools of the writer's trade, the colors he paints with, the clay he sculpts with, the essential materials with which he tells a tale, delivers a laugh or evokes an emotion. The English language is so rich in the sheer number of words the writer can employ to express precisely what he or she means to say, that there is simply no excuse for the numerous "ya know," "fer sure" and the "uh" that sprinkle the speech of too many people. We see them on television all the time. Athletes seem to be among the worst offenders.

Certain words that were once limited to the roughest of street talk seem to have found their way into everyday speech and thence onto the air waves. Even those who should know better seem to have lost their inhibitions regarding these expressions. As a writer, I never had any need of them. As a reader, I felt that there were better ways to get the point across. To me, the use of such words is not only offensive, it represents a poverty of vocabulary as well as a taste for vulgarity. While I am no prude, I still experience a sense of distaste when I hear or read them.

Flip the pages of time back to 1958, which now seems to have been a more innocent era. Our twins were about six months old, the three older boys were eight, ten and thirteen. All five were romping in the living room after dinner while Dan and I were preparing formula in the kitchen. Emerging clearly from the boys' cheerful chatter, I suddenly heard "the word." You know the one—the four-letter Anglo-Saxon verb beginning with F. It means . . . well, you know what it means. Here it was, under our roof, coming from the mouth of our thirteen-year-old.

"Did you hear that?" I gasped. "Did you hear what Ricky said?"

"Yes, I heard it," Dan replied calmly.

"Well, what are you going to do about it?"

"I'm not going to do anything about it."

"You mean you're not going to go in there and explain to Ricky that it's inappropriate to use that word? I doubt that he even knows what it means! You'd better go in there and explain that it's inappropriate and that he shouldn't use it."

"Oh, no," balked Dan. "I'm not going to do any such thing."

"Well then, I will!" Throwing down the dish towel, I marched into the living room, wrapped in righteous indignation, firm in my authority as a mother.

"Ricky," I said, as calmly as I could. "I heard what you just said. Do you know what that word means?" I believed that if I could get him to tell me the definition, he would realize for himself how inappropriate it was.

He just looked at me. "Tell me, Ricky," I urged, "what does that word mean?"

Evidently thinking that I was seeking information, Ricky looked around the room, avoiding my eyes. He looked at his brothers. They looked back at him. He looked at the twins crawling around on the floor. Then he looked straight into my eyes and said sweetly, "Well, you should know. There's enough evidence around here."

Feeling an enormous laugh bubbling up in my throat, I did an about-face and fled back into the kitchen where Dan was hanging on to the refrigerator to keep from falling down laughing. We fell into each other's arms and laughed until we cried.

Nothing more was said to Ricky about his language, but he never used the word again in my hearing range until he went off to college and got thoroughly corrupted, not to be reformed until his own small daughter gave him a bit of his own back.

And Dan and I still haven't stopped laughing. Which proves, I suppose, how a child's innate understanding can puncture adult pomposity and self-importance.

Florence Esten Kaufman

Too High a Price

Every man shall bear his own burden.

—Galatians 6:5

World War II was over. My brother, Paul, had returned from the Pacific Theater of War and the B-17 airplanes no longer flew in formation over the farm on a daily basis. I was eleven years old and the world was safe again.

A young couple with a beautiful five-year-old daughter moved into the house across the road but we never got the opportunity to really know them. The three of them returned to their extended family every weekend. Then, one Sunday night at church, word spread that the little girl had drowned that afternoon in the Watauga River.

Before the sun had set on Monday, everyone in our small farming community knew the details of the drowning. The little girl's family was a "drinking" family; a drink-bootleg-whiskey-'til-you-pass-out family. All except the grandfather. He was a teetotaler.

As the story was unfolded, we learned that on the previous Sunday afternoon the little girl was playing with a big rubber ball and it bounced into the deep and swift waters of the Watauga River. Unaware of the danger, she waded into the river to retrieve it. By the time her grandfather saw her, she was being swept downstream. With the entire family so consumed with alcohol they were unable to comprehend the crisis, much less be of any

131

help, he went into the river alone to save her but was unable to fight the current and was barely able to save himself.

Her body was brought home for the wake. Neighbors carried in food and stood over the casket and cried, and then retired to the yard to join in whispered conversation with their friends. Many would return again and again to view the little body before returning to the yard. A few chose to stay the night and sit by the casket with the parents.

I went with Mother and Daddy. I stood on tiptoe to peer into that small white casket. She was dressed so beautifully in blue and was wearing black, patent-leather shoes. Her dark hair lay in ringlets on her shoulders and her skin looked like wax. Tears filled my eyes and I vowed silently, "I'll never drink. I'll never drink."

When, as a teenager, I was offered an alcoholic beverage for the first time, the vision of that little girl in the casket flashed before my eyes and I said timidly, "No, thank you." In all the years since, whenever offered an alcoholic drink, I still envision her beautiful, lifeless body and say, "No, thank you," very graciously.

My lesson was paid for with a high price. Too high a price. But my lesson was well learned and has lasted over half a century.

Mary B. Ledford

Josh Sees

*Having the eyes of
your hearts enlightened, that you
may know what is the hope to which he
has called you . . .*

—**Ephesians 1:8**

For Josh Nicolai

His fingers are a guide
to the world.
He gropes, searches, finds,
caresses.
Mother's face
is branded into the palm of his hand.
He knows every smile line
at the corners of her mouth.
He feels father's strength
when wrapped around the broad shoulders
that carry him.
Josh sees the world
through his mind and his hands.
His eyes are his nose, his toes, his touch.
Colors are shapes and textures.
His sky the air.

Shades of light, though dim,
his shining sun.
But a small child,
he sees more through his blindness
than most of us do in a lifetime.
He penetrates the haze
the rest of us stumble through.
Josh sees . . .
He sees with his soul.

Kathleen Rodgers

Why, Susie, Why?

Child, you are like a flower,
so sweet and pure and fair.
I look at you, and sadness touches
me with a prayer.

—Heinrich Heine

It was the fall of 1940. My parents had made the move from the cattle ranch in the sandhills of Nebraska to Vashon Island off the coast of Seattle. They were to try their hands at fruit ranching with my grandfather. I was enrolled at the island school, which seemed quite large to a six-year-old who had attended the first two months of the term at a country school with only five students in Nebraska.

After being the "new kid" for the first few days, I was thrilled to be accepted as a friend by a little girl who walked the same route to school as I did. Susie and I were an unlikely pair. I was rather tomboyish with a mop of sun-streaked hair and freckles. Susie was a little bit of a thing with dark hair and almond-shaped eyes. You see, Susie was Japanese-American. Her family raised strawberries on the place just up the hill from Grampa's.

The Sumikos were "good folk," Grampa said, hard workers who kept their place up and made their kids behave.

Like most kids, we were usually hungry after school. We formed the habit of stopping for a snack at one of our homes

135

one day, and then the other the following day. At my house we usually filled up on homemade sweet rolls or bread and jam. Mrs. Sumiko fed us more exotic fare: tiny balls of rice seasoned deliciously, or bits of fish and sweet fruits. When we were fortified, we would jerk on play clothes to go traipsing off through the woods behind Grampa's orchard and tramp beneath the big trees that grew there. We watched for just the right size sticks to use for our stick horses when we played "cowgirls and Indians." I taught Susie how a bleached stick could be a palomino and a speckled one with bark, a roan. She soon had her own stable of mounts in her back yard.

We both loved flowers. Susie knew where all the prettiest ones grew. There were wild flowers and fields of commercial varieties. We would pick huge bouquets, holding them up to our faces, practically drowning in the sweetness. My favorites were the pussy willows that grew in pale green thickets along the road ditches. I could just imagine those fuzzy, gray buds as being itty-bitty kittens.

Miraculously, to us, one day we did find a real kitten huddled among a clump of willows. He was half-starved, obviously abandoned, so we were allowed to adopt him. Naturally, we named him Pussy Willow—Willy for short. Grampa's loft became his home.

The loft was a fine place for playing or, when it was rainy, to sit and talk, sharing thoughts and secrets. Children do a lot of thinking. They wonder about so many things. What seems logical to a child often seems silly to an adult. But then, what adults do may seem pretty silly to a child.

Susie was a great one for questions. She wanted to know the whys and wherefores of everything. Perhaps she thought because I hadn't always lived on the island I had the answers. I didn't. But, rain or not, we couldn't sit still very long and would soon be off with Willy at our heels to find something to do, such as playing the old pump organ at Susie's house.

We had a great summer that year, gorging on fruit and exploring, but as fall once again drew near, my father made the announcement that he would rather punch cows than wrangle fruit. He would settle for fruit from a tin can, he said. It was decided that our family would return to the ranch in Nebraska.

I took Willy over to Susie's the morning we were to leave. She had found a place for him in the tool shed. We sat talking on her front steps. She still questioned why I had to go. We promised we'd write letters, like grownups did, and tell each other everything. We hugged and pretended not to see each other's tears (cowgirls don't cry). The last I saw of Susie, she was standing on the steps with Willy cuddled under her chin, watching me walk away.

We did write those letters. I learned that Willy had caught a mouse and there was a new teacher at the school. I wrote about my pony and the baby calves when they came in the spring. We didn't write much about the war that started so violently in December, 1941, though Susie did write that her older brother had gone into the Army. She was very proud of him.

At first, the war had little meaning to two seven-year-old girls. In time, rationing would come. My family would move to war work, and I would watch the bloody newsreels at the movies which affected me so that I couldn't sleep without a nightlight. But none of this had happened yet on the day I rode my pony to the mailbox to find my last letter to Susie returned, and marked "Address Unknown."

Mother tried to explain. Our government didn't trust people of Japanese ancestry now that Japan was our enemy. Those along the coast were being moved to camps inland. She used words from the newspaper, such as spies and sabotage. I couldn't understand what those words had to do with Susie and her family. Weren't they Americans? Wasn't her brother in the American army?

I thought about the Sumiko's house standing empty, the organ silent and dusty, with no one to care for the strawberries, and the row of forgotten stick horses. I imagined Susie being led away. I hoped they had let her take Willy. I was certain she had asked a lot of questions. *Did anybody answer?* I wondered. *Did anybody have an answer?*

Maxine Bridgman Isackson

Our Four Inspirations

Children are the keys of Paradise.

—Richard Henry Stoddard

Many things about our family are unique. My wife and I met through the mail while living two thousand miles apart. Even before we met in person, we talked about having a family, a family which would consist of six biological children and six children with special needs who would be adopted.

Less than a year after our marriage we learned that we could not have children of our own, so adoption became the only option. Within weeks of attending our first adoption meeting, we had our first child, a six-week-old baby boy we named Joshua. Joshua has Down's syndrome. While being interviewed by the adoption agency, we let them know that we were open to just about any child—no matter what kind of disability—with age, sex, race and nationality all irrelevant.

We found such joy in Joshua that a year later we asked the adoption agency to help us find a second child. That second child turned out to be a two-month-old baby girl who we named Kristi. Kristi was a full-blooded Syrian, quite a contrast to Joshua, whose birth background was Irish and Russian Jewish.

We were so happy with our two children we decided to adopt a third the following year. Shortly before Christmas, ten-month-old, blue-eyed, blond Justin came into our lives.

There was a wait of almost five years before we got our fourth child. Joshua, Kristi and Justin have Down's syndrome. Our newest addition, Jacob, who was one-half Spanish and almost six months old when he came to us, was born with a genetic disorder called *Cri-du-Chat* (Cry of the Cat). Each of our four children is a great inspiration for us. Joshua is now eight years old, a brown-eyed boy who loves people and is very eager to learn. He is beginning to read, can count to fifty, knows how to do touchpoint arithmetic and can run a computer. These are not typical things that eight-year-olds with Down's syndrome can do. As I continue my own education at age thirty-seven, I am inspired by Joshua when I see him put the finishing touches on a piece of artwork or an arithmetic problem. If he can bring stars and smiling faces home on his homework, college algebra is less of a challenge to me. Joshua also serves as a religious inspiration in our family. Always praying and thanking God, he probably knows more about the true meaning of Christianity than many adult Christians.

Kristi is now seven, a dark-haired girl with big brown eyes. She is a little shy at first, but a real joy once you get to know her. She loves to stand in front of the mirror and admire herself in the pretty clothes her Momma has bought her. Yet she is not in the least conceited. Kristi, too, is a great inspiration for our family. She can sense when I am down, and comes and gives me a big hug. Like Joshua, she is also a great help for Mom and me around the house, eager to help with the new baby or help us carry in the groceries and unpack them in the kitchen.

Justin is now six, his blond hair more golden than ever, and his eyes the color of the sky. Justin has had the most health problems of our children (Kristi rarely gets sick and Joshua's worst health problems have been croup-related). Justin had open-heart surgery at fifteen months, and although fully recovered from that, he now has juvenile arthritis, which affects his hands and legs. But the arthritis doesn't get Justin down. Last spring, he brought home three medals for track in the Special Olympics. When I see Justin run and play, not letting his arthritis bother him, I am inspired that I, too, can overcome physical obstacles. If Justin can get up and go with arthritis, there is no need for me to lay in bed complaining about the flu.

Jacob is now eighteen months old. The experts say he will be the most severely retarded of our children. But experts are sometimes wrong. He is already doing things the Cri-du-Chat literature said he would never do at this age. Jacob has big blue eyes, brown curly hair and a constant smile. If my wife and I are worried or anxious about something, all we have to do is take one look at him in his playpen and see that huge smile stare back at us, followed by a giggle or two, and we forget our cares.

Our four children have brought us joy and inspiration which is immeasurable. We consider ourselves very lucky to have adopted them, and feel that we could have not done better had we had our own biological kids. In fact, we don't ever consider them adopted unless someone reminds us of the fact. We are sad that the birth parents chose not to keep these kids, but are so happy that we were chosen to raise them. Each night, we thank the Lord for our four inspirations: Joshua, Kristi, Justin and Jacob.

David Shipp

My Sister

*Always be a little kinder
than necessary.*

—James M. Barrie

I'm thrilled to be asked to help with the book you're creating!
I hope you'll like my ideas. I don't mean to brag or anything, but
I'd say I'm pretty excellent when it comes to writing and spelling.
Which, of course, is good for your book.

Here are some of my thoughts:

My own sister can be a pain. We get along okay and everything, but we're not the closest sisters we could ever be. Right
before her birthday, Carolyn began to realize that not everything
in her body worked right. So, a couple of nights before her birthday she signed to me, "I want new eyes, and ears that work."

Being the sister of a child with special needs can be hard. I
know it's hard on any kid with a situation like mine, but there are
times when I sit down and think "It's not fair!" And sometimes it
isn't fair. But it's just one of those stressful, unfair moments you
have to get over and then just move on.

My sister goes to a special school where they provide special
care and well-trained physical and occupational therapists. This
next year, my sister will be going into first grade, which will be
much harder than regular, fun kindergarten. At first, my parents
were worried that first grade would be too hard, but I'm sure

Carolyn can handle it if she tries. She'll just have to work hard. My family has faith in her, and she has faith in herself.

Every weekend our family has fun times together going to our grandfather's lake cottage. Carolyn has a great time swimming (her favorite sport) and doing all sorts of fun things.

Hope I helped!

Angela Sorrem

[EDITORS' NOTE: *Angela was eight years old when this article was written. Her sister Carolyn, who is six, is deaf and has a visual impairment and a physical disability.*]

My Brother

*A good heart is better than all
the heads in the world.*

—Edward Bulwer-Lytton

He walks funny as walks go, I suppose. He twitches his fingers whenever he stares at the interesting nothingness on the wall, which the rest of us cannot see. He asks God to bless all the good people when he says his prayers at night. He plants his feet on the dance floor and moves his hips back and forth when he dances at the local jazz bar. He can write only his first name. He thinks M&Ms and a house cost the same: $100. He has taught me about the human capacity for love, acceptance and friendship. He has autism and mental retardation. He is my brother, J. T. Turnbull.

I do not remember a moment when my parents set me down and told me about J. T.'s disabilities. I always knew he was different.

I do, however, remember the early disillusioning experiences of prejudice and discrimination when J. T. was laughed at, ridiculed, and shunned because of his differences. Because of this, I have spoken out for my brother and people like him at local, national and international conferences on the family and disability ever since I was seven years old. I even reported a special education teacher to the principal when I was in the sixth grade because I witnessed her abuse a peer with a disability. J. T.'s struggle did not embitter me—on the contrary, it empowered me.

When I was younger, my parents struggled to get J. T. and other people with disabilities included in "regular" classes at the local high school. They were told that they were crazy. I remember how, following high school, they tried to find places for my brother to live and work in the community—something other than group homes and sheltered workshops. "They are not part of the community living and working this way," my parents said. "They are not being treated as full citizens." My parents were laughed at.

Achieving their dreams for J. T. wasn't easy. J. T. had behavior problems, which included anything from choking to hair-pulling to hitting. After being asked to leave a group home, J. T. moved back in with my parents who "hired" a friend for him—J. T.'s first friend at twenty-one. Through this friend, J. T.'s circle of friends expanded. Today, he lives in his own house with two graduate students and works at the University of Kansas. It is my parents' advocacy and determination I will always remember.

J. T.'s many accomplishments and my parents' struggle have taught me to have great expectations for *myself*. If J. T., with his problems, can face his challenges with courage and a sense of optimism, then so can I. J. T.'s lesson is a universal one: We all have the capacity for human greatness.

J. T. has taught me about love as well. If a person who was homeless or terminally ill approached J. T., my brother would automatically extend his love and friendship. He would neither see nor understand why this person is different from the rest of us. He would probably ask this stranger to come to his house for lunch and include him or her in his prayers.

Yes, J. T. has a below-kindergarten intelligence level. And, no, he has never read a book on his own nor has he ever signed his last name. But he naturally understands something that the rest of us do not always recognize: Human beings are human beings and, although people may come from different parts of the world, different socioeconomic classes and different cultures, we will always have humanity in common. J. T. can make anyone smile when he is smiling. That is the simplest, best reminder of his common touch.

J. T. has taught me about struggle, about empowerment, about beating the odds and about love. These lessons are valuable to me as I grow up in a world where I turn on the news and see peace-makers assassinated, and families and communities despairing over the gang violence that has invaded their towns. I get angry.

But then I look at J. T., sitting in his chair with his legs crossed, gazing at the wall, twitching his fingers and giggling to himself every once in a while. The simplicity of his life—his appreciation for the innate humanity within each person and his pure, uncon-ditional love—is a lesson to us all.

Whenever he sees me crying, he asks me, "Katie, are you sad? Oh, let me give you a hug. Things will get better soon." Will they, J. T.? Okay, I trust you.

Kate Turnbull

[EDITORS' NOTE: *Kate was eighteen and a student at the University of Kansas when this article was written. Her brother, J. T., is eleven years older.*]

The Broken Angel

*See everything; overlook a great deal;
correct a little.*

—Pope John XXIII

CRASH! The sounds of shattered glass mixed with a little girl's regrets echoed through the ceiling from the upstairs bedroom. I bounded up the stairs and discovered a pile of fractured ceramic birthday angels with the dismounted shelf which formerly displayed them. My seven-year-old daughter, Erika, and her friend, Jessie, were wearing their best "I'm innocent" expressions. The figurines belonged to Erika's nine-year-old sister, Andrea, who was not home at the time.

Andrea's angel collection consisted of nine delicately painted ceramic angels of graduated sizes, bearing numbers from one to nine. Each had been a gift from grandparents on the corresponding birthday. This treasured collection now lay in pieces on the dresser and floor.

Knowing that rambunctious Erika and her equally energetic friend were capable of great mischief, I immediately demanded, "What happened?" Receiving only sketchy information, I became suspicious and began to interrogate. Details were never completely clear, but their main theme revealed that Jessie had somehow bumped the display shelf as part of a climbing/jumping maneuver involving the top bunk bed. This caused the shelf to fall off the wall and the figurines to tumble.

When Andrea returned home that afternoon, I gently told her of the accident with her angels. Surprisingly, her first words were, "Is Jessie all right? Did she hurt herself?"

I was deeply touched. What a picture of compassion and forgiveness from a nine-year-old! I felt a mixture of admiration for my daughter, and shame for my own harsh punitive attitude.

Using large amounts of Super Glue and a week's worth of evenings, my dear husband painstakingly reassembled the pieces. Most of the angels were restored to their former appearance. But Angel number five had many visible cracks and chips, even a few gaps where the pieces were too badly smashed to be reglued. Although Jessie's mother offered to replace Angel number five, I declined. The broken angel had taken on new significance as a visible reminder of Andrea's generous nature.

Years later, when the grandparents presented a replacement for Angel number five, I still could not bear to discard the original. It had, to me, become a monument. Now Andrea's birthday angel collection, complete from one to sixteen, has two Angels number five. One is perfect; the other is precious.

Ellen Seibert Poole

Stick Heaven

*The most beautiful thing we can
experience is the mysterious.
It is the source of all true art and science.*

—Albert Einstein

The following excerpt is from a letter Christine Kreitler Mellin
wrote to her son about an incident that occurred when he was
three years old.

Joshua,

I mentioned earlier that you enjoyed collecting sticks.
However, you were in "stick heaven" the day I decided to
trim the aspen trees. I kept sawing and clipping, and you
kept heaping up the sticks. By the time I was finished, we
had a rather large pile in our backyard.

You played with the sticks for days. You spread them out
and organized them. You gathered and rearranged them.
You stacked and positioned them, and cried when they fell.
You pretended to shoot, to dig, to sword fight, to touch the
clouds and to build homes for your imaginary dinosaurs.
You poked with the sticks and drew with them. You brought
them with you in the car, and even wanted to bring them
with you to bed.

After several days, unbeknownst to you, I placed all the
sticks in our garbage barrel and set them out for trash day.

Unfortunately, you were an eyewitness at the scene of the crime. You were standing in the driveway when the garbage truck arrived. I watched as you silently watched the garbage man throw all of your sticks into the truck and drive away. You turned around with tears brimming in your eyes and raced wildly into the house wailing, "He took my sticks. He took my sticks." You were sobbing so hard I was barely able to understand a single word you uttered. For many days afterwards, you cried each time we walked outside. It was a devastating occurrence in your third year of life.

As an adult, I momentarily lost the ability to notice and appreciate the diligence and intensity of a child's work. With your tears came the realization of my mistake. If I had spent hour upon hour, day after day working on a project; if I had poured my heart and soul into a task, only to have someone steal it, or toss it away, I would have reacted just as you did.

Most everyone in this world of ours—young and old alike—is working on an important project. I hope I have learned from you to value and respect the labor of others.

Love,
Mom

P.S. I'm sorry I let the trashman take responsibility for stealing your sticks. It seemed, at the time, like the easy way out.

Christine Kreitler Mellin

No Strings Attached

Property given away is the only kind that will forever be yours.

—Martial

My family was fortunate to live in a small community in Arkansas for about eight years when my children were younger.

One of my children, Jared, was in the fourth grade at our little community school. Jared had always been a sensitive and caring child. One day when he came home from school, he told me about a little boy in his class whose shoes had holes in them. Like a busy mom, I just sort of acknowledged the comment and went about my chores.

Well, Jared didn't let it end there. He kept talking about this child's shoes. To this day, I don't know why he was so concerned about the shoes, but I suspect it was because he knew Eric was less fortunate and the shoes were a visible sign of this fact. One day, he came home and went straight to the closet in his room. I was busy in the kitchen when Jared came in and said, "Mom, I think if we buy some new shoestrings for these shoes of mine we could give them to Eric." I was stunned, literally speechless. My eyes filled with tears. I will never forget that moment. I looked at Jared, holding the shoes in his hands like an offering, and said, "Jared, if it means that much to you, we will buy Eric a new pair of shoes."

And that's what we did. Jared and his dad went shopping the following Saturday and bought Eric a nice pair of navy blue jogging shoes with Velcro ties rather than shoestrings. Not only was Jared sensitive to Eric's need for shoes, but he was also concerned about his feelings. He very carefully told us how we were to give the new shoes to Eric. His dad was to go to school, get Eric out of class, and give him the new shoes privately so he wouldn't be embarrassed. That's exactly what my husband did.

I will never forget Jared's face when he came home from school that day. He said, "Mom, Eric wasn't embarrassed about his new shoes at all! He went all over the playground showing off his shoes and saying, 'Look what Jared's dad gave me.'"

Jared is now twenty-one and will graduate from college next spring. He is as sensitive and caring as he was in the fourth grade. Wherever Eric is, I hope he is having a good life—and is wearing good shoes.

Mary Short

The Safe Haven

*Train a child in the way he should go,
and when he is old he will not depart from it.*

—Proverbs 12:4

While preparing our son to go off to college, I felt so proud of him. Yet there was a sense of apprehension as to how prepared he would be for college life. I knew he was academically prepared, but I was concerned about campus life. Steven had led the typical teenager's life. He had been active in extracurricular activities at school, went to football games, was an honor student, went out with friends, actively participated in church and worked at a part-time job throughout his high school years. We had always tried to instill in him a strong sense of the importance of doing what was right; not necessarily what everyone else did. I hoped he would always remember those lessons.

The first year of college went well, even considering minor problems like roommate issues, dorm noise and late-night studies. Steven handled all of these in a fairly mature manner. Academically, he excelled. We hoped he was happy and still holding to those ideals we had established for him during his formative years.

Toward the end of the last semester of his freshman year, we were visiting with him and decided to see some of the local sights. Although Steven had suggested several places to visit, we

152

got hopelessly lost. After riding around aimlessly for about fifteen minutes, we decided to return downtown, where we had started and call him on his car phone.

Although the downtown area traffic was heavily congested, several minutes later we saw Steven approaching us from the opposite direction. When he rolled down his window, and we did the same, he yelled, "You're lost. Go to the church!" He did not say what church or where it was. He knew we would know. He did not care who heard him. There was no question in his mind as to where we would go. Steven arrived at the church parking lot a short time later to lead us back to his dorm.

All the apprehension we had as to how our son would do in college quickly evaporated. He had been pointed in the right direction throughout his life and would not lose sight of the church, which had been an integral part of his life. It was a lesson he had learned well enough to pass on to his parents: *Go to church when you're lost.*

Sonja M. Tomlinson

A Matter of Style

*"It's all that the young can
do for the old, to shock them and
keep them up to date."*

—George Bernard Shaw

I'm shocked when I see a current photo of myself. Is that me? What did you expect to see, Kirk—Champion? Spartacus? Doc Holliday walking alongside Burt Lancaster?

But I don't feel old. I feel like the best of life is still ahead of me.

In the Torah, all the patriarchs lived to ripe old ages—most of them died somewhere in their hundreds. Abraham became circumcised at ninety-nine, and after that he sired Isaac. Moses climbed Mount Sinai when he was eighty. I could do that too.

One day, while I was ruminating like this, my son Peter came into the room.

"Peter, do you think I'm old?"

"Hey, Dad. You work out every day, and you look a lot younger than people half your age."

A bit of hyperbole, but I accepted it.

"But Dad . . . your clothes . . ."

"Huh? Your mother picks out my clothes."

"They look like they came out of a geriatric thrift store."

"How can you say that? Your mother was voted the best-dressed woman three years in a row."

"Yeah, 1954, 1955 and 1956."

"But she has impeccable taste."

"But Dad, she wasn't voted the best-dressed man."

He had a point.

Michael had been giving me similar advice. He especially criticized the form-fitting sports shirts I was fond of. "They look like something Jack LaLanne might wear." Jack LaLanne was considerably older than I.

The hip way to dress these days, according to the fashion education I received from Peter, was to wear "deconstructive" clothes. "Deconstructive," I have come to learn, really means "sloppy."

At first I objected. I told him that I wouldn't wear what my grandson Cameron—age seventeen—deems fashionable. I hope by the time this book comes out, Cameron's style—wearing baggy pants with the crotch hanging down between the knees and the belt across the rear end—has gone out of fashion.

But finally, I was convinced that I had to update my wardrobe. And, at the urging of my wife, who actually agreed with him, I submitted to going shopping with Peter. We went to The Gap and I tried on a pair of pants he picked out. "They are much too baggy," I told him, but he insisted. "No, no, Dad, they are just the style."

Well, all right, I am going along with this.

I'm standing there with these pants that are so big and loose it looks like I just had an accident and am carrying a load in the seat of my pants. And he brings out a jacket to match, with shoulders down to my elbows. I grin and bear it. Then come the shoes. I can't believe it. Big and heavy, like boots. When I was a kid, farmers used to wear shoes like this, with big rubber soles, just perfect for trekking through slop.

"Peter, are you kidding?"

"No, Dad, this is what's in."

The only positive thing I can see about those shoes is that those thick rubber soles make me an inch taller.

"You look perfect," he is saying.

I look at myself in the mirror. Disaster.

But Peter is keeping up the refrain. "That's it. That is the 'in' look. Now you got it."

I didn't say a word to my kid. When I got home, I called the tailor. I had him take in the seat of those pants; I had him cut them down so the ankles wouldn't bag so much. I couldn't do much to alter the shoes.

I've resolved to try to be "with it," but I hope that God rewards me for trying and makes this style go away next year.

Kirk Douglas

Dan's Wish

Love, you know, seeks to make happy
rather than to be happy.

—Ralph Connor

My son, Greg and my nephew, Dan, were born a month apart. They've been joined at the hip since. Their relationship is comfortably smooth and easy, with barely a squabble. Today, at twenty-one years of age, they are still bonded in a way that is enviable.

Around the time of their fifth birthdays, I decided to take them on their first miniature golf outing as part of our celebration. At one of the holes there was the putt-putt version of a wishing well—a small pond with hundreds of pennies on the bottom. Deciding this would be a memorable moment, I dug three pennies out of my purse. I used one to dramatically demonstrate how you make a wish. Turning my back to the pond, I tossed a penny over my shoulder as I explained to the boys that you do this while making a wish.

The boys were eager to follow suit, and neither one hesitated a moment to think about their respective wishes. First Dan, then Greg, performed our little ritual. I was terribly curious about what they were wishing for, but I held my tongue.

Though I really tried to forget it, the entire way home I was just dying to know what they were so positive they wanted that there wasn't a moment's indecisiveness in their actions. I rationalized that I really needed to know so I could tip off my sister about what to get Dan for his birthday. I further justified it with the thought that Greg might be longing for some "ace in the hole" gift and that I needed to know to make the "magic" a reality.

Finally, I could stand it no longer and asked in the most nonchalant voice I could manage, "Hey Dan, what'd you wish for at the well back there, anyway?" Without hesitation, Dan replied, "Oh, I wished for a puppy." Visualizing myself as my sister's genie I responded, "Wow, that's really great, Dan. I wonder if you'll get your wish."

Glancing at my son I said, "So Greg, what did you wish for?" Greg's reply surprised, humbled, then instructed me. "My wish was that Dan's wish would come true."

Carole Lisson

To Mary Hannah,
on Her First Birthday

*Children are the anchors that
hold a mother to life.*

—Sophocles

A year. It can't have been a year already.

Such a short amount of time to have fallen so deeply in love. Such a short amount of time to have changed so completely.

Who was I a year ago? No . . . even better to go back two years, before you were even a thought. I'm not even sure I remember myself that long ago. But I see glimpses of her here, in this very room. I see her in the "dry-clean only" fabrics and the engraved glasses. I see her in the dust-covered fax machine and the picnic basket for two. Oh, yes, I remember now. I wore silk skirts and drank wine. I ran my own tidy little business and romanced my husband.

And then there was you. Or rather, the beginnings of you. I was beautiful for the first time, I realized one morning while examining the slight swell of my abdomen. Sure, your daddy said I was beautiful long before I cradled you in my body . . . but I never *felt* truly beautiful until you were a little seed inside me. The act of ultimate creation taught me to appreciate my body in ways I'd never imagined. I was not only alive, I was making life.

Each part of my being was busy, knitting you from cells and molding you from the DNA supplied by myself and your father. What a wonder to be female; what a gift to be a woman.

I remember the first time I felt you move. I had just showered, and was stretching like a lethargic cat on my bed. Then, BOOM! A distinct motion—a kick? a flip? just above my pubic bone. There you were, making your presence known. I called your daddy and then my own mother. We connected for the first time on a whole new level—motherhood.

There was so much more to think about, so much to consider, and only eight months to digest it all. Find the right doctor. Sleep the right way. Eat the right foods. Buy the right things. Take the right classes. I read five pregnancy books, each with different advice on everything from choosing a feeding method for your newborn to choosing a pediatrician. A flood of information was thrust my way from others: mothers, fathers, doctors, friends of people who had known someone who had had a baby once, ten years earlier, in a snowstorm near Peru.

Then there was the (obviously) unplanned preterm labor. Things about that day I'll never forget: sitting at my desk at work and watching the tally of contractions grow from four to twelve in one hour; your father arriving, breathless, with a friend's watch so that he could accurately time contractions; stopping at a convenience store so that I could use the bathroom; my paralyzing fear at being told that I was, indeed, dilating; the giddy, almost painful, rush of the breathing. "A trial run," my doctor said. "Consider it practice for the day you do go home with a baby."

In the end, nothing could have prepared me for the day you came. I thought I was ready. Maybe that was the *old me* coming through, trying to take control, make an outline, ensure the follow-through. The *new me,* the me that was handed just over ten pounds of newborn daughter, was ready to admit that she knew nothing, but that yes, she was willing to learn.

So what have I learned?

I have learned that strained carrots do not come out in the wash, but that clay and fingerpaints do. I have learned that mommies can still cure just about any hurt with a kiss and a well-timed

"I love you." I have learned that sometimes, in the course of life's ever-advancing pace, friends are left behind. I have learned to love so completely that its manifestations are physical. I have learned that breastfeeding does not come naturally, but the instinct that tells you when your baby is sick does. I have learned to tell a tired cry from a pain cry. I have learned to interpret emerging dialogue. *I have learned to trust myself.*

The *old me* never would have admitted it, but rarely, if ever, did I trust my own heart before you entered my life. There were too many opportunities to second-guess my feelings and inclinations. The *new me* doesn't have the time to weigh again and again things that aren't of major importance and so, instead, I have learned to work by new principles, new guidelines that allow me the freedom of mistakes. I trust that I will make the right choices. But if I don't . . . well, if I don't, I can be very forgiving. That's something else I learned from you.

It is with the freedom of trust and the joy of wonderment that I prepare to enter your second year of life and, in effect, my own second year. Thank you for giving life to the mother within me. Thank you for teaching me the deepest form of love.

Happy birthday. Let's celebrate life, daughter of mine.

Heather Mills Schwarzen

Afternoon Tapestry

*There is nothing like staying at
home for real comfort.*

—Jane Austen

Mottled leaves drift and spin, brightly flickering through clear, brisk air as gravity and wind play their autumn game. Our children run and shriek, caught in the wind-blown excitement of the first Canadian front. Its currents whisper sweet promises of candy apples and ghostly costumes, holiday feasts and velvet dresses, cold cheeks, muffs and cinnamon mingling with buttered brown sugar. *And something more,* I think, allowing a stillness to settle into my mood. On days such as this, children reveal innate truths, truths so quiet and subtle they often go unnoticed. I resolve this afternoon, to listen.

Our youngest daughter, Lauren, searches through piles of leaves for hidden treasures. She brings her finds inside and lays them across the oak table in our kitchen. We peruse them one by one: a maple's brilliant red star, a burning-orange crepe myrtle leaf, brown sycamore hands, a tallow's purple heart and one simple green leaf now prized for so persistently holding onto its summer color. We delight in their variety: flocked and papery thin, brown-crackle thick, waxy, serrated, smooth and perfect oval. It is impossible to choose a favorite.

Looking up from the table, we spy visitors through the bay window, a quail couple we've observed since early spring. This time they've brought their brood. Heads bob and tails wiggle as they promenade through the yard. "Oh, cute! Look how many!" We rush to count—nine, eleven, twelve . . . *twelve* babies! "Oh, no! That one's going off on its own." Our hands flatten against the window panes and we hold our breath, but the mother quail is no slacker. With the crispness of a drill sergeant, she runs after her errant child and nudges it back in line. Our lungs fill with air.

All summer long we have thrown offerings onto the grass—honeyed cereals, peanut butter and jelly sandwich crusts, the favored apple slices—and the birds have flocked. At mealtime they gather to share our sustenance, and in return, satisfy something more than our physical hunger. Fierce blue jays, conservative cardinals, vivid tanagers, shy brown thrashers, territorial mocking birds, nervous sparrows and the tyrannical crows who brazenly rule over our backyard world, we've come to know them all, and to delight in the beauty of their colors and the vagaries of their personalities. They are as unique as snowflakes, as diverse as the leaves.

We turn away from the window as the quail patter across the street and into the woods. Each family member follows his personal whim. I pick up a book, make a cup of espresso and choose turbanado sugar for its molasses punch. The turbanado is kept on a shelf in the pantry between the maple sugar we prefer for French toast, and the delicate confectioner's sugar we sprinkle on fruit fritters.

Five-year-old Anthony decides to draw a Martian city. He does a cursory inspection of the art shelf before snubbing the piddling pack of sixteen markers and reaching for the panoramic box of sixty-four crayons. He wants the paper worlds he creates to hold all possibilities.

Ten-year-old Kathleen heads out of the door on a bug safari, clutching a new collection case. The set is very official looking, sporting a magnifying glass, a net that closes with an impressive snap, and eight or ten clear plastic sections where budding entomologists can separate their discoveries by category. But soon Kathleen is back, rooting under the sink for a large jar. She leaves the institutional bug zoo on the table. "The bugs look lonely and scared in that thing," she says, hurrying back outside.

Squatting on the patio, she carefully crafts a small habitat in a mayonnaise jar: blades of grass and earth, twigs and leaves, even a bottle cap with water. Into this mini-Eden she places a caterpillar, a moth, several roly-polies, a few ants. It is a congenial group. The caterpillar snacks on leaves, the ants and roly-polies explore, and the moth lights spread-winged, resting on a stick.

My husband, Jim and our son, Matthew, the twelve-year-old fisherman of the family, sit at one end of the oak table, their heads close in conversation. They are plotting strategy for tomorrow's fishing expedition. With mind-numbing nuance, they discuss the many types of fish and their preferences. Should they try bottom fishing from a dock, patiently waiting with lowered fiddler crabs in hopes of capturing the elusive sheepshead? Or should they start with a wire leader and a shiny metal lure, add a little strip of pin fish and try surf-fishing for mackerel? Grilled mackerel is awfully tempting. Unable to resist the lure of a good fight, they finally decide to liveline for shark. Eternally optimistic, we all smile and accept on faith their promise of fried shark steak for tomorrow's dinner.

Sipping coffee, watching birds dart through raining colored leaves, and surrounded by the quiet hum of our blooming children, I discern a simple truth: Children are joyous because their hearts are open. Open to colors and cultures, opinions and tastes, the diversity that weaves texture into our lives. They stretch and grow by reaching for each new experience, embracing life without preconception.

They see beauty in the curve of an Asian forehead as it slips down into a small and graceful nose. Instinctively, they search and find the warmth radiating from the marrow of Arabic eyes. They know that sunlight on black skin releases marvelous colors, like rainbows from a prism, and that people, like birds and plants and moths, are unique and precious because they are heterogeneous.

Children know that separated by category, we are as directionless as the wind-scattered leaves, as dull as a box full of white crayons, as frightened as a moth in a glass cage, but gathered together, we are as full of promise as an early morning in fall.

Leigh D. Muller

Old Friends

*Out of the mouths of babes and sucklings
hast thou ordained strength.*

—Psalms 8:2

As the day of the operation drew closer, it became more and more painful and frightening to contemplate. In spite of efforts to protect me from the truth, I already knew that I had only a fifty-fifty chance of surviving the surgery. I lay on my back, frozen, unable to avoid thinking the darkest thoughts. Then, at an especially bleak moment, the door flew open and in hurried a squat fellow with a blue scrub hat and a yellow surgical gown and glasses, speaking in a Russian accent. He announced that he was my proctologist, and that he had to examine me immediately. My first reaction was that either I was on way too many drugs or I was, in fact, brain damaged. But it was Robin Williams. He and his wife, Marsha, had materialized from who knows where. And for the first time since the accident, I laughed. My old friend had helped me know that somehow I was going to be okay.

And then we spent time together. He said he would do anything for me. I thought: *My God, not only do I have Dana and my kids but I have friends like Robin and Gregory who truly care. Maybe it can be okay.* I mean, life is going to be very different and it's going to be an enormous challenge, but I can still laugh, and there's still some joy.

One day most of the family was together in the mailroom, busily sorting through stacks of letters. Will was on the floor playing. He looked up and said, "Mommy, Daddy can't move his arms anymore." Dana said, "That's, right, Daddy can't move his arms." "And Daddy can't run around anymore." "That's right, he can't run around anymore." "And Daddy can't talk." "That's right, he can't talk right now, but he will be able to." Then Will paused, screwed up his face in concentration, and burst out happily, "But he can still smile." Everyone put down what they were doing and just looked at one another.

Christopher Reeve

The Gift of Love

*The childhood shows the man,
As morning shows the day.*

—John Milton

As a teenager, I dreamed of being a mother. Deep in my heart, I was also convinced I would be a good mother. Little did I know, however, that it would take so long to realize my dream.

My husband, Earl and I had been married ten years before we were able to conceive a child. Elated at our good fortune, as soon as our first son, Brad, was born, we decided that we wanted another. Twenty months later, our second son, Curt, was born. As they have grown, both boys have given us much joy—along with the usual portion of worries and concerns, especially as they entered their teens. They have both been active in numerous team and individual sports and we have encouraged them, sometimes with our hearts in our throats, to reach for the stars. Along the way we have learned to trust them for their courage, independence and good judgment.

This past Christmas, we learned to trust them in a whole different way. We'd had a bad year, full of financial, emotional and physical setbacks. As Christmas approached, my heart was heavy with the knowledge that we could not afford to buy Brad and Curt any of the things on their wish list. It made me very sad because they had both performed so well all year and made every effort to behave according to the rules Earl and I believed were so important to keeping teenage boys out of trouble. Despite our confidence in how we had raised them, we had no illusions about peer pressure and the negative influences all around them.

Our sixteen-year-old, Curt, who was in his junior year of high school, nonchalantly informed us as Christmas approached that he'd lined up two part-time jobs; one just after school each day and the other selling Christmas trees in the evenings and on weekends. A few days later, Brad, who had graduated high school during the year and was employed full-time at a carpeting outlet, told us his employer was so pleased with his work that he was giving him a huge roll of carpeting left over from their office redecoration to replace our worn carpeting that was so dingy and depressing it made me want to cry.

What a joy it was to see Earl, Brad and Curt install the new carpeting a few days before Christmas! That same evening, Curt proudly brought home a glorious six-foot-tall Christmas tree which brought tears to my eyes.

As we opened our modest Christmas gifts, the soft carpeting and the twinkling lights on the tree cast a magical glow and warmed our hearts. Our boys reminded us that the greatest gifts we can give each other have nothing to do with what we can wrap in paper. All my dreams were realized.

Margaret A. McDonald

When Daddy Goes to Work

The author, Zoie Griffiths,
imagines what a five-year-old thinks when
Daddy goes to work each day:

He gives me a hug
And walks out the door.
I look out the window
And wave one time more.

There goes my Daddy.
He said that he must go
To a place he calls "work."
Where it is, I don't know.

But, he must love to go
Because he goes everyday.
Wait! I think I know
He must go there to play.

That place that's called "work,"
It's a castle, tall and grand.
Yes, it's a place where my
   Daddy
Is king of the land!

I'll bet it has hundreds, no,
Thousands of toys.
I'll bet no one shouts,
"Hey, cut out that noise!"
as Dad bangs on a drum,
or toots on a horn,
and sings with his teddy
That's tattered and torn.

Outside his castle
Dad has his own zoo
Full of lions and tigers
And clowns painted blue.

I know he must laugh
at the tricks that they do . . .
and if I were there with him,
I know I'd laugh, too!

169

But, here I am,
On my way down to eat
A breakfast I wish, just for
     once,
Could be something sweet.

Now I am sitting.
Here comes my plate.
Do I dare look? Oh no!
It's something I hate!

As I look at my eggs,
And I pick up my fork,
I think about Dad
At that place he calls "work."

There he eats ice cream,
So he uses a spoon,
And I'll bet on his wrist
He has tied a balloon!

Yes, ice cream and cake
And for lunch a sundae!
With it a milkshake
That's chocolate on Monday,
On Tuesday vanilla,
On Wednesday strawberry,
On Thursday it's peppermint
Topped with a cherry!

What about Friday?
Oh, I think I know.
Dad orders my favorite,
Thick, green, pistachio!

Hey! Now I'm mad
(and a little bit sad)
"Work" must be fun,
and if Dad's happy I'm glad.
But what if he goes
And plays there all day
And as he's laughing,
Dad chooses to stay?

Nah, Daddy always comes
     home
I think as I smile.
He leaves his castle, his zoo,
And he drives a whole mile!

If Dad leaves "work" to come
     home,
What fun I must be!
He must love nothing more
Than to hug and hold me!

Zoie Griffiths

Our Most Important Teachers

*A teacher affects eternity; he can never
tell where his influence stops.*

—Henry Brooks Adams

We get our messages in mysterious ways—perhaps in a lyric
of a song, or the words of a stranger, or maybe a passing remark
on television. I hear the messages more often now. Not all the
time, but more than ever before. It causes me to pay attention to
and value others in a way I might not have in the first part of my
life. Each person before me might be the carrier of information I
need to move forward in my evolutionary growth. We are all connected in this way. That's the beauty and joy of the life we have
been given and the reason to value all living things. By abusing
or ignoring life in any of its forms, we might possibly push away
important information relative to our growth.

What have I learned over the past twenty years? What was the
point of these experiences? These questions were going through
my mind one night while watching a segment of *Dateline NBC*.
The show featured a woman who had adopted two little girls into
her serene life. Because of the children's prior abuse, which she
had not known about, they brought chaos and misery to her
orderly and idyllic existence. They acted out, had tantrums, exhib-
ited personality disorders and were unable to accept love in any
form. It went on for years, and all the while the woman was trying

171

to change the girls, trying to make them conform to her idea of normal. She was never successful, and when finally, twenty years later, they angrily moved out of her home, the woman felt relieved. At last she could have her normal life back. But to her surprise, she found herself missing them. In the twenty years they had lived together, they had subliminally taught one another things they needed to know about themselves. The woman realized she had spent her life trying to change these children rather than accepting them as unique individuals. This kept her from giving love, which she now realized was the only thing they craved and wanted from her and the one thing she had wanted to give.

This made me think about my stepchildren. In the early years of my life with them, I was always trying to fit them into a mold of what I understood. I wanted them to act the same way as my child. I wanted them to conform to my ideal of children. No wonder they acted out in their different ways. I never accepted them for who and what they were. I never allowed myself to see their free and beautiful spirits. I wanted them to be like me. I now realize I was ignorant and close-minded.

But along the way, love grew. In spite of ourselves. It's not the same love I feel for my own son, Bruce. It can't be, no matter how much I might will it. It's a different kind of love, but it is love. I would miss them terribly if they were not in my life, they are now a part of me. They are my family and the love I now feel for my stepchildren is as deep and as important as that which I feel for my own child. My stepchildren have been gifts in disguise. They have taught me about patience and control.

I am always putting myself in situations to teach myself about control. It comes from a childhood where everything was out of control. As a result, in my adult life, I've always tried to control everything. But that thinking has limited me, not helped me. The time has come to be open to new thoughts, new ideas and new ways. My stepchildren were and are a big part of my learning. Today I love and admire their differences. I constantly learn from their unconventional attitudes. They approach life from another angle than I do, but now I enjoy it and am expanded as a person because of it.

The biggest surprise has been the growth we've all experienced as a family through our grandchildren. They have taught the family about love and acceptance. They don't know about blood connections or family divisions, they simply react to love. As I watch my stepchildren interact with their own children, I see what it would have been like to be loved by them without all the baggage we brought to one another's lives. I see their patience and attentiveness, their kindness, joy and boundless capacity to love. In watching my stepchildren, I am able to imagine what it would have been like to have accepted one another earlier on, and I find great satisfaction in realizing how wrong I had been about them. This knowledge allows me to love them without working at it. . . .

In turn, my relationships with our grandchildren have taught our children, including my son and daughter-in-law, about me. Through the babies, my stepchildren see what kind of mother I could have been. They watch me love their offspring without agenda, and as I love their children, it allows them to love me. . . .

Who would have thought that these three beautiful little beings were sent to us as our most important teachers? Yet the true gifts are in our ability to be open to learn from them.

Suzanne Somers

The Three-Legged Dog

*We love the things we love
for what they are.*

—Robert Frost

For as long as I can remember, Diana has had a love affair with animals. As I look back on so many incidents in her childhood and youth, I am stunned now to realize how much this devotion to animals has shaped her values and beliefs. Now that I've grown up considerably myself, I better understand what I once perceived to be a weird and uncommon fixation with other forms of life. Now that she has grown up too, I see with great clarity how that passion for dogs, cats, turtles, mice, squirrels, hamsters, birds, fish, monkeys, spiders, cows and horses—and virtually every other living creature—has been the source of so much goodness and generosity in her nature.

Now I understand why she brought home a captive mouse from school and secured it in a jewelry box when she was eight years old. She thought the mouse was going to be used for an experiment—like the frogs that were routinely dissected in science class—and wanted to rescue it. The poor creature suffocated in the jewelry box, which caused no end of grieving at our house, but that marked the beginning of her commitment to save any creature she thought was in danger.

To complicate matters, she was a highly allergic child who

could not have the usual cats or dogs as pets. Not that we didn't try to harbor a few, given the pressure she put upon us. But inevitably, we had to find other homes for them when it was very clear that removing carpeting and drapes to maintain an allergen-free environment didn't make any sense if there was a furry creature on her pillow at night.

It was years before she could safely have a cat or dog, and when that was medically safe, she compensated for all the years of deprivation. At one time, her household consisted of six cats and two dogs—in a New York City apartment.

These cats and dogs, I came to realize, were not chosen for their breeding or charm. While they all had some appeal, none of them would qualify for a place in her heart or her home unless they had special needs. That usually meant they had been abandoned or abused in some way, or were handicapped. Along with Schuyler, the cat with the severed tail, the black Lab with cigarette burns on his forehead, and so many others she adopted from neighbors or found on the street or could not resist at the ASPCA's overcrowded facilities, there was the three-legged dog with the unlikely name of Guillermo.

Actually, Guillermo had four legs, but one was paralyzed and in a splint. As a result, he had a makeshift doggy "wheelchair" secured to his hind quarters, like a little cart with wheels. She brought him home one day because the owners did not want him when they discovered he would need special care. "Couldn't we keep him, please, just for awhile, until he is strong again?" she asked tearfully. The sight of that valiant little creature racing joyfully after a ball, dragging his wooden cart behind, could melt any heart. Every time her father and I swore we would not yield to any more of her impassioned pleas, we would find ourselves opening the door, one more time. So often, as with Guillermo, we grew to love these creatures and to marvel at how Diana knew how to restore them to health—no matter what the ailment or injury.

She restored them because she knew how to love them, unconditionally. I remember so many times when she could barely pay her rent, but if Ashley or Cady or Teddy or any of her menagerie needed shots or food, she denied herself to take care of them. She was the kind of city kid who would cross the street at Central Park South because she couldn't bear the sight of the horses tethered to the hansom cabs lined up to take tourists through the Park. No matter how I tried to console her that the horses were probably content, and they were treated humanely, she would rail about the flies that covered them in the summer, or their empty oat bags, or sad eyes. I came to the conclusion that Diana saw things most of us didn't want to see and, years later, the treatment of these horses became a real issue.

We used to think this was some kind of madness and many times resisted the urge to help her pay the vet's bills or whatever expenses she had related to her animals. Those were tough decisions and, of course, we often did write the checks. In retrospect, I'm glad we did, because now I see that we were not indulging her in something frivolous or selfish. On the contrary, we were endorsing something splendid and fine in her. When she founded an organization called Creature Compassion, she put her heart and soul into it. It was obvious that this commitment to the welfare of animals was a passion of hers and I have no doubt that many animals facing abandonment or extinction found loving homes through her efforts.

We see these qualities of caring and compassion emerging full-blown now in her love for her husband. That same sensitivity and abundance of feeling she has shown throughout her life is now focused on Randy. How fortuitous that Cady, her canine companion for the past ten years, adores Randy and waits at the door for him every evening. On the other hand, I can't imagine Diana loving any man who didn't share her love for Cady. Love is contagious and has no boundaries, as my daughter taught me long ago. I realize now that there was nothing excessive or peculiar about her wanting to save a mouse, lie down in a field with the cows or cheer for a three-legged dog.

Joan Aho Ryan

The Mother's Day Party

*The supreme happiness of life is
knowing that we are loved.*

—Victor Hugo

It was a Mother's Day party for the second-grade class. My son, Austin, spent part of his day in a special education classroom, and was mainstreamed part-time into Ms. P's class. I was so excited about the party. There had been no parties or other special events in his special ed classes. Austin's entire school experience had been in special education classes until that year, so this would be our first celebration together in a regular classroom.

All of the moms were dressed in their finery. Most of them knew each other already and quickly got involved in lively conversations. I recognized a few of them from Austin's preschools. But he had been asked to leave: "His behavior is out of control, Mrs. Hughes." It hurt my feelings that they pretended that day not to know me, but I also knew by then that otherwise kind and understanding people could be quick to gossip, judge and exclude me and my child from their lives.

This day would be a happy occasion, I was sure. Each child had decorated his or her desk with special favors for their mom, and would be serving cookies and punch to her. Then, each child would read a poem about why he or she loved Mom, and loving songs about mothers would be sung. The air was festive, mothers beaming with pride. One by one, each child was called to the front of the classroom to read a poem. Some were shy, others confident. Moms were swelling with pride and shedding tears of joy. *When would it be Austin's turn?* I wondered. When would I share that proud moment with my child?

As it turned out, I shed a few tears, too, not from joy, but embarrassment. Austin could not even find his special poem, let alone read it. He was roaming the room, sampling treats from any desktop that caught his eye. He knocked over glasses of punch. When the group was singing in the front of the room, he was disruptive in the back. *Why couldn't he be like the other kids?* I asked myself, holding back bitter tears of disappointment. I wanted to be like the other moms, basking in their children's accomplishments. I wanted to enjoy the party. Instead, I felt like running away as Austin's teacher came toward me with a stern expression on her face. Perhaps it would be best if Austin and I left since he was not able to settle down and participate in the festivities, she said. Quickly, I gathered up whatever party favors remained on Austin's desk, grabbed him by the hand and left without saying a word to anyone. I could feel the stares of some of the other mothers and imagined their cruel comments. I was devastated.

Austin was too fidgety to even notice my silent tears on the ride home, and had great difficulty unwinding that evening. I wasn't in the mood to read him bedtime stories. Instead, I went up to my room and tried to read, but I couldn't concentrate on the book. I kept thinking about how much Austin wanted to be included in the party activities, and yet he couldn't restrain his impulses. Behavior that came so naturally to the other kids was something he struggled with mightily day in and day out. I knew how hard he tried.

Tired, frustrated and feeling sorry for myself, I decided to call it a day and just go to bed early. Maybe tomorrow would be different and better. Maybe, by some fluke, it would be just an ordinary day, not one full of trials and stresses. As I pulled back the cover on the bed, I saw a handmade card from Austin. In his childish scrawl he had written "Love, Mom" and "Love, Austin" on the front, and drawn a heart and flowers. Inside was "Love to Mom from Austin," with flowers and a blazing rocket.

It was a special Mother's Day, after all. In his own way, my son told me all I needed to know. I love you, too, Austin.

Jeanne Hughes

Notes to Myself

*Of course, there is no formula for success
except, perhaps,
an unconditional acceptance of life and what it
brings.*

—Artur Rubinstein

I was diagnosed with arthritis at the age of seven, my third year of T-ball, just before the second grade began. I have come to live with my disease and have become the person I am because of it. It makes me shudder to think of what I actually could have been without my arthritis. For all the things in life that happen, there is good to be found. I think you just have to find it.

Because

I guess I should be grateful to have my arthritis. I mean, who would I really be without it? I think I would probably be a person I do not want to be. Maybe a jock. Maybe I wouldn't have the mind and intelligence I have. Or what about my personality, would I be as personable? Would I be anything other than what I am? I still wish I could play catch with my brothers in the yard once in a while. I don't enjoy sitting in the window watching. It's not fun. Everything I ever did was

in the hopes that my arthritis would go away, but it's
not leaving. Maybe some day, I won't hurt so bad that
I can play catch with them when we grow older, or
maybe play catch with my children, as well. If not—
well, I didn't lose anything I already had. I suppose I
could ask why, but I don't get any answers. No replies.
The only answer I will ever receive is my own. And the
only one I have is—because.

A Poem

Everyone tells me I'm so strong
They say they wish they had my strength
But who failed to mention the two-hour drive in the
   country
With tears blinding my eyes
Who failed to mention the countless hours of lying
   awake at night crying
Who failed to mention the pain of being left out
or the feeling of not being able to even try something
Who failed to mention the mere pain.
I suppose it was me
I'm only a person.

A Prayer

Dear Lord, thank you for my arthritis. It has taught
me many things. I praise you for the strengthening of
my body when it is feeling pain, and for strengthening
my mind so I can deal with the obstacles I have been
given. Thank you for the life I have led that has
allowed me to observe not only myself but others as
well. I would just ask that you please continue to work
in my life as you desire, and allow me to continue to
learn about life. It seems crazy that you have given me
the ability to look upon this affliction as a positive
event and not a tragedy. I suppose I'm not supposed

to understand your ways, Lord, and I praise you and ask you to continue my life as you wish. I am ready.

Want Ad

Wanted: friends for a lonely and dejected child. Willing to accept that outside appearances aren't everything. Willing to play games that don't involve much physical contact. Willingness to just be a friend, nothing asked for, everything given.

Kyle Lawson

Bo's Eyes

*I know that I shall meet my fate somewhere
among the clouds above.*

—William Butler Yeats

It was a warm sunny September afternoon when Bo, our yellow Lab who had been a part of our family for fourteen years, died peacefully on our front porch.

My husband got the tractor and prepared the grave site. We laid him to rest in the backyard beneath a magnolia tree, burying him with his favorite blanket. We all wept as we said our last good-byes and put wildflowers the children had picked on his grave. The neighbor's horse, Annie, stood by the fence and solemnly watched. It seemed she too was mourning the loss of a friend.

That evening, we looked through our old photo albums at pictures of Bo when he was a playful puppy and our daughter, Nicole, now nine years old. They grew up together as best friends. Together, they enjoyed tea parties, afternoon naps, storytime, strolls in the park and many wonderful times. It was part of the healing process for us all. Nicole wept as she looked at the photos. "I've known him my whole life," she sobbed.

The next morning, our son, Trevor, who was three years old, said he needed to talk to Bo. I walked with him down to the grave site where he knelt and said softly, "I love you, Bo . . . I miss you and I hope you like it in Heaven."

Several weeks passed and I was driving Trevor to preschool on a beautiful sunny day. The sky was a vivid blue with puffy white clouds. I told Trevor how I used to look at the clouds and try to find animal shapes or other characters within the cloud formations.

He caught on quickly as I said, "See, that cloud looks like a dog." He responded excitedly, "It does! I think it's Bo!"

The idea evidently captured his little imagination and that night we were walking down the sidewalk to our house after a late evening shopping trip. It was a clear, starry night. My husband pointed out to the children how bright the stars were that night. Trevor stopped in his tracks and looked up at the sky. Pointing his little finger, he yelled, "See those two stars over there? I think those are Bo's eyes looking down at us!"

How beautiful that moment was to me. Trevor understood that death is a part of life and even though our loved ones are no longer with us on Earth, they are still with us in spirit. If only we could hold onto that belief, and see the world through a child's eyes.

Jodi Estes

The Year of the Beetleborg

Nothing is impossible to a willing heart.

—John Heywood

It was early September of 1996. My wife, Cheryl, and I were the proud parents of two boys: Danny, age five and Jay, age three. We asked the boys to start thinking of things they would want for Christmas since we knew how discriminating they were about what Santa would bring them. Danny, as always, had a quick response. His wish list included superheroes, Megazords, race cars and games. If he had seen it advertised, he pretty much wanted it. (If it wasn't for girls, of course.) Jay, more thoughtful about these things, contemplated our request. After careful consideration, he told us there was only one thing on his list. "I want only one thing—a white Beetleborg," he said emphatically. So began what I now think of as "The Year of the Beetleborg."

A Beetleborg, probably now extinct, was a hot item that year. A superhero action figure like the Power Rangers, it was very popular. Cheryl started shopping in early October at a leisurely pace. Danny's items were easy to find. She found a lot of things for Jay, too, but not the white Beetleborg. That was fine, we told ourselves. It was only October and she had only shopped locally.

November came and the shopping became more intense. The superheroes, Megazords, race cars and games were all purchased, but the white Beetleborg remained elusive. Three area malls had

185

been searched, to no avail. Our hopes rested on Jay forgetting his request or, at the very least, expanding his list. But not Jay.

In December, the shopping became frantic. The family was recruited in the campaign to find the white Beetleborg. As they branched out, word began to filter back to us, like reports from the battlefield. There had been sightings of red, green and blue Beetleborgs—but no white ones. Jay remained steadfast. He was reminded that Santa couldn't bring everything that he wanted, to which he responded, "That's okay. I only want one thing—the white Beetleborg." Maybe Santa will be too busy to find this one thing, we said, trying to reason with him. "That's okay. Santa's elves can make it," Jay said jauntily. If only our faith had been that strong.

It was now less than a week before Santa's arrival. Desperation had moved into the slot previously held by frantic. Then came devastating news from the front: A brother- in-law called the company that made the Beetleborgs and learned *they do not make a white Beetleborg!* The war was over. We had looked long and we had looked hard. Let's face it, we had been looking for something that didn't even exist. It would have been almost comical if it were not for the pleading, big brown eyes of our three-year-old son.

Something happened three days before Christmas. Now, I don't know if it was the devil in me, or the American never-say-die attitude. Whatever it was, a glimmer of hope began to develop in the midst of my despair. *What if I got another Beetleborg and painted it white,* I thought. Was it possible? Why not, I decided. Something had to be done.

Here it was just two days before Christmas. Cheryl was working late, and I was with the boys. I formulated a simple war game: Wear the kids out and put them to bed early. Then, drive to Wal-Mart, secure the goods in any color, and I'm home by 10 P.M. Simple.

Yes, simple, except the harder we played, the more worked up they got. Which, of course, made bedtime impossible and later than normal. When they finally were tucked in, off to the store I went. You don't want to know about shopping at 10 P.M. two days before Christmas. Suffice it to say, I didn't arrive home until midnight, and I was without a Beetleborg. So much for the best laid plans, and thank God I've never had to plan a real war.

On the day before Christmas, a friend of mine came into my place of employment. Casual conversation led me to believe that he was a little crazy. You see, on this day before Christmas he was going shopping in Pittsburgh. Yes, *Pittsburgh!* Downtown, in the city, the day before Christmas. I tried to warn him about my experience so far, but he was committed to the quest. At 10:30 that night, Christmas Eve, there came a tap at our door. There was the good soldier, proudly holding a blue Beetleborg, and there was hope.

Unfortunately, there was no white paint, but we were not going to be denied now, with victory at hand. Cheryl found some fabric paint in the attic and, for the next hour, I painted that blue Beetleborg. Still pale blue, it needed another coat, so I set the alarm for 3 A.M. to apply another coat. The transformation was complete, we had a white Beetleborg! The alarm was set again for 5 A.M. to wrap the precious gift.

Christmas morning arrived, full of excitement and anticipation. However, Cheryl and I were tense as we waited for Jay to open the one gift he wanted. We held our collective breaths as he opened the wrapping paper, stared at the contents and was silent. An eternity passed. Then he looked up, smiled and said with a big grin on his face, "I got my white Beetleborg." Relief. Joy. Happiness.

Our elation was short-lived, however, when Danny started to cry that he, too, wanted a white Beetleborg. He changed his mind quickly, though, when he examined Jay's gift and blurted out, "Oh, that's okay, that's not a white Beetleborg. That's a blue one that was painted white." Busted. Demolished. Downcast.

Little did we know that the color wasn't the only thing different about these toys. Each color meant it had a unique antennae and a different weapon. Who over the age of five knew that? Then, just as Danny's comment was floating in the air, threatening to ruin our victory, Jay saved the day. "I don't care," he said. "I like it anyway. It's really special this way."

Those words made the day. Jay had no idea just how special that white Beetleborg really was. So ended the Christmas of 1996: "The Year of the Beetleborg."

Tim Sager

"Thy Will Be Done"

God moves in a mysterious way
His wonders to perform . . .

—William Cowper

On the day our daughter was supposed to enroll in first grade, she was in a coma fighting for her life in a hospital forty miles away. "Bulbar polio," the doctor had diagnosed. "The worst kind. Few people survive it, but if they do, there is no crippling as in the other type." The year was 1950, just four years before the Salk vaccine became available.

We had followed the flashing lights and screaming siren of our police escort as we rushed Patty to the children's hospital in our capital city. As soon as we arrived, intravenous feeding was begun and Patty's condition seemed to stabilize, giving us a faint glimmer of hope.

Early the next morning a nurse rushed up to my husband and me in the cafeteria where we had gone for a cup of coffee. "Come quickly," she said. "Patty has gone into a coma and has been rushed to intensive care."

The first view of our daughter was devastating. Patty's once lovely little face was gaunt and death-like. Her eyes were rolled so far back in their sockets that only the whites showed. An oxygen tube ran through her nose, and an intravenous needle was attached firmly to her hand. A nurse bathed her constantly in an attempt to bring her soaring temperature down, and a doctor stood by her side aspirating the phlegm from her throat every few seconds.

Another doctor came toward us. "Patty's condition is very grave," he said. "Her temperature shot up suddenly, and she went into a coma. Her temperature is so high that she now has encephalitis. I'm afraid there isn't much hope. Even if she should recover from the polio, the chances are she would be a vegetable from the brain damage caused by encephalitis."

Inside, my vital organs seemed to drain from my body leaving only vast emptiness. Horror stricken, I looked at my husband. His face was completely drained of blood.

"There is always hope." The doctor's voice was kind. "Sometimes we do see miracles."

Dear God! my heart cried in anguish—but what could I pray? Could I pray my daughter live and be a vegetable? Could I pray that she die?

No, no never! my whole being seemed to shout. This was a dilemma far beyond any human solution. I could only pray in all humility, *Thy will be done.*

After four days, Patty's temperature did begin to come down. It leveled off at 104 degrees, hovered there for a while and then gradually came back to normal. Little by little our daughter came out of the coma. When she was awake, we were ecstatic about her intelligent responses, and when she looked at the clock on the wall and told us exactly what time it was, we felt sure our daughter was not going to be a vegetable.

Surely a miracle had happened, but our joy was short-lived. Further examination revealed that Patty had also had the crippling kind of polio along with bulbar and encephalitis. One arm was useless, stomach muscles were nonexistent, and her neck could not support her head, which simply flopped over like a rag doll.

Patty was removed from intensive care, and physical therapy was begun immediately. The doctors said children usually fought therapy, but from the beginning Patty was a very cooperative patient, trying to do everything they asked her to do.

When our daughter left the hospital one month later, she was able to hold up her head, and a month after that she could discard her arm sling. Thus began years of physical therapy and regularly scheduled hospital check-ups.

In the years that followed I realized that sometimes a child can handle adversity better than some adults. Patty never complained about her condition, nor did she ever use it as an excuse. Instead, she struggled to keep up with all the activities of the other children. For one year, when she had to wear a special corset with steel braces to correct her curving spine, she made no objections and wore it every day. When she began swimming lessons, she refused to enroll in the special class for children who had had polio. Instead, she signed up for the regular class. She endured daily physical therapy for six years without complaint.

What did I learn from my daughter during this experience? Patty taught me there is no place in life for self-pity, that excuses and complaints accomplish nothing, but that determination, persistence and an unwillingness to give up do bring results, even though they may be long in coming.

After eight years, the doctors declared Patty completely cured and she no longer required any follow-up treatment. The miracle had indeed happened. I am eternally grateful!

After such a fine example, how can I face life's adversities with less courage that Patty? Sometimes a child can show us the way.

Dorothy M. Reese

Free the Children

Free the Children is an international youth movement of children helping children at a local, national and international level. It is unique from other charities inasmuch as its young people participate in concrete actions and projects to assist their underprivileged peers. Through their efforts, children who take part in Free the Children projects learn empathy, self-respect and leadership skills.

Free the Children was founded by Craig Kielburger in 1995, at the age of twelve. He was moved by an article on the front page of his local newspaper. According to the piece, a boy named Iqbal Masih had been sold into bondage at the age of four as a carpet weaver. Six years later, he was killed, after speaking out against the horrors of child labor. Craig was touched by the differences between his life and the life of Iqbal. He gathered information on child labor and brought friends and classmates together to discuss what they could do about the problem. As a result of these actions, Free the Children was born. Since 1995, the organization has quickly expanded in scope, and, with the help of the media, has gained extensive national and international exposure. In excess of one hundred thousand young people in more than twenty countries around the world have become involved in various levels of the movement.

Free the Children works for the basic human rights of all children and has instigated many projects which are making a real difference in the lives of poor, working and marginalized young people. The organization has built a live-in rehabilitation center for freed bonded laborers in India and has constructed numerous primary schools in the developing world in order to help break the cycle of poverty. Many thousands of health kits and school

191

kits have been collected by young people in North America and shipped to countries such as Kosovo, the Philippines, South Africa, India and Nicaragua. Free the Children also works on the issue of peace building, because wars and refugees are very much a reality of our world. In addition, the organization fosters leadership development for young people.

Craig's first book, *Free the Children,* was recently published in the United States by HarperCollins. It is available in German, Spanish, French and Chinese editions. All of Craig's royalties from the sale of the book go to support Free the Children projects.

Free the Children needs your help in order to continue its work. It has charitable status in Canada, the United States, Mexico, Germany, England, Italy and Brazil. Your tax-deductible gift will do the following:

- $10 provides a health kit to a child in need.
- $50 buys a brick to be laid in your name or that of a loved one at the Peace Center for Children in Sarajevo, Bosnia.
- $125 provides the salary for a rural primary-school teacher in India for two months.
- $2,500 provides for the construction and operation of a school in rural Latin America. The school can be named as you wish and can be visited once completed.

To contact Free the Children for information or to send a donation:

Free the Children
1750 Steeles Avenue West, Suite 218
Concord, Ontario L4K 2L7
Canada
phone: 905-760-9382

(A portion of the proceeds from sales of *Lessons From Our Children* is being donated to Free the Children.)

Contributors

Sandra Ervin Adams, Jacksonville, North Carolina, a poet and young mother, contributed a poem entitled "Thoughts About My Daughter" celebrating the joys of motherhood.

Maureen Anderson, Detroit Lakes, Michigan, a writer and host of a syndicated radio program called the *Career Clinic*, realizes that imitation is *not* the greatest form of flattery in "Lessons from a Three-Year-Old."

Theresa A. Anderson, Batavia, Illinois, wrote a heartwarming story about her three children—Kerry, Allison and Neal—in "Famous for Your Love."

Janice Anthony, Shawnee, Oklahoma, submitted two wonderful examples of wisdom of the heart for this collection: "Rainbow Eyes" and "It's the Only Face I've Got."

Karen Augustine, South Connellsville, Pennsylvania, in "For Nikki," credits her daughter, Nikki, with helping her survive her battle with cancer.

Betsy Bee, Tallahassee, Florida, a contributor to *Lessons from Mom* and *Lessons from Dad,* served three governors of the state of Florida during her career. Now, launched on her second career as a writer, she has written numerous tributes to her family, some of which were published in the *Florida Democrat.* Her submission for this collection, entitled "The Daring Young Man," is about her grandson, Will.

Allen A. Bennett, Nampa, Idaho, displays his pride in his son, Dr. Andrew Bennett, in his poem, "Doctorcito."

JoAnn Blake, Auburn, New York, writes a weekly column and feature articles for her local newspaper. Her story, "Baubles and Bibles" describes the perspicacity of her twelve-year-old son.

Sally Brungart, Williamsport, Pennsylvania, eighty-five years old, is an avid reader and enjoys writing poems and stories about her great-grandchildren, as she did in "Blessed Events."

Virginea Dunn Cooper, Tallahassee, Florida, who was a contributor to *Lessons from Dad,* has been in charge of the Lafayette Park Writers Workshop in Tallahassee for twenty-eight years. A writer whose work has been published in numerous magazines and the *Washington Post,* she dedicated her poem, "Curiosity," to her niece, Brittany Virginea Dunn.

Pat M. Costner, Charlotte, North Carolina, submitted "Looking Inside," a story that reminds us to not judge people by outward appearances.

Mary L. Crain, Williamsport, Pennsylvania, relives the example of the enduring fable in her charming story, "The Hare(s) and the Tortoise."

Robin Czombos, Ansonia, Connecticut, reveals in "The Tender Heart" that a lesson learned from her brother, Wade, still touches her heart.

Patricia K. Deaton, Hilton Head Island, South Carolina, a writer and grandmother whose work has been published in *Woman's World* and other national magazines, describes in "Reflection" how the love for a grandchild is like no other love.

Wm. Richard Dempsey, Tallahassee, Florida, a poet, short-story writer and novelist, recalls the apprehensions of a parent whose son has just learned to drive in "Listening for a Volkswagen."

Jon Mikel Emery, Nevada, Missouri, one of our youngest contributors, wrote a touching tribute to his grandmother, Helen Emery, titled "Ode to My Grandma," when he was eleven years old.

Jodi Estes, Tallahassee, Florida, in the insightful story, "Bo's Eyes," reveals how her son, Trevor, came to accept the death of the family's dog.

Sarah Fernandez, Hollywood, Florida, a single mother of two who is working toward a degree in computer design, explains to her three-year-old daughter, Kaylyn, in "The Quiz," that God is truly in her heart.

Rich Fiegelman, Dallas, Pennsylvania, the father of Zachary and a writer currently at work on a novel about growing up in a small town in Pennsylvania, brings meaning to the simple task of feeding ducks in "Zack and the Ducks."

Janice Graham, Pleasant Grove, Utah, a published, award-winning author of fiction and nonfiction for adults and children is also a journalist, columnist, piano instructor, mother of seven and grandmother of two. In "One Small Step," she provides a dictum on how parents should encourage their children's creativity.

Zoie Griffiths, Owings Mills, Maryland, wrote an inspired poem about the world of work as seen through a child's eyes in "When Daddy Goes to Work."

Paul K. Haeder, El Paso, Texas, currently associated with the English department at the University of Texas El Paso, is a prolific writer, essayist and playwright. In his story, "Charlie," he poignantly describes the effect of a son's brain disease on the character of his father.

Peter Hawkins, Deerfield Beach, Florida, a British-born writer who recently became an American citizen, recalls a touching interlude with his daughter, Laura, in "Laura Takes to the Water." The experience described here, teaching her to swim, enabled him to face the reality of "letting go" when Laura died tragically at the age of eighteen.

Sam G. Higgins, Quincy, Florida, a former educator and member of the Lafayette Park Writers Group, describes in "The

Ice-Cream Cone" how two ice cream cones purchased for his daughters caused him to stop smoking cigars.

Lisette Hilton, Boca Raton, Florida, the single mother of Annie and Abbey and the owner of an editorial consulting business, recounts in "Laughter's Magic" how the antics of her daughters brought her to the verge of exasperation, but the sudden realization that they needed to act like young girls turned her into the "third girl."

Michele Pace Hofbauer, Trumbull, Connecticut, is a published writer and professional illustrator who also runs her own business, teaches, lectures and works for a small book publishing company. In "A Boy and a Fish," she describes how her fifteen-year-old son, Mike, revealed his innate compassion during a fishing expedition.

Lisa M. Horan, Germantown, Maryland, is a writer, editor, wife and mother of an infant son, Griffin, who teaches her how to savor life in "Just In Time."

Terri-Gayl Hoshell, Warrenville, Illinois, shows, in "Life Lesson," the efforts made by children with handicaps to be "just like everyone else."

Jeanne Hughes, Lafayette, California, has dedicated many years as a volunteer on behalf of children with attention-deficit/hyperactivity disorder, including serving on the board of directors of a national nonprofit organization for people with this disorder. Her story, "The Mother's Day Party" provides a powerful lesson that life seldom goes according to plan.

Maxine Bridgman Isackson, Brady, Nebraska, is a published writer who recalls the injustices inflicted on Japanese-Americans during World War II in "Why, Susie, Why?"

Florence Esten Kaufman, Palm City, Florida, has had a long career as a writer and artist. She was a reporter/editor in Detroit and was later involved in corporate communications in California, where one of the publications she produced won an award from the International Association of Business Communicators. She has contributed two stories to this collection: "As Young as I Used to Be" and "It's Only a Word."

Barbara A. Kiger, Tallahassee, Florida, explores the innate lack of bigotry among young children in "Incidental Teachers" as she reveals how her five sons fully accepted her sixth son, who was adopted.

Beckey Kite, Spokane, Washington, wrote "From a Distance" as a tribute to her children: Kelly, Shane and Kimberly.

Kyle Lawson, Caldwell, Idaho, the son of an employee at the Idaho Equine Hospital in Nampa, wrote "Notes to Myself" as part of a high school project. It was submitted by Jeannine Ickes, who works with her husband, Lionel C. Ickes, D.V.M., at the hospital.

Mary B. Ledford, Jonesborough, Tennessee, a contributor to the two previous *Lessons* anthologies, has written three books about her heritage and childhood for her children, Susan and Tom, and her four grandchildren. She is currently at work on a novel, and for much of her life she has served her local community as a registered nurse. It is through this latter experience that she movingly recalls her relationship with a young burn victim in "An Open Letter to Jackie."

Carole Lisson, Glen Ellyn, Illinois, tells an inspiring story about the friendship and love between her son, Greg, and her nephew, Dan, in "Dan's Wish."

Marjorie L. Lundgren, Plantation, Florida, the mother of an eight-year-old daughter and the stepmother of two older boys, ages twenty-one and twenty-four, recently relocated to Long Island. Her story, "Personality," reveals how her daughter cleverly defines the personalities of cats and dogs.

Margaret A. McDonald, Coral Springs, Florida, who contributed to both previous *Lessons* anthologies, shares "The Gift of Love," a Christmas gift to Margie and her husband, Earl, from their sons, Brad and Curt.

Vickie McGrory, Kennett Square, Pennsylvania, wrote a lovely tribute to her daughter, Amanda, called "Anything is Possible," which recollects Amanda's determination to overcome handicaps despite her paralysis.

Christine Kreitler Mellin, Eaton, Colorado, wrote a letter of apology to her son when he was three years old. "Stick Heaven" is excerpted from it.

Leigh D. Muller, Tallahassee, Florida, devotes much of her time to raising Matthew, Kathleen, Anthony and Lauren, and is also a member of the Lafayette Park Writers Group. Leigh was a contributor to *Lessons from Dad.* For this volume, she has written a lyrical ode to autumn and human diversity entitled "Afternoon Tapestry."

Rita Nearhood, Forty Fort, Pennsylvania, who has published her work in her local newspaper and in *Catholic Digest,* wrote about sharing the joys of "Indian Summer" with four-year-old Savanah.

Garnet (Jackson) Piatt, South Shore, Kentucky, reminisces about a visit from her four-year-old granddaughter, Trisha, in "Thoughts of an Old Grandmother."

Ellen Seibert Poole, Portland, Oregon, makes an important point about the unexpected kindness of children in "The Broken Angel."

Carole Williams Pore, Lexington, Ohio, a published author, discusses, in "The Trouble with Rear-View Mirror Living," a valuable lesson learned from her three-year-old son about keeping focused on the opportunities we can create for our own future happiness.

Dorothy M. Reese, Tallahassee, Florida, another contributor to the two previous *Lessons* anthologies, is a member of the Tallahassee Writers Guild and a former English teacher whose fiction and nonfiction has been published in several national publications. Her contribution to this volume, "Thy Will Be Done," recounts the long battle of her daughter, Patty, to overcome the effects of polio and encephalitis.

Gail E. Rigby, El Paso, Texas, writes compassionately in "You Were Right" about Steven, who was four years old at the time she was caring for him.

Kathleen Rodgers, Colleyville, Texas, is a writer whose work has been published in *Family Circle* and other national magazines. Her poem, "Josh Sees," was written about a blind boy who sees the world through his mind and his hands.

Tim Sager, New Bethlehem, Pennsylvania, in "The Year of the Beetleborg" tells of the frantic search just before Christmas for a child's toy action figure—in a color not made by the manufacturer.

Heather Mills Schwarzen, Macon, Georgia, is a published author of short fiction and children's stories. Her essay in this collection, "To Mary Hannah, on Her First Birthday," is a joyful tribute to motherhood and to life.

David Shipp, Nevada, Missouri, reveals the joy he and his wife found in their adoption of four boys with special needs in "Our Four Inspirations."

Mary Short, Vancouver, Washington, in "No Strings Attached," shares a story about the generosity of her son, Eric, when her family was living in Arkansas.

Erin K. Smith-Day, Orem, Utah, a writer of essays and short stories, explores her world through the senses of her young son in "The Perfect Little Tour Guide" and discovers wondrous things she had previously never noticed.

Angela Sorrem, Milwaukee, Wisconsin, wrote an endearing story when she was eight years old about her six-year-old sister, Carolyn, who is deaf and has a visual impairment and a physical disability. Entitled "My Sister," the story first appeared in *Views from Our Shoes,* edited by Donald Meyer.

Edward P. Stephani, Escanaba, Michigan, a writer of children's stories, short stories and poems, submitted "We Caretakers," about how his son, Steve, motivated him to help rescue a seagull entangled in a fishing line.

Melissa Sutinen, Calumet, Michigan, contributed a story entitled "The Real Meaning of Love" about her son, Uriah, who died at the age of sixteen.

Mary Ann Swenson, Cedar Hills, Utah, shares a stirring moment in the relationship between her husband and son in "More Than Dirt."

Charlotte A. Thomas, Ports, Ohio, describes, in "You Can't Get Lost, Mom," her lack of a sense of direction, and her son's confidence in her and in God.

Scott Tidwell, Athens, Alabama, the author of "WWJD? (What Would Jesus Do?)," and his wife, Melanie, own Harvest Field Christian Books, Gifts & Supplies in Athens.

Julianne Tilt, Brookings, Oregon, the wife of Dr. Samuel M. Rubin (who submitted her story) and a gardener, herbalist, Lost Valley community member and cofacilitator of its Apprenticeship programs, wrote an inspiring story, "Growing People," about their daughter, Ariel. When participating in the spring planting, Ariel admonished her mother to be "gentle with the babies."

Paula Timpson, Trumbull, Connecticut, is a writer of children's books, poetry, and spiritual pieces and the contributor of "Mango Memories."

Sonja M. Tomlinson, High Point, North Carolina, wrote "The Safe Haven" to describe how her college freshman son pointed her in the right direction.

JoAnn Townsend, Spokane, Washington, tells the story in "Homemade from the Heart" of the creativity displayed by her nine-year-old daughter.

Sharen Trembath, Angola, New York, acknowledges the

inspiration provided by her son, Jim, in "Making a Difference," a story about the "Great Lakes Beach Sweep" environmental program which began, as Sharen says, "because one child cared."

Kate Turnbull, University of Kansas, was a student at the University when she wrote "My Brother," an inspirational story about her brother, J. T. (Jay Turnbull), who suffers from autism. The story first appeared in *Views from Our Shoes,* edited by Donald Meyer.

Laurel Turner, East Wenatchee, Washington, is a published writer who is working on a novel about the *new* American grandmother. Her story in this collection, "Mad Dad," recalls a time when her three boys helped her to realize that she could not be a "buffer" between members of the family.

Jeanine Turpie, Hilton Head Island, South Carolina, is an English and speech teacher at Hilton Head High School and chairperson of the English department. In "My Hero," she tells of a lesson learned from her "hero"—her nephew who fought valiantly to overcome dyslexia.

All the stories selected for inclusion in *Lessons from Our Children,* with the exception of those from famous individuals, were submitted by "average" people from across the country. When I requested submissions, little did I realize how the idea of describing the impact of a child's effect on an adult would resonate with people from all walks of life. I am deeply indebted to all those who responded to my request for material, including those whose submissions were not included due to a lack of space.

I am now gathering material for *More Lessons from Our Children,* another anthology of lessons we have learned from our children. Any reader with a story, poem or essay can submit it to me at:

P.O. Box 8141
Atlanta, GA 31106

Joan Aho Ryan

Permissions *(continued from page iv)*

"You Can't Get Lost, Mom." Reprinted with permission of Charlotte A. Thomas. ©1999 Charlotte A. Thomas.

The Daring Young Man. Reprinted with permission of Betsy Bee. ©1999 Betsy Bee.

Life Is Precious. Reprinted with permission of Terri-Gayl Hoshell. ©1999 Terri-Gayl Hoshell.

Zack and the Ducks. Reprinted with permission of Rich Fiegelman. ©1999 Rich Fiegelman.

Reflection. Reprinted with permission of Patricia K. Deaton. ©1999 Patricia K. Deaton.

Thoughts of an Old Grandmother. Reprinted with permission of Garnet (Jackson) Piatt. ©1999 Garnet (Jackson) Piatt.

An Open Letter to Jackie and *Too High a Price.* Reprinted with permission of Mary B. Ledford. ©1999 Mary B. Ledford.

A Child's Pain Is Parent's Pain. Written by Ray Recchi. Reprinted with permission from the *Sun-Sentinel,* Fort Lauderdale, Florida.

Laughter's Magic. Reprinted with permission of Lisette Hilton. ©1999 Lisette Hilton.

Growing People. Reprinted with permission of Samuel M. Ruben for Julianne Tilt. ©1999 Samuel M. Ruben and Julianne Tilt.

Just in Time. Reprinted with permission of Lisa M. Horan. ©1999 Lisa M. Horan.

Curiosity. Reprinted with permission of Virginea Dunn Cooper. ©1999 Virginea Dunn Cooper.

Now That's Funny. Copyright ©1997 by Paul Reiser. Reprinted by permission of Rob Weisbach Books, an imprint of William Morrow & Company, Inc.

Personality. Reprinted with permission of Marjorie L. Lundgren. ©1999 Marjorie L. Lundgren.

Charlie. Reprinted with permission of Paul K. Haeder. ©1999 Paul K. Haeder.

Lessons from a Three-Year-Old. Reprinted with permission of Maureen Anderson. ©1999 Maureen Anderson.

A Boy and a Fish. Reprinted with permission of Michele Pace Hofbauer. ©1999 Michele Pace Hofbauer.

The Tender Heart. Reprinted with permission of Robin Czombos. ©1999 Robin Czombos.

Famous for Your Love. Reprinted with permission of Theresa A. Anderson. ©1999 Theresa A. Anderson.

Laura Takes to the Water. Reprinted with permission of Peter Hawkins. ©1999 Peter Hawkins.

From a Distance. Reprinted with permission of Beckey Kite. ©1999 Beckey Kite.